# BOTTOM FEEDER

## Stories of Partial Awakening

by Pavel Somov

**i-Catching Books**

To Alexa Frey.
Thanx,
P. Somov
2019

# Prologue

*"First, you are a god. Your kids look up to you and worship your almighty power. You gave them birth and you can kill them. They know your might. They know the power you wield. They know it long before they know anything else. It's instinctual. Those are the breaks. And then you begin to transmit this power to your kids. You praise them. You build them up. You make them golden. Each pat on the back, you transfer this immense power that you have onto them ... and eventually the powerless become the powerful and the powerful become powerless again.*

*That is the story of parenting – that is, when it is done right – it's a story of empowerment, a story of creating gods. Only gods can make gods. Powerless have no power to give. Each parenting moment is a voluntary zero-sum exchange: your power wanes, your kids' power gains. It's the thermodynamics of love, a dissipation of heart-heat into the Universe. In the end, roles have fully reversed: parent-gods are nothing but fallen angels, to be reminisced in passing through psychoanalysis, as the newborn gods edit their origin stories. And the kids, once helpless, powerless, and frail sail on into the future, with the confidence of immortals, leaving behind two broken parent-hearts, powerless to stop time.*

*And then, again, a moment comes – the wheel of*

*cosmos makes yet another turn – and the new power-drunk generation of gods gets bored with playing and the kids – they always remain kids to you – your kids go on to have their own kids, repeating the cycle of parenting Samsara. Whether you are there to witness it or not, doesn't really matter. You are powerless to stop this cosmic centrifuge. The undifferentiated proto-matter of sentience needs a monkey wrench to keep stirring it into becoming. Beings are born. The agony-ecstasy of love continues. The restless Universe keeps chasing its own tail. And, yes, sometimes – in fact, often, in this human realm, - things break down. When parents refuse to give up their power, they breed groupies, not gods. Groupies that worship them. That is what you folks on this planet call narcissism. And these empty ghosts, ever yearning for power, set everything on fire. With no fuel to burn, with no heart-heat to power their own lives, they see everything and everyone as kindling, not as kin ... "*

(from "Parenting Gods")

# TABLE OF CONTENTS

# The Karma of Karma

That night I never went to sleep. I just sat in the kitchen with the lights off, listening to Billy Joel's "We didn't start the fire" on a loop, on my waterproof yellow Walkman. Sipping unsweetened, cold black tea. Watching snow rise in layers like sparkling, stellar yeast-dust on the unplowed sidewalks of my little proletarian corner of Moscow. I was waiting for morning. It was one of those restless nights that haunt young minds – a frustrating night-pause in the cosmic order of things, an unwelcomed imposition on the racing cycles of a youthful heart. I finally made my mind to go for a run. I quickly bundled up – two layers of dog-wool socks, two layers of sweat pants, two long sleeve undershirts, tightly tucked, a hoodie, a lined windbreaker, a ski hat and gloves, of course – grabbed my music and the house keys, and went out as quietly as I could. I was pretty sure I didn't wake up anyone in the apartment and now I wanted to make sure I wouldn't wake up anyone in the building, so I skipped the elevator and strummed the stairs with quick light steps, navigating around broken beer bottles and puddles of piss. The entrance door into our high rise was missing and the ground floor greeted me with a powerful draft. I gasped, zipped up my hoodie all the way to my chin and got ready to breathe through my nose.

I ran fast, like someone trying to catch a bus, taking creative short-cuts through the courtyards of the projects, as I have done many times before whenever I would miss my bus at the corner stop and would chase it through improvised diagonals and "back channels" of my ghetto world. Powdery snow muted my steps and I moved through the sleeping suburbs like a mad shadow, unwitnessed, with no destination in mind. Fresh out of the military, my lungs were used to this sort of challenge. For the last two years I was used to running in full jacket with an RPK machine gun and a trench shovel slapping my ass every step, in any kind of weather, sometimes in a gas mask. But now, without any gear and without much light, I felt weightless, moving through the night with powerful, high-knee strides and kicking up my heels like a mountain goat. Thankfully there was no black ice under the snow to slow me down. But something did anyway.

First I didn't realize what I saw, I just zoomed by and then had to re-wind myself like a cassette. I was passing by a fenced-off dog park and at this time of the night it should have been empty. But it wasn't. In the dark, I made out a figure of a man, on the bench, sort of slouching to the side, and a dog laying down around his feet, sharp ears standing tall and on guard, panting, warm air billowing out of its muzzle. I turned back and came up to the fence. Taking off my headphones, I called out: "Hey, guy! Are you ok?" There was no answer but the dog bent her ears back and issued a whining noise. I jumped over the fence to investigate. Not knowing the dog, I approached the bench slowly. I took off my left glove, bent down a bit, and offered my hand for the dog to sniff, my eyes, however, fixed on the man, who seemed motionless. The dog did stand up but didn't oppose my advance and settled down immediately after sniffing my hand, its leash – I noticed - being tied to the iron-wrought legs of the bench. I poked the man with my left hand and, still not getting any vital signs, slapped him a bit harder on his shoulder. He didn't protest. The dead generally don't. For no reason at all, I started trying to straighten him up on the bench but Earth's controlling mistress of gravity wouldn't have it. The body kept falling over to the side, even worse than before. He was frozen. I leaned in to smell his breath and did pick up a strong odor but that means nothing in Russia – most older men, at least, where I am from, have a smell of hangover on them. I noticed the dog's eyes on me – she was watching my every move and I felt sure that, while it didn't know what to do and was now in a position to rely on human mercy, it still wouldn't allow me to physically disrespect her owner with any kind of careless gesture or movement. Somehow I knew in my gut that it was a she and I addressed her: "It's gonna be okay, girl. What's your name, love?"

I carefully reached under her face to see if there was a tag on her collar but there wasn't. I petted the dog on her chest, noticing the pounding of her heart. She was clearly distressed but had that built-in Stoic feel that all German shepherds have about them. She looked young, perhaps, a year old. Perfect in posture, with inquisitive eyes. I refocused on the man and sat down next to him – or, rather, next to what was left of him, that is, next to his body. I checked his outer coat pockets and found an envelope with a good bit of cash and a page-long note with neat smallish handwriting.

It said the following:

"This is not an accident. Nothing is. This is Karma. She is 13 months old. You will find her paperwork in my inner pocket. The money is for the dog. This is your Karma now – your dog and your destiny. What happened to me is my own business. Your business is what is happening to you right now. You are at crossroads right now. A choice is required of you. You can call police and let them take it from here. You can take the dog and the money. The dog is well trained, very social, she knows she needs someone right now and will readily imprint on you, she is still young enough. Or you can just take the money and go, in which case, fuck you. If you call the cops and let them take care of this, you know how it will play out: they will take the money and hand the dog off to animal control, which, I am sure, you realize is a certain death for the dog. Frankly, I don't have a preference since I don't know who you are. Maybe you are a sadistic vivisectionist … Maybe you are one of those fucks who will displace your frustrations on the dog every day … I have no idea who you are and that's why I don't know what's best for the dog. Perhaps, dying at the hands of the animal control is a better option for her than to put up with you. I don't know because I don't know who you are. But you know who you are. So this is now on you. Whether you act or not act, you are acting. There is nothing else to it. It's on you now … "

The message took up about two thirds of the page, the quality of handwriting getting worse towards the bottom of the page, words sliding off the lines and the shape of the letters becoming less and less legible. The tone too had also seemingly de-evolved from formal to rather informal, as befits a parting mind. I wondered if the note had been started at home but was finished right here, in the dog park, on the bench. Did he take something to overdose and then went outside with his dog to wait for someone to find him? It seemed probable but also somehow irrelevant.

As for the dog, I already knew what I was going to do but I turned over the page to see if there was more. There was. There was a short post-scriptum. It read:

"Underneath my shirt you will find a monograph on the concept of karma, "The Topology of Karma," it is yours if you are philosophically inclined and if you are interested. Take it if you want. I hope it helps you in your life."

I looked at Karma, she was starting to tremble from the cold – who knows how long she had been on this strange post-mortem guard duty; she seemed, however, calm and accepting of my presence. I folded the note and put it back inside the envelope, and then folded the envelope and stuffed it inside the first layer of my wool socks. I untied the pup and petted her a little. She seemed to be finally calming down. A few moments later I looked around to make sure there were no passersby and began to unbutton the man's coat. It was a cheap padded *vatnik* "body-warmer" with tight buttonholes. I finally reached inside and unbuttoned his shirt, feeling his cold and clammy chest with the back of my right hand.

I stopped for a moment, not in doubt, but in a strange state of awe. I looked at the man, studying his face, and thinking about the mystery of death. Here he was – a multicellular microcosm – a home to trillions of cells, some of which had clearly already died but some of which were still alive. His nails and hair would still grow for days, and, given the freezing temperatures outside, I am sure there were still plenty of organ cells that could be revived and transplanted – and reincarnated? – into other bodily homes. So, was he alive or was he dead? "He sure acts dead," occurred to me. This thought struck me as new and very strange, cascading into unfinished fractals of word-fragments and images, finally re-emerging as a question to self: "Is death an act?" A question that in a moment answered itself in a rhetorically elusive manner: "Life is an act, isn't it?!"

I sort of came back to myself and refocused on the task at hand, namely, on locating the aforementioned manuscript on the man's body. Like the man had said in the note, the papers were on his body, inside a plastic folder, with about forty or so typed up double sided pages inside. I looked at the front page in the dim light of the streetlights. It was a title page, which read: "Topology of Karma and Reincarnation, a Non-Dual View." I skimmed through the table of contents and returned to the front page, looking for the author's name. None was included. "Strange," I thought to myself again: here I was, knowing the

11

name of the dog and not knowing the name of her owner.

I got up from the bench and stuffed the manuscript under my hoodie, into my sweat pants. Then I sat back down and re-buttoned the man's coat. I stood back up and stepped back, having a moment of doubt. I remember I wanted to ask the man: "Are you sure?" But dead men typically don't answer questions, let alone change their minds, so I said nothing.

I looked up into the sky, at the stars, - no, not to consult them, not in search of guidance, but just to see if they were paying attention, and it felt like they were, - and closed my eyes for a moment. I felt the squeeze of the foam covers of the headphones on my neck. I felt the gentle wet kisses of snowflakes landing on my face. I felt that somehow it was all just right, just so in that moment. The Universe that didn't make sense to me for so long finally started to make sense. It was the right night to be awake. And, yes, I was "philosophically inclined." And, yes, I preferred to have a running mate that morning. So, I picked up the leash and pulled Karma away from the bench. She obeyed. As we walked away, she kept stopping and turning back to look at the man, tightening the leash; but then the leash would slacken and she'd heel and follow me. When we were a hundred or so feet away from the bench, I tugged on the leash harder and started running.

And Karma ran with me that morning, through the snow, through uncertainty, until the morning sun re-infused the world with its illusory reassurance of light. Eyes make fools of us – yes, they do. Half way through the run I realized that Billy Joel had been on pause now for quite some time and I pressed the black "Play" button on my racing-yellow, heavy-duty, water-proof Sony Walkman. And Billy shouted into my ear: "We didn't start the fire … It was always burning, since the world's been turning …" And I felt he was absolutely right, in a karmic sense. We are all innocent as we burn through our lives. And it dawned on me that there is no such thing as sin, there is just "topology of circumstance" and "parameters of ability" and an interplay between these two cosmic factors.

After an approximately two-hour run, Karma faithfully bonded by my side, I circled back to my apartment complex and took the elevator, not wanting the pupper to cut her paws on the bottle glass from in the stairwell. I opened the door and let ourselves in. My mom was already up and happened to be in the foyer, getting dressed to go to the store. "Oh," she said with a jolly lift in her voice and bent down to greet the newcomer: "Now, who do we have here, Pash?" "Karma," I said, introducing my mom to a destiny that she and I, and my dad, and my brother were all yet to share. Karma was my first German shepherd. In years to come she was followed by Sherpa. And, finally, Zoya. But back then, in that moment in time, there was only Karma.

Without missing a beat, my mom decisively took off the wool shawl from her shoulders and used it to towel off the snow from Karma's haunches. The tail wagged and I realized that I was no longer needed at this moment.  I went to the kitchen and put the darkened copper cezve on the stove to make thick Turkish coffee, my dad's favorite, and plunged myself into the man's unsigned manuscript on "The Topology of Karma."  I knew my dad and I would have much to discuss that morning and I wanted to get a head start on the matter.

# The Silt of the Lotus Pond

Akatugawa* put out the cigarette and stepped out onto the balcony of his hotel room. Paris was asleep. Or, perhaps, having sex, which is rarely more than a pretext to eat. He leaned onto the filigreed ironwork of the railing and closed his eyes. He now knew he had written his best story. It was still embryonic, nothing more than a conceptual skeleton, scribbled on the back of a theatre programme. The writing of it took but a few smoking minutes: Akatugawa knew, perhaps, like nobody else alive, that when you stop controlling your breath, you will inevitably become inspired. The universe that is a seamless oneness has no protagonists. That was the secret, the thin red line through all of his writings. And such was the case with *The Spider's Thread*.

--

Akatugawa walked back into the room and buttoned his white shirt before going out. He wished to re-read what he'd just written. As always, he was going to be his own first reader. He picked up the theatre brochure with his writing on the back of it. And here it was, the short and sweet of it, a handful of sentences that had only a few minutes ago had crystallized into a story** out of the cosmic clouds of unknowing that we have so conveniently call our minds.

*One glorious day in Paradise, Buddha was strolling along the rim of the Lotus Pond. It was morning. The merciful Buddha happened to peep down through the lotus leaves into the shadowy abyss of the Hell down below the crystal clear water. There at the lowest recesses of Hell, he saw a man named Kandata, a notorious robber and murderer. Buddha remembered Kandata's one and only good deed many years ago, when Kandata, while walking through the forest, caught a sight of a spider and restrained his impulse to crush him with his foot. "Although it is only an insignificant creature, life must be dear to it, it would be cruel of me to take its life for no reason." Having remembered Kandata's good dead, Buddha decided to give Kandata a chance of escape. Just at that moment, a spider of Paradise happened to be close at hand, weaving its beautiful silvery silken web. Taking the spider's thread softly, Buddha let it fall into the bottom of Hell, amidst the pearly white lotus leafs. Kandata clapped his hands at the sight of this chance to escape and grasped the thread tightly. As Paradise is a million miles higher than Hell, Kandata climbed up for some time and eventually grew tired. As he rested he looked down and saw thousands of his fellow sinners down below also climbing up the thread after him. Afraid that the thread would not support the weight of all the sinners and their sins, Kandata yelled: "You damned sinners. The spider's thread is mine.  Get down!  All of you get down!"  And just as he said that the thread snapped right where his hands had previously gripped it and Kandata hurtled downwards into the abyss of the Hell at the bottom of the lotus pond.  Sorrowful, Buddha looked at Kandata's black heart and walked away, while the white lotus flowers of the Paradise, caring nothing about the happenings of the world, kept waving around the feet of their merciful Lord.  In Paradise it must be getting on towards noon.*

--

Whether Paris is paradise or hell is a matter of perspective but there is one hour of the day when this dubious distinction is particularly hard to make and that hour is midnight – that inconspicuous hour when the womb of darkness begins to incubate the idea of light, the very hour when life role-plays death, when the wick of dreaming starts to smolder with oblivion.

Akutagawa, wearing his oversized white shirt, un-tucked like some kind of sari, stormed out into the night with no destination in mind.  He was finally free – free from his pen – free from the compulsive need to write and re-write, free to roam the night, free from his own mind.  The street welcomed him with the sucking eagerness of vacuum – you know, that seeming ethereal nothingness that is the womb of everything.  Everything yearned to be him.  And, as if on wings, Akutagawa filled the world with himself,

moving through it like a knife moves through a stick
of butter.

--

New York – they say – never sleeps. Paris, unlike
New York, sleeps all right but it never jumps out of
its bed. Akutagawa filled the desolate foothills of the
Montmartre with himself, threading his info-essence
up the cobblestone streets that led up to the Sacre-
Coeur and sat down on the steps of the basilica. He
never liked the pretentious leg-spread of the Eiffel
Tower. Torso-less, the structure reminded him of a
pair of elegant legs for sale in fuck-me- stockings of
filigreed ironwork. The observation tower itself had
to be observed – it commanded everyone's eyes,
stealing the show of the cityscape, like an attention-
hungry debutante.

Akutagawa noticed a still burning prayer candle that
someone had left on the steps. He got an idea. He
stood up and started looking for a cigarette butt, one
that'd be long enough for at least few drags. He
hadn't smoked in a while and for some reason now
felt the urge. He chose a Gauloises – it was nearly
intact. He was familiar with the brand. Aromatic,
silky and unfiltered – just like Gaul women -
Gauloises was packed with dark Syrian tobacco leaf,
dark as the elusive dark matter itself. Akutagawa
walked over to the candle, ran the cigarette through
the sterilizing powers of the flame back and forth,
stuck it into his mouth, bent over even deeper and lit
it up off the candle. The space toyed with smoke the
way it toys with anything. The smoke didn't diffuse

into nowhere – it became nowhere, just as nowhere became it.

--

Someone coughed somewhere near, somewhere behind Akutagawa and Akutagawa suddenly was no longer alone. As he turned around he saw a tall, thin, dark man, probably a French Algerian, leaning with his back on the red doors of the church. Strangely, Akutagawa hadn't heard his footsteps – had he been standing there all along, watching Akutagawa? But whatever the context might have been, Akutagawa could tell that the cough was either a "hello" or a non-smoker's "fuck-you." The hypothesis was easy enough to test. Akutagawa stood up, walked up to the man, nodded a hello at him and offered him the still burning cigarette. The man took it and brought it to his lips without any sign of aversion. His cough – it was clear now – had been a hello.

--

"Name is Meursault," *** the man introduced himself.

"Akutagawa … You can call me A.K. for short." said Akutagawa.

The two – almost in sync – sat down on the top step, side by side, looking at the flat Parisian horizon. The silence dragged on but neither seemed to be bothered. Both were strangers to Paris and that self-evident silent bond seemed to be enough for them for now.

"Do you write?" Akutagawa finally found the question that interested him.

Meursault shook his head and asked: "Do you?"

"I do," said Akutagawa and added: "In fact, today I think I have written my best piece – just a few paragraphs, a sketch of a story but I am not even sure if I need to do anything else with it."

"What's it about, AK?"

"It's about … what matters and what doesn't matter … it's about a collision of free will and determinism … about –," Akutagawa didn't finish his thought, he suddenly stood up and offered: "Up for a cup of coffee?  My treat."

Meursault acquiesced.

--

The two walked down the winding streets of the Montmartre, with the lightness of those who are always hungry and in a decent enough mood.  It wasn't long before they spotted a café that was open – or rather opening up.  A man in a white apron was flattening out the wrinkles from a white tablecloth with a callous, shovel-sized palm.  When he finished, to his satisfaction, he went inside without saying a word.  There were no chairs yet and Akutagawa and Meursault stood in front of the café, hands in their pockets.  Five or so minutes passed before the man brought out the chairs.  "Please, sit down, I'll be right back with some coffee," he said, sounding gruff and with a heavy accent.

"I think he's Russian," noted Meursault. "There are a lot of Russians here, I noticed."

Akutagawa nodded: "Yes. I heard Paris is some kind of center for organizing the anti-Bolshevik movement. Their aristocrats and White Army officers are still plotting the return of the Romanovs. Perhaps, our waiter is one of those counter-revolutionaries, you know … "

Meursault seemed surprised by how much Akutagawa seemed to know about this Russian matter.

By now the two sat down. The coffee – unlike the chairs – arrived without a delay. It wasn't exactly hot but it was certainly not cold. The waiter poured each a small cup and disappeared without a word.

For two men who still barely knew each other, the two seemed unusually comfortable with prolonged silence. Akutagawa was now able to take a better look at his companion – dark, North African skin, Caucasian features with a prominent straight nose, broad shoulders and sinewy forearms.

Meursault decided to speak: "I want to thank you for the chat, and the stroll, and the coffee." Akutagawa issued a graceful nod. Meursault continued: "And I want to know more about this story that you mentioned … "

"Oh, yes, of course," said Akutagawa and proceeded to retell the vignette. As Akutagawa began to speak, the Russian waiter now came outside with another chair. He put it next to the entrance door, on the other side of where the two men were sitting, but well within the hearing distance, and sat down. He lit a cigarette and closed his eyes.

--

"So," said Meursault, seeming genuinely intrigued, "A bad man is given a chance of salvation by a benevolent god and he blows it – eh … - because he doesn't want others – sinners, just like him, – to be saved? Hmm … "

"You could say that … I am frankly unsure … The story just came to me … I am yet to understand it myself … "

Meursault looked at Akutagawa with surprise: "Is this how you write?"

"I know," said Akutagawa, "In fact, I even question the idea of authorship – some of the best stuff I've written – not that it's any good – just came to me. Writing for me is very much like reading – it's as though I am simply transcribing what already exists and as I write it down, I feel that I am nothing more than the very first reader of the story that I am also supposed to transcribe. Naturally, I add my own voice to what I hear, but it's just like with any translation. You know how they say 'lost in translation'?"

Meursault shook his head.

"Well," Akutagawa continued, "The reason why the original message is lost in translation is because it is usually embellished. It is very hard to translate without adding some unintended meaning."

"A better phrase, I suppose, would be 'gained in translation'?" proposed Meursault.

"Absolutely! This is, in fact, very, very good. Are you sure you don't write, Meursault?"

Meursault smiled baring a row of strong white teeth: "The only writing I've done of late is a letter to my mother."

"Oh, yes? You write to your mom? How sweet!"

"I really don't. It's been years since I've written her. She sent me a letter a few months ago, telling me she wanted to see me. I replied with a promise to come and visit. I didn't hear back. A week later I got a notification that she passed away. I buried her two weeks ago."

Akutagawa jerked his head back as if from an uppercut. He didn't see this coming – an innocent conversational detour and – bam! – you are in a conversation-ending cul-de-sac. Where do you go from here? Akutagawa seemed to reflexively look up to the sky, as if for guidance.

The Sun, still somewhere behind the horizon, has already adjusted the dimming switch of the night to a rosy haze, bleaching out the stars and setting the bottom of the sky on a slow fire, rolling out a red carpet of light for its own arrival. The Russian waiter, still with his eyes closed, was on his third or fourth cigarette. And the proletariat class of Paris was already rolling up their sleeves.

--

"No, I don't miss her," said Meursault rather bluntly. In the last few minutes, Akutagawa had clumsily navigated the obligatory small talk that follows the revelation of death. Meursault seemed utterly unperturbed by the exchange.

"I want to get back to your story," said Meursault, "I find it very interesting … Would it be accurate to say that the man in your story, the protagonist, who was given a chance to escape out of hell … would it be accurate to suppose that, perhaps, he felt that he was not a sinner after all, that he had been misjudged, misunderstood, mistreated by the system, if you wish, and, because of that righteous sense of innocence, he felt that it would be simply unfair for other sinners to take advantage of the escape opportunity that had been given only to him?"

"Oh, I see where you are going with this, Meursault," said Akutagawa, checking his empty cup of coffee, in the hope of one more sip. The Russian waiter, uncannily, opened his eyes, as if operating on some kind of sixth sense, and stood up. "More coffee, messieurs?" Akutagawa nodded with relief and the waiter left. At this point there was no doubt whatsoever that the Russian waiter had been eavesdropping on the entire conversation between the two early-morning patrons.

Akutagawa continued: "I think that this is an entirely legitimate interpretation of what might have been guiding Kandata when he cut off the spider thread ... "

"Oh, yes, Kandata ... I've been trying to remember the man's name," echoed Meursault.

The waiter returned with more coffee and an unsolicited opinion. He pulled up the chair he had been sitting on, turned it around so that the back faced the table and straddled it in a highly informal manner, with his beefy forearms overlapping each other on top of the chair-back. He forcefully cleared his throat and unapologetically butted in.

"I've been listening to you, I am sure you noticed," he began, his tongue working out the nuances of French the way a child's hand might struggle when digging a hole in tightly packed wet sand. "I think Meursault is right, AK, but there is a twist here, my friends, a very important twist that both of you are missing."

Meursault and Akutagawa were both startled by the brutish informality of this encounter: not only did the Russian eavesdrop on their conversation, he memorized their names and unceremoniously used them without the slightest of pretexts. The Algerian and the Japanese were witnessing a classic Russian case of poor boundaries. Only people that hail from the largest geographical territory on planet Earth can be such presumptuous trespassers. And yet both were instantly sucked in: the Russian – no doubt – had a share of self-affirming magnetism.

"My reading of your story – so to say, since I haven't actually read it, - is that Kandata couldn't help but play god. Buddha gave him a spider thread to escape from the Lotus Pond. God giveth, right? And Kandata, now in possession of this divine gift, chose to take it away from his fellow sinners. God taketh away, right?"

Meursault and Akutagawa, dumbfounded, both nodded, not necessarily in agreement with the message, but simply yielding to the Russian's uncompromising categoricalness.

The Russian, without missing a beat, continued: "You see, the reason why Buddha noticed Kandata in the first place is because he recalled that Kandata had once saved a spider, right?"

The Russian looked at Akutagawa to confirm the plot-line. The latter nodded, this time clearly in consent.

"Right," continued the Russian, "So, Buddha saw himself in Kandata. How so, you may ask? Well, when Kandata had spared the spider's life, he – Kandata, that is – played god. God giveth, remember? It was a Buddha moment. And that Buddha-moment was the karmic basis of Kandata's salvation. Buddha remembered it and decided to let Kandata cash it in. But here's the glitch. Kandata is fucking innocent: he is perfectly consistent in his conduct. When he spared an innocent spider, he was playing a benevolent god. When he cut off the spider thread to deny a chance of escape to his fellow sinners who he felt were undeserving of salvation, he was trying to be a fair god. Kandata – and I think it is very important to appreciate here – was simply doing his shitty human best. I – for one – have absolutely no problem with Kandata as a character, as a fallible human archetype. My problem – if I may call it so – is with Buddha. It is Buddha who is the asshole here, he is the sinner. If by Buddha, my friends, we mean god – a creator god, an all-powerful, all-pervasive god – then what the fuck, my friends?"

Meursault – strangely calm – sipped his coffee. Akutagawa, oblivious to a cup of coffee that he began to bring to his lips and left hanging in mid-air, was looking for an opening to break in.

Unstoppable like Russian T-34 tanks, the waiter continued: "Gods, my friends, if they exist, they are the sinners. They throw us into this reality, without an informed consent, without consulting us. Not one of us asked to be borne. And this shit-head Buddha first takes pity on a life that he himself created and then castigates Kandata back into hell just because the poor schmuck wanted to play fair."

"But," Akutagawa tried to protest. The Russian interrupted him in mid-speech: "Listen, my friends, the coffee is on me. The owner isn't even here yet. There are three men in the back and they don't need me today. I decided I need a long weekend. Let's get the fuck out of here and I have a proposition to make to you. What do you think about that?"

The Russian stood up, took off his apron, hang it up on the back of the chair and looked at Meursault and Akutagawa expectedly. He was of average height, stout, the type you wouldn't want to fight if you ran into him on the streets, but most likely kind and gregarious, the type that'd probably hug you to death before he'd hurt a hair on your head. He was exuding impulsivity and cheer.

Meurault smiled, got up and quickly finished his coffee. Akutagawa was still sitting, struggling to digest the Russian's forceful informality. He looked at Meursault and made his mind, sort of: "I am game if you are, Meursault."

"I am Pavel. Friends call me Pasha. You can call me Pasha since I've already addressed you as friends. Anyone is a friend unless proven otherwise," the Russian rattled off like a machine gun and disappeared back into the restaurant, probably to notify his coworkers of his unexpected departure. He popped back out for a second with a question: "Have you guys seen the knife from the table? I thought I brought out the set of utensils ... for the bread and butter ... but then, perhaps, I didn't ... since I actually didn't bring out any bread and butter ... "

Akutagawa lifted up the napkin: "I am pretty sure you did .... Here's the plate for the bread, and I do remember the silverware ... " Pavel looked underneath the table, shrugged his shoulders, and walked back into the restaurant with "Oh, well."

Meursault said nothing. In a moment Pavel was out, with a jacket flung over his shoulder and a dazzling smile of a single man with a long weekend ahead of him and seemingly nothing to lose.

--

The three made reasonably fast "friends" – the term that Pasha seemed to insist on. They had promising common denominators. All three were fundamentally strangers to Paris, to each other and even to themselves. All three were existentially adrift, with not a hint of an agenda. And all three had seemingly nothing to lose, or gain, for that matter. Meursault made no pretense about having no money on him. Akutagawa seemed to have some pocket money and a hotel room with a view. And Pasha made it clear that he was in a mood to party and that he was not above the idea of bankrolling whatever had to be bankrolled. They spent a day, walking the streets of Paris, discussing Akutagawa's story, deepening their respective disagreements about the "true" meaning of that vignette. As the differences in their interpretations grew, they seemed to be growing closer, more intimate, more informal. Pasha – already informal at a baseline – was openly touched by this trend.

"Look at you two, gents! No, look at us three – we are making fast friends, yes?"

Meursault and Akutagawa no longer nodded. Having long regained their voices, they slapped each other on the shoulders, jokingly shoved each other with elbows, and laughed at the silliest provocation. Fact is the three had graduated from coffee to port wine and, eventually, to some strong cognac.

--

They just returned to Akutagawa's hotel room. They had been in and out of his room throughout the day – getting liquor and cigarettes. But they have now returned back, this time to stay. They picked up meats and baguettes and a few apples. Meursault, clearly tipsy, was setting up the table while Akutagawa was wrestling with unruly curtains that kept getting in the way of a spectacular view. The door onto the balcony was open and the evening breeze was forcing the curtains into a risqué tango. Akutagawa, standing on a chair, was trying to wrap one of the curtains around the curtain rod above the opening and not having much success. Pasha just walked into the room, wiping his wet hands on his shirt. He yelled, laughing, to Akutagawa: "You don't have any clean towels in your washroom, but that's totally fine, I don't like towels anyway, that's what shirts are for."

Suddenly, he stopped in mid-laugh, looking at the knife in Meursault's hands. Meursault was cutting the loaf of bread into neat pieces, crusty bread breaking up into crumbs all over the newspaper that served as a tablecloth.

"Wait a second, bud, this is the knife that I was looking for this morning, Meursault." Meursault stopped cutting the bread, while still holding the knife in his hand. It was no butter knife. A butter knife is useless with French baguettes. Baguettes require nothing less than steak knives. Meursault was holding a stolen steak knife. Akutagawa, looking a bit shocked, stopped messing with the curtain and the cloth got sucked outside by the wind that picked up in strength. Meursault put the knife down but offered no explanation.

"That's a deal breaker, my friend," said Pasha, widening his stance for some reason. His hands, now dry, slightly went up to his waistline, as if ready for possible defensive action. "You have to explain yourself, Meursault."

"Yes, Meursault," Akutagawa chimed in, "you really do."

--

A few tense minutes passed by – too slowly for Akutagawa, too fast for Pasha. The explanation was refreshingly straight-forward. Meursault explained that he needed a knife for a stick-up. "Unlike you two, I have no money. How am I gonna get any money without a knife?"

"So you were gonna rob someone? At a knife-point?" asked Akutagawa, and then it dawned on him: "Were you gonna rob me the other night, on the Montmartre?"

"Yes, I thought about it, AK, but I didn't yet have a knife. I did size you up. But it didn't feel right, you know … "

Meursault was unflinching in his unapologetic transparence. Pasha, still standing, grabbed one of the chairs that was within his reach and turned it around, just like he did earlier today, with the back of the chair now being a protective barrier between him and Meursault. He did nevertheless sit down and extended his hand towards Meursault.

"I want my knife back, I'll need to take it back to the restaurant … " he said to Meursault.

"No problem," said Meursault and handed Pasha the knife.

"And I have a question to you, only one question, but it's important … " he said, motioning to Akutagawa to get off the chair and find a place to sit down somewhere.

"Have you," said Pasha, once again clearing his throat, "Have you ever killed anyone?"

Meursault didn't rush to answer. There was something elastic about the silence that ensued – it felt both fast and slow, depending on whether you felt the moment in real time or in retrospect. Meursault finally open his mouth and simply said: "Yes and no."

--

The answer was somehow enough for Pasha. The answer had enough information for Pasha to recalibrate his attitude to Meursault. It was now clear that he could not continue to get more drunk in the company of the Algerian. But everything else that

Pasha had come to feel about Meursault so far buffered against a rash decision to bring the evening to a close.

Akutagawa, on the other hand, took over the questioning: "How do you mean, Meursault? It's a binary matter – you either killed someone or you didn't."

"It is not binary, AK," said Meursault. "Just like your story about the Lotus Pond isn't binary. Nothing is binary in this world. Binary implies an "emptiness" between black and white, between one and zero (Meursault put "emptiness" in air quotes). But there is no emptiness. Everything is intertwined, like the web of that silver spider in your story."

Neither Akutagawa nor Pasha had yet heard Meursault say so much in one breath. Which is not to say that Meursault spoke fast. Not at all, he took his time, punctuating his speech with the micro-pauses of a radio narrator. It's just that Meursault's level of contribution to the conversation so far - in the last 10 or so hours since the three had met – had been quite minimal, ranging from simple questions to monosyllabic grunts. The most he had said was early on when he shared his interpretation of Akutagawa's story.

"Ok," said Akutagawa, "I want to know more, the specifics, please." Pasha didn't weigh in, he was simply witnessing life unfold as it always does, without our permission.

--

Meursault explained – in his characteristically laconic way – that a couple of weeks prior, after he buried his mother, he killed a man on the beach. "No, not out of grief, of course. There wasn't anything to grieve. Just because … "

"Just because? I am sorry I simply don't follow," protested Akutagawa.

"That's what I meant earlier when I said 'yes and no,' it just happened, the same way the stories come to you."

Akutagawa gasped: "I am sorry, but when I am talking about 'stories just coming to me' I am talking about being visited by a muse."

"It's the same thing, AK. It was just like that: you had a pen in your hand, and I had a knife in my pocket. We both took dictation."

"From whom?" pleaded Akutagawa, struggling to defend against the irrefutable parallel that he already glimpsed between his doing and the doing of Meursault.

"From the fucker upstairs," Pasha finally chimed in.

Meursault nodded: "Yes, from the guy upstairs." Unlike Pasha, the Algerian didn't seem to switch to the informal mode even while divulging self-incriminating information to complete strangers, even if they insisted on calling themselves as his "friends."

--

"Question is," said Meursault, addressing primarily Akutagawa, "Are you, AK, going to snip the spider thread that I am climbing on right now?"

Akutagawa shook his head, obviously confused: "What are you talking about, Meursault?" His voice betrayed both fear and frustration, arguably, the worst combination of feelings that one can combine. Fear and frustration.

"I am asking: are you going to call the police, AK? Now that you know, are you going to cut me off? Are you going to let me plunge into the abyss of your moral judgment?"

At around this moment, Pasha broke out into uncontrollable laughter. Meursault cracked a smile, his thin lips spreading apart just enough to betray the strong white teeth, like the window curtains, unable to hold back some internal wind of humor that – if you, reader, pay attention – blows through us almost non-stop. Akutagawa – AK, for short – simply stood there, vulnerable, with his back to the balcony and the evening Paris. Not yet amused but already bemused. The cosmic humor – when attended to – spares no one.

As soon as Pasha caught his breath, he slapped his shovel-like palms on his respective knees, got up from the chair and proposed: "Let's drink to whatever this fucking moment is, friends! Drink with me, you strange motherfuckers, or I am myself gonna cut you up."

--

Threatening toasts like that – among strangers – must only be taken with the benefit of the doubt. Otherwise, how else can we exit this kind of situation alive?

"I'll be frank with you," said Akutagawa with thick cognac breath, "If I live through this curious junction, I am going to write a hell of a story about this."

"No, you won't," said Meursault, and added with complete seriousness, "It's already been written."

--

The three drank through the night like nothing happened. But, of course, something definitely did. And the conversation reflected the occurrence. For hours, Akutagawa kept grilling Meursault on his motives. And as it often happens with conversations like this, clarity finally hinges on the right type of question. A good question is half the answer, as they say. And the question came from Pavel, most likely as an attempt to escape the ascending spiral of intellectualizing that the two – Meursault and Akutagawa – kept climbing.

"Meursault, here's what I wanna know – I want you to describe the setting, the moment, the knife. Put me in a state of mind that you found yourself in that day."

Akutagawa, red-faced from alcohol, shook his head with disapproval: "What fucking difference does that make, Pasha?"

"None! Obviously, none to you, AK. But I – for one – wanna know. Is that ok with you, friend?!" roared Pavel who, by now, seemed to have reached that point of intoxication that delicately borders on aggression and universal love.

Meursault intervened, as asked: "As I said, I was on a beach. It was late morning. Scorching sun. Pounding waves. Hot sand that you could cook in. Deserted beach, except for a few folks here and there."

"What were you doing on the beach, Meursault? You, Algerians, don't tan," said Pasha rather tactlessly.

"Ocean is the only truth. Each wave is like a big eraser for the mind. That is, if you pay attention. I often come to the water to reset my mind. To return to that baseline radio silence that is so hard to hear behind the static of modern life … "

Akutagawa started rummaging around for a piece of paper and a pencil. He wanted to take notes.

"Stop fussing, AK," said Pasha, "Just listen, friend. He's about to tell us."

But Meursault grew silent again. The inconsistent cadence of his narrative was both frustrating and jolting. His mind seemed to work in spurts and starts, like a diesel pump that is about to die.

The Japanese and the Russian listened.

Finally, Meursault spoke again: "I think I was simply at the mercy of the place. I sat there, thinking about my mom and how little she knew me. For years, for many, many years, when she'd ask me about how I was doing, I would only say 'ok,' and that seemed always enough for her. So, I simply assumed that it didn't really matter to her since she didn't want any details. She didn't press for them. So, I was just sitting there by the ocean, listening to that occasional clap that waves make when they hit the shore, thinking about that. And each time I heard the clap, it was as though the ocean hit me with a stick, right upside my head, like some kind of rascal Zen teacher. For a moment, I'd feel shell-shocked. But pleasantly so. It was working is all I can say. So, I kept sitting there, feeling the burn of the sun on my skin and the hiss in my ears, after each clap."

Meursault retreated into himself again. Suddenly, Pasha clapped his hands and Meursault and Akutagawa startled.

"Why the fuck would you do such a thing?" demanded Akutagawa.

"Easy, pal, easy," said Pasha, deploying the rest of his attention on Meursault.

Meursault, unlike Akutagawa, was smiling: "Yes, just like that. It was working. And then I heard that Frenchman start fiddling with his pocket radio. He was looking for music. And he wanted to find a good signal. He kept going back and forth trying to fine tune the signal to get the best reception. And I just got up, got a knife out of my pocket and went up to him. You know the rest … "

"Yes, we do," said Pasha, "we do."

--

Paris was dark again. The three now stepped out onto the tight balcony of the hotel room and, leaning on the railing, smoked.

"What you said, Meursault, certainly makes sense to me. But I think there is more to it. I think it is simply in the nature of space that we inhabit."

"How do you mean, friend?" asked Pasha as Meursault spat from the balcony at the sidewalk below.

"As long as I've known myself I've had this feeling that space is pregnant with possibilities. Space is karmic, it has a history to it. And as we step into a given coordinate of space, we enter an unconscious circumstance that presents us with what we experience as an impulse or a choice or a sudden mood. I am convinced that had you been sitting just a few yards away, Meursault, on different sand, in different wind, you wouldn't have done what you did. Something had happened in that space before and you got high-jacked by its history, reinforcing it, making it likely to reoccur again. Of course, it'll take a different form next time. Maybe a kid, playing in that very sand, will one day watch a jelly fish evaporate in the sun instead of taking it back to water. Or, perhaps, someone will cast a fishing rod there, on that very spot, and turn that spot into another gateway to death. The place, I am convinced, had a will of its own, and that's why you felt what you felt. You were right when you said 'yes and no,' that it 'just happened,' same as I myself get randomly inspired with 'this' or 'that' story.' Each coordinate of the Universe has its karmic signature. Is this making any sense to you?"

Pasha yawned and offered: "That's more like it, AK. I think you've got something there. Something that definitely rings the bell ..."

Meursault flicked the cigarette butt into the street below and said: "Would either of you have a few franks that I can borrow?"

Startled, Akutagawa, checked his pockets. Pasha did the same. The two handed Meursault a handful of bills. Meursault, nearly expressionless, pocketed the money, picked up the stolen knife from the table, cupped it with his right hand, and hid it, with the blade up, inside the long sleeve of his shirt. He then walked out of the hotel room without a good-bye.

Pasha and Akutagawa walked out onto the balcony to watch Meursault re-enter the night of his estrangement. In Paris it must have been getting on around midnight.

--

But not in Paradise ...

*In Paradise, the glorious noon-time Sun was shadowing Buddha on his stroll around the Lotus Pond. As always, Buddha made it his business – but only in passing – to peep down through the lotus leaves into the Hell below. In between the lurking shadows of the catfish, deep down at the bottom of the pond, Buddha saw a familiar face – a man named Kandata. Buddha knew Kandata's story all too well, his seeming ingratitude for the recent chance at salvation, his utter lack of insight into his sins, his righteous sense of entitlement for another chance. Kandata seemed beyond redemption. But once again, Buddha remembered how long ago Kandata spared the life of a spider. Buddha replayed that moment in his mind, trying to understand how such a beautiful seed of compassion could fail to blossom. This time Buddha decided to send no emissaries or proxies on his behalf. He himself – with the agility of an acrobat – slid down the silver spider thread that happened to be nearby. And as soon as his feet touched the silt of the lotus pond, Buddha addressed Kandata directly.*

*"Kandata, my child, I want you to tell me why you cut off the spider thread the other day when I gave you a chance to escape from hell? Did you not feel sorry for your fellow sufferers? The thread was strong enough to empty the entire population of hell had you not cut it off to spite the others."*

*Kandata, expressionless, suddenly produced a serrated knife out of his right sleeve and stabbed Buddha in the ribs, right under Buddha's heart. Bewildered and breathless, Buddha slumped over and*

*then fell onto his knees, his hands now submerged
and slowly sinking in the black silt of the lotus pond.*

*"Why, Kandata?" Buddha asked sorrowfully.*

*"It is the will of the place, my friend. The nature of
the medium, you might say. Silt is silt. And clouds
are clouds. What did you expect would happen in
Hell?"*

--

Buddha, of course, didn't die. Buddhas – if they exist
– cannot die. A Buddha's heart is emptiness in the
highest degree. No, not the proverbial emptiness of
the atom, but the emptiness of non-bias. To love all
is to love no one. A heart like that is impervious to
knives.

*"Why did you try to kill me, Kandata?" Buddha
asked again.*

*Kandata smiled, the lines around his mouth parting
like stage curtains: "Gods belong in Hell, don't you
understand? Hell is where your work is needed, you
princely asshole! Hell, not Paradise, is the
vivisection chamber of the soul. If you are a true god,
you belong with the sufferers, the sinners, the broken.
Paradise needs no micromanagers, it'll run on its
own just fine."*

*Buddha, washing his hands off the black silt of the
lotus pond, was back on his feet, the lotus roots
obsequiously wrapping themselves around his
sculpted calves.*

*"Kandata, if you are so high-minded, so concerned about the wellbeing of your fellow sufferers, then why were you so eager to escape this Hell the other day? Why were you groping your way up the spider thread?"*

*"I wasn't trying to escape this Hell, you moron. I was coming after you. I have been watching you from down here, waiting for a chance to pounce. And when I saw the silver spider thread, I knew it was my chance, my chance to get you. Had I reached the surface of the Paradise, I would have stabbed you until you were unconscious and would have dragged you down below, to Hell where you belong ... "*

*"That's what you would have done?" asked Buddha clearly surprised. "That was your plan all along, Kandata? To bring me down below?"*

*"Yes, so that you'd minister to the ones who suffer rather than witnessing the ones who don't ... What else are gods for?!"*

*Buddha demurred.*

*"I think I have underestimated you, Kandata. I might have totally misunderstood you. That time when you spared the life of a spider ... that was no fluke ... That compassion you showed is your true nature ... And the actions – the robberies, the killings – you have had to do in your life ... all these are just the necessary evils – the will of the place, as you say ... the package deal of life ... "*

*Kandata's shoulders – tense his whole life – suddenly relaxed. For the first time in his existence, he felt absolved, his motivational innocence final witnessed.*

*Buddha continued: "You and I, we are the same. I, the prince, and you, the untouchable – no fundamental difference between us, only a gap of circumstance. I feel it is now your turn to live in Paradise, and my work – you are right – is here. "*

And with these words, Buddha touched the taught dark green stem of the lotus plant that had woven loops around Buddha's legs. The roots relaxed for a moment and sprang out another shoot.

*"It is for you, my friend," said Buddha with a familiar raspy Russian accent, for some reason.*\*\*\*

Kandata grabbed the shoot and was carried, amidst a whirl of bubbling contrails, to the top. The stolen serrated knife fell out of his relaxed hand and sank down into the deep, as he himself ascended to the serene surface of the Lotus Pond. Buddha picked up the knife from the soft black silt. In Hell one is wise to have a knife in hand, even if one is a Buddha.

--

Notes

\* Ryūnosuke Akutagawa – a Japanese author (1892-1927), "father of the Japanese short story," died of suicide

\*\* This is a full text of Akutagawa's story "The Spider's Thread"

\*\*\* Meursault – this character is meant to be the same Meursault as the one in Albert Camus' novel "Stranger"

\*\*\*\* The text in italics, starting with *"In Paradise, the glorious noon-time Sun ... "* and ending with *"It is for you, my friend ... "* is Somov's elaboration on Akutagawa's story

# Bottom Feeder

When you drown, your mind becomes a bubble of air that rushes to the surface, while de-fragmenting into ever smaller bubbles as your body keeps moving down, like the dead weight that it has always been, in the opposite direction. The marriage of matter and consciousness, as indivisible as it seems, is the flimsiest of all. Consciousness is in a constant state of infidelity: eyes see, ears hear, and skin touches the things out there, while the matter that makes these eyes, these ears, and this skin remains mostly unattended to, taken for granted, and ignored.

I learned this strange perspective from Dimka Tokarev, a 7 year-old pal of mine back in Moscow. He drowned in 1976.

When he came to my mind one day, I asked him: "How can this be? How can we defrag into a myriad of pieces? Isn't there a oneness of some kind in there, inside of us? Aren't you, Dimka, one? Aren't I?"

"Yes, of course. Of course, you are one. But it doesn't mean that you have to be in one place at all times," he said, turning over on his side. His long-decomposed body seemed blurred at the edges, his facial flesh almost gone and swaying, in ragged blotches, in the jet burst of a nearby fish spooked by his ghostly presence.

"I don't understand," I said to him. "How can you be one, but not in one place?"

"I don't know how but that's how it is, at least, that's how it is for me," Dimka bubbled out a few muted words, slowly morphing like a sunken lava lamp at the bottom of the Moscow River.

"Tell me more, Dim, tell it to me from the beginning."

"Ok, Pash, but this is the last time. I am done with this, you know."

"With this 'what'?"

"With this reincarnation, Pash, with this footprint I've left in your mind. You have to let me go, you know. Erase me from your thoughts. Maybe write it down somewhere; just get it out of your mind. Get *me* out of your mind!"

"I'll try, Dim. Maybe I'll write it up as a story."

"Anything, pal. Anything! To think about what no longer exists is to not think about what still exists. Don't you get it?"

"I do, at least, I think I do, Dim. Please, go on, friend. From the beginning, ok?"

"Ok, Pash. But you've heard this before and frankly I don't know why I have to go over this again and again and again." Dimka paused, his murky eyes lacking any inner focus.

He eventually continued: "Vovka (from the fifth floor) and I were taking turns going out into the water on a tire-tube, in Izmailovo. We hitched a ride with his dad who was going to work. He said he'd pick us up on the way back. We had almost two rubles between us so we knew we had a day of fun ahead of us, with enough money for snacks when we get hungry. It was my turn and Vovka decided to pull a prank. When I wasn't looking, he loosened up the valve and I went out into the water not knowing that the tube was losing air. As you know, I can't swim. I was out a good distance from the shore, paddling around like an idiot, when I realized what was happening. But it was too late: the tube was losing air too fast and I was too far and Vovka, the shit-head, ran off the moment I started yelling for help. I guess he panicked. I would have panicked too. There is a chance he ran for help but I wouldn't know. By the time he would have returned, I would have already gone down anyway. Have you talked to him? Do you know why he ran off?"

This was different. Dimka hadn't asked me that before. I felt taken aback as I stared into his unfocused eyes inside my mind.

"No, Dim, I haven't," I said, adding, "He hasn't been

48

out to play. He might be transferring to a different school after this, maybe even to Orphanage. But I think you are right. He's a shit-head and he probably did piss his pants and ran off to change them first. So, you drowned, huh?"

"Yes, Pash, I did! You are an effing moron, you know. You saw me in a coffin, you heard my mom wailing. Why do you keep asking the same silly questions like a fat catfish that you are?"

I didn't object. Being called a "moron" by Dimka was par for the course. This was the thing between us – words. Words, come to think of it, *are* the thing between most of us. Language is more of a barrier than a bridge.

"This reminds me, Dim," I said pensively. "I used to give you so much hell when you called me 'fat catfish.' I used to chase you around the school yard for hours. You knew I could kick your ass but you also knew I could never catch up with you because you were a fast bastard. Who's a bottom-feeder now?"

Dimka seemed uninterested, his eyes disappearing from view. "So, what else is there to know, Pash?"

"Tell me what the realization was like, you know, when you understood that you were going down?"

"Ok, but for the last time, you know. I am tired of these thoughts. You asked me this before. As soon as I was in the water I knew all there was to know. I was going down. I knew I couldn't swim so there was no point in trying. Frankly, I was just curious. Remember how Vaska's brother jumped off of the third floor when his parents were fighting? Since then I was somehow really curious what it was like to die. Fact is, neither then nor now do I believe it's even possible. Whatever already is has nowhere to go. It's all a change of form. Mutation. Transformation. Arising and cessation. The fact is, you never were, never are and never will be any one thing that you can call 'you'."

"Are you a Nothing then?"

"No, not a Nothing, Pash. No such thing-less thing as a Nothing, you effing moron."

"What then?"

"A nothing-in-particular, maybe, something like that…"

If I didn't like Dimka before because I could never catch up with his body, now I liked him even less because I couldn't catch up with his mind. Language was failing us. He and I were using the same set of words but we seemed to share entirely different experiential reference points. That's how it always is, between any two minds.

"What happened next, Dim?"

"Nothing happened, Pash. I watched myself drown."

"Tell me."

"It's hard to explain," continued Dimka. "First, I was focused on my body. Then I was focused on my mind. And then I was kind of unfocused. You know, like right now, if you were to study what you are, all you'd find is that you are a field of awareness, a space that is aware. And so was I – just under water. But it didn't bother me. While my body was wet, my mind was dry as ever. While my body was drowning, I, my mind, wasn't. It's hard to explain. The bottom-line is, nothing ever really happens to you. Whatever you think you experience, you really don't. If you are aware of 'it,' you aren't 'it.' There is a geometry to observation. To observe is to be separate, to be aside, to be perpendicular to whatever it is that you are observing, to be apart from 'it.' You follow me?"

"I think so. But I am not sure."

Dimka released a series of muted bubbles, savoring them like one would a series of perfect rings of smoke with each successive one threading itself through the pinhole of the prior ones. There was a hypnosis to this, and he seemed to know it as he returned to his point, his eyes once again shining for a second with a familiar gleam of teasing: "So, there I was  under water. And yet I, the way I know myself, the way I experience myself, was a field of being. Then this field that I was began to break up, to bubble up, to de-fragment, a piece of me, one bubble at a time, rising up to the surface, making its own twisting and spiraling way up above, and, once reaching the surface, vanishing in a pop. And so, bubble after bubble, a thousand pieces of my being at a time, in swarms, I kept de-fragmenting and vanishing as the pseudo-entity that I thought I was. Yet, I never seemed to disappear, fizzing out as I was, like a bottomless bottle of soda, I lasted and lasted and lasted."

"How can this be?" I asked again.

"I am not sure, Pash. I really am not sure, not at all. Here's what I think, but what I think doesn't really matter. This thing I am talking about is beyond words, before words, has no more to do with words than a hang-nail on your thumb. You know how we think we have a brain? We don't. There is no brain. The brain is not an organ. It's an organization. An army of stand-alone neural cells, each a micro-organism in its own right. So, when we die, or drown as is the case with me, we don't die alone, we die as we live, as a community, as a crowd, as a neural colony. When drowning, I didn't die just once, I died a billion times. Each neuron that 'I' collectively was, was giving up its own ghost, informationally de-fragging all of its personally encoded experiences, scattering itself, a life-page at a time, like a file folder that is blown off the café table by a gust of wind."

"How long did this last?"

"It's still ongoing, Pash, never ending, you know. You see, just like there is no brain per se, there are no neurons. These are all constructs, abstractions, mind-forms, semantic approximations. We package entire bottomless universes of thing-less things into single words such as 'neuron' or 'brain.' When my "neurons" de-fragged informationally, they continued to de-frag structurally. First, on a molecular level, then atomically, now sub-atomically. I am still de-fragging as we speak: everything 'I' ever collectively was is still un-dancing all of its vortical twists-of-determinism, in an infinite half-life overture of cessation. 'I' am still here, as completely, as I ever was, just not in one convenient place, but all over, even in you, through you."

"How do you mean, Dim?"

"Some of the calcium that I am (and am not) has already become your so-called bones. Not much, but enough for these silly notions of 'you' and 'me' to lose their meaning. It's just like the criss-crossing of ripples in a pond: waves of transformation pass through each other. Identity is a myth."

Just as Dimka finished this brooding train of thought,

I suddenly lost sight of him. Neither he nor I were any longer rolling around in the silt of the Moscow River. And then he re-appeared, with a question in his hollowed out "eyes."

"How's my Mom, Pash?"

At this point the tables of story-telling were turned. He had heard me explain this before and yet somehow what I, the living, knew in this here-and-now world that you, dear reader, and I share, this world was somehow stuck in Dimka's other-worldly mind. He and I shared this dance of fixation, like particles married to each other through some non-local bond.

"I don't know, Dim. I know I met her but it was before you drowned. I think just once. She told me to stop bugging you. I might have seen her when I saw your body on the day they buried you."

"Oh, so I was found? They found me?"

Coming from him, this question was insanely rhetorical. But what do I know? I feigned doubt. My doubt, I knew, was his hope. And his hope, I think, was my doubt.

"Yes, I think so. They had some kind of body in the coffin that day. Looked like you, Dim. I know that much. That's all I know really. I didn't even know you had died. It was a Sunday, I think. Summer, of course. I was out in the street playing and there was all this noise and mournful music. Women were wailing; many, many voices. I think some were professional wailers. I went up to your building and there was this big crowd around a Zil truck. They carried you out in a coffin, on shoulders, slid you into the bed of the truck and drove away. That's all."


"So, you didn't see my Mom?"


"Nope."


"You know, Pash, I don't even remember her. She is an idea. I was too young to ever know her as her, if that's even possible. She was always an idea for me. We never know our parents because they are parents to us, you see? Somebody who feeds me or somebody who makes me go to bed when I don't want to. We never met. Same with you, Pash. We, too, never met. These fields of being, they are non-overlapping."


We, whatever that means, looked at each other, separated by nothing more than the illusory dichotomy of "self" and "other." And I realized that we never have been apart. We are just a boundless, bottomless, beginningless ocean of bubbles of one and the same oneness, divided by nothing but words.


"By the way, Pash, are you still training in water

polo?"

"No. That is (was?), like, thirty years ago. But I still know how to swim, Dim. I just don't yet know how to drown."

"You fat catfish, you! One day you'll know."

Yes, one day we'll all know. There is a time to swim and there is a time to drown.

# Swatara

Mind is as fertile as alluvial soil, like the kind of soil you find around the Nile or the Volga, after the rivers spill out of their waistlines in spring. Mind is a receptive medium, a field to be ploughed and sown. But Mind-land must lie fallow for a while lest we lose our capacity for regeneration. Too much information chokes us up. You'll probably experience that in a few pages …

The field of am-ness that I am, has been doing just that, it seems, for months, digesting the indigestible, while asleep; but in its moments of lucid near-awakening, I knew I needed a three-alarm wake-up call, and so I called Bill Hayworth, an Iroquois medicine-man I know, to see what he had up his magic, star-studded sleeve.

"A trip to Swatara," he proposed.

"By car, plane or spaceship?" I asked.

"Car will do, Paul. It's just a few hours from Pittsburgh. You pay for gas, Paul, and I'll bring some home-made jerky," Bill chuckled into the phone and hung up.

--

We pulled over to the side of the two-lane road in the boondocks of Pennsylvania, about an hour's drive from Hershey, the Chocolate Country, and got out of the car.

"Hold on a sec," I said to Bill who was already out of the door. "Let me put the flashers on … "

Bill, a *Ho-de'-no-sau-nee* descendant of the famous Hiawatha, said nothing. Bill was a medicine man and silence, he once told me, was the best medicine for the mind. I met him at his sweat lodge a good while back and over the years he grew on me – the moss of consciousness. A mostly silent type with a pre-cirrhotic liver, Bill didn't say much except for when he told the stories of the past or philosophized. In those moments, he was unstoppable, a real force of nature to reckon with, a rolling barrel of a cosmic wave, full of foamy argumentation and preaching.

"This is Swatara," said Bill, spitting out a wad of Copenhagen on the ground. "This is where we once fed on eels … "

"That's what Swatara means, right, Bill, in Iroquois?" I asked catching up with him as he walked through the weeds towards a thin forest line.

"That's what Swatara means in Ho-de'-no-sau-nee," Bill corrected me with a sideways glance. "We ain't no Iroquois, that's a white man's term. Actually, a Basque pidgin name for my people. That's what those Spanish fishermen used to call us in Northeast way back when. They'd pronounce it *Hi-lo-koa* – the killers – the murderers … "

Bill chuckled to himself. He didn't have to verbalize the bitter irony that prompted the chuckle – it was self-evident, even to me.

"Hi-lo-koa … Ee-ro-quois … " I muttered to myself, playing with the Grimm's law of phonological change, my tongue rolling "l" into "r" like a fisherman from Okinawa trying to speak English.

--

We made our way through a thin forest and came out to a creek, cockle-burs – nature's Velcro - all over our pants. And here it was - the Swatara creek, not worthy of a postcard, but, to Bill, a sacred site nevertheless, and for me, an intriguing pretext for Bill's obscure point, which he was yet to make.

"Swa-ta-ra," said Bill again, savoring each syllable, and added after a pause, "This is where we – the killers - fed once on eels and where we fed on ourselves … " It was classic Bill – he was ever ready to integrate and own the very item that he had just fought. The derogatory term for his tribe – when spoken by him – was no longer an affront. Like a master street fighter, he took the word-knife away from his opponent, licked the blade clean, and put it into his own hip pocket for keeps.

--

We sat down. Bill found a spot on a rocky slab; I – on a log covered with dried up, crumbling moss.

"Just look around, Paul," he said with a commanding voice. "You can pick off the burs from your pants later, plus it's pointless, ain't it? You'll get all burred up on the way back anyhow … "

I looked up, ready to take in the moment: the afternoon Sun was forcing its way through the tree leaves, my eyes cutting up the blinding onslaught of light into a manageable asterisk of white rays.

"Swa-ta-ra," Bill said again, mantra-like. "This is where we stopped eating eels, you know … "

--

On the drive from Pittsburgh Bill explained that the eels are bottom feeders and that they particularly love feeding on drowned men, and that, because of that, eating eels was a form of auto-cannibalism. He also said that there was "much more to it than just that" and wanted me to come to the Swatara creek to explain his thinking further. In passing, he also clarified that the taboo on eating eels didn't last – like any diet the imposed self-restriction fell prey to desire rationalized as necessity.

"But that's not the point of it all, Paul … " he said with a flicker of irritation in his tone, once again letting me know that his star-studded sleeve was still full of surprises.

Right off the bat I knew the auto-cannibalism story couldn't be right: there couldn't have been enough drowned humans to sustain a population of eels, and how could have we – humans – know that eels consider our rotting flesh a delicacy – it just didn't add up.

I didn't necessarily believe Bill, certainly not every story that he told me. Half the time, I thought Bill was full of shit. The other half of the time, Bill would say as much himself. But my time with Bill was always well spent. And, after all, as many historians tend to admit in rare moments of intoxicated candor, history is not a collection of facts but a mess of self-serving interpretations. Bill was an eccentric and needed an audience. His mind was an evolving metaphor in which history intermingled with fantasy, fact married fiction, and cosmologies tangoed with botany. His mind was my kind of mind, a fellow mind and a fellow no-mind.

(Are you like that too? Just asking, you know.)

--

"It's a fool's errand to pick off the burs, Paul," said Bill while, nevertheless, helping me out. "There, no – right there," he said pointing to my shoulder, "and another on your elbow … " He reached way over, half-standing from the stone he had been sitting on, and picked off a bur from my back. Bill was a helpful guy even if he didn't believe in a given cause. The kind of guy that would help you collect kindling for a fire under a pouring rain, just to be helpful.

"So, how do you plan to get the burs off, Bill?" I asked in earnest.

"No need to, Paul, they'll get off on their own, like you do from a Greyhound bus when it's your stop. A bur is a bundle of seeds. Seeds are alive. All living things know where they are going. What do you think – they are just being sticky for no reason?!" He chuckled and added: "They know when it's their stop."

Indeed, the Universe travels without a GPS. Desire is its own map, its own compass. Burs do get off wherever they want to.

--

A while back Bill told me about how he figured out what the coffee plant "wants." Here's what he said: "The other day I had nothing to do, so I laid down on my bed and wondered – what is it that makes coffee so addictive? And then I had a vision of being a coffee bush. So I asked myself the same question. And then the truth was revealed to me … "

"Do tell," I egged Bill on.

"Well, it's simple really. As a coffee bush I knew I had to propagate. So, I asked myself: what's my advantage over other plants? What will I have that others can't have? And I thought to myself: I am gonna make those who eat me – mountain goats and the like – fast. I am gonna give them energy, so that they can run far and run fast, away from predators. And the benefit to me is that they will carry my seeds in their stomachs far, far away to the places that I haven't yet been and never will go to. So my coffee-bean energy will keep the goats fast and safe, and they will know it, and come back again and again to graze on my berries. Speed is safety, you know, and that matters in the wild. And then I also thought to myself: I am going to make goats shit as they run. Because if they don't shit, the husks of my children-seeds inside the goat's belly will soften up and dissolve and my offspring will die. Because, you know, the stomach juices are acidic and corrosive. But if the goats get diarrhea, they will poop out some of the seeds intact, undigested, and the coffee beans – my children – will find themselves in the new soils, already pre-fertilized with goat-poop for a healthy, long life. So, I saw this in my mind just as I see you now: a decision to be stimulating and diuretic – " Bill laughed out loud like a kid and added with a comically serious expression: " - because, as you well know, Paul, coffee makes you all energetic and makes you shit, right?"

"Right," I said and added: "You know, Bill, this makes good sense. Must be true. I just don't know how you figured this out."

"Everything we say is 50% true and 50% not true. And the only way to know true from un-true is to put the two together and to see what floats to the top. Bullshit floats to the top, we question it, we wade through it, looking for clean water … but the truth – the truth sinks deep into our hearts, like a stone, and we don't question it, we just nod along."

And I nodded along that time, not questioning the truth of the coffee bean.

--

On the drive, with the window down and his callous palm surfing the wind, Bill talked and talked about eels and humans. He talked about how female eels live to be 50 years old, "same as catfish!", how no one has ever seen an eel spawn because they only spawn in the ocean, "away from human eyes." Bill talked about fishing eels with chicken livers and how it helped to dip your hand in dry river sand when you try to hold onto them because "they are slippery bastards." And how to flip them on their back to calm them down before you kill them. And about how those "electric eels, who can deliver 900 volts" are not really eels. And, of course, about how majestic they can get – "6-7 feet, can you imagine?!"

But – Bill finally said - he saved the best "tidbit" for last. He wouldn't tell me now, in the car, but only when we reached Swatara.

"There is a point I want to make to you, you see, – an ancient point – I think you'll like it. But I ain't gonna spill the beans till we get to Swatara. Info for gas – that's the deal, white man. You pay for gas to get us there and I pay you back with a word of wisdom." And, at this, Bill chuckled, as usual, at his self-serving smart-alecky ways, as befits a modern-day shaman.

The informational priming – before the final coat of wisdom was to be applied – consisted of a few other, less interesting factoids about the life cycle of an eel. I'll relate those to you in a page or two.

--

A good while back, around the time I first met Bill, I asked him about his way of referring to white men as "white men."

"Don't you think it's kinda racist, Bill, not that I mind, you know … "

"Not at all," he said. "When I say 'white man' I am not referring to the color of your skin, Paul, but to the color of your mind, which is white. Plus, you got more tan on you than me most of the time."

"How so, Bill? What do you mean by 'white mind'?"

"White man's mind is blank, it's white like a blank sheet of paper. No history on it, no ink. Brown man's mind is black with ink, black with history. Non-white man remembers his past. White man doesn't. White man looks ahead into the future. Non-white man looks back, keeps his past in the rear-view mirror, you know – "

As was his way, Bill seamlessly merged from one metaphoric highway to another. Who was I to tell him to use his narrative turn-signal?

" – White man's mind is a blank sheet of paper, perfect for blueprints, for future designs, for sketching out the visions. We need minds like that. Brown people too now and then give birth to an albino-mind. We all need to reinvent ourselves now and then. A white mind – a blank mind – sketch-paper-mind is essential to survival. But your race took this too far. It began with the exodus from Africa – your kinfolk ran up North so fast, you never looked back. So the ink of the ages just faded away. Mind became blank and skin got bleached."

"What color is your mind, White Man Bill?" I asked.

Bill chuckled: "You are right, I - a descendant of Hiawatha – too now am a white man pretty much. But my mind isn't blank … No, sir … "

"What color is it, Bill?"

"It's the color of glass – every color, no color at all. Reflective of what's inside and of what's outside, like a living mirror."

Bill repacked his chew, smacked his lips a few times, dried them off with his tongue and finally added: "White man looks ahead because he doesn't get it that time is a circle. When we want to know what's next we just look back. Past and future are one seamless time. We've been here before, Paul, you and I, we ate those eels already … "

That was the end of that conversation.

--

So, the other few eel factoids that Bill had primed me with on our trip to Swatara, are as follows. Eels begin as transparent larvae in the sea. They see you but you don't see them. Then, as they mature and become elvers – still somewhat transparent and, thus, called "glass eels" - they move into freshwater rivers and travel upstream, climbing obstructions of various kinds. Nature's little perfectionists, "strivers," as Bill called them. With time they turn big and brown, eating voraciously anything in sight, hanging out on the bottom with catfish and other bio-waste-disposal fish-crews. "They are nighttime fish," said Bill, "just like my people – we too liked to hunt at night."

Eventually, the grown eels return back to the sea to spawn. Which is why back in the days of Aristotle, eels had a mythical status – no one had seen them as young. They seemed to have come into existence fully grown. Were they water-snakes or giant earth-warms who learned to swim? "Nobody knew back then. And now nobody cares."

But, most importantly, "an eel is good eating," explained Bill. Tossing a river-stone into the Swatara creek, he added: "A mature male eel easily – easily! - feeds three! So, this was no easy decision for us to stop eating eels, you know, and as to why, I am yet to tell you … "

--

"The Swatara tale is like that bur seed on your jeans – it gets off the bus when it's ready. This tale resurfaces every so often among my people, a few times in a generation, not every time we eat eels but once in a while. The story gets off the bus of our unconscious, collective mind and steps into our waking mind when necessary, when the time has come."

Bill could be poetic, a wordsmith, no less, when he wanted to be. He seemed interested in that now, in telling a good story, in putting some ink onto the blank page of my mind.

--

Bill pulled out a pack of jerky he had bragged about. Offered me some. I accepted the offer. We sat there for a while, watching the creek. It's amazing how long we can stay preoccupied trying to get out a piece of food stuck in between the teeth. In my life, I've wasted entire days like that until I finally got home and was able to floss out the annoyance. Sometimes to the point of jaw muscles feeling sore, as the tongue tries to pretzel itself into some out-of-reach dental corner.

Something like that might have been happening in Bill's mouth as well. He was grimacing a bit.

Jerky was gone, so I asked: "What's on your mind, friend?"

"Just the rest of it. There is a bigger point to Swatara – you know how I said we stopped eating eels because they had been known to feast on drowned men, that wasn't the main reason. There is a bigger point here. A bigger tale. Not quite a tale but an insight, an epiphany, a big realization."

"Yeah?" I said to let Bill know I was ready to hear it.

"The bigger point, Paul, is that we ourselves are eels, just eels on legs and with hands."

"What do you mean, Bill?"

"I'll tell you what I mean – we are toroidal."

"Toroidal, you say, or hemorrhoidal?"

It was an imbecile joke but Bill cracked up; it typically didn't take him much.

Suddenly Bill got serious. That's how it was with him. He started talking with the verbal precision of a graduate philosophy student on meth. His eyes now seemed to be connected to mine with two invisible clothing lines that tensed and slackened as he spoke but never broke contact.

"Toroidal beings are oral: we erroneously over-identify with our contents, unable to stomach the emptiness of our essence. Toroidal orality is insatiable. Accepting our emptiness is fulfilling – "

"Wait, wait, wait, Bill. Back up a mile, will you, please?" I asked.

Bill smiled: "Ok, Paul, let me start over … "

--

"What is "toroidal"?" Bill asked himself and proceeded to answer: "That which is in the shape of a donut, with a hole in the middle. That's what we really are like. If you imagine any human body without limbs, just a torso, you will see that there is a hole/tube running through us. It's the GI (gastrointestinal) tract."

I nodded to show him that I understood. The invisible lines of the eye contact slackened but tensed again.

"What is oral?" Bill asked himself again in a professorially rhetorical tone and answered: "Consult Freud regarding the meaning of this term, Paul."

"I know what oral means and you know perfectly well that I know … "

Bill nodded to show me that he understood. "Do I need to back up any more?"

"Sure, maybe a foot or two."

I knew what had happened: Bill hated being interrupted and he was on a roll. But I didn't drive all the way to Swatara just to be lectured. I wanted an understanding and an understanding is impossible without an exchange.

Bill continued:

"Animals – humans included – are, in essence, trees on legs, we are mobile plant-life. So, our root is on top, where the mouth is. Pour in water up there, stuff that mouth up there with food and, look, body sprouts at the bottom. Just like trees, we are living input/output tubes, only oriented differently, and on legs. Mouth is the root, the root of all your bodymind growth. You literally sprout from these very lips that kiss reality with every bite, from these two rows of teeth that mill the matter of reality into the consciousness with which you right now are trying to understand what I am saying – "

This was Bill's favorite conversational maneuver – to engage his listener in a moment of self-referencing. He was a conversational hypnotist that used confusion as a clarification strategy. Whenever this happened, my mind would come to a stall: a moment ago I was just listening to a story, but now I was listening to a story in which I – just like you are, my dear Reader, right now – realize that I am the very subject of the story that I am listening to or reading …

That's how Bill got around my insistence on engagement: feeling confused, with a taste of clarity in my mouth, I had nothing to say, so I just listened just like you – right now – keep on reading.

Bill carried on, unstoppable in his spiel: " - Before you eat next time, notice your mouth. Clench and relax your jaw, smack your lips, let your tongue maniacally sweep around its cavernous abode, chomp your matter-milling teeth. Check the equipment of your growth. Get rooted in the mouth. Realize: this reality you are about to process is the very ground you sprout from."

He reached into the cargo pocket on his pants and pulled out a banged-up, bent-out-of-shape granola bar most likely years past its expiration date. "Here, Paul, eat and notice! Eat and notice. Shit in – shit out – you are a living tube, nothing less, nothing more!"

--

Like all medicine men and women, like all shamans and motivational speakers, Bill had that capacity to turn on the energy on demand. He'd probably say that he simply summoned the Cosmic forces or the wind of his ancestors. At any rate, invariably, as befits the moment, Bill would transform into a rock-star TED-talk speaker and dish out non-stop pearls of wisdom like Spinfire tennis ball machine. I decided to stay silent – Bill demanded an audience and I was the only pair of ears around.

"So, what does all of this have to do with eels, you must be wondering?" Bill once again went rhetorical.

"I am, Bill," I dared to chime in.

"This is where we understood our toroidal nature, Paul. Or rather this is where we remembered it. It's a tribal memory that revisits us once in a while, a Jungian kind of memory … "

Bill's tone suddenly softened. The change was remarkable – same as the rapid temperature change that happens when you are in an open-air city pool in early fall and it is sunny one moment and then the sun disappears behind the clouds and you realize that you are warmer in the water than in the air and you sit and wait for the sun to come out again so that you can get out of the pool, dry off and not come back until next

summer. The TED rock-star was gone. Bill –
relaxed, conversational, non-academic – was back.

"Here, look here, Paul," Bill said drawing with his
fingertip a wiggle line in the tightly packed yellow
sand by the creek-bed. "This is the eel, right? Now,
add a couple of arms and a couple of legs, and what
do we get?" He paused like a diver would at the tip
of the jumping board and back-flipped into the
conclusion: "We get a human figure – a tetrapod with
a GI track, with four oars that first became four legs
and then became a pair of legs and a pair of arms ... "

Bill skipped another beat and continued: "And now
see what happens when we take these four limbs
away – " Bill cut straight lines across the limbs as if
severing them – "we get our eel back ... The
difference, Paul, between you and an eel is inessential
– the four limbs ... "

"And the brain, Bill." I added.
"And, yes, the brain, Paul ... But the reason why have
such a big brain is because we have four limbs to
manage and all the additional degrees of freedom to
process and make use off ... But our basic anatomical
blueprint is that of an eel – we are living tubes, just
like an eel – but on legs and with arms which, by the
way, also used to be legs, you know ... "

--

"When I smoke my pipe and think deep I see my ancestor, Hiawatha, sitting here, looking around at his people and having this insight."

Hiawatha, Bill told me before, was a famous ancestor of his, not at all a killer but a peace-maker. One of several mythical Iroquois who didn't just smoke a peace pipe but lit it too. According to Bill, Hiawatha and Jigonsaseh, also known as the Peace Queen, had to do with the Great Law that united half a dozen of Northeast tribes.

"So, I see that old chief sitting here, looking around at his people, eating eels, having a good time. And then his eyes come upon a wounded man laying on the ground, maybe his leg had been chopped off with a battle ax or his arm or both ... And there he is writhing on the ground, in pain, limbless ... And then it dawns on Hiawatha – we are just like eels, we are no different, we are just like the ones that we are eating now, and just like the one that we just tried to kill in a war party and just like the ones who tried to kill us the other day in a war party ... We are all living tubes, some with mohawks, some with fins ... Some of us, living snakes, walk upright through the grass with spears and bows, other snakes that we are crawl around with forked tongues, and others – freshwater eels – hang out at the bottom of a pond, in the murk of the water, eating the water snow of rotting debris ... "

Bill stood up and tried to mime, dance-like, the animal spirits that he was envisioning in his mind – swimming, crawling, prancing.

"And I see Hiawatha getting up and kicking the dirt into the cooking fires, yelling and shouting, telling his people to stop eating eels. And the next morning, I think, he woke up and decided to bring the Six Nations – Mohawks, Onondagas, Oneidas, Cayugas, Senecas and Tuscaroras - into a peace treaty, into the Great Law of peace and nonviolence … The Basque were right in calling us "hi-lo-koa" – "Iroquois" – the killers. We are all Iroquois. All of us – Americans, Brits, Russians, Mongols, French, Poles, Maoris, Sudanese, Dutch, you name it – all of us all killers. We are all scalping and skinning each other … We are all Iroquois … "

Bill walked a few more laps around this invisible point of truth, kicking up river sand with his boots.

--

As always Bill was convincing and dramatic, the point itself was clear. I imagined myself as a quadruple amputee – no legs, no arms, just a torso. I raised my chin up in the air and envisioned an empty tube running right through me, my digestive track. I saw myself as an eel, a land-dwelling eel. I thought about my brain as a kind of GPS in a backpack, a computational device necessary to move the living tube that I am here or there. Bill, off his shamanic high, was now watching me process this information, digest this ephemeral mind-food.

"That's what I mean by saying that we are toroidal – take this living tube that you are and slice it up like a stick of salami into coins … " he said.

"Coins?" The word didn't sound right in this context, so I repeated it out loud.

"I mean circular segments – imagine an eel sliced up like a stick of salami – and now look at each slice – it's a coin of sorts – a hole of the GI track in the middle, body around it … that's the donut, the basic toroidal architecture of any living body … "

I nodded again, the imagery was sinking in.

"And what's the implication then?" - I asked – "What's the big picture, Bill?"

"The big picture is that the picture is quite small – we think of ourselves as this or that but we are nothing but living emptiness – glorified earth-worms is what we are, on legs, with phones and car keys in our pockets – we crawl around, eating shit, making shit … "

It was my turn to chuckle. I remembered the tale of the coffee bean.

"It just occurred to me, Paul … Imagine me as a living tube, no legs, no arms, a human eel … A garden hose, in a sense … And this living coffee bush is holding me in its hands, feeding me this stimulating and diuretic concoction of coffee grinds and using me to spray it around like a fertilizer … "

I was laughing as I spoke and Bill was smiling: "You are getting weird on me, Paul. Did you eat some berries on the walk that you weren't supposed to be eating?"

I kept on laughing and Bill joined me in my laughter as we kept talking shit about the shit tubes that we are. Because that's what a living tube is, isn't it? Just a shit tube. The Cosmos feeds this tube Form on one end (say, a carrot-form or a chicken-leg-form) and this Form is turned into Formlessness on the back-end. But the Universe needs this Formlessness so that it can be deposited and made into Form again. Call it metabolism or circle of life. It's uroboric – an eel eating its own tail. We – the living tubes – are like garbage disposals in our kitchen sinks. We are de-formers. Living black holes that swallow the Universe and spit out dark matter is what we are. And that process is war – a constant war of eating.

--

Now that Bill was done, he was back to his old kooky self. He invited me to go down towards the creek. Swatara was low and we waded down a bit, not worried about getting our boots and pants wet.

"Would be nice to see an eel," I said and asked: "Do you think they are still here, Bill?"

"You are looking at them, Paul. You are looking through them. Elvers are transparent when young – glass-like – and that's the thing of it, pal, to see through the invisible, to see what others fail to see, to see even if you are blind ... "

"To see Form in Formlessness and Formlessness in Form," my mind completed his thought while my legs walked.

We waded on and the burs miraculously let go of us, and floated down the stream, some alongside us, some rushing ahead in search of fertile alluvial soil.

# Piano Tuner

*W*ait a moment, I need to refill my glass of wine.

There!

As I was saying, or was I saying anything? I guess not. Well, there we go. Let's start. The official story is that I didn't have my first drink of alcohol until I was about 35, although that's not quite true. I had my first drink when I was 16. This story is not about that, but about what moved me to do it, not that it's a big deal for a culture where the word for water (voda) is almost identical to the word vodka.

It was 1985, I was 16 and I needed to get laid. Well, actually I first needed to get a job and save up a little money to buy a pair of stone-washed jeans. That would help me get laid. In those days, a pair of Levi's in the Soviet Union would get you laid faster than a rocket launch without having to take them off. So, I needed a job. My dad, a ghost writer, made a few calls and a ghostly lead of a job with a piano mover materialized pretty much overnight. It wasn't going to be my first job, but it was going to be my first nighttime job.

I met the guy on Tuesday at a pelmeni place where men in winter coats stood around chest high tables and quietly ate without looking at each other. Now and then they would take a stealthy sip of something from military-issue flasks and put them back in their coat pockets. I approached a man in a red artificial fox fur hat. He looked like Atlas with a powerful torso showing through layers of winter clothing and a wool coat. Or perhaps his coat was simply too small. I was impressionable in those days and looked for giants wherever I went.

"Red hat?" I asked.

He nodded and introduced himself, "Sergei."

"Why do you want a job?" he asked with an accusatory tone.

There was no point in b.s.-ing. "To get laid," I said, cutting to the chase.

He must have liked the answer and, having picked up a pelmen' with his fork, stirred it around a yellowish pool of bubbly butter on the plate and offered it to me.

I shook my head. "I am full," I lied, ruining my just renewed record of honesty.

"Flex your biceps," he suddenly ordered, and I was pleased to oblige, posing like Arnold. His hand descended on the sleeve of my coat like a pneumatic vice, cutting off my blood supply. He had one hell of a grip.

"About 38 centimeters?" he asked, guesstimating the circumference of my arm.

"40!" I said with minor triumph, "I go to sports school, you know," I rushed to share my athletic qualifications.

"What sport?"

"Rowing. I used to play water polo but busted up my wrists when I fell off a skateboard."

"What's a skateboard?" he asked, but instantly shook his head, "Never mind. How's your wrist?"

"All healed, I am good."

He took another look at me, as he ate the pelmen,' sizing up my physique and finally concluded, "You'll do."

"Meet me at 8:00 pm tonight," said Sergei, "At the apartment complex outside the Avtozavodskaya metro station, by the Zil plant." He took out a memory of a pencil, the kind that old folks carry around in their pockets for years as they work on crossword puzzles. He handed the pencil to me and pushed a napkin my way. I wrote down the street address.

Hours later, with my homework done, we met at the entrance to the building. "Did you know that this is one of the very few buildings in Moscow where apartments are on two levels? In fact, it might be the only one," he said, wistfully looking up into the dark winter sky.

"You mean like a house or something?" I asked, not believing my ears. I had never seen anything like that. I grew up in a commune apartment, on Arbat, with six families and one bathroom. And then we moved to a "separate" apartment, with our own bathroom and kitchen, all to ourselves. I pretty much assumed that it doesn't get any better than that. But an apartment on two levels, that's just unheard of. I was excited like it was New Year's Eve.

"Yep," he said. "We are going in for an estimate."

"Estimate of what?" I asked.

"Of how much to charge to move the instrument," he replied.

Instrument. What a curious word, I thought to myself. Such tact, such delicacy, such nuance in the name.

We took the stairs as he didn't trust Soviet elevators, he explained.

"Are Western elevators better?" I asked.

"I don't know," said Sergei. "They have Westinghouse elevators in the Kremlin, at least that's what I heard."

"With toilets?" I tried to joke but he shot me down with a look.

"Listen, Pasha, you keep your mouth shut. I talk on the job, got it?"

I got it.

We buzzed the ringer two or three times. A sleepy looking man in a kitchen apron opened the door. He had kept us waiting because he had to go turn the stove off first. We walked in.

"Let me show you the instrument," he said, and led us down the hallway. I was looking around for the stairs to the second level. I was dying to see the layout of the apartment.

He beat me to the punch: "This isn't the two-tiered apartment that they have on the upper three levels. You've probably heard about the building, right?"

We nodded, I, with disappointment, Sergei, with nonchalance. "Just your regular apartment," the man said with an apologetic tone. "Well, actually, this used to be a communalka (commune apartment) which is actually why I called. Let me explain, I guess."

Still in his apron, red in the face, in home slippers over dog-wool socks, he stopped and barricaded the hallway with his stocky body, telling us an unnecessarily long story about how he and his wife purchased this former commune apartment and converted it into "a separate" except for one room. "You'll just have to see," he said, once again showing us the way through the labyrinth of the corridor.

We made a right and walked into, I wanna say into a room, but it'd be more appropriate to say "a closet," or to be more precise, *into* a piano. This was a space no larger than a grand piano, in fact, identical in size, windowless, completely and entirely occupied with an amazing concert piano. He finished the story: "This self-taught musician, you could say, a carpenter, you could say, used to live here. Back in the day the room was much larger, but he kept selling off the space and the neighbors kept moving the walls until this was all that was left. He slept right here, under the instrument, had a lamp there and a sleeping bag. Believe it or not, he had, back in the day, crafted this instrument himself at a piano factory, then found the guy that had bought it, they come numbered you know, bought it back, and had it moved to this apartment. Then this whole thing happened with not having money and selling his space in the apartment and the neighbors moving the walls…"

It was clearly a mission impossible. A box of a room with too narrow of a door, without a window, with a grand piano inside. "I'd hate to have to break it up, you know," said the man, confessing further: "I've had the instrument appraised. It's a masterpiece. Furthermore, it has quite a history, I won't bore you with details but I'll tell you this much, Tchaikovsky played it." He looked at us with a triumph.

Tchaikovsky who? said my face. Sergei's face once again said nothing.

"I've had a few movers come and give me estimates. The prices are too high. They have to take the doorway down and then charge for moving it out down this mess of a hallway. Others don't want the job, too much hassle, they say. I see where they are coming from, but I hate to have to break it up. You are my last hope."

Sergei stood motionless, a faint, very faint smile could be seen in the corner of his mouth and I had no idea what that meant. He crawled underneath the instrument and re-emerged on the other side of the room. "May I?" he asked lifting up the key cover.

"You play?" asked the owner.

Sergei shook his head but did raise the cover and struck a cord or two. He seemed to listen rather intently as if he was a piano tuner not a piano mover. He said nothing and took a dive back under the instrument and re-emerged back in the doorway.

"I'll move it," he said, and added, "for free."

"For free?"

"Yes, for nothing. And I'll tell you why. If I mess it up I don't want to be responsible…"

"But why would you bother?" asked the man, essentially reading my mind.

Sergei, by now, was leaning against the wall, relaxed, reclining, like a Greek Atlas, half-supporting the world, half-risking to tip it over. There was no doubt: he had an amazing upper body, with the coat off, hanging on his arm, he looked like a real life giant. He seemed to totally not give a fuck: he had all the cards, it was a take it or leave it kind of moment,. He had offered to move "the thing" for free – "the thing" is how I was thinking of this instrument of theirs in my own mind.

He looked at me with a reassuring look as if to say "Worry not, kid, you are covered, you'll get yours."

The man was drilling Sergei with his eyes. Finally, he lighted up as if he finally got it and cracked Sergei's secret code: "Oh, you are hoping to keep the thing, huh?" I noted that he too was now calling the thing "the thing."

Sergei shook his head: "Nope. Just moving."

"But why?"

That was, indeed, the question of this particular moment. Mine, this man's, the moment's question. "I simply am interested," said Sergei, "Intrinsically."

There was no satisfaction in this answer. At moments like this, when you are selling some kind of mystery to someone, you have to find the right words, to keep them listening, to keep them wanting, to keep them reading.

Sergei tried again: "For practice sake, to get this one (he motioned his head at me) familiarized with the process of things."

That did it. The man sighed, smiled, and said, "Ok, I guess."

The man and I were instantly relieved. The world made sense again. And it had to. The human mind can't handle a lack of meaning, a lack of sense, a lack of pattern. We are junkies for order, for the expected. We expect what we get and we get what we expect. The human mind doesn't like to dice reality into bits and crumbs of the unknown. It takes years for clarity, for theories of everything, it likes to arrange and can't stand mystery.

But the relief didn't last as long as was hoped for.

"On the condition," began Sergei.

"There we go," I thought to myself. "Now he's gonna ask for something ridiculous, like to sleep with the man's wife or whatever," I half-expected.

"On the condition that the job will take place at night and there will not be anyone in the apartment. You are to leave me with a set of keys and to show up the following morning. The piano will be outside, in the foyer of the building. You take it from there and do with it what you wish. Pavel and I (Sergei motioned at me) will move the instrument out of this room, free and clear, no charge."

He finished as calmly as he had started and I felt a strange sense of pride. The man in front of us was looking at a couple of Houdini movers that could apparently, with obvious confidence, make the impossible possible.

The two picked a day, the coming Thursday, a

duplicate set of keys was given to Sergei, and we left.

The next two days, Wednesday and Thursday during the day, I worked out with a special kind of vigor. I borrowed a pair of work gloves and even meditated for a moment, a trick I learned from my dad. I left home at 11:00 pm on Thursday and I was not to return until the next morning I would return a changed man.

The door into the apartment was unlocked, Sergei was in the kitchen, naked except for black boxer shorts and flip-flops. He was a flesh-and-bone Atlas, sculpted like no man I had ever seen in a locker room, a David on steroids.

Sweating on the kitchen table, was a defrosting bottle of Stoli. He locked the door behind me and poured me a short one. "Drink!" he said and I drank my first.

"You don't need to undress," he preempted my question. He poured another one, there were no chasers, and said, "Finish this and come with me." I swallowed the strangely oily, transparent liquid and followed him out of the room. We walked down the corridor to the room with the piano.

"Here," he positioned me in front of the open doorway, pointing at the piano. "Take a look." I did.

"I have no fucking clue how we are going to move

this monster out of this rat hole," I said.

"Watch your mouth," barked Sergei, smiling. The alcohol was clearly starting to take effect on my youthful flock of neurons that had been hiding out inside my skull like a bunch of microscopic bats.

I eyeballed the door opening, then looked at the thing and shook my head. "There is simply no way in hell this thing is coming out of this room in one piece. We either have to take the wall down or call it a night."

Sergei smiled. "Stay put."

He came back with the rest of the bottle and gave me another swig.

"Here's what's gonna happen, my little friend," he said mischievously, squatting down alongside the wall like a prison inmate, perfectly balanced on the balls of his feet. "Do you like physics?"

I shook my head, mixing up the eddy of a buzz inside the liquefying field of my consciousness. I dumbly sat down to listen. I could tell I was in for a lecture.

Sergei, without any warm up, fired off, "We are composite creatures. You and I, and this piano, each of us is a suspension of monads, each of us is a plurality of sovereign monads, each of us is a 'many of' which means that each of us is 'none of,' which means that each of us is an illusion. You, I, this piano, there is not a bubble of emptiness between us, all this is but an informational matrix, a matrix of consensual, agreed-upon relational infrastructure."

"What's a monad, Teach?" I asked, feeling like I was sliding downhill all the while sitting in stuporous stillness.

"Good question, Pasha. A monad is a conscious particle, a particle of self-aware space, a field of awareness limited only by the event horizon of duality. We think we are many and in some ways we are, but, but, objectively we are one. Here, have another swig," he finished with quiet triumph somewhere amidst his bushy brows that seemed to be on a collision with each other.

I was starting to feel dizzy, like a Sufi after a meth-induced marathon counterclockwise spin. But somewhere inside me there was burning a pair of eyes, not a set of fast-approaching headlamps, a locomotive of a question tearing apart the darkness of my confusion: "But what has all this got to do with moving a piano?"

"Nothing and everything. First, there is no piano. Second, the piano that you and I see can't be moved, can't be forced, can't be force-moved, it has to be engaged as a conscious entity. It has to be moved by the intensity of our predicament! It has to relate to us, as a monad to a monad."

With these words, Sergei stood up and climbed up the wall like a spider. He looked at me, while hanging upside down and said, "This is not magic realism, my little friend. It's vodka and cosmology, cosmology and vodka. That's the whole thing-less thing of it!"

I closed my eyes to reboot. When I opened them a couple of hours later, the room was empty. I was still where I was (was I?). Sergei's voice could be heard from the murky labyrinth of the hallway. I looked at the room. It was perfectly intact, the doorway, the walls, even the bare light bulb hanging at the end of the wire.

I discovered that I, too, was now in nothing but my boxers. I didn't question the why of this or the rationale behind anything else. It was safer that way. I stood and swam up the length of the hallway. The piano, in all of its black lava-lamp concert triangularity, was standing upright, sideways, that is while Sergei was sitting, spider-like, on one of the walls, playing it. I couldn't believe the sound. It was no piano, no matter what keys he struck, he seemed to be playing it as some kind of Tibetan organ, sounding out periodic harmonies of various permutations of Om. Each and every alveoli of my swimmer's lungs said "wow." I inhaled deep enough to almost curl right into my own body, head, tongue and body, almost coiling inward like a snake chasing its own tail. Any question that I had in my mind simply vanished. I forgot what questions were, that is how relaxed and detoxified I felt.

"I need you to hold the door," said Sergei, dropping down to the horizontal, his legs for some reason now striped with black-and-white like he was a zebra-based reincarnation of the Greek god, Pan. "I had to metabolize quite a bit of duality," he explained. "Walls put up pretty serious objections to seeing me and the piano and themselves as a trinity of divine sameness. Walls tend to be like that, built to divide, they take a long time to melt their self-other duality."

Any thoughts that bugged me about what he just said splattered against the windshield of Sergei's pantheistic definitiveness. My mind, dead on arrival, got wiped off sideways with a flicker of his suggestion.

"Hold the door, Pash." I knew how to do that and did exactly that. The piano slid right past me, hovered rather, with Sergei after it, walking, not levitating.

"Un-ask the question, Serpent Mind," Sergei said to me with a wink, effectively gagging the SOS of my "how-is-this-possible-mind" dead in its tracks. To empty a room is trick enough. But to move the thing down a dozen of flights of stairs in the middle of the night without dropping the damn thing and waking up the whole apartment building. That, that was the next thing I couldn't fathom.

"Empty your mind, Pash," said Sergei from somewhere inside. "Heck, even that is overkill. The mind is already empty. Just notice it, notice yourself, past my voice inside your so-called head. See?"

"I see," someone other than me said to someone other than me with my so-called mouth. And I checked out, to reboot, I guess.

This time I didn't idle too long. When I was back, Sergei-the-Piano was somewhere down below, a good few flights down. I looked through the chicken wire of the elevator shaft. Sergei, with the piano sitting on one step, and himself a few steps below, had the piano resting on his shoulder, and was standing, seemingly asleep. He wasn't. He was being a piano, moving himself from within, below the Planck's scale of distinction. Suddenly he reached over the set of keys, lifted the cover with two or three of his fingers, and using the remaining fingers struck a key, the same primordial sound of om-ness, of am-ness escaped the instrument like the throatal groan of a Tuvian monk. The piano lifted up, slid over the edge of the step and dropped down almost a flight of stairs, without a sound. Yet the sound of that chord, like a shock wave, spliced into my psyche. And not only my own; half a dozen doors opened up and a motley assortment of sleep-walkers greeted each other with a "Namaste" and then returned to their respective apartments.

"You see," commented Sergei, seemingly on an

esoteric lunch-break, "An instrument is a tool. The mind is an instrument. The mind obeys. Everything is the mind: each and every one of us, not that we really exist as separates, each and every one of us has an entire eternal, boundless Universe at its disposal. The universe is a collective mind. When you wake up to that, when you collapse the duality of being and non-being, of matter and consciousness, of you and me, of self and other, you realize that the piano wants to move. Think about it, my little friend, it's been cooped up in that box of a room for all those years. Tchaikovsky, for crying out loud, played on it. And there it was, collecting dust."

"Tchaikovsky?" I protested, showing the limitations of my secondary education.

Sergei lifted the key cover and found a key to strike. When he did, I was, and that's the only way that even begins to approximate the experience, I was withdrawn from inside, out of awareness, emptied out from within, like a bagel that swallowed its own hole.

Two days passed. I didn't go to school. My mom thought I was running a fever. "You have a visitor," she said. I got up and dressed. Opening the door of my room I could hear my Dad talking to Sergei in the kitchen. They were smoking up a storm, I could see it. I walked into the kitchen, rubbing my eyes. A battery of port-wine bottles was standing empty on the windowsill, like on a parade.

"You ok?" asked Sergei. I nodded. "Here," he said handing me 70 roubles.

"What for?" I asked realizing that the piano move was no dream, "I didn't do shit."

"Watch it," said my Dad.

"You didn't get in the way. That's a lot," said Sergei.

I waited for more. Nothing else was coming: they had been having a deep conversation, I could tell. Men of ontological depth, a depth I finally glimpsed and almost drowned in.

"I know you don't like questions, Sergei, but may I?" Sergei and my Dad smiled with some kind of secret smile, as if to say "He's finally digging it: questions never got us anywhere useful."

"Shoot."

"Why did you need me in the first place, Sergei?"

"Oh, that. Think about it, Dr. Watson," said Sergei, with a mocking tone, and since I finally knew the reference, I appreciated the irony. "Who would have hired me to move a piano without a crew?"

"Gotcha," I said and bowed out. I had phone calls to make. I was back on a hunt for a pair of bootleg Levi's, with a distant prospect of getting laid finally one logistical step closer.

# Into the Next Moment We Now Walk In

For the longest time I couldn't understand what people meant when they talked about the so-called illusion of invincibility that happens to characterize the teenage mind. Does that mean that I have only now, at the age of about 40 or something, stopped being a teenager? I don't know. But as I start to look back at my earlier days, I am gradually beginning to see the fearless mind that I once was – a walking zombie-god no less. I acted as an immortal. And, therefore, I was.

When I think of this seemingly endless, never-ending now of fearlessness, an image pops into my mind of walking along the pier of a subway station, from back to front, right along the very edge. To my left is a rioting mass of hurried commuters waiting on a train. One clumsy push somewhere and the crowd can burp out a sudden pulse of motion that can easily knock me right onto the subway tracks. This could have happened any number of times but even though this possibility now and then occurred to me, I never minded it. I had thought it through. I'd simply run towards the front of the tracks while I had time and if the train were to be already upon me I'd simply lay down in between the rails and wait for it to roll over me. "No biggie," was my mindset on this issue. I felt immortal. And, therefore, I was.

Gods and zombies are funny, aren't they? They have no choice but to be what they are. And in this self-chosen pre-determination there is a sobering existential clarity. A clarity I now envy, but also laugh at.

"I was working on a manuscript," said Michigan, a streetwise pal of mine who made his pocket money twenty different ways. He was now sitting in the back of my Moscvitch hatchback as I was jitneying around trying to scrape up enough moola to buy my way inside the Margarita Café, which is only three or four blocks away from the Moscow KGB headquarters. Margarita was a hip little dance place and I got lucky there every time. As always, I was horny pretty much from 7:00 am and now it was coming up on 6:00 or 7:00 pm. I only had about half a tank of gas left and about three more hours to hustle to get a few good fares to afford the cover fee and to have some money to refuel for tomorrow.

"Tomorrow never comes," someone somewhere said sometime. Indeed, we are born into now. The whole life is one life-long now. We are born into the present, we stay and stew in it, and "then," while still in this life-long now, we die in it, never knowing non-being. Subjectively immortal even if objectively perishable, we are.

"A manuscript?" I echoed from the front, turning down the raunchy Malchishnik rap track.

Michigan, whose name harkened back to a little line he had when accosting foreigners, said, "Yes." He was glad to have my ear but he couldn't have my eyes yet. A sooty, patched up Volga with Benz hubcaps suddenly cut in front of us and I slammed on the brakes. The passenger to my right, some out-of-towner with a giant plastic bag full of Adidas socks, came alive from his nap on the front seat.

"Hey!" he said, and then nervously chuckled as soon as he realized that all was fine. "I don't know how you can drive in this mess all day," he added and closed his eyes again. But it was clear his nap was over.

And now there were three of us in the car. Sort of. When we are asleep, are we really we? Does sleep count as life? Does life itself count? Not when on autopilot; or maybe only then. This, by the way, was a point of some contention, behaviorally, not conceptually, between Michigan and me. He preached self-awareness and I preached awareness. There is an ocean of difference between these two. But it's only an inch or so deep.

If I were to break in here with a subtitle it would be: "How Michigan Got His Name." And since I already have (broken in), here's the scoop: Misha (as his real name was), in his teens, would hang around the Red Square and use his limited English to drum up a buck or two. He'd spot a mark (in, say, New Balance sneakers and a Nikon on his neck) and roll up to him with the question, "Are you from Michigan?" That was his line; he invented it. What would follow didn't matter. He was utterly unable, then and now (not that there is a difference between these temporal planes), to carry a conversation in English any further. This question was a pattern break, a maneuver of conversational hypnosis to get attention, and to confuse a mind. Ignoring the answer, he'd open up his shoulder bag and show off his wealth of cheap souvenirs – Matreshka nesting dolls, Soviet Army lapel pins and other crap.

The narrative detour over, the Volga got out of the way. The passenger in the front seat was clearly awake and showing interest in us, and Michigan was eager to finish his train of thought.

"So, as I was saying," he reminded me of his presence from the backseat. "I was working on this little opus of mine, it was going to be about how time really flows from the future into now, not from the past into the present and into the future." He emphasized the "into" and in so doing he sucked me not just in, but into his train of thought. It pulled the passenger in, too. Both of us, I suspect, were swirling around this cognitive eddy, not knowing how to orient ourselves to it.

Michigan held a longer pause than was typical of his chatter mouth. Instead of adding any further explanations he returned with a question, "When I just said this, what happened to your mind?"

"Hmm," the nameless passenger said opening his eyes and his mouth at the same time. He felt, for some unknown reason, that the question, from the backseat, was addressed to him personally (Michigan had that effect on people). "I kind of went into a stupor a bit, it sort of made sense but …"

"But it was too Copernican to process, right?"

I now knew what this was all about. Michigan wanted to use the word "Copernican." He was looking for a context to plug it in, to then have to explain it, to pilot it. It was a semantic souvenir, a beginning of some future spiel that he was working on. So, I threw him a rescue line, "What do you mean, 'Copernican'?"

"Well, you know, right, good ol' Nick woke us all up a while back when he said that the Cosmos doesn't revolve around the Earth but that it's the Earth that revolves around the Cosmos. Or was it Galileo?"

I wasn't sure but it sounded coherent enough so far. "Your point, Misha?"

"My point is, that whichever fuck-wad it was that said that, that proposed that, he provoked a near-instantaneous Copernican paradigm-shift. Near-instantaneous, historically speaking, I mean. We, all of us, the humanity at large. suddenly realized that A isn't A; that A is B. And bam, all has changed."

We all sat in silence for a bit, I tailing a tricked-out Lada with a disproportionate spoiler, my passenger in confusion, and Michigan, in my hunch, a moment of triumph. This cheapskate, mind-luddite that he was, he once again succeeded in arresting the free-flow of human consciousness. But I wasn't interested in these conversational hypnosis shenanigans. I wanted to know more about his little premise about time.

"So," I said, trying to restore the vector of cognitive organization, "You said that you were working on a manuscript about how time comes from the future, right? How it flows into the present, not from the past, but from the future, into the present, right?"

"Right," said Michigan. "It's obvious, self-evident, and self-explanatory, really." he added, rattling off as many synonyms as he could. (People do that when they are trying to sell a point.) "Time can't flow from the past. Time flows from a source of change which can only be found in the future. Past is known, there is no change, no variability, no variance in it. Thus, it is impotent; it cannot be a source of unpredictability, of chance, of luck. It is known, a given, a 'was.' There is no 'maybe', no 'possibly' in it. I don't know. I see it plainly, do you?"

"I think so," said the passenger, still under an egocentric illusion that everything that is happening now was about him. And, in some pre-Copernican way, it really was.

"Time has to flow from the future – that's where the degrees of freedom are, it flows into the present. But it's really just a word-game, you see."

This was an exciting point in our little talks. There would always come a moment in which Michigan would begin to collapse his premise, on his own, with utmost dialectic integrity.

He said: "You see, there really cannot be a future. Reality is always now, present, present-tense. But we are a phase behind. The information-processing creatures that we are, are always a click or two behind what is happening right now. This future that flows into us is really our present, the Big Now, and we are discovering it a subjective moment too late. It is still accurate to say, that future flows into us, because informationally-speaking we are always behind, in the past of what just was. But one goddamn thing I am sure about is that time cannot flow from the past, you see what I mean?"

I did. I also saw the municipal Kamaz truck dripping liquid filth in front of me, so I tapped the breaks to put some distance between us, and shifted lanes.

"So," chimed in the passenger, "the so-called arrow of time flies not from the past, but in reverse, from the future into the past?"

"Exactly!  We are walking into it, running into it, like a slab of living, breathing, deluded steak into a hot shish kabob poker!  Right into your chest!" Michigan was pounding his ribcage with a fist for added effect.

Life often doesn't leave room for comment. The passenger stuck out his index finger and drew my attention to a grey high-rise on the right. "Right there, please," he instructed and I turned on the right signal to park. I stopped a few feet behind the bus stop and the guy pulled out his wallet. He had already opened the door and I was ready to be cheated. Michigan on the backseat perked up, it was his job after all to make sure this shit doesn't happen. As a jitney, I've come to certainly expect that my passengers would now and then make a run for it without paying me the fare. That was part of the risk. The problem was that over the last few months I had heard one too many stories of guys getting jumped and having their cars taken away from them. I asked Michigan if he'd keep me company now and then, for a commission, of course. It wasn't much of a living for him, but, frankly, the real currency that I paid for his time was my willingness to listen to his crazy ideas.

The passenger proved to be well behaved. He paid his fare but also made an interesting proposal. He explained that he was new to Moscow. "No shit!" we thought. It was painfully clear from the way he spoke and carried himself. "So, here's the deal," he started. "I got these keys to this apartment, a buddy left them for me at a train station locker box. But I have no fucking clue what I am gonna walk in on. In sum," he said, cutting to the chase, "I need a crew for a few minutes, to back me up if I walk into some shit or something."

Michigan looked at me. I was game. "How much?" asked Michigan, "for emotional support?" We spent the next few minutes negotiating "physical support," as I parked.

The elevator was down so we had to hoof seven or so floors, carrying some of this guy's plastic bags "as a courtesy," to use Michigan's ongoing itemization of our ad-hoc services.

"That's the one," said the guy, stopping in front of #702. It smelled like bacon. "Someone's home," concluded the guy, frowning. It was his understanding, we understood, that he was going to have the flat all to himself for a week. But these kinds of fly-by-night scenarios often don't work out the way they are scripted. He turned the key, he had to force it and almost lift the door a bit to get in. The door opened and the smell of bacon hit a bit harder. We walked in, first, to the right, into the kitchen; nothing was cooking. Then through a side door into the dining room. Again, nothing and nobody. Next we went into a small bedroom, which is where the cooking was apace.

Ok, I am now going to describe something that you probably shouldn't visualize, but here it is: a bed, a naked dude duck taped to the sides of a single bed, with duck taped legs and hands, and duck tape running over his neck, but not over his mouth, with a clothing iron duck taped to his stomach; the iron, plugged in, obviously on, sunken into a coagulating, sizzling mess of his stomach. Half of his tongue bit off from pain on the side of his mouth. Dead. Probably from a heart attack.

This is what the three of us saw. Three fields of open-minded awareness, suddenly organized into one instant flash of an impulse to run. We bolted.

Back in the car, we were aghast. A bit panicked, excited, and somehow unified. A crew at last.

I floored it, cutting in and out of traffic like a steak knife through a half-melted stick of butter.

"Shit! I left my stuff there," said the guy.

"I wonder what the fuck happened there," started Michigan. I could already see how he was going to spin some kind of fairy tale about some out-of-towner who didn't pay a call girl a time or two and how a

106

couple of brothers dropped by for an inquisition into his poor commercial ethics.

This kind of analysis, I felt, was well beyond the point. I am no Sherlock Holmes or Jules Maigret to try to solve mysteries. I like encountering mysteries. Solving them never interested me. Before too long we ditched the guy back at the train station, his visit to Moscow cut short, and headed back out into town. It was time to eat. No, no bacon tonight, though!

We rolled up to the Margarita Café by about 11:30pm. The place was hopping as it always did back then. A crowd of humanoid tadpoles exorcizing the demons of libidinal energy. "Everything already is," I kept thinking to myself. This music already is and I am only now hearing it. The girl I am yet to hit on already exists and I am yet to cozy up to her in this bouncing, pulsating quantum field of psychosomatic am-ness. The guy in the apartment was already dead and that future that we were to walk in was already his present. "Everything already is," I kept thinking to myself, discovering each pseudo-moment of "now" as a future-given fact.

Michigan and I, the zombie-gods, kept on dancing for another two or three years, never looking back, but only looking into this already-present future that pierces us right through our chests, the silly little sizzling shish kabobs that we humans are.

# Tir

The river of life has no fords. We simply cannot wade through shallow water on our way to the other side. To get to the other side we have to first learn to breathe under water and then dive deep. One life is almost never enough to master these skills. So, we keep dying again and again. As we die, we assemble, like log booms on a river, into massive hordes of transmigrating souls. Friendly neighborhood psychopomps – the mythical soul guides – like log drivers, direct us *en masse* to the other side. This is the safest passage that we can buy for the information that we carry within ourselves. Information is buoyant. The more we know, the more we have experienced, the less water-logged we are, and the faster we get to the other side. Otherwise, empty-minded, we sink into the deep and have to be dredged up through the silt and the rot.

Or maybe it's the other way around. Must be.

Anyway, there are many living rivers in the world and many psychopomps working them – Charon, of course, the ferryman of the river Styx; then there's Jizo who works the Sai-no-kawara river-crossing; and, let us not forget, the ever-mystical Herman Hesse with his assistant Siddhartha on the banks of the river Rasa, a tributary of the Indus river. I don't know about you, but I haven't yet been to any of these underworlds, at least, not that I can remember. But I've been to the Armenian Highlands and that's the Tir turf – a real old-school soul-guide, I must say.

--

We were stationed in the gymnasium of an old school, in the middle of some residential neighborhood of Yerevan, the capital of Armenia. The digs were good enough, the local food was supreme, and I was an utterly self-involved 20 year-old draftee who was single-mindedly preoccupied with the forthcoming demobilization – my two years in the Soviet military were coming to an exotic end. And I welcomed any twist of fate as a perfect way to quicken the viscous fabric of time.

It was the spring of 1989 and the war between Armenia and Azerbaijan was heating up. We – the OMSBON – based out of Leningrad, were just around the corner for all this excitement, and were airlifted to Erevan to patrol streets and guard the TV broadcasting tower. Just two months earlier, in December of 1988, we had been airlifted to Spitak in Northern Armenia after a devastating earthquake. It was a post-Pompeii kind of scene: a true apocalypse. As many as 50,000 people were killed in that earthquake and over 100,000 were injured. Spitak, Gyumri and Vanadzor were wiped out almost completely – the shoddily built Brezhnev-era high-rise apartment buildings laid down on the ground like folding chairs. These were the last years of the Soviet Empire and Gorbachev threw all he had at Spitak and neighboring areas in terms of humanitarian relief. He had even invited foreign help – the region crawled with international do-gooders and good-samaritans, which was unprecedented. We – the OMSBON – were there not to help out with the clean-up effort but to make sure that no one else would interfere with it. But we weren't alone – the place was teaming with VDV, the airborne troops, with their signature zebra-patterned *tel'nyashka* tank-tops under the winter coats.

--

I couldn't care less about any of that – I was 20, as I said, and completely self-involved. I was only two short spring months away from demobilization and the two years of military service, with all of the hazing bullshit and maddening inefficiencies, were about to be forever behind me. Bunked on top, as befits a self-respecting second-year Soviet soldier, I was searching for sleep somewhere in the nebulous clouds of consciousness behind the curtains of my eyelids. But sleep was nowhere to be found. So, I opened my eyes and looked to my left to see if Sashka, our medic, was still awake. As I turned my head, my eyes met his – he was wide awake, and eagerly so, I must say, as though waiting for me to look at him. He lifted up on his elbow, reached underneath the pancake-thin army pillow and pulled out a roach.

"You know I don't – " I protested.

"Don't be a moron, Pash, we are *dedi*, aren't we? Who gives a fuck, man?!" Sashka was referring to the long-awaited status of the second year soldier in the last quarter of his military duty. *Ded* in Russian means "grandpa" and grandpas don't do shit, as you know, they just sit around and swat flies away at a family reunion while sipping on sweet ice tea.

"Where did you get this shit?" I asked.

"From a kid in the neighborhood. He was selling. I just took it away from him … I told him it was illegal … Just watching out for a kid, you know, " Sashka said with a smirk and a scowl.

"Bad karma, Sash … "

"Shut the fuck up, Pash, what the hell do you know about karma anyway, city-slicker?!"

"I know this much, you freckle-face-country-bumpkin-nut-sack: we are in the holiest of holies – Armenia – the Caucuses! Just a hop and a skip from where the Indo-Aryan race reached enlightenment. This is where the Vedic teachings began, you know. Armenians are the "white devils from the North" that poured *en masse* into India thousands of years ago. The Vikings of the Caucuses, so to say. The soma-drunk Brahmin charioteers!"

"*En masse*? *Soma* what?" Sashka asked, sounding suddenly self-conscious as he repeated the unfamiliar terminology. He suddenly remembered that I was an educated Moscovite and he – well, who the fuck cares which Central Russia village he had hailed from … (That's how I thought in those days, dumb-ass blow-hard that I was).

I knew Sashka loved when I threw some Latin into my Moscovian dialect but he'd never admit it. "Did you just come up with this shit, Pash, as you always do, you overcompensating bumble-bee dick? No need to answer, Pash, I know you did – this "soma" thing gave it away, sounds too much like your last name to be true, you self-promoting fuckwad."

"Soma, Sash, was a ritual drink, a psychedelic concoction that the Aryan warriors drank before battle – it made them immortal. Or so they thought …"

"Yeah? Well, Pash, I'll tell you what – get your pimply lazy ass up, make us some tea, and then we'll share this Armenian spliff. I bet it'll make you feel immortal too!" And then in a frenzy of alliteration, Sashka added: "While Frankie goes to Hollywood, Lance-Corporal Somov is gonna have some Soviet-spun soma…"

While Sashka sure knew his MTV, I had majorly overstated the Armenian role in the Indo-Aryan migration theory. Armenia was way too mountainous for war chariots – those ancient analogues of tanks had come into existence in the Caspian steppes, a good bit north of Armenia. But what the hell, I needed to shut down my loud-mouth friend and the only way I knew how to put a gag in Sashka's mouth was to play the academic, I-know-it-all card. It usually mesmerized his provincially self-doubting mind into a stupor. Not that he'd ever show that. But I knew.

--

Now, Sashka jumped off his top-bunk, dragging my army-issue blue wool blanket down with him to the floor and started dancing a jig right on top of it. A few sets of eyes opened up on the lower bunks and prudently reclosed themselves, choosing to mind their own business. When *dedi* partied, the young bloods would keep their mouths shut and eyes averted. That was the axiom of survival in the military barracks in those days. And I am pretty sure this nasty tradition is still alive and well. Whenever you give 18 year-old kids guns and a mandate of power, you always get a lord-of-the-flies nightmare.

--

The base was unguarded ... because there was no base. A first-year soldier, half-asleep, stood guard in the doorway. He perked up as he saw us, first probably thinking that it was his relief partner and then simply to look alert so as to not catch flack from a couple of jolly-looking dedi.

"You know you're not suppo – " the guard tried to protest as we walked right through him. He might as well have been made of immaterial ether: no resistance was felt.

"Hey!" he ventured another muted vocalization of protest but was immediately chilled by Sashka's "Shhh, boy!"

--

It was warm outside. Heck, by Moscow standards, a true summer night. We stood outside the school building looking up at the star-studded sky. All around the school yard were apartment high-rises, just like the ones that collapsed in rows in Spitak, – wet clothes strung in rows on balconies, a few windows flickering with reflections of TV, and a set of abandoned swings on the playground inside the fenced-off school yard. Erevan at night had the smell of freshly cut up cucumbers, with humidity bordering on mist.

We turned the corner and demonstratively ignored yet another sentry at the main entrance as we walked off the base. Sashka lit a cigarette, un-tucking his shirt from his pants. I unbuttoned mine. Neither of us had a *pilotka* on – these foldable vagina-shaped side-caps that completed Soviet uniforms. Everything about us was against code. Had we run into an MP patrol we would have been taken to the brig, no question about that.

--

But the city was ours. And so was Earth. And, heck, the entire Universe, with its mind-boggling bottomlessness. We owned the moment. And the moment owned us. We slowly walked around the block, listening to the echo of our own steps, looking for a place to land. We found a clean-enough bench to sit on in front of one of the high rises.

But before casting an anchor on that concrete slab, we walked into the building and got into the elevator. You can never be too careful when you are in a uniform, you know. The elevator smelled of take-out food and piss. As the elevator doors closed, Sashka took out the spliff, smelled it with satisfaction, and pushed the button for the 10th floor. He lit the roach, and took a long drag. The Soviet-era elevator thought for a long electric minute and jerked us upwards, contributing to the launch effect. Sashka handed the roach over to me for my turn. The skunk-weed burned the throat bad and we coughed up a storm, laughing it up in between the coughing spasms. After a couple of turns, Sashka put out the roach and saved the rest.

We rode the elevator up and down a few times, laughing and coughing. And finally got out on the ground level and returned to the bench. At which point we looked at each other ponderously, then at the black, star-studded mountain-sky above us, and yielded to that insidious disappearing act of consciousness, each sinking into our own mental elevator shaft.

--

"What are you up to, *soldatiki* (soldier-boys)?" said a gritty voice out of nowhere.

Sashka and I were startled out of our respective numbness. The question – turns out – came from an Aladdin-looking genie-of-a-dude, in a patched-up bathrobe and a pair of stinky house slippers with turned up toes. The Aladdin had a handle-bar mustache on him and a pair of fiery eyes, framed by bushy black brows. He was absolutely bald, exposing a perfectly shaped skull, a nice gleaming disco-ball for moonlight to ricochet off.

116

"I heard you boys talking down here, from my balcony ... I am on the 5$^{th}$ floor ... So I came down to check on you two young fools ... "

It always amazes me how quickly we size each other up. Just a moment ago, the man's tone was cautiously respectful; and a moment later he is already calling two strangers "fools." Truth is if we just sobered up a bit, we could easily kick his shriveled ass, but – and he knew it – as of now, we were no threat to him. We, humans, make these kinds of safety assessments intuitively, in a flash. And, boy, do we miscalculate sometimes!

"Sit, sit down with us, old man," I said to Aladdin, scooting aside to make room for him on the bench. I looked at Sashka to see if he'd mind. He didn't seem to mind at all – minding of any kind was simply not his thing. "Yes" was his perpetual, unrevised default setting on any – I repeat, on any! – occasion.

--

"How do you like Armenia, friends?" asked the old man, circling back to the safety of the small talk. By now I realized he didn't need safety. As he sat down and I got a closer look, I could tell he had nothing to fear from us: strong veiny forearms and calves gave away his athletic or deeply proletarian background. In his past life – which might be still ongoing – he had to have been a gymnast or, maybe, an acrobat. Straight back, broad shoulders, a pylon of a neck – he still had plenty of juice in him. It was no surprise: Armenia has always been a land of weightlifting and wrestling giants of average height. So, the

117

miscalculation of his threat potential was definitely on my end: the Aladdin was here to mess with us. But I still didn't mind.

"Armenia smells good, except for your stinky slippers, friend," Sashka countered clumsily. The old man, not feeling the love that he felt he deserved as an elder, shook his head, but stayed put. Probably, because he saw a quick look of disapproval that I shot at Sashka; so, perhaps, the man felt he could still count on me as half the audience. Put differently, since I had not yet burned any bridges and had invited him to sit down, I was not yet lost to him.

--

With fatherly tenderness he slapped me on my knee with a large muscled hand, the kind you'd find on a geriatric blacksmith, and looking me straight in the eye, said: "I can see that you boys are stoned, but don't worry I am not gonna tell your commander about that. No way. But I'll tell you what, boys, now, right now, right this very second, boys, while your bull-headed Russian minds are learning the Armenian nuance with a little bit of help from ancient Caucasian herb, right this very moment in your life you are better positioned to comprehend the meaning of stars. Let me, boys, be your guide for the evening. Let me journey you around the Universe, if time permits … "

As I said earlier, Sashka didn't have the word "no" in his vocabulary. And I myself was simply too plastered to articulate any objections. I nodded in consent as the genie's hand relocated from my knee to my shoulder.

"I am not gonna reveal to you all the secrets, boys, the night is too short for that. But I will tell you about the three hells and one tiny little hidden door – a gateless gate, to be precise – called Nirvana."

"You got anything to eat there, pops, on the 5th floor?" asked Sashka. The old man ignored him, while staring at me. I tried to bleat something in response to his inquisitive, piercing look but nothing human came out of me except for a meaningless "baa-a-a … "

Sashka laughed and tried to bury his head into my shoulder, yawning. I shoved him off gently, helping him find a more comfortable position on the other end of the bench.

The old Armenian looked at me – he was all patience.

--

"Each form of hell begins with desire, my friend. Desire is always a rejection of What Is. Let me say this again, because it's important that you understand this – hell begins with desire. We can only want What Isn't. Wanting is always about rejecting What Is in favor of What Isn't. Wanting is always teleological, goal-driven, future-oriented. Do you follow me, soldier-boy? You do, I know you do."

I shook my head and Aladdin continued. As he spoke, I felt I needed to ask him for his name, but my tongue felt as heavy as a set of pliers. And I had a metallic taste in my mouth.

"Wanting takes us out of this moment, it transports us into the moment that isn't yet. Wanting rejects the present moment as somehow insufficient, as somehow not enough, and focuses us on that future moment in which we will hopefully have whatever it is that we think we right now lack. The irony is that as we take our eyes off this precious present moment, we create the very deficit that we hope to address through wishing. It's a feedback loop: the more we want what we don't have, the less we want what we do actually have; as we want what we have less than we did a moment ago after we started wanting something other than what we have, we end up wanting what we do have even less than we did a moment ago, and, of course, we end up wanting what we don't yet have even more than we wanted it a moment ago. And so the wheel of desire goes round and round, emptying us out. Do you understand what I am saying, my boy?"

A part of me did, and the other part of me didn't. The part that didn't shook my head, and the nameless Aladdin continued.

"That is the first kind of hell that we inhabit. The name of this hell is Ts'ankut'yun." The old man spelled the word with his finger in the air, in Armenian alphabet, tying my focused eyes into a Cheshire-cat pretzel.

"What's Ts'ankut'yun?" I asked.

120

"That means thirst. In India – which I refer to as "East Armenia" - they say Tanha or Trishna. All these words mean thirst, thirst for something other than What Currently Is."

I don't know why Aladdin referred to India as "East Armenia" but it peaked my interest since it was giving some credence to my erroneous belief about the origins of Indo-Aryan migration into India. Wrong as I was then, I shot a triumphant look at Sashka – he couldn't care less, curled up on the bench in deep reverie.

Meanwhile, Aladdin droned on: "This thirst is never-ceasing. It's endless: the more we want, the more we want. The more we seek, the more we seek. This circle of thirst knows no satisfaction. Each time you try to satisfy this thirst, you become even thirstier. In Buddhism, they speak of pretas – hungry ghosts – their throats are thin as a needle and their bellies are as big as hot air balloons. Each time a preta tries to satisfy his hunger, his throat gets even thinner and his belly gets even bigger, so he hungers even more intensely than before he tried to satisfy his hunger. Buddhists call this hell Hunger, we call it Thirst. But the idea is Desire – the self-emptying nature of desire … "

I looked at Sashka – he was smacking and licking his lips, the word "thirst" probably getting to him bad, traveling into his brain down some subliminal underground railroad.

--

"This thirst dries us up. It evaporates our cosmic soul. We start out as beautiful and powerful acacia trees and we dry up into pitiful shit-sticks. We start out as Processes, and we become Things. Things is the name of the second hell, my young friend. You understand what I am saying to you, soldier-boy?"

I shook my head, my tongue beating around inside my mouth, from a cheek to a cheek, like a led clapper inside a bell. The nameless Aladdin continued.

"We started out as living, animate, cosmic processes and we dry up into dead, inanimate abstract things. Another name of this hell is Abstraction. As we become obsessed with What Isn't, as we thirst for something other than What Currently Is, we get lost in abstraction, our minds become fixated on ephemeral goals that are completely divorced from the business of daily living; we start to close off to anything that seems irrelevant to the potential satisfaction of our desires, and we dry up – we lose touch with the wet-work of reality. We become an idea. An idea – you see – is a thing. An abstract thing. And an abstract thing is not a thing except for only in abstraction. Another name for this hell is Patrank. An Illusion. A world of mirage. A world of Maya or Mara, as they say in India, or Eastern Armenia, as I call it. Surely, you understand?"

"I do not," I managed to mouth, my lips feeling rubbery and not mine. He continued.

"But that's not all that happens in this second kind of hell. Not only do we become things in this Hell of Things, but we also turn everything else into Things.

It's simple, really, if you think about it: when you want something, you develop a goal. A goal is an end. Once you have an end in mind, everything else turns into a means, into a method, into a thing. When you fixate on something, the reality becomes an instrument of satisfaction. Take eating for example, when you want to eat, a pig ceases to be a living sentient being and becomes "pork." A cow becomes "beef." A person you know becomes a "connection." A young beautiful woman – a "score." And so it goes. I bet you soldier-boys know this better than I do: you do know, don't you, that you are nothing more than "cannon fodder," right, nothing but a means-to-an-end … "

I chuckled like Beavis and Butthead. The Aladdin said "score." Just in case, I shook my head again. And Aladdin continued.

"So, the thirst of desire dries us up, deadens us into things. Then, we lose touch with the Living Oneness of All That Is – that We Ourselves Are! – and we deaden everything around us into things or abstractions. We start out as luscious acacia trees and shrivel into dried-up shit-sticks and then we look around and start seeing everything as a means to an end. And that is a deadly way of seeing the Cosmos. Dead ourselves, we kill everything else through abstraction and reification – "

"Wait, wait, wait there!" It was Sashka – he woke up for a second, finding himself amidst a perfect polysyllabic storm of unfamiliar terminology, and slammed on the brakes. Except that he wasn't the

123

one driving.  The old man, paying him no attention, continued to preach.  By now he was standing, feet apart, hands on his hips, a veritable starfish in a raggedy bathrobe.

--

"The third hell is – how do I say it? – is really the beginning of the first hell.  Just like the second hell is the end of the first hell and the beginning of the third.  As we dry up and turn into shit-sticks and turn everything around us into dead "means" to our hopeless "ends," we begin to realize that we are dead.  It suddenly dawns on us that we have killed ourselves.  We begin to regret and reminisce and mourn and yearn for the precious lives that we have taken for granted and wasted on chasing our abstract desires.  Instead of making peace with the fact that we are dead, we – you guessed – start wanting to live again.  At this moment – Buddhists call it "bardo" – we could just accept this new state of reality for what it is, but instead – just like when we were alive – we fight it, we don't want What Is, we want What Isn't.  We are dead.  We could just say, "Oh, well, so be it.  I was gonna be dead anyway, eventually, so why not now?"  But, instead, having learned nothing, we want to live again."

At this point I tried to get up from the bench, as if trying to escape from my own hell, but my ass seemed to be nailed to it.  The weed – it occurred to me – was surely laced with something heavier-duty.

"This hell is called Antenghyakut'yun or Avidya in Sanskrit, which is just Eastern Armenian, you know.

124

Ignorance – in Russian. What we fail to see – again and again and again – is that to live is to suffer. Why? Because to live is to want. To live is to desire. It's very difficult to be alive and not to want, not to desire. To be – without wanting to become something other than what one is – is enlightenment. And very few want that. Why? Because that kind of being is like non-being, that kind of living is like dying each and every moment. You see, life is just a dress rehearsal for death. Dress rehearsal for the true death, I mean, not for that thirst-ridden bardo-death … "

The old man took out a little leather-wrapped flask out of the side pocket of his bathroom robe and took a swig.

"Want some, soldier-boy?" he offered me a turn. "No worries, it's just chai." But I wasn't buying it. At this moment, I wasn't gonna trust anything Armenian. Even Armenian gravity. So, I shook my head, and stayed put.

--

For a while the Aladdin said nothing. I neither shook my head in confusion nor nodded my head in agreement. I stared at the old man like the stars above us stared at me – vacantly.

"It's a circle, my friend, a circle of three hells, a hellish trinity, if you wish, but there is a way out."

I summoned all my strength, thinking that he was talking about helping us get back to the barracks.

"The way out – the little trap door that I had mentioned a while back – is ..." he began, but was suddenly interrupted.

An obnoxiously loud female voice bellowed from above: "Tiran – T-iii-r-aaa-n - where the fuck are you hiding out, you dog-dick ... " It was clear from her tone that she had the necessary clout to cork this genie back into this bottle, no questions asked.

Instantly, everything changed: Sashka, perfectly sober, raised himself from the dead. The Aladdin was transformed into a pious ole man under the firm thumb of his woman, and I was thirsty to know about the little trap door at the end of this hell, about the way out.

"It's super late, boys, I gotta get up in an hour or two ... Gotta check in with the mistress of the house and see if I can catch some z's ... "

"What's your full name, Aladdin? I wanna come visit you some time, when I am sober, before we ship out," I said watching him re-wrap his bathrobe tight and neat.

"Gurdjieff ... Tiran Ivanovich Gurdjieff ... Sure, soldier-boy, come back any time. And bring your boy with you – he is still a sleeper ... But you – I can see – not so much ... "

--

I watched Tiran Ivanovich disappear into the building, his bathrobe flashing momentarily in the staircase windows of each of the five levels, as he ran up the five floors.

"What's the deal with that dude?" asked Sashka, trying to get his situational bearings.

"That old dog, he's been bending my ear for at least an hour, maybe two, and he is probably gonna get laid too, before he has to get up to go to work, but not us, pal, not us. Not yet, that is! But two more months, my friend, and we are outta of this aromatic hell!" And I laughed and hollered all the way back to the base.

# Fog of Nothingness

**A** stained carpet with two, maybe three bare feet on it. A sunken-in sofa, with a man, a mind, on the edge, naked, slumped over, head in the hands, moaning, "Horror! Horror." It is, of course, the middle of the night. A literary mind poisoned by poetics might fine-tune this as happening "in the wee hours of the morning." Style, with all of its trivial sensitivities, is utter, utter nonsense.

Whatever pity, whatever touch of sympathy you might have just experienced for this desolate, unknown figure in its unnamed state of distress, is about to fade away. Details have the power to change a reader's mind, to make it skeptical, to brace it for a cynical revelation. That pesky issue of two, maybe three feet on the floor. "What's that about?" inquires the mind, perhaps, even re-reading the opening sentence in disbelief. Surely, the author of this little midnight opus owes an explanation. But no explanation will be given; reality just is. It owes us absolutely nothing.

I will nevertheless explain since the digital page I am typing on, like a bottomless Nietzschean abyss, yawns with whitish emptiness. The man is not alone. Next to him is a one legged prostitute, Klava, a long-time neighbor in his Soviet-style commune apartment. A prostitute by day, we must add, but by night, an uncompensated lover. That's right, love doesn't pay, in case you haven't noticed. A point of thought, if not ideology, that is part of the very horror that has just overwhelmed Sergei's mind.

Still naked, Sergei gets off the sofa and begins to pace around the room, stepping over a couple of quarter-liter bottles of vodka, still populated with the faint spirit of well distilled Stoli vodka. Life in a commune apartment has two focal points – the kitchen and the john. When unrelated people share these two facilities on a daily basis for any duration of time, inevitably they become related. If you cook together, you are likely to drink together. If you wait on each other to take a shit, there's a good chance you might end up talking about the shit you have to deal with. Social psychologists have long commented on the bonding power of proximity. Love, as Sergei was saying just a few hours ago, while still in the loving embrace of Klava, was an illusion of bias, nothing more, and nothing less.

"Why an illusion?" Klava asked.

"Because we are all, without exception, inextricably self-serving. Self is its own bias. Each mind is its own religion!"

But this exchange, however provocative or flawed, was a long time ago, A few hours can feel like an eternity when you are sobering up from what in the final analysis is always a moral hangover, an original sin of confusing form for essence.

One thing, however, could not however be denied. Sex with a one-legged woman is a commonly underestimated pleasure. Legs get in the way of intimacy. The basic nut-and-bolt mechanics of most forms of sex conceal a strange ontological truth of being and non-being, of space and matter; a thought that Sergei could see himself developing later that morning, over a cup of coffee, but not at the moment.

With nothing less than demonstrative disgust, he stepped right onto an open page of Emmanuel Kant's book of pure reasoning like it was a stray sheet of newspaper somewhere on the streets of Moscow. He couldn't stand Kant. Had he thought in English, he would have delighted in the phonetic connotations of Kant's name: Kant as a thinker had that refined intellectualizing bitchiness that Sergei couldn't stand since his days as a student. Yet he could never get rid of Kant. His two-volume collection of pure reasoning still had the promise of shedding some kind of clarity on this murky existence that right now horrified Sergei.

He finally found his black socks; the kind that men in dress shoes pull up almost to their knees. He put them on and somehow inexplicably relaxed, as if finally organized, and settled back down on the sofa.

"What's up with you this morning, sweetie?" asked Klava, her breasts reflecting the fainting moonlight of the soon-to-be morning.

Sergei once again shook his head: "Same thing-less thing as always."

"What's that?" Klava probed.

"That's the thing of it. Its thing-less-ness, it's a name-less thing-less-ness that escapes any definition, any label, any logic or explanation. It's like the eye of the storm. A focal point of everything that is a nothingness in and of its it-less self-less self."

He went on like this for a while as Klava listened. The mind, she thought, is just like an ant-hive, ever crawling with information, particularly, a mind like that of Sergei. She herself did not have this problem. Selling her body taught her how to ignore her own mind. She lived on a riverbank of meta-cognitive distance, more in touch with her ineffable, cosmic self than Buddha or Mahavira, or any one of all these Krishnamurties that baby-sit human restlessness.

There was only one grounding truth that she knew and that was touch. She leaned not against Sergei but into him, as if she was intending on walking through him – hard, heavy, forcefully, as if she lost her balance and fell. But Sergei didn't even notice. His neural ant-hive was teeming with coiling serpents of self-referencing circular logic. In saying nothing, at least, as he thought, he was saying nothing false.

Klava allowed herself to fall back and stretch out on the unwashed bedsheets, her hand suddenly stumbling upon an object somewhere in the crevices of the cushions. She pulled out a party book, a KOMSOMOL membership pocket book. "Look!" she said handing it over to Sergei. "And look at you! Such a handsome bright face!" she said drawing her index finger down the middle of Sergei's back.

Sergei took the pocket book and looked at his picture. It was clear he was pleased, this sudden, out of the blue, ego-stroke coupled with an erotic touch, worked its shameless magic. The fog of nothingness vanished and suddenly a strong craving for coffee was on his mind. Life was finally organized into a cohesive, albeit illusory, whole.

"Let's get up and clean up. A new day is upon us, Klava!  It shouldn't be wasted!"

# Un-Inc.

A land-locked Viking, he was forever moored to the axis of existential gravity, that ran straight down his spine. Diffusing consciousness anchored in a weighted down body.

He was ensconced, better yet, "Brahmanically enthroned," amidst a still well-upholstered mid-century modern Danish chair that used to sit, an eternity ago, in the foyer of his last house, by the fireplace. A kind of cozy place for thumbing through the writings of mad-man Kierkegaard or something, a fantasy that had never played out.

The coffee swirls of the hardwood floor were brewing up a metaphysical storm around his feet somewhere down below, miles below, while his am-ness, that field of awareness that you and I are, was somewhere up-up-up, almost butting up against the ceiling. He was larger than his immediate world. Not in size, but in the radius of his identification.

He was the dogwood tree in front of him, through the window – each and every blossoming quartet of purple-white clovers.

He was the rigid piping of the cushion of the chair he was sitting on – each and every hidden stitch and roll of fabric.

He was the sound of the May rain outside the stain glass – each and every un-witnessed drop of it.

The world around us is the world we choose to see. But we can't see the choice itself. With predetermined blindness, we suffer the karmic consequence of our own freedom, incarcerated, land-locked, moored amidst the luxury of our ignorance.

His am-ness (that undifferentiated field of awareness that you and I are), long freed from any anchor of ego, like a cloud, levitated, propped up by the musculoskeletal chassis of this life-vehicle. It (am-ness) was all colors at once; a self-unaware spectrum of radiance and darkness. The body was nailed down, more literally than metaphorically, to the mid-century modern chair that used to serenade his house visitors with moments of respite that never materialized. The dogwood tree, across a dusty pane of glass, had long withered down to a skeletal silhouette. Spiders, in checkered golf pants, lounged in the cobweb hammocks that they had fastened around the two Viking horns that had grown out of his mottled hair. No pulse to be found in this rotting pile of flesh. Blood, now free, coursed his now totally relaxed "system" without the slightest lock or impediment.

The heart never ticked. The brain stopped waving.
The lungs were wide- open gateless gates.

This field of am-ness (that you and I sometimes are)
stood still, like a primordial lawn, lush with potential.
But suddenly, finally, it rippled. With powerful waves
of reminiscence. The mind filled with an endless
stream of moms and dads, brothers and sisters, dogs
and cats, pet parrots and pet dinosaurs, the lovers he
loved and the lovers he hated. The mind, a self-
illuminating informational lava-lamp that it is,
became a fractalizing circus of distorted mirrors, a
meta-feedback loop, a Moebius labyrinth of self-
referential duality.

The coffee swirls of the hardwood have finally
soaked through his house slippers, and only found
handfuls of desiccated bones and ligaments. The
coffee colors of the hardwood floor surged upwards
in search of a beating heart. But to no avail. The times
and causes for arrhythmia had long gone. There was
no one left for the heart to beat for. No one left to
pine over. No one left to ache for. Only iridescent
ghosts filled this unincorporated am-ness.

Karmic winds blow. But not like physical winds.
They suck. But not like a vacuum. They draft up the

possibilities of what could have been, but really couldn't have been. They stir up the dust of the imagined and settle down with a sediment of fact. Gusting, gutting you out, with a chilling realization of what actually is.

He saw himself rowing on a wreckage of a ship, kneeling down on a deck board, paddling along, reaching down to the bottom of this liquid oneness with his sinewy forearms and shovel-like palms. Head fallen, his Viking horns leading the way. This was a parade of accountability. Shores upon shores were crowded with endless lives, all seated calmly and in judicial contemplation, in shaky mid-century-modern chairs. Familiar faces on the outside, and totally unfamiliar on the inside. He loved them all. He lived them all. He…

He shook off the mirage, once again back in the room, he was now nothing but a space, a space of awareness; the last dream awakened from; the last memory erased. Movers are walking through him, carrying furniture and boxes and rolled up carpets. He didn't mind. He wasn't there. A pixel in an informational matrix he knew. There is no movement. The effect of a running light is just an artifact of our perception, a series of mental events in an otherwise perfectly static and seamlessly monolithic oneness of all that is.

But he wasn't done yet. A garland of black bile and guilt was weaving a knot around his neck. What was

he being dressed for? What murky gala was he to
attend?

Eras passed. The fairy of time, rocking up and down
on a tick-tock swing, has sanded down the last rocks
of the Himalayas with the train of her dress, one
momentary pass at a time. A lonely Sherpa was
dragging a sled with a Viking up a prideful molehill
of Earth. A sky burial was in the offing.

Space rested while light played with it. Time rested
when there was no mind left to fill it with passage.
Her Brahmanic Highness of Am-ness sat on its mid-
century Danish lotus, ripe for another sowing. But no
seed of reincarnation came. Interested parties stopped
by and sniffed around. Some found too many
excesses of historical guilt. Some were spooked by
the last owner's preoccupation with unconditional
acceptance. Others made offers but asked too much or
too little. Terms could not be negotiated. But all, all
loved the setting – the coffee swirls of the hardwood
floor, the withered dogwood in the window, the mid-
century modern chair that housed these long
disillusioned bones. The setting was spectacular.

Just like the sunset of the day. The moon cut into the
sun, turning the blinding halo into a sharp enso. A

finch swayed on a rigid limb. A spider continued to crochet a striped sweater for a Viking horn. The field of am-ness was almost fully defragged and ready for another karmic programming. The future loved itself again. The past, sullen with its loss of freedom, binged on sour grapes. And somebody was finally thumbing pages of Kierkegaard in the empty foyer.

# The 20ᵗʰ Century Catfish

# (or the Hard Problem of Space)

Space – be it personal, physical, or conceptual - is a hard thing to understand for a catfish, let alone for a human. As a fish, I am a bottom feeder. I live and play at the philosophical ground of what exists, just a breath above the ontological bottom-line of matter, in the silt of the ineffable. I know, believe me, that when I babble like this, spewing out unfamiliar polysyllabic terminology in rapid succession, when I make these kinds of obscure proclamations in that smug categorical tone of mine, you are likely to shake your human head in disapproval, dismay and outright scorn. But I take no offence to such reaction. None at all. So, let me rephrase my thesis here: as a fish, I believe, I understand space better than you, human, do. The reason is simple: my space is more palpable than yours. Water is more concrete than air.

-

But you, human, do deserve some credit for my insights. Over my many years in the rivers of Earth, I've learned a good bit from your kind. The knowledge I've picked up from you has however come at some cost. Oh, how little you think of the rest of us who dwell on this planet! But I've learned not to mind your unsolicited patronage of us. In fact, I've come to enjoy your childish delusions of grandeur, your daring appetite for knowledge, and your unshakable conviction in your evolutionary supremacy. You, humans, have a very peculiar kind of charm – the charisma of neoteny – the irresistible cuteness of the little one who keeps asking "why."

But the time has come for me to share what I've learned over the years. I know my time is near, I know it because no catfish that swims so close to shore can be lucky for much longer. Curiosity doesn't just kill cats, it kills catfish too.

-

I was spawned in the slow-flowing womb of the Seine, before the Great War; Paris is my home. The Seine was the promenade of my youth. But my resting place will most likely be in Thailand, in the Mekong, where I currently spend my dwindling days. Just like there are many kinds of cats, there are many kinds of catfish. In Europe, my kind used to be known as a Wels. A Wels catfish is a biggun, the eighteen-wheeler of the deep. We grow all of our lives, both in size and wisdom. No reason not to. And we travel widely. But, of course, not widely enough to migrate from Europe to Asia, which is what happened in my case. There is a story of human intervention here which I will eventually tell, I promise, but not until I share the notes from my journey.

Parenthetically, when I recently surrendered myself into the care of a certain Buddhist monk in the North-West of France, before I was transported to the Mekong river, I checked in at about 650 pounds. But I am even bigger now. And if I ever get caught again,

I am sure, I will feed a whole village. But until that day I have no plans to stop growing. Keep in mind that back in the day, before you, humans, came along, we, the catfish, shared the burdens of the world alongside with a few tenacious whales. Back then the world literally rested on a much more solid foundation than it does now, in this age of relativity and epistemological uncertainty.

-

Each species of fish has a philosophical question to solve and all of these questions have to do with space. Skates, for example, contemplate non-Euclidean geometry. Sharks study the philosophical implications of origami. Minnows generally tend to mull over the possibility of a geometrical point. Tilapias study the topology of toroids. But we, the catfish, the bottom-feeders, burrow as deep as we can – we ponder space itself, from an ontological perspective. We keep peeling its non-existent surface like a street bum that spent his last money on an unlucky scratch-off.

So space – in all of its conceptual, physical or personal manifestations – has been on my mind ever since I can remember myself. In fact, this autobiographical fact goes right along with one of my key insights: I propose that self-awareness is space-awareness. A self, as I think it, is a space that is aware of itself as being separate from the rest of the space "out there."

A self is a "here." Everything else is "not me," out there, in that space outside of "me." And it is exactly by knowing what I am not and where I am not that I get to experience myself as a self-referenced "here" and a self-aware "this."

I have no idea what this means to you. But that's ok since I also have no idea what "meaning" means.

It took me a while to arrive at this first realization about space. I'd swim entire rivers from start to finish and back, up and down the stream, just thinking and contemplating, like some kind of peripatetic Michael Phelps on 'shrooms doing one philosophical lap after another.

Breathlessness, by the way, is a better source of inspiration than breath itself. And like you, human, I, fish, too, can control my breath. Just because I extract oxygen from water rather than air, through the gills rather than mouth, it doesn't mean that I can't benefit from the breathless revelations of self-imposed anoxia. And I believe I have. My keenest insights would come when I would swim entire rivers on a single out-breath. But enough drumming and stridulation! Swim on with me, human mind, until we meet at the common denominator of liquid oneness.

-

One of my early memories is two sets of human feet, dangling in the water, off the embankment behind the Notre Dame cathedral, in Paris. As I lurked around this intriguing sight, I soon learned that the four feet belonged to two seminarians who seemed to be in love and were right now in the midst of pouring out their hearts to each other. The two men were sitting in the shade of a tree, next to each other, with their pants rolled up knee-high and their feet in the water, their beaten up and dusty black shoes heaped together to the side. They were experiencing – it seems – a crisis of faith and that unique sense of trepidation when you realize that you have found yourself in a pirouette of mutual self-disclosure. Their topic wasn't space but the space between them was nevertheless relevant to my philosophical investigations. Here's what I heard:

"Religion, my dear friend, at its worst, uses a child's imagination against himself. When working with kids, the fire-and-brimstone dogmatics know that they have a unique opportunity to convert an impressionable mind, not through logic, but through imagery, through the horrible image of hellish fires and unquenchable thirst … These commis-voyageurs of faith, these peddlers of morality know that a rational mind will inevitably correct its own cognitive distortions. They know that and, instead, they, quite prudently, choose to invest into imagery rather than into reason or logic. The fact is, my dear friend," continued the young man on the left, "one could make a logically irrefutable argument for God, but these pirate-priests don't want to bother with theosophy. They know that logic – even good logic – is a low octane fuel… With kids, they aim for the stars – they try to hijack their imagination, to turn a child's mind against itself. And it is all too easy to do. And when that is accomplished, the water of logic can never put out the fire of imagination… A young mind that has imagined hell in detail can never truly break away from that kind of indoctrination. This is emotional faith. It lives deep within, below the thinking, analytical mind. You can cut the leafy limbs of logic but you can never uproot this limbic stump. The conceptual space of the mind, my friend, is pre-populated, pre-configured, and pre-shrunk ... A mind that is afraid is too small to appreciate the all-forgiving implication of divine omnipresence ... If God is everywhere, as I believe, then God is everyone and everything ... But the mind that has been cornered by the four tigers of fear dares not to leave its cage of alienation ... The tragedy here is that in selling God, such tactic also manages to sell separateness ... The conceptual space, my friend, must be liberated if we are to successfully share the word of God ... Only an open mind can be spacious enough to accommodate the vastness of God ... but a mind that is afraid is too conceptually small for a true epiphany, don't you think?"

"Is that what happened in your case?" said the seminarian on the right and put his hand on the other man's knee. A silence ensued, and then more human words followed but I no longer listened to them talk. I remember shuddering with a strange vibration, moving just enough to counteract the lazy flow of the Seine, which was quite easy so close to shore and so near the surface. The question that I wished the other man would ask was to clarify the phrase "conceptual space." So, I got even closer, now and then tickling their feet with my rubbery black whiskers. But I waited in vein, eavesdropping on their touching fall from grace; no clarification of the term came; they themselves now became a topic to each other, their

144

feelings and fears of what they felt; they were now talking about expanding their hearts, not minds, which too, they said, was very important… But, by now, I gave up on listening to them, and I went down deep, as far as I could go, until I came to the other surface; no, not the one between water and air, but the one way below, between water and bedrock.

-

The phrase "conceptual space" made me think of furnishings, clutter, and inner décor. Is consciousness a space that we populate with objects of abstraction? Is consciousness like a belly for thoughts? Do we digest information the way we process food? Is there a limit to how much we can hold in our minds and learn? Is our inner life a kind of limitless self-storage? As I burrowed into the silt of the Mother-Seine, I also thought about thinking itself; I thought about thinking as a kind of spawning, and I thought of thoughts as some kind of "conceptual caviar." And then I thought of thinking about thinking, and I discovered that there was yet another kind of space, a gap of sorts within me between my own thoughts and my awareness of them. And I thought of that gap and realized that this meta-cognitive gap was a kind of "non-conceptual space." A "pure space," perhaps? A field of primordial awareness?

And then I thought to myself: "Who is thinking this thought? Where is this thinking coming from, how is it emerging, who is generating it?" And I studied this question waving my whiskers back and forth, like so many pairs of oars, stirring up clouds of river sediment while trying to purify my mind. And it dawned on me that I was trying to swim up a stream of thoughts inside my own mind, as if I was swimming up an actual stream, like some kind of suicidal salmon, chasing my own origins. And I felt the danger of that: "What if I get to the very top of where this stream of consciousness flows from, and what if I come ashore, on some other side of myself, out there, out of this "here" that I am into some kind of out-there, out of my own mind, into that ineffable wellspring that gives rise to my being …"

Imagine that, human, a Wels catfish about to discover the wellspring of its being!

Eventually I had to give up trying to understand myself through this so-called "conceptual space." As many times as I tried to get ahead of my own stream of consciousness and swim up to the very top of where it flows from, I would inevitably sink, in mind and in body, which is an actual limitation of the catfish species. We are negatively buoyant, which means that we sink instead of floating. Like all bottom-feeders we sport – a funny word, isn't it? – a rather heavy bony head and we have a rather small gas bladder. So, we tend to sink instead of effortlessly staying afloat. We suck at staying on the surface, which gives us – bottom-feeders – a philosophical advantage, which we secretly treasure.

-

Having plumbed the depths of "conceptual space" for the better part of my youth, I was next interested in trying to understand "physical space." The physical manifestation of space seemed like a fitting question for a middle-aged, empirically-minded catfish. So, one day, I decided to leave the Seine behind, and headed down towards a labyrinth of mid-European tributaries that I knew like the back of my tail. My destination was LHC, the Large Hadron Collider that lassoed a huge swath of land on the borders of France and Switzerland.

Back in the day, when LHC was nothing more than a 75 meter-deep trench, it was a man-made circular river during the rain season. Navigating by stars and zen, I made my way down the Rhone and started to hang out there, waiting for a chance to learn about space from particle physicists themselves. With enough snowmelt or rain flooding, I figured, I might be able to make it directly from the Rhone into the LHC ditch while it was still under construction. But that seemed like a … last-ditch effort, without a clear way out. Was I really ready to die to learn something new about space? I didn't know. I mean, I knew that I wouldn't know if I am ready or not until the opportunity actually presented itself. I never was the one to get all excited over hypotheticals. I waited but the opportunity, as I had envisioned it, didn't materialize. Something else did, however. Did eventually while I took the time to organize my thoughts on the matter of "physical space."

You need to understand that, as a catfish, I experience space as variable – variable in density and … variable in taste. Sometimes space is edible and I eat it, sometimes it tries to eat me and I flee it. I, of course, don't actually see space, I only butt into it or against it. A while back I realized that it is impossible to see space. Eyes are not for seeing space but for seeing objects, which we can only see by not seeing space. And this isn't just about where I dwell – in the water – but it's about the ontological impossibility of seeing space, regardless of where you dwell. Whether space is liquid or gaseous, it – by definition – cannot be seen. Space – to function as space - has to be invisible. True, when space hardens, it becomes matter. It becomes visible and objectively impenetrable. After all, what is a wall if not hardened space? But then, space stops being space.

These were my musings. And I think there was some merit to these conclusions. But with no one to consult, I was left to my own limited devices, trying to sketch out the philosophy of "physical space" on the easel of my "conceptual space." And that, on some level, seemed like an impossible feat. Indeed, to map out physical space inside a conceptual space seems akin to a goldfish swallowing a whale. How can a finite mind grasp infinity? How can one mind encapsulate the entire Oneness of All That Is? I needed help and I had to fish for it.

-

The flooding that I had been counting on to get into the LHC construction site didn't seem to be in the cards. But one day, while coursing impatiently up and down the Rhone near the provincial city of Bellegarde-sur-Valserine, I started trekking a small fishing expedition. The folks on board had the latest-issue out-board motor and the kind of expensive fishing gear that most locals couldn't afford. "Physicists!" I thought to myself, with hope. Indeed, it is common knowledge that particle physicists have all the money. Somehow the smaller the unit of study is, the bigger is the financial reward. Frankly, particle physics strikes me as a big racket. I think of particle physicists and the industrial engineers and the construction contractors that they work with to built all of this massive custom-made testing machinery and facilities as a kind of scientific mafia. But that's a separate topic, of course. Perhaps, a tad too political to tackle it here. Point is, I was jubilant at the opportunity to learn at least something about what was going on at the Collider and, as it often happens in a state of excitement, I got too close to the well-rigged fishing expedition. Before I knew it, I had a gaping hole in my lip with a metallic aftertaste from a hook, and, next, two pairs of surprisingly muscular arms dragged me out into the boat. My curiosity has finally found itself on a collision course with a couple of overcompensating brainiacs.

The two guys that fished me out threw me on the floorboards, letting me thrash myself into exhaustion, and were now resting, each sipping a beer and shooting scientific shit.

While gasping for air in the bloody slush of the fancy fishing boat, I overheard them talk about neutrinos – the so-called "ghost particles" – about how these particles would pass through Earth without ever colliding with any other particle. "Imagine that!" I thought to myself, temporarily distracted from the task of saving my life. I knew they weren't going to gut me – too much of a mess - and that I was too big to be simply knocked out cold with the back of an oar. I knew I had time, so I took my time to think.

"If you were a neutrino," I thought to myself, "you'd just zip right through the entire density of Earth's matter never knowing you just passed through a planetary object. If you were a neutrino kind of catfish, you'd slip right through the hull of the boat and back into the murky depths of safety. Which means … which means …"

The priorities of survival were starting to finally kick in. You, humans, say that fish rots from the head down. That's technically not true. But what is true is that a fish, just like a human, goes mad from the head down. And if I didn't do something soon, while I could, I'd be mad enough to deserve to die. So, I decided to put on a show. I put all of my back into it, nearly rocking the boat. One of the guys, frustrated with all the racket that I was making, grabbed from behind and lifted me up by my tail as high as he could, my head now resting awkwardly on the floor. This was a successful little maneuver on his part: it was hard to thrash this way, but not impossible. I knew they were getting ready to finish me, probably, by cutting through my spine. And, indeed, the other guy disappeared out of sight for a moment and returned with an electric fillet knife in his hands, and started advancing at me. As a catfish, we are scale-less and big and kinda slimy; and this helps in these kinds of moments; we make pretty slippery bastards. For all intents and purposes it is easier to subdue a Brazilian ju-jitsu black belt than one of us. And, it goes without saying, in this moment I had everything at stake, unlike these human schmoes. For me it was a life-or-death moment. For them, it was a matter of sport. With my tail high enough in the air, I realized I was exactly in the right position to wrestle my way out and, with any luck, slip out over board, which is exactly what happened. As the electric buzz of the reciprocating blades nicked my spine, I convulsed with all my might and fell overboard with a big splash.

"Was zur Hölle?!" exclaimed the one in with the electric knife while the other man scratched his head. And the two burst out into uncontrollable laughter.

I couldn't care less, however. Back in the softer space that you, humans, call "water," I screwed myself deep down and away that day, into the colder and darker realms of the Rhone, escaping a very close call with a mix of terror and glee, tunneling through the pliable medium of my world, like an oversized neutrino flying through Earth, unimpeded, until I could no longer feel the centrifugal tickle of the vortices of the overboard motor above me, somewhere up there on the surface of an entirely different world with its entirely different conceptions of space and matter.

-

But no sooner than I escaped, I returned to my preoccupation with space. Enriched now by this idea of a neutrino, I tried to plug this concept into my worldview.

In my reality, space has a feel, a touch, a taste. It's all around me just like it's all around you. But for me space is so much less abstract. For a human space is a thought, for me it is a sensation. When you move in your human world, space yields and disappears. When I move, space stands in my way and reappears. It's only when I don't move that the medium that surrounds me – my reality, that is - disappears and becomes conceptual space. It's only when I hang still that space for me becomes what your space is for you – an emptiness, a non-thing, a no-thing, a nothingness, i.e. an abstract, impalpable reality.

But even then I still have a taste of it on my skin. As a catfish, in case you didn't know, I am covered – head to toe – with taste buds. For all intents and purposes, I am a swimming tongue with a brain attached it. I eat space. And now and then it eats me. But not that day.

-

I was finally leaving the Rhone behind, with all of its non-sense talk about neutrinos. How could such a thing be ever measured if it can pass through any matter and, thus, through any sensor undetected? I couldn't fathom that. But, perhaps, my imagination and knowledge base were too limited. One useful conclusion did however occur to me on the way back to Paris and that is that speed creates space. A hand touching a brick wall discovers a barrier. The same hand, moving at karate speed, turns brick into space. Speed creates space. Speed turns the impassible into transparent. A karate hand can do that to a brick. A bullet can do that to a body. A hungry catfish swimming downstream can do that to water. An object in motion turns its surrounding medium into a gateless gate. It's all about speed: a photon passes through a pane of glass whereas a slower fly, trapped inside, head-butts the invisible hard surface until it runs out of energy and dies, not ever understanding how previously malleable air suddenly solidified into an impenetrable invisible barrier.

-

Back in the Seine, I decided to check under the bridge behind the Notre Dame. It was a sentimental thought, a simple desire to reminisce and to see if the two men I had seen long ago would somehow still be there. And, to my surprise, there they were, the same two men, sitting on the edge of the river embankment, like two gargoyles frozen in time, with their shoes off and their feet dangling in the black-green water. Except that they were unmistakably older now, their feet showing the age with knobby bunions and hints of varicose veins. The guy on the left once again had his hand tenderly resting on the other guy's knee. But, strangely, he wore a wedding band. My guess is that their connection managed to remain largely platonic – another tragedy of forbidden love. The shoes by their side also showed a divergence in their existential paths. One pair was an expensive Italian loafer, the kind you might expect a Vatican official to wear. The other was a pair of worn-out Birkenstock sandals, with skin-polished insoles. One had a Catholic collar, the other an unbuttoned Hawaiian shirt. It all made that peculiar 20th century sense. Things sure had changed but their hearts seemed just as young as before. And they seemed to be having the same conversation as before – the one about religion - but this time they were approaching it from an altogether different angle.

The one on the right just said: "But what if that imagination – that child's immense capacity for fancy – could be turned on in some positive way? Towards a sense of awe, rather than fear?"

"I know!" exclaimed the one in the Hawaiian shirt. "You know how much I was into Herman Hesse in those days when we first talked about these things as young seminarians? After I read Hesse's "Journey to the East," I knew I had to go there for myself, I had to join the movement … Well, you know all that, about my leaving the seminary, and all that jazz. My point is that what you just said about imagination as a way to kindle a religious passion is what I discovered there in the East – God without church, love without judgment, the Bhakti way – a kind of ecstatic, dogma-free worship that taps into the child's imagination, in a pagan way, turning everything inanimate into animate, energizing, invigorating, illuminating everything and anything. Just imagine growing up like that, with your mind full of awe and your heart in constant ecstasy …"

"So you are not against religion after all?" asked the one with the priest collar, as I quietly circled around their feet.

"No, not at all. I am against the abuse of imagination. What I am for is the trinity of spiritual space …

There must be room for all of us in this world, for all of our thoughts, and all of our desires, for our inner and outer lives, for the objectivity of our deeds and the subjectivity of our intentions … "

-

It is as if they read my mind. Or, as if I had projected myself into their minds. Somehow these two humans and I seemed to be on the same brain wave. I swam around for a while longer but became eventually tired of their intellectualizing. Once again I felt profoundly changed by this random encounter. Random? Was I really sure it was random? How would one know for a fact?

Anyway, I left, with trinity of space on my mind. As usual, I looked inside myself for answers. Here I was, as before, a living space – a space of awareness – a field of am-ness – a subjective or "conceptual" space that … existed objectively, and, therefore, physically. Was this space that I was my personal space or did I share it with All That Is Alive? And if I did share this plane of being with All, then how could I assert any claim of ownership of this coordinate of being? How could I possessively claim that this space of being is "mine"? And so, lost in thought, I slid across the riverbed like a gloomy rubbery torpedo, not knowing where, not knowing why.

-

The river of time passed, evaporating as it flowed, and to my own surprise I found myself in Normandy, on the other side of the Channel, swimming along the right bank of the River of Epte, my mind still on the mysteries of space. And who comes down the stream? Douglas Adams of all humans! That whimsical Brit who penned "The Hitchhiker's Guide to the Galaxy." Doug's reputation in the Waterworld preceded him like the prodromal signs of a migraine. Famous for his catchy phrase – "So long, and thanks for all the fish!"- that belonged to dolphins as they left Earth before the planet was demolished to make room for a hyperspace bypass – he clearly thought of maritime creatures as sentient, and, perhaps, even superior to humans. So whenever he got close to water, he was the center of attention.

That day he was floating down the slow and methodical river Epte on an inner tube with a beer in hand and a companion in a similar set-up. I made a quick u-turn and followed Doug and his friend down the stream, wondering how in the hell such a tall man – and Douglas had an imposing height of six feet five inches – could be such a clever writing gent. Verily, the history of literature knows practically no tall authors. Somehow the Muse prefers shorter human antennae for reception.

"So," I hear Douglas say to his companion, "I've had this idea for a new book, The Salmon of Doubt … about this salmon that refuses to swim back to its ancestral birthing ground just to spawn and die. So, this Salmon is a kind of Camus character who questions the absurdity of life, defying Freudian postulation that Thanatos is stronger than Eros …"

"Thanatos, is that some kind of dinosaur?" asks the other guy with a smirk, after a long and slurpy sip of beer.

"Yes, of the early Freudian period" says Doug, "No!" – he then corrects himself and shoots an inquisitive are-you-pulling-my-leg kinda glance at his friend, and adds: "Thanatos, you know, the will to die, the death instinct … Freud, I think, went off his rocker when he concluded that it is the death instinct that is the primary motivational driver, not the libido, the life instinct …"

"That's what I thought," I hear the other guy say as he – can you believe it?! – drops his now empty beer can right into the water. "But what about all these other salmon who swim to die … voluntarily … what guides them, Doug?"

Doug took a sip and scratched his head: "Lack of self. There is something inherently Buddhist, undifferentiated about them, something impersonal," he says and continues: "But my salmon, a Doubting Thomas of a fish, questions this blind evolutionary mission. On second thoughts, I think I'll go another way with this – perhaps, it'll be just another Dirk Gently novel, but I love the title and want to find a way to use it."

And with these words another empty beer can splashed into water while two new beer cans cracked open almost in sync. I noticed a little blue plastic beer cooler tied to Doug's inner tube, bopping up and down behind, and a school of star-struck minnows swarming around the man's size 13 feet.

-

Appalled by this almost demonstrative littering I broke away, in a silent protest. Furthermore, I heard enough. Enough to last me a while. Enough to process. My catfish mind – just like your mind – started connecting data-dots. In particular, the phrase "personal space" that I had recently heard under the bridge behind the Notre Dame and this notion of an impersonal, Buddhist sense of self - or should I say "non-self"? – were now comingling in my consciousness.

Swimming ahead of Doug and his companion, and moving downstream, I began to notice that the river of Epte was narrowing its clay shoulders, getting shallower and more crowded, reducing – it occurred to me – itself into an eventual tired trickle, as some rivers do, in an act of topological self-annihilation. If so, I was now likely coming to the end of my own lifeline too. A fish of my size needs a lot of water to live comfortably. I am no lungfish that can burrow in the mud and wait on the rain to come. But things – fortunately for me – played out quite differently. The Epte ended up not in a whimper but in a kind of watery cul-de-sac, not big enough to be called a lake but a tad too big to be called a pond. A sprawling reservoir of sorts. And this pond-like terminal happened to feature a levy that was currently spilling over into an altogether different realm.

I took a chance and navigated over to the other side, into what turned out to be a rather picturesque waterhole, bedecked all around with boulders and stepping stones and mystical bridges. Unknowingly I found myself in an immaculately landscaped oasis of a little known Buddhist center in the North-Western France.

A welcoming committee of plump ocher-white koi surrounded me on all sides. The koi are the Buddhist monks of the waters. Reared for centuries for decorative purposes, these meandering contemplative fish have long served as merchants of enlightenment. As they swim around near the surface of man-made ponds, they flaunt their frilly orange skins like monkish saris, following each other around an invisible underwater labyrinth.

Fish typically don't talk to fish, but exceptions do occur. Sniffing and tasting my way around this picturesque pond I soon found out the name of the place – Perche Zen Centre of Normandy, also known as Daishugyoji. I asked the koi about the place but received but a few answers, mostly of little use. The koi said something about Soto Zen but couldn't elaborate.

For a while I preoccupied myself with the sound of the place. I swam around the luscious water lilies, now and then tugging on their stems as if strumming a base string of a sitar, and listened to the muted sounds as they traveled and crisscrossed the pond down below. Once or twice I poked my rubbery blunt nose out of the water and watched the trembling beads of water scattered on the round green lotus-leaf coffee tables. The koi minded their own business, filing along in an underwater kinhin procession, mindfully mindless of the point of it all.

-

There was, however, one memorable encounter that still lingers in my mind. Given my exotic size, I was the talk of the pond and one day a baby koi tried hard to make friends with me. I ignored him but he wouldn't give up. He followed me for days until I finally faced him nose to nose and demanded: "What do you want from me? You've been following me for days now, aren't you tired of this?"

The baby koi hesitated to answer but finally mustered up his courage: "I want you to eat me."

"Why?" I snapped my mouth with unmasked irritation.

"I want to become you. I want to be a part of you – "

"Because I am big and you are small and afraid and you think that if I eat you, you become me or a part of me and lose your fear, right?"

"Right, and- " began the baby koi.

"The problem is," I cut him off again, "the problem is that I don't want to become you."

"Why not?" asked the baby koi, quivering from the intensity of my stare.

"Because if I allow you to become a part of me, your fear becomes my fear and I don't want that."

"But – " baby koi tried to protest.

But I wouldn't have it: "Furthermore, as you ought to know, as a catfish, I don't eat live fish. And before you ask me why one more time I'll just come right out and tell you: because I don't eat fear. I'll eat you when you are dead, when you have nothing to fear. You'll taste much better then."

With nothing to say, the baby koi finally left me to my own devices. And so I circled the air bubbler and strummed the taught stems of the lotus leaves and measured my time with questions rather than answers.

-

Eventually, one moonlit night I sensed a distant vibration of approaching human steps and, full of curiosity, I swam up to the edge of water and held in place, in the shallows, wafting my pectoral fins.

A hand reached into the water and petted my back.

"Who are you?" said the voice and I looked up. "I am Taisen Deshimaru, the Head Monk here," the voice introduced himself.

I wasn't at all surprised at this inter-species act of communication. Most creatures on Earth know that Buddhists – only Buddhists – can communicate with all life-forms. Catfish too possessed this knowledge.

"Who am I?" I repeated the man's question to myself, "I am not sure how to answer this," I said. I forced my way up the warm sand like a black sub that ran aground, to get a better look at the man, and sized him up. Dressed in orange, stout but quite ancient in look, the monk seemed to radiate a glow. His chiseled, high-cheeked face had a hint of dimples that eagerly morphed into an exaggerated smile-emoji of a face. This was no ordinary monk, I could tell. A Lama no less. Or a Zen Master, which he was, as I soon found out. "Help me back to the water," I asked for assistance and the monk kicked off his sandals, picked up the bottoms of his robe with one hand and gently shoved me down into deeper water.

"Thank you, brother," I vibrated in return.

"My pleasure, Boddhisattva!" whispered the monk, squatting down low and looking straight at me, the bottom folds of his orange robe now hopelessly soaked through. "I know you. You and I, we have the same Buddha-nature, don't we, friend?"

I rolled over like a dog offering the monk to tickle my scale-free rubbery belly.

"I have no idea what you are talking about, human fish," I vibrated back with my abductor muscles, and added: "But I am eager to learn from you."

"No worries, fish, I will explain," said Taisen. He backed up a few feet to the shore and sat down into a half-lotus on the big warm flat top of a nearby boulder. "You are a catfish, friend. And as a catfish, you are a vegetarian of sorts … No, let me rephrase

162

that," he continued, "Not a vegetarian, but a non-violent opportunist eater, you are the vulcher of the deep, a scavenger fish rather than a fish of prey, are you not?"

"You are right, two-legged fish," I said, experimenting with how to address the man. "It is true that I avoid the violence of predation. I do subsist on what is dead and no longer suffers. I am a cleaner, if you wish, a janitor of the riverbeds. A living broomstick of the silt."

"That is exactly what I meant," said the Master and added: "And that is what makes you and I such close kin. You and I, we are both practitioners of the ancient principle of non-violence. We are both the ideologues of Ahimsa, of that original morality of pacifism. And that makes you, talking fish, a Boddhisattva of the Green Abyss."

"No one has ever called me that, man," I bubbled back, "But I see no reason to object. A name is a name is a name."

"Oh, dear fish, I see you too love to speak in circles. In saying nothing, you are saying nothing false, huh? Commendable!"

-

And so the exchange between a man and a fish unfolded, between the two life-forms, one land-dwelling and the other waterborne, about all kinds of matters and non-issues. Various points were brought up – that we are all fish, that humans prenatally

163

breathed in the waters of amniotic fluid and sported tad-pole like tails at six or so weeks post-gestation; that to this day, each human cell contains the exact saline proportions of the waterworld humans evolved from – "We – human fish – brought the ocean with us, in our cells!"

We talked about reincarnation – of the literal, metabolic kind and of that other speculative metaphysical kind, of course.  About how we all continuously reincarnate – fish into humans and humans into fish – ants into sequoias and marsh-mellows into volcanoes; about how all – verily all! – is alive and sentient and shares the same impersonal space of oneness.

And we babbled on about how "this" and "that" are not really two, about how all dualities are mind-made be they of animate or inanimate origin, and about how there is no such thing as "self," that self is but the behavior of the Universe at a given location, and about how the subjective and the objective are two sides of one and the same side-less coin.

I also remember making a point to correct the monk's notion that all catfish are non-violent carryon eaters. I told the Monk about a curious recent phenomenon that I had witnessed where some catfish in Paris would hunt pigeons: they would lurk right under the surface near the banks, waiting for birds to wade in for a drink, and then, all of a sudden, would lunge out of the water, like jungle crocks, sometimes even coming ashore, trying to capture an unsuspecting pigeon, and not without some success.

"Unbelievable!" said the man when he heard this. "Unprecedented, that's for sure!" I agreed. "So, I guess," the monk continued, "It would be incorrect to call these rogue catfish bastards bottom-feeders any more." "Indeed," I echoed, "Surface-feeders would be the right name for these young turks." And at this moment the Monk broke out into a belly-shaking laughter as I tried to match the sounds of his laughter with the sounds of stridulation.

-

But the topic that intrigued me the most was the idea of a "rainbow body." According to this monk, there were practitioners in Tibet who could disband – dematerialize - their bodies at will. Apparently, over the centuries there had been a few documented cases when advanced practitioners would announce that on such and such day they would cease to exist. But not by hanging themselves or through self-immolation or some other known method of suicide but merely through a top-down command to disintegrate. In fact, the explanation went, they would turn their body into a rainbow of light that would then dissipate, with nothing left behind but their shoes and robes.

"I don't understand what you mean by that," I said to the Head Monk, feeling utterly fascinated by this possibility.

"It has to do with the idea of self-as-space," he said, with moonlight gleaming in his eyes, "Your mind tells you that you are a thing, right? That you are a fish. Mine tells me that I am a human. But these are all words to describe things. Nouns that describe objects. The truth is that there are no things, there are only processes. A thing or an object, in order to be a true thing or a true object, would have to be separate, it would have to totally stand alone in space, sovereign and independent of everything around it. But that's impossible. The Buddhist doctrine of Dependent Origination clearly states that there are no independent things, that all is inter-dependent, and therefore connected … Not even connected, but seamlessly intertwined … In fact, that all is one. So, a thing is just a process … But these processes look like things to us, due to the limitations of our sensorium. You see, what we experience as things and label with such nouns and pronouns as "fish" or "I" – all these are but various processes of the Universe happening at a given location that you experience as you and I experience as me … Nothing is static in this Universe … Everything is a process … The whole dynamic living system evolves in its entirety from a moment to a moment to a moment …"

There must have been a fog of misunderstanding in my eyes, a veil of confusion, so the Head Monk offered to demonstrate what he meant right there and then.

"Do me a favor and whip your tail right now."

I did.

"Now, notice this vortex that you created. When a mind sees this it sees a thing – it focuses on the most differentiated, most informationally-rich part of the picture and sees an eddie, or a vortex, and calls it that.

166

Mind objectifies the process into a thing. But as you yourself know, this vortex that you just created with your tail is not separate from the rest of the water in this pond. In fact, this vortex is the behavior of the entire pond – all of the water in this pond has been affected by your tail whip and now all of the water in this pond is participating in the behavior of this whirlpool."

I was beginning to understand what he meant.

The Head Monk continued: "To you space is water. To me space is air. To a worm tunneling through the soil, space is soil. To a neutrino flying through a mountain, space is rock. There is nothing but space. Space is everywhere. Space is what connects us all. And space is what we are made of. What we call a thing or an object or an entity is but space in motion. Here, where you are, space behaves as you, and as water around you. Here, where I am, space behaves as me, and as air around me, and as grass and soil beneath me. When you look up and see the sky, you see space acting like air and the sky – "

"But how can space move? How can space be in motion?"

"It doesn't. But it can change from 'this' to 'that' and that's what we experience as motion … Like those running lights on a movie marquee – they are not really running, are they, from one side to another, they are just changing state from 'this' to 'that' in sequence and our senses gives us an illusion of motion …"

"But what about that Rainbow Body that you mentioned?" I chimed in again.

"Yes, yes, I am getting there, buddy. So, an advanced practitioner realizes that self is space, that each and every part of us is just a pixel of space with its own identity, that each and every cell is but a small region of space with a conceptual self, that even the particles that constitute those cells are mini-selves too, that even the proto-particles that make up the particles are mini-selves too, and that all these sub-atomic, atomic, cellular, and organism-wide selves are self-imposed illusions. So, this practitioner decides that he or she will let itself go – that it is time to dis-organize this metazoan living organization of composite selves – through an act of will, which is really a final act of truth, a fact of liberation …"

"But how is this actually done?" I pleaded, totally intrigued.

"I can only speculate on the basis of the witness accounts that I have read or heard. One day you decide that you are done. You seclude yourself. And you meditate deep down to the bottom of your mind, where you had for years fed yourself with this idea that you are separate, and you tell yourself the truth that you are not. And you sit with that truth until every part of you hears the bugle call of liberation. Neurons in your skull are the first ones to hear it, then the other cells, then all of the cells, then all of the molecules that make up your cells, then all the atoms that make up these molecules, then all the proto-particles that make up the atoms that make up the molecules that make up the cells that make up the organs that make up the body that make up the illusion of self … And when the totality of you has finally realized that you are not separate from All That Is, you issue a final top-down command to all these pseudo-selves to awaken to their true emptiness, to their spatial nature …"

The monk's voice was trailing off …

So I picked it up from there: "And, I guess, if you were there watching this person meditate like that, at some point, at a critical point of truth, at the moment of their system-wide awakening, you would see them simply disintegrate, de-materialize, vanish, with not even a pile of flesh left, just shoes and clothes, right?"

"Exactly! Except for hair and nails, I am told. Apparently, the cells that grow hair and nails are very hard to communicate with, they are, in effect, unreachable, which is why they still grow after the rest of us dies." And with a chuckle, the Monk ran his hand over his bald head and added: "Stubborn, uncooperative hair cells!"

-

These exchanges went on for hours or maybe for days or even weeks or years. Neither of us kept track of time. But eventually the conversations came to a curious proposition. It was birthed in the middle of a starry night when otherwise crazy ideas acquire a degree of cosmopolitan feasibility, at that passing moment in time when there is just enough moonlight for the eyes to see but without a focus on details.

-

"Have you ever ..." asked the Monk, "thought about taking a journey to the East?"

"I haven't, my human friend," I said, my whiskers mixing the liquid blackness of the surface into tiny vortices, as my head gently bopped up and down like a rubber tug boat, "but I certainly have heard a thing or two from those who have," I said and shared about the conversation I had the fortune to overhear under the bridge behind the Notre Dame.

"What would you say to the following arrangement: I will charter a flight to Thailand, where we have a sister monastery, and I will pay to transport you there ..."

"On ice? To be filleted?" I half-joked.

"No, no, not at all," the monk protested, "Of course, not. Not on ice but in a carefully maintained, temperature-controlled water tank. Heck, I'll accompany you on the flight. I'll have to, really, because it's going to be a long one."

"Why not?!" I said without a moment's hesitation. And so was my destiny sealed.

-

In the next several weeks I swam alone, accompanied against my will, by a curious retinue of koi. We circled endless laps around the air bubbler in the middle of the pond, sometimes going deep, sometimes cutting through the thin film of surface

170

like a school of scissors. The monk had disappeared and at some point I began to wonder if that proposal was a flippant joke or if the plan simply fell apart for logistical reasons. I couldn't care either way. The swimming tongue that I am, I like the taste of reality just about wherever I am. Truth be told, I like the taste of the Seine the best. It tastes of wilting bouquets – too many of them are thrown off bridges by the romantics – and of sour wine. The pond of the Zen Centre, however, had the taste of a perfumed fish tank. The pretentious koi insisted on being fed and passively awaited for handfuls of fish food generously sown atop the watery furrows each night. The pond smelled of freeze-dried water fleas and human hands.

-

Eventually the day of the big move came. All went as planned. I was airlifted to Thailand. The head monk did break his promise. He never came along on the flight. With no one to talk to, I tried my best to hibernate at the bottom of a sizeable steel tank that had been filled with the now all-too-familiar taste of the pond water from the Zen Centre. Not knowing the meaning of flight – except for a rather faint conceptual representation of the idea – I simply rested, trying to integrate my understanding of space the best I could. Eventually, I was let loose into a tributary of the Mekong river somewhere in Thailand, near another Buddhist monastery. The taste of Mekong, which I could feel with every chemoreceptor of my skin, had an utterly unfamiliar quality. The river flowed from the snows of Tibet and had the freshness of the land that borders on clouds. I imagined that I could almost taste the feathers of migrating cranes. Not that I would ever allow myself to hunt them like those urban surface-feeders in Paris. Time passed and I learned to make a home in this distant corner of the world. The twentieth century was coming to an end and I had grown to the size of a submersible dirigible. I was beginning to slow down, favoring the same shady spots, day after day, until one day I have noticed a silly little silver hook dangling in front of my nose, with a pitiful worm on it. I couldn't believe my eyes. The scene was textbook. No self-respecting fish of any experience would fall for this cheap trick. And yet, they did. I stayed and watched one minnow after another, bass and carps too, take shots at this measly offer. "What a scam!" I thought, watching little fishes and bigger ones too come and nibble on the worm. And every so often, the hook would jerk and one unfortunate bastard after another would be violently yanked out of the depths, only to be thrown back into the water a moment later, albeit with a bleeding hole in its lip.

This puzzled me to no end. Was there a catch-and-release sportsman of some kind, in an expensive fishing vest, with a hundred pockets and a safari hat, smothered in sunscreen? I had to see what was going on and so I swam up to as nearly to the ephemeral line of surface that divides my world from yours, and I looked up. To my surprise, I saw a local kid, in dirty cotton shorts, squatting on the riverbank with a primitive fishing rod in his hands.

"What are you doing, little fella?" I asked him from the depths.

He startled as if he understood me. He looked around and waded knee-deep into the water. I made my presence known once again by bumping into his knee. He once again startled and began to talk. Most catfish of certain age and maturity understand children, regardless of the tongue they speak.

The explanation given was as charming as it was pitiful. "I am here looking for a fish that can feed my entire village. And that is why I keep throwing all this good-for-nothing mackerel back into the river. I am waiting for a big one, the one that can make a difference. The one like you."

"Hmm," I vibrated, kicking up the river sand with a tail splash. "You have a good heart, boy, but a silly mind. A big fish knows better than to bite on a silly little worm."

"I was suspecting that," said the boy throwing the fishing rod back on the grass. He squatted down right into water and stretched out his hands: "I beg you, Big One, come to me. I know I have nothing to offer you. But without you everyone I love will go hungry tonight. Have mercy on me, Fish."

I backpedalled a tad, burrowing myself backwards into the slimy safety of silt. "Let me mull this over, little brother," I said and added, "I promise I will consider your request but only on one condition: break your fishing rod in half and stop harming the little fish with your bait and hook. Can you do that?"

"I can," the boy agreed eagerly and did as he's been just told. He picked up his improvised fishing rod and busted it up in half against his knee. "There!" he said, holding two broken sticks. "I'll sit here and wait for your decision, Mr. Fish."

I smacked my lips and swam away.

-

I retreated into the cold depths of the Mekong and thought of Zen Master Taisen Deshimaru. Oh, how much I wished I could consult him now. But he was nowhere to be found. Was he even a thing or did I dream him up? I could no longer tell. So, as befits a bottom-feeder I took another final dive within myself.

"What is space?" has been the question on my mind as long as I can remember myself. Conceptually, space is a nothingness. Personally, space is me, myself and I. Physically, space is that unifying medium that connects me to everything that exists. That is the trinity of space – it is what keeps us separate, and what keeps us united, and what makes us who we are."

"Yes," I thought to myself, resting in the cold silt of the Mekong, passing water brushing my rubbery sides, "I've come here to learn the Way of the Rainbow Body – to let go of myself in a literal sense, through my own choice – but isn't allowing yourself to be cut apart into a hundred pieces and to be eaten the same? Isn't that too a rainbow body, minus the ego illusion of total body control?"

I knew it was.

"Have I solved my koan? Have I understood space?" I asked myself, feeling the water rush out of my gills. "Have I really understood that space and self are the same and that in letting go of myself I am simply letting go of the idea that space is somehow out there, around me? Have I plumbed the depths of my emptiness to know that I own nothing to call it my own? Have I accepted that I, myself, am space, and that there is no letting go of space, that space has nowhere to go? Have I really grokked it that no matter what happens to me conceptually, nothing really happens to me personally because there is no personal stand-alone, sovereign, independent me in any physical sense of the word?"

"I have," I thought to myself and swam up to the shore to see if the boy was there. He was.

I backed up a bit and with all the power of my body ran myself aground. Gasping for air, I looked up at him and said: "Kid, do me a favor, please. Turn around. You see that big rock over there? Pick it up. Bring it over right here. Now, lift it up as high as you can and, when you are ready, hit me on my head with it. But don't do it just yet. There is something I want to tell you. Before you drag me by my tail back to your village, and definitely before you cut me up and throw me in the caldron, promise me one thing: promise me to contemplate one question …"

"What is it?" asked the boy.

"What is the taste of space?" I blabbered, choking on the river sand in my mouth.

"Ok," said the boy and turned around to pick up something big and hard to hit me with. I closed my eyes and awaited my reunion with space.

-

That evening I was distributed among a dozen or so households of a small river village. I was fried and consumed with gusto. And I was finally all in one and one in all, omnipresent, nothing more and nothing less than space devoid of its illusion of self.

# Triptych of Am-ness

"*I* wanna ask you for a big favor," she yells into her phone, pacing around a park bench as I happen to walk by. A moment later the demand is drastically dialed down. "Ok, listen, I' m gonna ask you for just this one thing…" A tick later, the apparently unmet demand is suddenly reversed into an angry counteroffer: "I'll tell you what! A) fuck you! and B) I'm gonna do *you* a favor and hang up right now." She doesn't hang up. She keeps on shouting into the phone but I am already too far away to pay attention, or to give a fuck. I moved on (even if she hadn't) – returning to my recollections of *what once was and no longer is*. (I know: italicizing is a tad controlling. Indeed, *who am I* to place emphasis on your thoughts?)

In the summer of 1989 I had my best body, and my best mind, resulting in a series of three reincarnations – from a demigod to a demagogue and back.

A freshly demobilized 19 year-old Russian soldier is

an unstoppable sex machine. At least in theory. Just imagine a stomach full of vasodilating, nitrogen oxide boosting borsch and a case of chronic tumescence in your nether regions. Two years in a military uniform has a way of turning a libidinal pupa into a sex-obsessed pterodactyl.

This one, that I was once and no longer am, with an ego wingspan as wide as the Kalininsky Prospect was out on patrol that day, looking for romantic road-kill wherever the wheels of life could find it. I was beating around every possible bush (pun half-intended), but not much was happening. Only 24 hours out of the uniform, with two long years of sexual deprivation behind me, I was already feeling at an impasse. Life wasn't cooperating. Old girlfriends weren't returning my phone calls and new girlfriends weren't yet giving out their phone numbers. I tried and I tried and I tried, but, alas, the first day out brought no relief. The next morning, however, was to hold some promise.

I woke up with a brilliant idea. I would revisit my old stomping ground – the rowing club in Serebryanni Bor, a little summer oasis in the suburb of Moscow, a paradise of sandy beaches and dachas. I finished my mom's borsch for breakfast, readjusted my crotch, and grabbed a gym bag that had been left unpacked since about two and a half years prior.

On the way to the metro station I tried to remember the last time I exercised out of this bag. I couldn't recall. The contents of the gym bag were, in effect, unknown. So, I carried it the way airport security folks would handle an unattended bag, with care and suspicion.

I arrived at the rowing club by 9:00 am and looked for my old coach. He was easy to find, drunk and asleep in the boat repair shed. He remembered me although it had been almost three years; at least, my face, if not my name. He asked for a couple of rubles "for the hair of the dog, you know" and tossed me the keys to the hangar. "Take #28," he said and closed his eyes.

#28 was a familiar single racing shell. It had long been retired from any competition, if it ever competed in the first place. Even back in my so-called day, it was a practice boat, beaten up and patched with swirls of glue here and there, and in hopeless need of sanding. The good thing about it was that it was dry. I had my choice of oars, however. I didn't compromise and picked a good one. On the way out of the hangar I grabbed a Styrofoam knee-mold from a heap of them by the door and headed out.

With the canoe against my side, I walked up to the dock and looked around. The Moscow River seemed to sprawl as wide as mythical Volga – an endless table of liquid steel. I remembered about the gym bag and thought to myself, "Fuck it!" I took off my shoes and my t-shirt and was now down to nothing but a pair of jeans. I rolled up the pant-legs, placed the boat into the water, stabilized it with the oar across the hull, and stepped into my rowing past.

I cut into the liquid depth with forceful digs, shoveling out the river's liquid intestines by the bucketful. I turned right and headed upstream for the beaches, trailing along the shadowy shore, in and out of the willow archways.

Kneeling on my left knee, I'd explode into a stroke like a spring-loaded cobra, thrusting the boat with myself in it far forward, against the viscous current, and then recollect myself with a straight back, like I had been taught, sweat running down my chest and back. Behind me was a wake of violent white water eddies.

The river was empty and so were the shores. I plowed and plowed and plowed, my lungs filling up with the silence of the morning and my mind totally AWOL. Having picked up speed, I steered away from the shore and headed out for the middle of the river where the current was the strongest. I was looking for resistance.

But I found the resistance back on the shore. I spotted two naked bathing beauties who were gingerly wading into the river. When I first spotted them, they were only knee deep. As soon as they spotted me they hurried in deeper and were now standing half-covered by the flowing water, their breasts still in plain sight. I slowed down and steered to my right, towards them.

180

Like a Greek god Pan, a half-man-half-boat chimera, I had come upon them out of the watery nowhere, a Poseidon of sorts with a canoe oar instead of a trident. I slid across the blue corduroy of water to within talking distance and put the oar down across the boat, halting it to a stop. We looked at each other, speechless. They, seemingly a bit shocked but totally unembarrassed. I, bewildered, out of breath, erect. The river flowed between us, through us as we watched each other. They smiled. I smiled. But neither party dared to break the curious silence.

It suddenly occurred to me that they were waiting for me to leave. And with uncharacteristic chivalry I yielded, like the very last Mohican to the eventual inevitability of the New World Order.

I turned around and, showing off, exploded into a rapid series of turbo-strokes. Now finally heading downstream with nothing to resist, I let the river do most of the work. No longer horny, I felt transformed.

Serebryanni Bor beckoned like a magnet. Next day I was back, in search of more nudity. And I found it on one of the many hidden beaches of this suburban paradise.

But, let me backtrack a bit. It was already a week

since I had gotten out of the military and I still haven't gotten laid. Unfathomable! Unacceptable! I had made calls to old girlfriends. All were out of town or otherwise engaged. I had made calls to old buddies in the hope that someone would play matchmaker. Again, all were out of town or otherwise engaged. It was clear, getting demobilized in the late spring, on the cusp of summer was a curse. Love waits for no one. It germinates all winter and, come spring, un-winds its swan-neck of libido through the snows of rejection and the leaf-rot of anticipation. I had, it seemed, missed the train. I arrived too late. All the flowers were picked, all the stems cut, a melancholic bumble bee buzzing above for romantic road-kill.

I walked through the empty sandy beaches of Serebrynni Bor, maneuvering among beer bottles, cigarette butts, and crumbled paper plates. The beaches, all nameless, all informal, were punctuating the shore of the island, separated by narrow growths of hedges and bushes. Swaths of sand fenced off from each other with short walls of green.

It was still early. Way early for a beach day, around 9:00 am or so. I spotted a volleyball game a distance away and could hear the thumps of the spiked ball, and the call outs. What I couldn't see, however, is any swimwear. A motley crew of young men and women were playing naked. I sped up my pace.

A few minutes later I joined the game, with my shorts

still on. Martyr that I was, I immediately proved my worth by diving for the ball a few times. This "self-sacrifice" didn't go unnoticed. The folks asked for my name. The game came to an end and the folks spread out, some went for a dip, others returned to their blankets. My attention, however, was on a particular girl. She had her swimming trunks on but no top, and had long curly hair. She headed out to the water and I followed. She seemed to be around 19 or 20. She was self-conscious, which she managed by giggling and joking as she carried on a conversation with a couple of guys that stayed back by the net, over an increasing distance. She'd turn around and say something and cover up her breasts and turn around to face the river and put her arms down again. I walked alongside a few meters to her right. We both walked into the river slowly, stopping waist deep. It now seemed as though both of us stood entirely naked, I bare-chested, she bare-breasted.

We talked a little and stepped in deeper for a swim. A connection seemed to be forming. I told her about yesterday, about the canoe. She talked about college and her plans for the summer. It was all utterly irrelevant. What mattered was that I liked her and she seemed to like me.

In a sense the story ends there. We never got any closer than that. The sandy beach remained between us. We did, however, spend almost an entire day there. We played volleyball, chatted, and ate. The naked crowd left. The properly dressed crowd replaced them. But the girl never put on her top.

Women cursed. Men watched. And the two of us just fooled around until we both turned red under the sun. We ran circles, kicked the ball, swam, laid on her double-wide blanket, and talked and talked and talked. She knew my name but I didn't ask hers. I didn't ask for any contact information, either. Somehow I could tell from the very beginning, like Heraclitus, that I was not to enter this human river of spontaneity not just twice but even once. She was a forever elusive target. It seemed that each moment of flirtation set me back a step and I'd have to keep re-approaching her through honest coexistence.

People came and went. An older lady came up to shame us and we only laughed. She flaunted her partial nudity with complete abandon and I, it seemed, was both her private audience and her private bodyguard. She was Marilyn Monroe and I was JFK, a beauty and a gentleman, a siren and Odysseus.

On the walk back to the station, fully clad, I had my arm around her shoulder and her arm around my waist. Our skin burned. Mine on the inside as much as on the outside. Even though we were heading in the same direction, she asked if I minded taking a different train. I did and didn't. But I agreed, once again practicing this new art of letting go. The train doors hissed shut and she blew a kiss at me as I sat down on the ice cold marble bench to wait for another train.

This body that you and I are, it reincarnates continuously, with each breath, with each choice, with each encounter. To say we live is a misnomer. There is no "we." No "I." Not a moment that continues unchanged long enough to constitute an uninterrupted essence. Once a demigod of mindlessness I have since denigrated into a demagogue of mindfulness, into a self-amputating sophist. But enough of this prelude. On with this triptych of reminiscence.

Flesh is not a thing but a living process. We are living, conscious, dreaming flesh; a living, conscious, dreaming process of self-guiding matter. We think of rivers as horizontal processes. But we too are rivers, living, conscious, walking rivers. The body-mind that you are is a constantly morphing lava-lamp dressed in a pair of jeans with a credit card in your hip pocket. In the span of reading this sentence, tens of thousands of cells that you thought you were have died and/or divided while the rest of this seemingly immutable you has mutated and continues to mutate, just like the ceaseless flow of a river. We flow and flowing inside us are billions of microscopic and not-so-microscopic lifeforms, just as you'd find inside the Mississippi or the Volga. Each of us is a fluid, mostly self-unaware microcosm, a world in passing never to be witnessed in its bewildering complexity. What re-incarnates this flow? What re-enters this flowing, living field of awareness with an occasional glimpse of presence?

That is what I was pondering while sitting on a bench by the Gorky Park subway station. Or something along those lines; certainly not in those very words. But the quality of my questioning, the stupefying intensity of awe of that moment was so very similar. It lingers in me to this day, easier to bring up in my memory than any of my previous phone numbers. I was waiting on Romka, a great buddy of mine, a pal that I had betrayed a few times, inadvertently, out of the ignorance of my youth. I finally had gotten hold of him and we were to meet up at the Gorky Park station. He was running late and I got up and went to a cigarette kiosk. No, I didn't smoke but I had a pyrotechnic urge in me at the moment and bought a box of matches. I sat back down on the bench and watched a thin river of street filth run a vanishing course along the sidewalk curb. This street brook, if you wish, perhaps, too shallow to qualify as a body of water of any depth or direction, was drying up under the hot summer sun. But what caught my attention was that this stream of street filth was covered in white fur, in "pukh" from poplar trees. I lit a match and set it on fire. I'd done this many times before as a kid. Now 20, with nothing to do, it still seemed like a great idea.

It was hardly a fire, more like the slow burn of a cigarette, a glowing red creep that worked its way "up the stream," along the curb. A couple of pedestrians slowed down to watch, some with disapproval in their eyes, some with curiosity. It was a non-event. And it soon ended. A bus pulled up to the curb a distance away from me and the burning fuzz disappeared

186

under the black rubber of a giant wheel. The show was over.

I struck another match and startled. It was Romka. He had arrived unnoticed and slapped me on my shoulder from behind. I hadn't seen him in two years. He was also back from the military service with the same skinny, toned, bald look. The same hunger in his eyes. He had a couple of tennis rackets which caught my attention. I didn't know he played.

He explained that he didn't. He had just bought them off a drunk who needed money for the hair of the dog. "Probably his kid's. I felt bad. But what the heck, you know."

He had a tennis ball, too. "It was funny. He really thought it through, the moron," said Romka. "Two rackets, one ball; a package-deal he said." We chatted, had some food and ended up behind the subway station, banging the ball against the wall. It was an advantageous spot, we could see a two-way flow of constant human traffic in and out of the subway station, in case somebody caught our attention, but also had the privacy of an improvised racketball wall.

Having exchanged every possible war story we could think of, we refocused on the matters of horny youth. We were on the prowl, striking up conversations left and right, with anyone who even vaguely met our aesthetic criteria. Time went by. And then time came to a standstill. A Natasha (for some reason I've known many over the years) stopped over. On her own initiative, more or less, with zero prompting. She was interested to know if we "really" played tennis. She agreed to go back behind the building to test our skills. We played a few rounds of racket ball instead, taking turns. And she concluded that we were cheap show-offs.

She couldn't have been more right. We were, no argument about it. The theme of tennis was dropped and flirtation began. Romka soon realized that Natasha was interested primarily in me. She was taking summer courses from nearby InYaz (the Institute of Foreign Languages), and I claimed that I spoke English. She immediately tested that and I passed. Romka excused himself with a grin and disappeared, with the rackets, of course. Natasha and I, however, seemed to have time to kill so we headed out to Gorky Park, over the bridge. A powerful breeze blew right through us. I told her about my first kiss under this very bridge. "Really?" she said and grabbing me by the arm, pulled me in and planted a kiss of her own. "Tell me about your latest kiss now," she demanded, laughing.

Things could not have been going better. She said she lived in Prigorod on the outskirts of Moscow and asked if I'd see her off to her home. I called my folks and fibbed that I was gonna stay up late and, if too late, I'd stay over at Romka's. I knew he'd back me up if need be.

The ride to her place was crazy. An hour on the subway, two bus transfers, and a long walk. Finally, her high-rise apartment was in sight. Her place was on the 3rd floor and the elevator wasn't working, of course. Inside, she finally undressed and asked if I wanted to shower with her. Now that was an offer I had been waiting for!

We took turns stepping under the showerhead. She soaped me up but didn't allow me to touch her. I was harder than rebar. She enjoyed it. "You look beautiful, you know," she said to me. I had never thought about this. I had never really taken stock of what I looked like. Two years in the military did use up all of my fat reserves. I was lean and young, a demigod. But I had never been complimented. It was a shock, a shock of self-awareness. I wasn't prepared to be aware of myself in that setting, at that moment. A total mind-fuck. Did I have to be awakened at that moment? Was it necessary to tap my consciousness on its shoulders?

But tapped I was.

"I am not interested in sex but I can help you out," said Natasha. I shook my head. "Then I'll leave you to it," she said with a wink and stepped out of the shower to towel off.

There was seemingly nothing left of me in that moment. Just a body of horny flesh under a showerhead of someone else's aesthetic appreciation.

She clearly proved to be more "corrupt" than me, wiser, more distanced from life, able to marvel at it from a distance, a mind-space I was yet to learn to inhabit. I didn't feel thwarted or disappointed. I stood there, wet, confused, certainly flattered, but, most importantly, awakened to my own presence. Sometimes gurus come into your life wet and naked...

"Here I am," I thought to myself, finally incarnating this throbbing flesh with a field of self-awareness. A body of life finally inhabited by self-presence, awakened by a random, long-legged, tennis-playing avatar named Natasha. "What is this, this stuff that I am?" I kept asking myself. This questioned smoldered inside me on the way home, like that creeping, crawling burn of the poplar tree cotton fuzz along the sidewalk curb.

A reincarnation of myself is what I am.

# The Dragon of a Question

I've resisted fiction for years. Reading it and writing it. Until I recently realized that the boundary between fiction and nonfiction is itself fiction, like the boundary between a beach and the ocean. Waves of interpretation wash over the sand of facts and the self-serving double-helix of the mind's narrative replicates itself until it runs out of life. Language is a detour of consciousness but a detour that you and I are currently on, Reader-Writer, in all of our illusory separateness. So, keep this preamble in mind as I tell you a story of how Ivan Vasylievich (better known to you as Ivan the 4th or Ivan the Terrible) went about schooling himself in the wisdom of life.

A bad temper is one thing, a mad temper is another thing. It enfolds everything that bad temper ever has to offer and adds a pinch of creativity. Each mind, at least once in a lifetime, stumbles upon an inscrutable question, a question that keeps it awake, a question that puts it to sleep. Ivan's question was of the tsar's caliber. Is life worth living? And, secondarily, is life worth preserving?

Already mad with wisdom, he broke no teeth of his own on this nasty little bone of a question. Instead, he instructed his bodyguards to round up twelve upper class boyars with the longest beards. This approach to sampling was not without its own logic. He rightfully presumed that a higher income would correlate with a higher education and that the length of the beard would correlate with piety and life experience. He further instructed his loyal servants to dig twelve six-foot deep holes, arranged along the periphery of a circle, like a clock. He also ordered that the twelve selected boyars be buried up to their necks along the outline of this circle. He subsequently demanded that a special scythe be wrought out of the best iron, with a long handle, so as to look like the kind of scythe that Death itself would be armed with. Once the preparations were all in place, on an auspicious date per the advice of his royal astronomer, he positioned himself in the middle of this circle with a scythe in his hands and delivered his instructions.

"Fellow countrymen and fellow minds, I, the Tsar of Moscovia and the Tsar of Russia, summoned you here today to wrestle, alongside with me, with a dragon of a question that has bemused me and has kept me awake at night and has kept me asleep during my waking hours, with a question that you yourself no doubt have pondered in your own time, with the question that I, as your Lord, demand an answer for, not for me alone, but for all of us caught bewildered and unknowing in the seven winds of Russia's steppes. But before I put this question to you, let me first be assured that you have been treated with utmost kindness so far, that you have been fed and catered to. Have you?"

The boyars, near terrified to death and some truly speechless, only nodded in consent, afraid to cast any shadow on the graces of the royal court.

Ivan continued.

"I am sure you will find much solace in the following good news. Having summoned you so forcefully from your loved ones and from the lives you have so carefully constructed and no doubt treasure, I owe you bottomless grace and gratitude. So, let it be known that I have instructed my court to issue you each and all a degree of financial assurance, a trust for a hundred years, to be dispensed to you or your kin, as a recompense for your time and wisdom."

Forced smiles of gratitude distorted the mouths of the boyars as some flat out pissed their pants, some even soiling the soil they were dug in.

"Now, on to the question at hand. This is what I pose to you, fellow minds and countrymen. Is life worth living and, secondarily, is it worth preserving? As for one, I do not know. At times I even think I dare not to know or presume. So, I will rely on your life experience and wisdom to make my final mind. Your life depends on it. Convince me that it is and you get to live. Fail to convince me and you die."

Ivan walked around the circle studying the faces in front of him, his leather boots kicking up autumn dust right into the faces of the boyars. Not on purpose, of course, but out of necessity. He squatted down in front of a familiar face.

"You are Vasyli, are you not, the son of Feodor?"

"I am," answered Vasyli.

"You have my father's first name, so you have my first attention. Tell me, brother Vasya, why do you choose to live every day? Why do you now tremble in fear of losing this life? Is life worth living, you think, and, if so, why?"

All eyes were on Vasyli. Should he succeed, thought the boyars, we all live, we all go home, we all survive this peculiar philosophical inquisition.

Vasyli thought deep and hard and Ivan waited and waited.

"I think I know, your highness," he started but it was too late. Ivan pulled his hand back and swung the scythe from left to right, cutting Vasyli's head clean off its dust covered neck, like a lonely stalk of wheat. A fountain of blood spurted up in the air as everyone around gasped. Ivan kicked the head with bulging eyes with the toe of his boot and roared.

"If you have to think this long, if it takes you this long to come up with an answer, then, surely, you do not have one ready, then, surely, you are reaching and making up falsehoods. I did not gather you here to play philosophical games with me or to placate me with niceties or to wax poetic. I have gathered you here to learn from your vital signs. You all live. You all want to live. Why do you live? What's your basis for existence? What's your living philosophy?"

"I wanna know!" Ivan kept roaring, circling around like a dog in a cage. Finally he seemed to have quieted down. He picked up Vasyli's severed head and stuck it onto a pointed post in the center of the circle.

"Look at him. You are next. Look into yourself and tell me, without hesitation, without false intellectualizing, why are you afraid to be next? What's the basis of your fear? Why do you want to live?"

Ivan turned around and around and around looking at the dust covered faces. They seemed bewildered and mesmerized, most looking at what used to be Vasyli's neck.

"Never mind him. He's gone as if he's never been." Ivan went up to the clean cut of the neck and stomped on it with his boot to stem the blood trickle, blood mixing up with the dirt of his boot.

"Any takers? Any answers?" he asked, looking around. Someone at 11 o'clock gasped and Ivan came up to him. The old man, with a chiseled, exhausted face was gasping for air. Ivan kneeled down in front of the man and stared into the man's ashen face. The man convulsed, gasped a few more times like a fish out of water and gave up his ghost.

"See that?" roared Ivan. "Did you see that? He died of fear of dying, never having found out why he wanted to live and why he was so afraid to die. Will that, too, be your fate? Will you also finish out your time with nothing but a mouthful of clichés about God, about love, about meaning?"

Suddenly, the terror set in like a morning fog, the remaining heads started thrashing and moaning and praying. The rhetorical zeal of Ivan's last words made it brutally clear that he had already heard all the answers and none had satisfied him. Ivan knew this too. He grabbed the scythe and without a moment of hesitation dropped the edge down onto the ground and swirled around mowing down head after head after head. When he stopped and looked around, he was standing amidst a fountain of blood, covered in blood and dust himself. He turned around staggering from dizziness, tripping over tangled beards and contorted faces. He was checking to see if there was anyone left. And there was: a man he had known almost all of his life, a distant cousin, more than acquaintance, but definitely less than a friend.

He came up to him and addressed him, "Illarion, we share blood, you and I. We are leaves of the different branches of the same ancient tree. Our clans fought together and fought each other since days immemorial. What I want to know is why. What drives us? Why do we so stubbornly crave to live? Why do we fear non-being? You are my last hope. You are your last hope. Tell me if you know. Just don't patronize me with the usual horseshit. Don't tell me that we live because of our faith. You and I know not all of us believe, yet all of us want to live. And don't tell me that we live because of our love. You and I know that not all of us love, yet all of us want to live. And, pray, don't tell me that we live because of our search for meaning. You and I know that there is no meaning to be found on this random rock of a planet. We make meaning – we don't find it! We make it. We make it up, like the fairy tales of the old. Meaning is a rationalization to go on but not the Reason. You and I know that even in the moments of meaninglessness, like this one that you and I now share, we still crave to go on, meaning or not. So, tell me, my fellow mind, why live? What makes life worthy of pursuit and preservation?"

Illarion smiled but said nothing. Ivan waited. But nothing was coming. Illarion, with his eyes closed, waited too.

"Is this it?" asked Ivan, "Or are you thinking? And why have you smiled, Illarion? And why have you stopped smiling?"

Illarion opened his eyes and spoke, "That's what happens, Ivan. Questions do not beget answers, they beget more questions. There was a time I too tormented myself with questions like this. But that time is over, that time is long gone."

Illarion seemed to be in no rush. His speech was measured and calm. He seemed neither shocked nor afraid.

"Tell me more, Illarion. Do you mean to say you found the answers?"

"No, Ivan. I did not."

"What then?"

"Nothing, Ivan. When I didn't find any answers that I could honestly accept as absolute in their veracity and self-evidence, I had no choice but to drop the questions. And guess what? Life continued without answers. Our search for answers is a search for reassurance. Certainty is an escape but, as you see now for yourself, there is nowhere to run. We are lost in the woods of language. There is nothing to know outside of ourselves. You and I are but two faces of one and the same faceless coin. Truth be told, truth is silent, unknowable, ineffable. But you already know all this. You have heard the startsi talk about this kind of thing-less thing and it wasn't enough for you and neither will be my non answer. Plus, as you can see, I am rambling. Not because I am afraid to die but because I pity you and want to help you find that magic semantic formula that you will stick in your mouth like a thumb, a mantra to suck on, a verbal lollipop to sweeten your nihilistic bitterness. But enough already: I am not your wet nurse and you are a grown man. Face yourself, Ivan. There is nothing to know, nothing to learn, and nothing to pursue. All that can be, is. And that is always enough."

Ivan didn't seem to be listening. He had slouched and folded down onto the ground, with a strange passivity, as if a hand had been pulled out of a glove puppet, the scythe, however, still clasped in his hands. Illarion, too, was full of horseshit and he knew it from the moment Illarion opened his mouth. Ivan wished he hadn't. He already missed Illarion's simple silence and his simple smile. A non answer was perfectly enough but the non answer grew into an answer, into another mouthful of clichés and Ivan felt a seething stir within. He rose to his feet and commanded his servant to arrange for a pot of molten metal. This was arranged. Ivan dipped an iron ladle into the pot and ordered Illarion to open his mouth. Illarion obliged. "Thank you for trying, Illarion," said Ivan, "I mean it." Illarion nodded with his mouth open. Ivan brought the ladle over Illarion's head and slowly poured the metal into the last throat of falsehood.

# Mr. Goff

*H*e was high, clearly. But he wasn't flying. He was crawling, literally. And muttering to himself. He kept referring to himself as Mr. Goff. But he wasn't. He was simply Vadik, a late-80s Soviet playboy.

I don't remember how I got invited to this little soirée in Serebryanni Bor, historically, the dacha enclave for the Soviet elite, and most recently, a community of people with means, on an island of wilderness. The house we were in was rented, I was told, by Vadik's dad who was a medical administrator in the Kremlin hospital. But, as many times as I have partied there, I have never seen him there, not even a logistical trace of him. The place was a sand-box for his son. The house, surrounded by sequoia-ish looking pines was a crash pad. People came and people left. Call girls and low-level drug dealers. The ones that stayed had some kind of implicit invite. And Vadik, when sober, would be the one to enforce it. In the day, this mini-collective of hipsters, punks and otherwise well-connected youngsters would play cards, eat, and go to the beach. At night, they'd keep on playing cards, eating, and going to the beach – high and/or drunk. And, of course, through it all ran two other thin red lines, music and sex, through the days and through the nights.

I must've driven someone there and was invited to stay, gotten that vague invite to stick around. And I would. For a couple of weeks, I jitneyed all day to drum up pocket money and then I'd drive out there, hopefully with a passenger going in that direction, to pay for my own trip. I'd stick around till morning. I liked the conversations, the Dionysian energy of the place. And I was on home ground. I had spent several years in Serebryanni Bor on the nearby rowing base as part of my athletic training. The location had a special significance for me. I knew the island from the outside out, I had rowed circles around it. Now, too, I was still in its orbit, but somehow from within. I was more of an observer than a participant, or maybe an observer-participant. I think this relational buffer, this distance had its own charm. Vadik and company thought themselves to be special, an elite, of sorts. And they were. We all are, in a sense. And they wanted to be studied. So I studied them.

I had been now baby-sitting Vadik, sorry, Mr. Goff, for about an hour. High as he was, he was down on the ground, crawling around like a well-dressed worm, sometimes pausing to arch his mid-section as if to send a peristaltic, propagating wave through his body, like a break dancer. It never worked out, but, I got the point. First, we all laughed, then it got tiring and people spread out around the house to do their own thing. I stayed with Mr. Goff, baiting him with questions about what he was experiencing. I was intrigued.

Mr. Goff was finally onto something, I thought, when

he said: "We will, all of us, one day be gods."

"Didn't know you believed in gods, Mr. Goff," I said.

'I don't. There are no gods. But one day we will, absolutely, be gods."

"But not today, Mr. Goff?" I teased.

He squirmed and started to crawl away from me towards a bookcase full of empty booze bottles, carefully positioned side by side, like books in a row, a prank that this gang had been working on all summer.

I got around him and sat down on a chair by the bookcase, waiting for him to crawl up my way. He was frustrated, I was faster than him.

"Not fair, Pavel, not fair! You can walk but I can only crawl," he said while making his way in my direction.

"I know, Mr. Goff, and I am sorry. It is, indeed, very unfair."

"You see, Pav, a while back I was really into medieval medicine. You know my dad is a doctor and he's got these amazing illustrated books on how medicine used to be. I was obsessed with it. I kept imagining what it'd be like to live through the Black Plague, to have your doctors bleed you; to undergo surgeries without analgesia. I had nightmares about all of that. Has all these papers and notes on the future of medicine and he talks about it all the time, too, about the amazing advances that we are yet to make. And, it's not just him, you know. It's in the movies, in the sci-fi books, in our own imagination. So, when I lay out there in the sun, on those sandy beaches I sometimes think as far into the future as I can and what I see is gods, immortal, all powerful, cosmos-faring gods."

He rolled over and was now trying to arch his back, his head now almost in between my feet. He was looking up at me and I was looking down at him through my knees. I knew I had a smile to suppress and I could always count on my poker face – my trigeminal nerves have always obeyed me without fault.

"When I look at you now," said Mr. Goff, "I see a future god. When I compare the lowly little wreathing worms that we are with who we are destined to become, I see gods."

And with these words he suddenly got up. The gig was up. The mind-game that he had staged for himself had run its course and he was now hungry and ready to eat.

"Let's drive out to the subway station and get some

shashlik," he said.

"Sure," I said.

Vadik, not Mr. Goff any longer, yelled into the house, "We'll be back," located his car keys, and tossed them to me with an "Ever drove a Mercedes?" I shook my head.

"Good," he said and headed out for the door.

My car was parked on the street. Vadik's red 190 was behind the wooden gates. I knew it had no papers and wasn't registered. It was something that Vadik bought last week on a whim from someone who happened to be passing through his little abode in the Bor. None of that worried us. We all got pulled over by cops all the time in those days, no matter what we drove. Not for traffic violations, although those were plenty, but just because, just for the mere fact of our existence. You'd roll the window down and hand the cop your little driver's booklet with money in it  They'd take a ponderous look at it, nod, salute you and hand the papers back to you. And you'd be on your way.

I played with the car for a minute or two. I'd been inside a Benz before but never drove one. The thing about cars is that once you start driving they tend to disappear on you. At least that's what happens for me. What's left is just a mobile field of awareness that I myself am, my mind, the windshield, the road. a simple trinity coalesced into a moving fact.

We sliced through the flat main road of the Bor like a hot poker through a slab of meat, and got flagged down by cop as soon as we rolled over the bridge. They are almost always there. I reached into my hip pocket for the driver's license and the money but found nothing. The cop was already by the door smiling at us and checking out the Benz. Vadik, in the back seat, was in his head, not giving any fuck to this roadside show.

"I am sorry, officer. We'll take care of you on the way back or tomorrow morning, ok? I left my wallet back in the dacha. My bad."

The officer looked at me for a beat. "Ok, bud. I am back on here on Wednesday night, make sure you do that and I wouldn't mind a little something-something, an extra, you know, for my troubles, you know."

"I know," I said and added, "We'll bring you some beer, ok?"

"Sounds g-oooo-d," he mooed, saluted, and headed back to his blue Lada.

We peeled off, with demonstrative indifference.

"How are we gonna pay for shashlik?" asked Vadik from the backseat.

"No worries, Mr. Goff," I said and turned on the radio.

At the subway station, I parked and popped the trunk. While back at the dacha, when I gave the Benz the once-over, I had spotted an empty metal gas canister in there and a rubber hose. In those days, most drivers in Moscow were prepared for running out of gas and not finding it at a gas station. I closed the trunk, and leaned on the side of the car to rock it a bit. I heard an ample splash of fuel from inside and figured we could sell almost a can. I siphoned off the gas, making sure that we had at least a splash left for the way back and went out to the curb with Vadik still chilling in the backseat. I sat down on the can and waited. A couple of drivers pulled over and asked how much I wanted for the gas. I said I was selling the gas and the can as a package. We needed as much money as we could get because I didn't want to come back to the Bor on Wednesday. If I could take care of the officer by the bridge today, I'd rather do so tonight on the way back.

Twenty minutes or so went by and the shashlik vendor who'd been watching the show from his trailer came out and asked me how much I wanted for the can and gas. I told him. He offered a good price and threw in three extra servings of shashlik.

We were heading back home, Vadik asleep in the backseat, the shashlik, wrapped in a foil blanket, on the passenger seat. As I was coming up on the bridge I slowed down and made an illegal U-turn. The officer, still in his car, was startled but already smiling. I handed him over some cash and a serving of shashlik. Made another U-turn and shot across the bridge back to the dacha.

Back at "home," I made the executive decision to let Mr. Goff sleep it off in the back seat of the car. After all, man of luxury that he was, I am sure he would have preferred the choice of a leather couch, but this red 190 Benz had the only leather couch in the vicinity.

I went inside, played cards, fooled around with a girl named Marinka and went to sleep. In the morning, I learned that the god was dead. One of Vadik's pals decided to take the Benz for a ride in the middle of the night and wrapped it around a utility post, with Mr. Goff inside. The driver was unharmed, but Vadik, from what I was told, never woke up in the Kremlin hospital that he had been taken to, with his dad-doctor in attendance.

All summers come to an end. And so did that one.

# The First Soviet Skinhead

It was 1987. Before Christ or after Christ doesn't matter. There was no Christ in Russia at that time, at least, not that I could see. I know many would disagree, with over 500 churches in Moscow alone, how could there be no Christ somewhere? I don't know. We see what we see and I saw no Christ anywhere. Not that I was looking for him (her? it?). Nor would I recognize One if I saw him/her/it. I capitalized "One" because it just doesn't feel right to capitalize "I" and not capitalize All That Is (if there is such a thing-less thing). All I remember is that it was early, around 8:00 am or so. I had been directed to show up to the regional military recruitment "collection point" by 7:00 am sharp. I didn't. I showed up for my first day in the Soviet military almost an hour late. No, I didn't have a seeing-off party the night before, there was no fanfare about my leaving for the army. And that was fortunate. I am sure I would have gotten someone pregnant, maybe even a couple of someone's. I sure didn't need that kind of drama then, or, for that matter, another 20 or so years. A male mind takes a long time to mature (and I am not sure it ever does); and looking back at my life from the so-called "advantage of the years," I see too many close calls and a very spotty record of decision-making. Put simply, I am surprised I survived and I am very glad I didn't widow or orphan anyone in the process. At least so far.

My late arrival to the collection point (not far from the Bicycle Plant Farmer's Market) was a catalyst "to saddle up." A tired looking officer with a pillowy face and a cum stain on his pants looked around a sleepy waiting room and directed a motley crew of ten or so Soviet 18-year olds to get the fuck out into the green army van outside. Without having a chance to try out the strange red new plastic chairs in the waiting room, I turned around on my heels (like I had seen in the war movies) and energetically strummed up two flights of concrete steps with my feet. Back in those pre-coffee days, I'd have enough, shall I say, intrinsic energy in the morning to break Earth's gravity in a vertical jump. But self-consciousness kept me securely grounded not to ever try (but I do levitate nowadays no problem – at least I dream I do).

The driver of the idling van impatiently flicked the half-finished cigarette out of the window, indicating a long-ripened readiness to "just fucking go" (an existential malaise so typical of professional drivers) and we climbed into an army-green UAZik that had never known safety belts. There weren't enough seats, of course, so some of us had to sit on each other's lap. Not me, though.

The officer, I think his name was Ivanov (as is so often the case in Russia), looked at me and said,

"Since we've been waiting on your slow ass all morning, we now don't have the fucking time to stop over at the barber's. So, you'll be in charge of cutting hair." He handed me an electric shaver and told the driver to stop over at a beer kiosk where we could plug in. The other boys looked at me with a grin of acceptance, the "adventure of the military service," that had been culturally promised to us, was beginning all right, and getting a buzz was a logical starting point.

A few right turns and about a dozen major potholes later, we came to a screeching halt in front of a beer kiosk. The uniformed two (the driver and Ivanov) got themselves each a quart-sized mug of beer with aggressive foam. The shaver was plugged into an outlet inside with the extension cord and I was set to go. I had never cut any hair but a buzz is a buzz: there is nothing to it. Choose the setting, push the button and follow the bumpy landscape of a man's skull. It was called "pod noolek" (down to zero), The boys didn't argue, it was silently understood that there was already something exotic to write home about, having your hair cut behind a beer kiosk. Man-oh-man, the fun days are sure upon us!

I took a brief break (I was told that there was no rush after all as Ivanov and the nameless driver re-upped on beer) and let one of the guys reciprocate. He mowed down my own curls as the rest stood and chatted. Nobody seemed to miss their hair; it was neat to run your hand over the sand-paper stubble of your skull. All in all, with some really big exceptions, men's skulls look good. There is something inherently athletic, aerodynamic, and vibrant about these bony cupolas we live in.

Now it was time to do the last fella. I'd been saving him for last because this strange-looking homie had an afro. Not a jewfro like my older brother once had, but a solid afro. He had dark skin like a southern Georgian, and perfectly Caucasian features. It took no guessing on my part to add two and two, I instantly figured that he was a child of the International Youth Festival, a kind of student orgy, under the guise of spreading socialism internationally (like some kind of ideological venereal disease), that had taken place some time in the late 60s and produced quite a few out-of-wedlock biracial kids. I had known a kid like that before; he was on my water polo team and when we traveled to the restricted-access city of Nikolaev on the Black Sea, with naval bases and shipyards, he got questioned by police as soon as we had gotten off the train from Moscow.

What happened next is the reason I sat down to write this little story on this windy fall day. I am outside right now, next to a cup of Yerba Mate tea (two bags). I had a buzz cut yesterday and feel the sobering brush of the chilly autumn breeze on my skull. That's how this whole little story popped into my mind, through a chain of associations. That's right, a week ago I had no plan to write this down and I probably never would have. That's how random and cliché we are with the winds of circumstance, the winds of memory, and the winds of associations. It is nothing but chaos, nothing but chaos, and the illusion of order.

I started from the neck, plummed down the centerline and worked my way up, to the bony crest of this guy's head, then up and down to his hair line on his forehead, in a kind of reverse Mohawk. The boys, the officer, the driver, the guy from the beer stand and a couple of early morning beer kiosk patrons gathered up behind to see me shave this guy. I am sure he was dying to see himself in the mirror, but there was no mirror, he had to rely on the reactions of this random audience for a reflection of what was going on. His tightly wound, almost wiry curls fell down on the ground, into the oozing puddle of beer foam and general street slush. I swerved the shaver to my right, it was an executive decision of primitive aesthetics. Having done the reverse-Mohawk, I was now going for a half-and-half – half bald, half afro.

As fun as that was, the real fun was about to be discovered on his left side. "Oh fuck!" said a few guys in sudden sync, as I mowed up his curls from the neck and up to his left ear. No, it wasn't a scar, it was a swastika. A fucking bluish tat of a swastika right above and behind his left ear. Small, but distinct, each of its arms about 1cm long.

"What the fuck?" was heard all around. The kid might have blushed but I couldn't see it from behind. With dogged determination I simply continued to do my part letting reality play itself out as it had to. The beer

212

man was sent back for more, a suggestion that he silently dismissed as he himself had to stick around to satisfy his own curiosity. What followed was nothing less than a mini press conference except that the kid was answering no questions. You have to understand, a swastika in Russian meant only one thing, as it does most everywhere: a Nazi. But even more so, in those, still Soviet days, we had all grown up on the stories from the Great Patriotic War against Nazi Germany (which we fucking won!). A swastika on a Russian kid was unheard of and, as dark-skinned as he was, to us he was a Russian kid, living in Russia, speaking Russian, about to put on a Russian military uniform. So, the surprise, the shock even, was perfectly understandable.

Then, one of the young bucks whose head I had just shaved broke into ugly, hysterical laughter. "It's in the fucking wrong direction," he yelled, half-laughing, half-neighing like a horse that had been just goosed. How people laugh, not just when, says a lot about human nature. This guy was a degenerate, no doubt about it, if not technically, in essence for sure.

"What are you talking about?" someone asked and he, pointing a finger, explained, "It's supposed to be right-turning, the Nazi swastika, this one is turning left!"

People leaned in to check but no one was quite sure. And that's when Officer Ivanov in a rare, probably once-in-a-career strike of wisdom, interfered, "All in the van!"

The mini press conference continued in the same spirit while in the van, with questions but no answers. The kid held his own, and I felt respect for him, his newly shaven skull serving well as a safe and secure harbor to his peculiar secret. In a few minutes we arrived at the district collection point, a makeshift village of sorts, for all the 18 year-olds of 1987 Moscow about to be shipped off into the Soviet military.

I immediately lost sight of the kid without even getting his name, but not entirely for good. Having spent the night in the collection point, I caught sight of him the next morning in the washing room. His face was bloodied. Not so bloodied that it hurt to look at it but bloodied enough to be on the inside of the swollen business. I am sure he had gotten very little sleep that night. His future seemed uncertain in my estimation, and I tried to show interest. After all, through a strange twist of fate, I had played a role in this unveiling. Somehow, I think he felt it, too; a connection to me, I was a person of significance, I hadn't asked him any questions, and I sure didn't bust up his lips. I was a friend of sorts, you could say, in the loosest sense of the word.

We stepped behind a maintenance shed and sat down on a couple of old tires. He smoked a few, we chatted, and then he explained. "I am no fucking Nazi, you know.  Dumb is what I am, fucking dumb."  His dad,

214

as I thought, was a participant in one of those International Socialist Orgies. A student from Southern India, his dad got his blond Russian mom pregnant and left, leaving behind, for some strange reason, a Tibetan Buddhist flag with swastikas.

"Swastikas on the Buddhist flag, what for?" was my first and last question that day.

He explained that at first he didn't know why, but eventually looked up. "Swastika," he said "in Sanskrit means 'well-being.' That's it."

"That's it?" I asked rhetorically. It seemed he still didn't know what the hell he was talking about.

He admitted, he wasn't sure about the Buddhist connection. I myself know it now, but that's not the point of this writing, if there is a point to it at all. He explained that, of course, he felt that he did not belong, that he didn't fit in, and he wanted to connect to his dad somehow. He asked a neighbor of his, a con from the communal apartment he lived in, to do a tat and the con agreed, in exchange for letting him play with this guy's you-know-what. We didn't go into that. We didn't go into anything else. We just sat there, the first inadvertent Soviet skinhead (who was sure heading for two years of now super-complicated hazing hell) and I, not knowing what to say and rubbing my hand over the sandpaper stubble of my head. It was a head-scratcher, while somewhere up above us, beyond the blue sky and the black vastness, there was a four-armed spiral galaxy tightening the transparent sheets of proto-matter into a knot.

# Reader-Writer

This was the most frustrating book that he had ever read. It was called the "Manual On How to Become a Reader-Writer." The book came in a bottle of exactly six pills, with dosing instructions of "two every two hours for the rest of your life." Obvious inconsistencies aside, he dutifully gulped down the first two pills only to discover that the green bottle with the child-proof cap instantly replenished itself. He decided to take another look at the fine print on the back of the bottle, but it was too late, the book started reading-writing itself.

A built-in breeze flipped the pages of his consciousness with the roaming chaos of a draft that's been lost in some abandoned apartment building somewhere in Chernobyl, slamming doors and banging window-shutters. Words wrote themselves like a self-possessed type-writer, read themselves to themselves, manually backing up the carriage and generously self-censoring with swaths of white-out.

He grabbed his own ear with two fingers and folded it down, roll-pressing the crease with his other index finger back and forth. Having dog-eared himself on more pages than not, he cracked flat his own book-spine to finally allow himself to calmly lay open on page 37, which read:

> *Being a reader-writer is a basic pre-condition for existence, a mind corrects itself in an endless recursive feedback loop of adaptive self-awareness. Each thought becomes a free-wheeling eddy amidst an ever-dynamic ocean of undifferentiated oneness that we each, collectively and privately, are. Like a myriad of Brownian flurries, this morphogenic lava-lamp of consciousness defragments and reunites itself in an unborn and undying game of Lila, divorcing and remarrying itself in a frenzied agony-ecstasy of self-referencing.*

He stopped; he couldn't stand himself. He closed himself shut and slid underneath a saucer plate with bagel crumbs to hide. Tired of hiding, he shrugged off the saucer plate along with its crumbs, off the table and down onto the floor. No sooner had the plate shattered, his unfed dog ran up to the table to investigate what was going on and cut one of its paws on the broken china, trailing paw-prints of blood all around the living room on the whitish carpet.

It bothered him but he had to, *had to*, return to himself. He opened himself at random and started tearing out pages and pages of memories ("All false anyway!"). He was fierce with himself like that ouroboros snake if it ever caught itself, clawing mouthfuls of paper out of his own cellulose guts, like a swarm of mad bees at war with themselves. Pages upon pages of still self-editing text were flying off in every direction, landing breathless all over the kitchen floor. The ink, that just a moment ago was penning itself, suddenly froze in mid-flight, cut off from its organizing and experience-binding book-spine. Words and letters were dying unfinished. Whole sentences gasped and gargled with coagulating ink, forever unexpressed.

He was almost finished with himself, except for a handful of heavy-count illustration papers. He paused, looking at his own reflection in the black-and-white gloss of the surface and suddenly felt spent.

A photo caption caught his eye: <u>A young reader-writer on a vacation</u>.

The picture was familiar, a similar image of himself from a long-time ago instantly popped into his mind. It was at the Black Sea, in the Crimea, on one of the beaches in Yalta. He is on a towel, with a book and a pen in his hands. From the perspective of whoever took that photograph it couldn't be seen but he knew, he remembered, he saw it in his mind right now, that just a moment before this photo of him was snapped, he had doodled a nude on the margins of the book. It had excited him and his swimming trunks would have surely shown that had he answered his brother's call for a swim. Instead, he was waiting out the erection, lying on his stomach, and pretending to read.

As he read, the image of the memory in his mind, a new caption popped into his mind. The letters on the book page started dancing and rolling through like an odometer, spinning up and down in search of the right combination, editing the existing caption into the emerging, better one: <u>A future reader-writer, in the first moments of self-editing</u>.

He recalled what happened next. When he lied to his brother about wanting to finish the book (instead of admitting the real reason for why he couldn't get up for a swim), his first conscious lie, his first act of self-editing, his brother grabbed a camera and snapped a photo while yelling, "Picture of a dork! Picture of a dork!" and ran down towards the foaming water, self-unaware as he still is.

The book-bottle was finally empty. He was looking straight into the emptiness of the enso: the ouroboros of his self-narrative was finally uncoiled. Sobriety of self-acceptance followed. A scary, non-neurotic sobriety…

# LM002

"1986 was the best and the worst year of my life," he said, staring out the window. A small bird was prancing on the snow-covered deck outside the sliding glass door, possibly confused by its own reflection in the glass.

"It was the year Lamborgini came out with its Lambo SUV." He motioned at a framed picture of his younger self next to a metallic Lambo with a wrap-around deer guard.

LM002, dubbed "Rambo-Lambo," was a monster of conspicuous consumption, a grotesque splash of Italian car design on a four-wheel drive platform. It was sexy in its own cocaine-80s way; car porn, no less.

"I paid cash for it. Don't ask me how much."

I had heard plenty of wheezing in my life, delivering oxygen bottles to people's homes. But his was in a category of its' own. His lungs nearly gargled as he inhaled and hissed as he exhaled. He was alone now, and recently. "Wife died, kids don't give a fuck," he had explained the last time I dropped by to swap out his oxygen supply.

"1986 was the best year of my life," he repeated.

"Because of the Lambo?"

"Yes, because of the fucking Lambo, why else?"

He looked at me as if we were suddenly as foreign to each other as refrigerators and stiletto shoes, as if to say, "Don't you understand, you stupid fuck? With a ride like that, how can it not be the best of times?"

He asked me to light up a cigar for him. No, he wasn't going to smoke it, "of course." "I just like the smell."

"Take one, no, take two, fuck, take the whole box if you wanna," he said, sucking in the dancing ghost of the smoke from the smoldering cigar on the table. "But if you do take the whole box, I want you to promise me one thing."

"What?"

"I want you to promise me that you will remember this year, this fucking 2013, as the best year of your life."

"Why?"

"Because you got a box of fine cigars for free, that's why."

I chuckled. He chuckled too.

"We are fucking apes. Just apes. We call ourselves human. But we are apes. They should drill this into us from day one. We pot around like some kind of fucking pinnacles of evolution, but we are just fucking apes. Smart, self aware apes. And that's what I was in 1986. An ape king. A king ape. A King Kong. Did I mention that I paid cash for that Lambo? Don't ask me how much though. But if you want to know I'll tell you this, I didn't pay nearly enough. It was worth every penny and ten times more."

I was long done, but I knew he wanted me to stay around for a bit more. Heck, I had already gotten a box of great cigars out of this, so why not.

"We are apes, just fucking hairless apes. In 1986 I was a fearless ape. I wasn't even wiping my ass with money, I was shitting money, on a regular basis." He issued a brief laugh, cracking himself up with the pun but immediately choked and regretted the laughter. He shook his head as if to say, "Can you believe this shit?" and zoned out.

The bird was still prancing around on the snow covered deck outside. The view was amazing, good enough for an album cover. It was a cliffhanger of a house, a custom-made modern module of Nordic austerity, sitting alongside the distant horizon, clouds moving from the side in the endless wall-to-wall window to the other side, as vivid as TV.

The house, basically an open space, with no stairs, was ideal for the man's motorized wheelchair.

"You know, everything on this planet lives in fear. But we, the puny, hairless apes that we are, managed not only to survive but to even experience fearlessness. 1986 was my year of fearlessness. Until it wasn't."

He lowered his eyes. The bird outside finally flew off. And I instantly knew it was time for me to go. We both knew that there was a question in the air. It had been in the air for the last year that I'd been delivering oxygen to this swanky, brooding place on the edge of the world. Perhaps today was the day I'd finally ask.

"What happened in 1986?"

"A stupid thing happened."

It was clear from his tone that he was ready to tell me but there probably was not much to say.

"I was walking down a flight of stairs, in my summer home, in Connecticut. It was late and I was sober. It was the  most usual moment you could think of. But, for some stupid reason, while I was still walking down, I started to take off my pullover, I guess to save time or something totally inane like that. At any rate, my sleeve caught on the banister, I tripped, fell down the stairs, and broke my fucking neck. Just another stupid ape that fell off the tree. A fitting end, don't you think?"

You dare not correct statements like that. You just witness them, the agony that they are. There is nothing to dispute here or to alleviate, the narrative is set like a prehistoric bug trapped in a drop of amber.

He glanced again at the framed photo on the wall and said, "I am sure you gotta go."

"Yes," I said, taking the hint.

"Take the cigars with you, I mean it.".

I picked up the box. It was a deep box, with a separate compartment at the bottom. The drawer slid out and I saw a .45. Probably loaded.

"Not the box. Leave the box on the table, but still take the cigars, all of them."

"See you next month?" I offered my default goodbye.

"Sure," he muttered with total indifference towards my pretense at optimism.

I walked out through the garage, just as I had come in, past the Rambo-Lambo. Half an hour ago I had asked him about it, hoping to learn his story, the story I knew he had.

"When is the last time you took this baby out for a spin?"

"1986," he had said, just a half an hour ago, beginning his story.

And now I knew how the story ended.

The window of the Lambo was down. I looked inside this Italian monstrosity out of curiosity. "Low miles, mint condition," I thought to myself, guesstimating how much it would bring at an estate auction.

1986 was nothing special in my life, this particular hairless ape, the one that I still am, is still driving the same old Ford Taurus wagon that I bought in 1986, the year it came out.

I put the Taurus in reverse and backed out of the gravel driveway. My gut was telling me that I was here for the last time.

# When Brezhnev Died

"You know how when you happen to drive through some farm land, you might suddenly notice the stench of manure?"

I nodded, maneuvering in and out of traffic like a sardine in a can jockeying for a better position. What I was doing made no objective difference but all this "active" driving created an illusion for me and my passenger that we weren't just taking the rush hour laying down, we were doing something about it, asserting our own, however misguided, path of self-determination.

My passenger, a graying man with a wrestler's build and a leather wrapped attaché case in between his knees, sat with half of his body spilling out of the passenger's side window, looking directly into the eyes of other drivers as we inched by, with a steely challenge, as if trying to hypnotize them into surrendering their place to us. I asked for no help but he simply stepped up to the plate and started to use the weight of his presence and a meaty forearm in a rolled up sleeve as a kind of traffic controller. Now and then, he'd growl "Hey, hey, hey!" as he'd put out an open hand stop sign to a fellow driver to my right. The other driver would eventually give up and let me in. Only a fool would have not complied with this burly man hanging out of a car's window. With a guy like that you don't need a cherry top to command the right of way.

But, he also kept talking:

"…and so you drive into this stench, this smell of cow shit, and for a while you can't wait till it's over. But then a part of you begins to realize that its not that bad, that you even kinda like it. There is a sweet kind of sourness to it. Particularly, if you had grown up on a farm or in the country. I didn't, but I suspect if I had, it'd be even more so. Regardless, you go on and on, and before too long, you really don't mind the smell. Like I said, it sorta grows on you."

I was wondering where he was going with this. For a second I tried to wind back our conversation in my mind to see how he got on this train of thought. We were talking politics, I think. It was 1990. I whiled away two years of my precious life in the Soviet military while the country that I was "serving" had essentially ended. I put "serving" in quotation marks because I don't believe in altruism, no such thing-less thing. But now is not the time for me to step dance on this rickety ol' soap box.

The point is, we were talking about "the changes." Well, mostly, I was listening to him talk about "the changes." As a jitney, I'd stir up the conversation and let it cook on its own. It made the time go faster and also helped with tips.

"So, this stench, this smell of manure, you know, the smell you initially couldn't quite stand, you

228

eventually come to like, as you keep driving through it, mile after mile, year after year."

There always comes this moment in an evolution of a metaphor where language turns the final trick and your mind suddenly finds itself in bed with a set of unexpected connotations. And it's always a one night stand, a semantic encounter never to be repeated. A moment I was hoping for and it arrived when "miles" became "years." My passenger was now finally up against the very point he had been so deliberately setting up.

"Hey, hey, hey!" he first barked at a driver to my right, who dared to put on a turn signal in a stillborn hope to ease in front of me. Then my passenger continued.

"It's the same with propaganda, you know. It's actually even worse. You grow up in this stinky shit of a smell so you don't even notice it. It's everywhere. It's subtle. It's hidden in the color schemes, in the narrative, in what people say and don't say, in the jokes. And, now and then, they, whoever they might be, even make it sweet, sentimentally poignant to remind you that you don't have to just 'not mind it,' but that you can even 'like it.' As you grow up it's in your skin, like a shit tan that won't wash out. It's internalized, you know? And, say, Brezhnev dies and you cry like a little girl, like Americans cried when JFK died. You get this flashbulb memory that illuminates the moment like it's the most important moment in your life. And then you are stuck with it. You remember it better than your first kiss. Fuck, you remember it better, more vividly than your last kiss."

"I know what you mean," I chimed in. "I also cried when Brezhnev died. I was ten, eleven, or something like that. They gathered us up in the gym to make an important announcement. They said it just like that. We were all gathered up in the gym, all grades, lined up, waiting for something. I remember thinking, "That's it. Must be war." And then they told us, 'Brezhnev passed away.' I remember thinking, "What now?" And I had a tear or two."

My passenger cut in. "Heck, you were ten, you say, or something like that. I was in my late twenties and I cried. That's the fucking nonsense of this. That is how deep this shit gets into you. We are all susceptible to this. No exceptions. None!"

We sat in silence for a moment. He even waived someone in, acting, in a sense, as a driver. It was clearly in his blood to take command, to usurp it wherever he could. I didn't want to pry and probe. As young as I was, I had already learned the lesson of not rushing to satisfy my curiosity. It was, and still is, a lot more fun to stumble into the unknown rather than drill your way into it with a hundred questions. At the end of the day, you are still in front of one and the same wall of not knowing. Each question, even if answered, simply moves it an inch back.

"So, yeah, we stew around in this stench and then one day. bam!, everything has changed. You have left the farm country. The smell of manure is over. You can now roll the windows down and it's fresh air, perestroika, glasnost, a new future, all that new sweet shit, right? That's the change I am talking about, little brother, that's the change. The question is, 'Now what?' Same question you asked when Brezhnev died. Same question we are all now asking. And the scariest thing is that there are others that know the answer to this question. They've been working on it for a long, long time. But we, the schmucks that we are, we have no fucking clue. We are about to be sucked into yet another historical eddy of bullshit and we have no fucking clue. But someone somewhere does. They've orchestrated the changes, they have the schematics, the vision, the blueprint. We've all already been sold down the fucking river but we don't know it yet. Why? Because this new shit doesn't stink yet. It's odorless."

He went on like this until we finally broke through the Garden Circle, picked up speed and finally had Vorobiev Hills in sight. I knew these hills like the back of my hand. An old buddy of mine, Mishka Teplov, aka Khan, and I, spent endless Saturdays and Sundays skateboarding these slopes, down along the gated government villas on the bluff, overlooking the Moscow River, and in the nice summer shade of the towering Soviet goth cathedral of the Moscow State University. Those were amazing days. But now is not the time for me soak in this sentimental bubble bath with details.

I couldn't believe it! I was actually driving into one of these gated villas on the bluff. Who was my passenger? The time to ask was quickly coming to an end. Was he an apparatchik, a body guard, a colonel in the KGB or some other clandestine cold war figurehead. With those meaty forearms, commanding tone, and a wrestler's bowed legs, he had to be someone important. After all, he had the keys to one of these compounds. I saw it with my own eyes, he got out of the car, opened the gates, and waived me in.

I pulled up to the three storied staccato villa and he paid. He sat in the car for a moment and then said, "Wanna come in?"

I nodded.

"Park there," he instructed, and I obeyed.

I followed him upstairs to an open floorplan with the kind of living rooms that you expect in a cliffhanger house on the Adriatic. Hardwood everywhere, Persian carpets on top, a balcony with a colonnade overhang with a breathtaking view of Kremlin way, way down below, across the river, like a pearl on an open palm.

I realize now, as I write this that I remember this moment better than the one when Brezhnev died. The flashbulb of that moment burnt even brighter. I was now seeing, first hand, the hidden luxury that hid behind the Soviet doldrums.

He offered me coffee. He offered me to listen to music on a barely used Sony ghetto blaster, inviting me to rummage through a heap of cassettes of Aha! and other new wave stuff. He could see I was mesmerized and I think he could appreciate that I asked no questions. My tact of keeping my mouth shut was working, for a change, to my advantage.

He made a couple of phone calls. Then, to my surprise, he went downstairs and returned with a good-looking woman. Apparently we weren't alone in this mansion and I didn't even notice. He had changed. Gone was his tired suit and wrinkled rolled up sleeves. He and his companion were dressed to kill. They were going out. I figured that's why he had asked me to stick around. I figured he wanted me to drive them back to town. But I was wrong:

"If you want," he said, "you can stick around for a while. Listen to some music, eat whatever you find in the fridge. Take it easy with booze."

I shook my head: "I don't drink."

"Whatever," he continued, "If you want to do that, if you want to hang out a bit, just re-park your car outside the gates now and when you are done, just climb the fence over there on the back to get out, understand?"

Of course, I did. Without further ado, he and his woman trotted downstairs, her stiletto shoes echoing in the stairway. I went out to the other side to look out the windows. She came out alone, graceful in a red dress and immaculately toned calves. As she waited, an underground garage door opened up and a black 300 Benz, lacquered like a shined shoe, pulled out of the building.

She got in and they left.

"What now?" popped into my mind as I noticed the faint lingering smell of the woman's perfume.

I walked down the hall, found a shower, took my clothes off and started to jerk off.

# As Is

He was waiting on a symptom, for something to feel wrong, for a sign of distress or, better yet, for pain, to justify the invasive brain surgery that's been recently proposed to him. But he was healthy as the runaway ox in the darn ox-herding series.

His seven years in Tibet have long turned into fourteen and recently into twenty one. Lean, toned and flexible as a break dancing cobra he would surprise no one if he one day lived to be immortal. His daily regimen of a bowl of rice, twenty cups of tea with ghee, and hours of meditation shaped the Western clay of his body-mind into a living, breathing obelisk of Buddha-basalt. An envy of local fakirs, a reincarnation of Houdini, an embodiment of an Amish-grade space heater, he could sit naked amidst Tibetan snows, in a state of self-induced tummo hibernation, melting radiating Target-store patterns like crop-circles out of ice. He wrote books, with the focus of a modern-day luddite dead set on deconstructing the Great Mindwall of Western Duality (most notably, Nothing More Than Nothinglessness), he regularly blogged on Huffington Post, and had a burgeoning Twitter fan-base.

His acquired name was Genpo Nga, Tibetan for "undiluted salt" or the Mongolian slang for Splenda, or something like that.

But he was best known for the concept of "literal enlightenment." It went something like this. Matter and consciousness are not two; consciousness, he'd say, is the inner experience of matter, proportionate in its felt complexity to the organization of the said matter. We are all eddies, he'd say, body-mind vortices "unless!" we awaken to our true nature, which is "Light!" With Gurdjieffesque iconoclasticism, he insisted that enlightenment is literally just that, the experience of self as a field of self-illuminated awareness. When pressed by skeptics to drop the metaphors, he'd calmly insist that "enlightenment is literal, like a fire in a cave;" he'd point to the temples of his skull and say, "Consciousness sees!"

There was a lot of appeal to this teaching; indeed, to think is to see. Test it out for yourself. Close your eyes and see your thoughts. "To think is to see," he'd say and add "But that's only the beginning of it. Not to think is to see, too, to see more clearly." He'd explain, "Unencumbered awareness, free of info-eddies and mind-forms, the informationally sterile consciousness of Buddhamind is brighter than the sun itself, it is the inner peace of the stardust that we cosmologically are."

Some understood, some thought it too kooky, but all in all, books kept being written and speaking fees flowed.

The bliss came to a startling stall when, in the course of the recent Harvard study that was to use the cutting edge brain scanning technology in order to investigate his claims of "literal enlightenment," he was told that he appeared to have a golf ball sized tumor right in the middle of his forehead.

"But I don't feel a thing," he protested.

The surgeons were unimpressed.

"The good thing is that it's benign. By the size of it, it's amazing that you are still able to see. We are not sure why the optic nerve hasn't been affected. But it's going to have to come out. Better sooner than later."

So, he was now waiting on a symptom, on a sure signal that something was wrong, on something that would force the decision. But no such luck. The finely tuned machinery of his body-mind kept blossoming like a lotus on meth.

A year went by, a repeat scan showed minor growth, but still no symptoms.

"How can I justify cutting into my skull when I don't feel anything?" he'd vent to his confidants. "It just doesn't make sense. I'm feeling better than before." And the aging experts agreed: his age markers were continuing to improve: his hair was still jet black, his cardiac infrastructure was as tumescent and void of cholesterol as the Holland tunnel on a Sunday morning. Everything ticked and everything tocked, as if time itself decided to take a break in the marvelous geo-coordinate of his micro-cosmos.

But the decision eventually came, motivated mostly by the vestiges of his Western marketing savvy. He was now set to perform a pay-per-view televised brain surgery with no anesthesia whatsoever, on nothing more than the power of his literal enlightening. For a good cause, of course, to free the already psychologically liberated Tibet from… well, you know whom.

He had nothing to lose, after all, as he's been reassuring us all along, we are nothing anyway. Correction, not a nothing, but a no-thing, a nothing-in-particular. An informational process-in-formation, an eddy of Eternal Now amidst this unborn and undying Ocean of Boundless Oneness.

Per the contract, the OR was decorated with Tibetan prayer flags. The surgeons made their first tentative cut into his forehead as he laid serenely on his back, as sober as an addictions counselor at a rehab farm on Monday morning.

"How are you doing, are you in any pain?" asked the lead surgeon.

"The pain is there but I am not this pain," he said, with a blissful half smile and winked his permission to proceed.

A few moments later, when the top of his forehead looked like one of those metal loading docks that we gingerly step over, the lead surgeon looked right into his eyes and said, "We need to discuss something."

This never sounds good, not when you hear it from your wife as you walk through the door after work, not in performance evaluation meetings with your boss, and certainly not when you hear it from a brain surgeon who just cut a manhole into the top of your head. If there's ever a time for the art of heart-open acceptance it was certainly now.

Cameras zoomed in and so did the attention of the global pay-per-view sangha.

"The golf ball that I was talking about," said the surgeon, "isn't a tumor."

"It's not?"

"No, it's not."

To say that the tension of the moment was thick enough that it could be cut with a knife is to be primitively associative in this narrative. And right now I am glued to TV, I was seeing the Seer, a bloody, vitriolic, literal Seer that's been reporting on this phenomenon of "literal enlightenment" for years, whose signed books I have carefully displayed on my bookshelves, whose insights I've been regurgitating to my therapy clients for years.

"So, what is it?" came the inevitable question.

"It's an eye."

"An 'I'?" followed the clarification request with a couple of air quotes.

"No, not an 'I' but an eye," clarified the surgeon. "What we thought was a benign tumor is an actual eye, a third eye, in a manner of speaking, right in the middle of your frontal lobes. Can't you yourself see out of it?"

Understandable confusion followed. But a mind, better prepared for confusion, hasn't ever lived. Confusion, after all, as the teaching goes, is the courage of uncertainty, a letting go of the known categories; an openness to What Is.

"So, you are telling me that I have not two but three eyes? That you are looking at an eye ball inside my head?"

"Correct. Your optic nerve appears to have an extra branch and I am looking right now at a perfectly fine eyeball that's sitting right in the middle of your frontal lobes. And, it would appear, that this eye is moving and tracking. This is really not entirely surprising, your third eye sits on top of the pineal gland, exactly where you'd expect it to be, in the only other area of neural photosensitivity. The question is, can you see out of it, I wonder?"

"What color is it?"

"Right now it's black, like an eight ball. It's starved for light and is effectively blinded right now from overstimulation."

Brain surgeons are notorious for their compartmentalized curiosity, a human brain becomes a whack-a-mole machine to play with, poke here, see what changes, poke there, see what changes.

"No, I can't seem to see out of that eye."

The surgeon motioned to his attendant to turn off the overhead light.

"How about now?"

"Now I can!"

The hypothesis was instantly re-tested and re-re-re-re-tested.

Lights on. "How about now?"

"No."

Lights off. "And now?"

"Yes."

Lights on. "Now?"

"Nope."

Lights off.

"Yep."

The picture of the "literal enlightening" was beginning to emerge. It was a mix of vindication ("I told you consciousness is self illuminated!") and reductionism ("But, if it's anatomical, it's not metaphysical.") The light was kept turned off for a few minutes, out of courtesy, to help the patient see how he felt about this. The thoughts flashed through his mind like vintage slides against a square of projected light onto a cave wall.

Open holes in the head are as dangererous as missing manhole lids. The moment to close up the matter finally came. Plus, the surgeon's 4:00 pm split-brain epilectomy was approaching fast and he was itching to check his email before then.

"Whatcha thinking?" he said with sudden tone of familiarity. "Do you want it out or do you want me to close you up 'as is'? After all, it isn't hurting nothing, right?"

Seeing what to do, at a moment like this, is no simple matter. But 21 years in Tibet are no joke either. A mind conditioned for acceptance is the peak of evolutionary nonchalance.

"Leave it as it is," muttered the super monk trying to hold on to his "literal enlightenment."

Months went by and while the world moved on with its daily media IV of the Kardashians, a fierce debate ensued in such Buddhist publications as "The Tricycle." The chicken or the egg koans abounded. What came first, the eye or the enlightenment? Isn't "leaving it as is" a form of clinging to the status quo?

Twenty one years in Tibet, it turned out, were not to become twenty eight years in Tibet. The teacher repatriated his recovering body-mind to a modest loft in Manhattan, afforded by the proceeds from the infamous pay-per-view. He changed his acquired Tibetan name of Genpo Das to his "maiden" name before he married into Buddhism, that of Nathan Meyer. The age defying Benjamin Button vector of his life took a sudden u-turn. In the next seven years his age markers quickly caught up with his age cohort and the bottomless inkwell of his inspiration managed to produce one final mediocre seller (self-published on Kindle of all virtual places), entitled "Darkness That Sees Itself."

Don't get me wrong, he wasn't broken. His product of "literal enlightenment" was still good. But, stripped of metaphysics, nobody wanted it "as is." And that's what his last book was – is – about. His best book, I must add.

We met a year ago in a coffee shop. I had been calling him for months after his last book came out. He agreed to meet me for an espresso if I was buying.

"What do you want with me, smart ass?" he asked looking into my eyes with the serenity of a double barrel gun.

"I wanted your autograph."

"The book was never in print."

"I printed it out," I said and pulled out a home bound copy of his monograph and a pen.

He took a pen and swooshed a blitzkrieg enso on the cover: a perfect form of emptiness.

"Good enough?" he asked.

I nodded.

"You are the one that gave me the four stars on Amazon?" he asked referring to the only and only rating of his book.

"Yes, I didn't want to give you a five. It would've looked like an arranged review."

We took a few sips in silence.

"I still stand by everything I've been saying over the years, you know. 'Literal Enlightenment' checks out. It's irrefutable ontologically, cosmologically, and psychologically. I didn't need the third eye to see it. Heck, I didn't need any eyes to see it. Matter sees. Plain and simple, matter sees. Understanding that is enlightenment."

"I shouldn't've ever had that surgery," he said.

"Shouldda, couldda, wouldda, Buddha," I ventured a word of consolation.

He glared, "What's your name again?"

I opened my mouth to answer just as he slapped me on my face.

"I gotta go, smartass. I have a meeting with Keanu Reeves."

I wiped off my face, feeling (seeing?) a taste of blood in my mouth. I wasn't angry since I had been previously baptized by this strange form of Buddhist affection.

"He still sits?" I asked about Keanu.

"He still sits," said Genpo Nga, nee Nathanial Meyer. "The last Hollywood Buddhist, you know."

# The Questions of a Self-Seeing Eye

*I* walked all morning through the boondocks of the Moscow city underbelly. The wind gusts of my libido had blown me overnight into an unfamiliar territory. Unfamiliar in a geographic sense only, but seemingly familiar in an experiential sense. "Seemingly" is where it's all at, I now realize as I look back at my age of categoricalness.

That summer I roamed my Russian microcosm with nothing but my dick for a compass needle. That morning I was trekking through an ankle deep field of pinkish clovers, blades of wet grass covering up my boots. It was around 5:30 am, way too early to call anyone to plan another day of debauchery. But not too early to think, in fact, it was a perfect time to think, sunwise.

Now and then I'd stop and squat down to look at a dandelion or to lick half a sip worth of dew from a glazed green leaf. I had plenty of time to find my way back home to Moscow and being lost is how I found myself in those days. Last night was fading fast in my mind. And so was the fog of the morning. The gray walls of the projects were looming ahead, choirs of alarm clocks inaudibly going off somewhere. I felt a curious advantage over the millions of bodies that were still asleep. I felt the advantage of being already awake.

The Tretyakov opened up at 10:00 am and it was coming up on noon now. An art gallery was just the right place to cool the engines and formulate a plan. I had decided not to stop at my folks' place, another broken promise, and to continue my rodeo of consciousness without interruption. This impromptu pilgrimage into self was now unfolding into its third day.

A few blades of grass on the round toes of my Doc Martens seemed in strange contrast with the polished marble of the gallery floor. I didn't mind the contrast. I thrived on it. Contrast is what gives life a feeling of friction and friction is how we know we are alive. Armed with an admittance ticket I felt immune to the scorn of the hall curators who are always, for some reason, opposed to loitering despite loitering being the very mandate of the place that they curate. I'd sit on a bench for about half an hour and then, to ease the tension of the pacing curator, I'd pick up camp and move through a hall or two, out of sight, until I'd find another empty marble bench to crash on.

In those days, sitting for me was like lying down. My twenty year old body was a generously appointed temple for my consciousness. Heck, it was a five-star hotel in which my mind could comfortably rest in just about any physical position. Nowadays, it's a different story entirely. Tired of this parasite of consciousness, the landlord of Soma mercilessly fumigates its tenant Psyche with arthritic napalm, chasing the plague of self awareness out of its aching nooks and crannies, out and away from a joint to a joint to a joint.

But then, sprawled on a marble bench, I was watching a curious couple. An exotic-looking young woman and an older man in a wheelchair. They spent ridiculously long moments of time in front of every painting, exchanging but a few remarks now and then. The woman's patience however was beginning to thin. I could tell that she was well aware of my eyes. As I had followed them from a hall to a hall, her stride grew more springy, more deliberate, more athletic. Once she even raised up on her toes, for no apparent reason, as if to showcase her taut calves. I was dialed in.

Mila (as I came to know her, later) swayed on her long, toned and tanned legs like a tiger lily. She wore an ochre silk scarf, in an echo to Jackie O, and an unbuttoned raincoat. And, oh yeah, bitching red beach flip-flops. Her companion, ensconced in a wheel chair like a sphinx wore black jeans, a white v-neck, and an undershirt of ink. He had a curiously pained half smile on his aristocratically gaunt pale face. He was most likely in his early 50s. She, half his age, at most. At the moment, he was studying the *Passage* by Odille. She was studying her nails.

Sure, she stood out and I had already imagined how, at the end of our hypothetical flirting, if she were to ask me, "Do you want to sleep with me?" I'd tell her, "No, honey, of course, not! I want to stay awake with you, and if we ever, after all, decided to sleep together, I wouldn't just want to sleep with you, I'd want to dream with you, of us staying awake, late into the night."

"Enough!" I interrupted my own marasmatic fantasy. Truth be told, I was intrigued more so by him than by her, and, definitely, by the "it" of this seemingly strange union. The flash of a fantasy that had just played out in my mind was a reflex of my seeking age.

Suddenly Sergei (as I came to know him later) scowled as if he'd just circumcised himself by zipping up too fast, the foreskin of his quivering lip curling into a grimace of scorn. Did he not like the painting so much? I wondered to myself as they moved on to another piece, a few steps closer to where I was sitting. The proximity turned out to be of no coincidence.

"Young man!" Sergei unceremoniously called out to me, recruiting me in his moment without any introductions (which instantly pissed me off): "What do you think of this so-called art?" Having said just enough to obtain my attention, he immediately offered an apology, but for an entirely wrong thing.

"I apologize, I am rushing to influence a young mind, aren't I?" he said somewhat to me and somewhat to his companion. "A mistake I make too statistically often to write it off as chance." Twice now he had referred to me as "young," a gutsy move for a dude in a wheelchair. As they say, "them are fighting words." Young egos are the dinosaurs that still roam this Earth. I suspect he knew it. He ruffled my feathers on purpose, I believe, as a test of my flexibility.

Take this from me as advice, or a pearl of wisdom, or as a nagging post-modern narrative detour – never address this Reality on the basis of age! Any aspect of Reality you encounter, a just baked cookie or a stone-stale loaf of bread, is as old as the Universe itself. You see, the Eternal Cosmos in us, the beginningless and the boundless in us, accepts no prejudice of age. There is a reason why young turks feel immortal, it's because they are. We all are. But then we all conveniently forget about our cosmic immortality, buying hook, line and sinker into the cultural conditioning that we *have* to die, that death is inevitable. Sorry-ass culture-wide self-hypnosis is what kills us in the end. That's what I thought then and still think, notwithstanding the fact that one of my legs is stuck knee-deep in the fast setting concrete of the time- grave. But let's get back to our sugar-coated ponies of reminiscence.

"Sergei," he finally introduced himself and without missing a beat tried to suck me into yet another little eddy of his thinking out loud. "Not that we can name the nameless, right?" There it was, the assertive rhetoric that he had just apologized for. I knew he wasn't sorry at all, he was the type that has no interest in learning curves. Un-learning is what his type is after.

"And I am Mila," said the brown stem lily, cocking her right foot on a heel like a folk dancer.

Their overture in my direction was a seamlessly polished fly-fishing cast. Plop! The moment radiated through me with the power of a first sunrise. I offered no name in return for now. I was taken aback, pleasantly so, and definitely dialed in even more. Right then and there, I realized that she was the bait and he was the hook. But what were they fishing for? Surely not for the mackerel that I was. I was on the hook anyway, with Mila's legs and Sergei's tactlessly assertive entrance into my little clover world of treasured thoughts and insights, and, of course, the indeterminacy of their mission. There was a magic to it that I couldn't resist. Perhaps, even more than magic, maybe, even magnetism.

The three of us were now in a cab, heading to their place, a dacha, ironically back in the very same southern direction that I had trekked from earlier that morning. All good things in Moscow happen outside of Moscow, I was learning. At the dacha, the beefy cabbie, whom they seemed to know by name, helped Sergei out, carrying him with nursing aid savvy, two perfectly limp legs swaying noodle-like in sync. The cabbie accepted a quick shot of vodka "for the road" and left with a wad of rubles in his hand.

What followed, through the night, was a series of conversations, teachings, really, and mostly Sergei's thinking out loud, interrupted by periodic statements of boredom from Mila and occasional provocations from my yet to be plumbed withins.

Sergei had a tone of bittersweet molasses, an unstoppable viscous drip of one out loud thought after another. There was a grit in his voice, too, a very interesting grit. Silky, finely ground, espresso grit, but grit nevertheless. It sure held your attention. Mila, on the other hand, like a bookend to a shelf of satanic verses, sported an entertainingly insatiable appetite. For example, before taking a shower, "because it was hot and muggy," she had put a large pan of corn on the stove. After what seemed like indelible masturbation groans in the shower, Mila re-emerged, fresh, glowing, and carelessly wrapped in a bath towel. She plunked down on the couch next to me, and proceeded to inhale one phallic yellow corncob after another, now and then tucking her about to runaway breasts back into the towel.

The whole thing, this collective body-mind of the Sergei-Mila duet, had the feel of a game, a game they were good at, a game with an unknown outcome. While Sergei shamelessly vied for my attention with a commanding "Listen!" and an "As I was saying…"

Mila treated me to an IV of coy nonchalance. It was clear that she didn't want me per se, at least, not in the way in which I wanted to be wanted (as myself, nothing more, nothing less); she wanted me to want her, that's it, and I didn't want to be an arrowhead on yet another one way arrow of infatuation. She'd turn to me and offer me a corncob, "Want one?" I'd shake my head and she'd say with a pouty smile: "Fine, more for me!"

"Listen, Pash, as I was saying…" Sergei tried to corral my runaway attention back into his sphere of influence. He had the gaunt square face of the Buddhist god of death, Yama. He peered into you with Gurdjieff intensity, and you had a sense that there was nothing on the other end of this stare, except for some sterile, all knowing conviction. You had a feeling that you were locked into a gaze with a telescope, you on one end of it and the entire lively emptiness of the Cosmos on the other. He had "three teachings," as he put it, about the negligible difference between men and women, about the fact that we are worms, and, last but not least, about the illusion of separateness. The theory of nothing-less-ness," that is.

When he talked, I had the feeling of a piggy bank with Sergei's skillfully chosen words being deposited into me, meme by meme. I was a field of awareness, ploughed with rhetoric and sown with logic. The effect of these informational handouts was that of cognitively catalytic coagulation, the undifferentiated am-ness that I was would suddenly crystallize into a poignant sense of clarity. That happened again and again, like the sharpening of a pencil. A Tetris flash of consolidated insights would zip nto being, lightening-like, and the lush grass of my illusions would suddenly turn into Sumerian clay bricks. I was being civilized.

"Watch it, Pash, watch the degrees of freedom go!" Sergei would say, shaking his head as if in disapproval. "It's all shit, illusion, nonsense, you know. Never agree with a damn thing. The Universe is mind-made construct. Deconstruct at will! Illusion, nothing but illusion. Society builds jails of abstraction and then entices you in with promises of freedom. It's an occupancy business. The few, the elite, are domesticating the rest of us, the wild. With nothing but the mirage of freedom."

All of this sounded good and fresh. It had a breezy feel to it, an awakening quality, the kind you have when you stand at the ocean side, watching millions of shells wash out, and you ponder about what was the big fucking evolutionary point of us, of life itself, crawling out of these watery depths onto these burning shores of existence. Instead of evolving Form, we should have focused on evolving Essence. But, I guess, it's not too late, was Sergei's message.

The first teaching, the sociological point about the "negligible difference between men and women" went as follows. "The only difference between men and women is that when women are having an orgasm they curl their toes and when men are having an orgasm they bite their tongues. That's it, Pash! That's it! Nothing more, nothing less, the entire fucking difference is in how we fuck."

This made immediate sense to me. But not to Mila.

"You are kidding, right?" asked Mila with that contemptuous familiarity that you find in an older married couple.

"Of course, I am. When am I not, sweetie? The whole thing, this fucking life, this Universe, all of it is a joke. The Universe laughs at its own self-less self, shedding its seriousness with universe wide metamorphosis every nanosecond," was Sergei's counter. He could go on like that for hours, in metaphysically verbal diarrhetics, working himself effortlessly into a self-referencing double helix of ecstasy-agony. "Language is a tongue that kisses itself, you know," he had said earlier in a dismissal of a query. Sergei used language like some people used a rolled up newspaper for swatting flies.

Mila got up with dismissive decisiveness and headed out of the room, with a demonstrative mutter of "Blah, blah, blah!" leaving me and her bath towel behind on the coach. "Watch this for me, will you?" she said and added: "Don't listen to him, Pash, he's full of you know what." A moment later, Mila made an abrupt u-turn and stormed back in, stomping across the room. She came right up to Sergei, bent down, grabbed his square jaw and pried it open like a jewelry box.

"Show me this tongue of yours, the one you bite after fucking me! Show it to me! Where is it?"

Bemused, Sergei put up no fight. He smiled at me with his eyes, letting Mila display his open mouth in my direction with "See, Pash, it's all stupid little metaphors from him! Nothing but words!" Satisfied with the show of force, she once again left the room shooting a triumphant glare in my direction.

"But, of course, I am being metaphorical, Pash. Listen, you and I, we had a good share of sex in our lifetimes and, " he stuck out his tongue again for evidence, this time voluntarily, "and we are fine, right? What I mean is that men don't understand pleasure, we are too cognitive. We chase the abstracts, we thrive on duality, on divisions, on separateness, on war, in all of its immediate and symbolic permutations. Women seek nonduality, a felt sense of unity rather than agreement. They thrive on touch, on connection... It's not just maternal, you know, it's generative."

"How do you mean?" I asked.

"It's generative in a cosmic sense. It's a cosmic reflex, an echo of primordial identification with all that is. A bio-existential vector of enmeshment. Hard to explain, really, for a man to a man." He paused and continued, "Men, on the other hand, we are filthy polyps of consciousness, extrusions of premature differentiation. Each of us, you, me, and any Ivan Ivanich and Joe Schmo, we are all trying to sneak build our own empire of flesh and abstraction... We are divisive, and that's normal because it is cosmically necessitated. The Universe needs un-lubricated friction to finger fuck itself into another Big Bang of an orgasm."

It was clear to me that he had his own vocabulary, his own set of connotations that I didn't yet understand. Nor was I really interested all that much in the details. The difference between men and women was a long understood reality for me. There was no magic here, men don't leave their towels behind on a couch while prancing around naked in the kitchen. At least, not the men I had met.

That was the first teaching, a teaching Mila vehemently opposed. She scoffed and hissed and made disgruntled noises. She sat by my side, staring and scowling. She resented the generalizations of gender. I, too, had a problem with that. But I could see that Sergei was not really talking about gender, per se, but about the yin and the yang, about the dialectic of what is – yes, in his own provocative manner. All in all, this "teaching" did little more than entertain me. Well, maybe not just that, there was a kernel of an idea, the notion that consciousness had a geometry to it, a vector. Not just the "arrow of time" vector but also the "vector of interest." I'd come back to that idea again and again in the years to come, but at that moment I was nothing more than a field of awareness sown by memes without awareness. At the time I just watched and, frankly, enjoyed the friction between Sergei and Mila and knew that as soon as I'd leave, they'd be rolled back into a tight 69 of yin yang harmony of their baseline relationship. I was a guest, maybe, a pupil, but certainly a third party and a show was being put on. not for me, but for all of us, an interactive show, a show in which each pinnacle of this ad hoc human triangle was dynamically recoiling and re-approaching some kind of ineffable center. After all, each triangle is but a wannabe circle…

A day that began last night has become a tomorrow and now, that I noticed a nice breeze, it became a now. We were sitting out on the porch, a crazy night of conversation behind us. It was coming up on 11:00 am and this nice breeze, the kind that used to drive Van Gogh nearly mad, was bringing the news of a coming storm. We kept commenting on the dark sky and the thunder in the distance.

"It'll be here by noon," predicted Sergei. But he was mistaken. Noon came, but no rain. Tired of waiting for the rain we went inside, bringing in with us, like a couple of mosquitoes from the outside, the verbiage of yet another "teaching," an existential sob story, if you think about it. Here's the tale of it. And its sting.

"We are worms, Pash. Yes, worms! Living tubes, in fact."

"How do you mean?" Mila threw him another gauntlet.

"Just look at me, Pash," said Sergei, ignoring Mila's challenge. "I lost the use of my legs, and I am glad you haven't asked me how yet. And do me a favor, don't!  All I can say, it was a stupid thing. Regardless… "

He moved his head as if trying to shake off an

autobiographical tangent and apparently managed to do so. He returned to what seemed his original point, "Say, I also lost the use of my arms too? What am I then? Lemme help you out, literally, imagine me without these useless appendages, what am I then? A torso with two holes. A conduit, an input-output metabolic system, a tube! Right?"

"What about the brain?" came another challenge from Mila.

"The brain is irrelevant. The brain, for all intents and purposes, is but a leg itself, an inner leg, really just a biological GPS designed to move this living tube from point A to point B, towards food, away from becoming food. This brain," Sergei knocked on his head with the knuckle of his index finger, like on a door, "It's an auxiliary device, a cephalized neural net, a mega-ganglion of neurons designed to optimize the survival of this living tube that I am. The real brain, if you want to know, is right there," he pointed to his stomach, "in the gut. That's what it's all about."

Mila, who was now cozied up to my side on the couch, was preoccupied with navigating my hand down into her loins. She had Levi's on but was topless. Just a moment ago, she had willfully taken command of it – first by wrapping my arm around her shoulder, then by scooting up closer to me, and, through a series of gradual postural readjustments, she was kind of laying on my lap and was now maneuvering my hand, nudge by nudge, into her loins. Reflexively, I had unbuttoned her 501s.

"The point is," continued Sergei, "ignore the skeleton, the musculature. Just focus on the simple fact that your mouth and your anus are but two apertures of one and the same conduit. And just like worms we crawl out of some kind of crack of circumstance onto the hot summer sidewalk and we begin to fry. But we are slow, my friend, very slow. Phase delayed, informationally speaking. We don't even realize this until it becomes irreversibly too late. We have no fucking clue that we are being roasted alive. And when we finally catch on, we start squirming, turning this and that way, looking for an escape, for shade to hide in. But to no avail! Like hotdogs on a grill, we scorch and coagulate and scar. It's agony, utter fucking agony and we make it worse by chasing relief. This is where Buddha comes in, "suffering is inevitable," he said, "and accept it." The pursuit of wellbeing is but a flip side of suffering. The more you seek, the more you suffer!"

"Did Buddha say that too? Was that a direct quote, Sergei?" Mila aggressed again, my hand by now officially expropriated and lost in between her legs.

Sergei continued sermonizing without missing a beat, "Somewhere in this process of existential seasoning, we glimpse the hopelessness of our trajectory, we start asking the questions of meaning, we try to unravel the domino effect of our predicament, we start living in the shadow of our past. Then, if we are lucky, a cloud comes over, the sun retreats for a moment, and all cools off for a timeless second. And we breathe a sigh of relief. But then, of course, it starts all over again."

I respect metaphors, but only as auxiliary devices, as necessary crutches for a complicated narrative. What I have no respect for is a sloppy synergy of ends and means, of literal and symbolic. I was feeling that Sergei had by now once again crossed that flimsy little line and he was starting to lose me. Good thing was that the middle finger of my right hand was now also lost but in a kind of slip and slide, rubbing out a rhythm of inconspicuous pleasure somewhere inside Mila's pubic jungle.

"We are nothing but living skin, a touch sensitive surface folded onto itself, a Moebius bottle of living flesh ever trying to differentiate the inside from the outside. Life cooks us alive. To the point when we can't stand to be touched. Irreparably defensive we recoil even from a cooling breeze. Neurologists call this allodynia – a miscalibrated sensitivity to normal stimuli. Everything hurts, a kiss from your girlfriend, a wink from the Sun. Everything! It's an existential condition, not a neurosis or a neurological thing. Buddha got it, the dead beat dad that he was. It's what happens to the living ones, in the course of living normally, just as it should, under this merciless sun of being."

Mila was living proof that Sergei was wrong on this

point. Not everything apparently hurt.

"Hasn't happened to me yet!" spoke Mila, and I smiled in confirmation. I, too, had apparently not climbed this learning curve of suffering that high.

I was starting to tune out Sergei, he was too verbose, too dry in his intellectualizations, too attached to his point. Mila, on the other hand, was simply moist. Like a black hole, she kept sucking me in with the power of her vacuum, her emptiness growling with the soft persistence of a trash disposal motor in a sink.

Sergei was cluelessly unrelenting, lost in the illusion of the audience, which happens to narcissists a lot. "You are young, friend. I don't know how, but you are still not too scarred. You don't say much. Mila's magic doesn't seem to work on you as it does on most. I have a feeling that the worm that you are, you've been hiding out under some nice rock, making friends with the moss of consciousness. But listen, this, too, is a dead end. There is no way out from this frying pan. I, too, a good while back, looked inside. I spent years trying to shed the parchment of scars, layer after layer, looking for that inner diameter of nothingness. It ain't there. Nothingness I mean, no such thing-less thing as 'nothingness,' you know? We'll come back to this yet if you stick around."

Sergei finally caught on to the fact that that I was losing interest, or having it stolen by Mila. Same result. a narcissist ceases to exist without a mirror. With a righteous effort, Sergei started to wheel himself out onto the veranda, to leave Mila and I alone. She started to get up to help, out of a commitment that seemed to be far more fundamental to their relationship than any erotic or intellectual common denominator.

"I'll manage," said Sergei stopping her in her tracks, adding, seemingly to both of us, "Enjoy each other, living tubes." And so we did. For a tick and a tock and a long Moscow minute, studying each others' psychosomatic innards like two nesting dolls on a job interview.

There is no teaching without questions. Without questions, lecturers wilt like late summer flowers without water. Sergei seems to have exhausted himself with his ranting metaphors. Mila, eventually dissatisfied with the limited dexterity of my hands, decided to take a nap, coiled like a cat inside a hammock in a window bay.

"So, what do we do?"

"Nothing, Pash, nothing!"

Sergei's eyes lit up. It was the perfect bait of a question. A perfect exit ramp for a nose dive into some tautological conclusion of the "it is what it is" kind.

"Imagine," he continued, "that you are a line, a geometric line, a living line of infinite extension but of zero diameter, an abstract geodesic of cosmic consciousness."

"I don't like to imagine, Sergei."

Sergei didn't mind the interruption, he studied me for a good moment or two and concluded, "You are right about that, imagination gets us nowhere." Then he continued with a perfectly tangential link, "Which is really what I am talking about, nowhere, I mean. So, the line of continuity that you are, worming your way through time, building the rungs of your existence out of the ever renewing illusion of self. Imagine that one day, the line that you are, you look inside, like I think you like to do, which you probably call meditation [here he added air quotes] but this meditation is really nothing other than that same ol' imagination in its subtle most form. So, you look inside and you finally feel a center of sorts, a kind of fixity, a swerving, tunneling stability. And you ask yourself, what is this? Is this the 'I'? Is this my true self, my innermost essence? My fifth element?"

Mila, in the window bay, began to unceremoniously snore.

"So, you keep looking inside, like that self-seeing matter that you are, into this sense of phenomenological stability, into this baseline of am-ness. Suddenly, instead of seeing yourself you see the entire universe, and this universe speaks back to you, like a mirror, reflecting your own question back to you. It is saying who is this? It is asking you who am I? You hear it ask itself the very same questions you just asked of your self (he once again added air quotes to the word "self"); is this my innermost essence, my fifth element, my true self? First you panic and dodge the conclusion, this isn't me you say to yourself. You are dis-identifying, disassociating, and distancing yourself from this 'object of consciousness.' With time, as you listen to this voice inside yourself you begin to let go of the secondary question of, 'Is it me talking to myself or am I being talked to?' And you realize that you are both you and not you. That you are both this conscious subject that experiences this object, and that you are this object of consciousness being experienced by some other subject. That both you and not you are one and the same self-seeing mirror that has met itself at an existential perpendicular. A mirror that reflects itself internally, in an infinite regress of self same identities. Or you realize that you cannot possibly rule out the possibility that you are not a creator of your own thoughts but merely a receiver, a station!"

"I am sorry, Sergei, but I am confused about, how shall I say it, the geometry of this."

"Of course, you are, because all geometry is really

just an imagination. There are no lines, no circles, and no dots. But, if you can stay with me for a bit longer, at this crossroads of communication, then maybe you and I can meet *outside* these limited words, outside these shitty little words we play with as we try to show each other the ineffable. So, if you look at this geometrically, here you are; an ever metabolically renewing pattern, really, a straight line through time, if there is such a thing-less thing."

I was done. Sergei had lost all clout. I felt that, each time he came to a vulnerable point in his improv, he'd roll out a new construct, a new term, a new something that would allow him to leapfrog a gap in his presentation. I was seeing the pattern all too clearly. I was seeing through him. He had the ambition of a guru but no courage to face his own non knowing. True, I was a sucker for the philosophical. But I was an even bigger sucker for thinking out loud together. This wasn't going to happen with Sergei. He was a record broken into a myriad of shards. A kaleidoscope of erudite associations and nothing more!

He did, however, flag a little something that stayed with me for years, a question about whether there is such a thing-less thing as nothing-ness. He never got to that point, merely alluded to it, with that off-putting categoricalness of a nerdy teenager who scoffs at the idiocy of the adult world. I was done with Sergei even if I wasn't yet done with Mila.

I remember a moment when I looked outside through the windows. The sky was pouty with clouds and the gray-green of the trembling leaves had the pleading look of upturned eyes. I borrowed a cigarette from Sergei and stepped out for a piss. Out in the country, with the sky like that, it seemed like a perfect moment to relieve itself. Sergei watched me for a second through the window then turned away. I went out in the field, into the tall uncut grass, unzipped and had a nice long piss.

When I came back up onto the porch I realized that the door had apparently shut locked behind me. I tugged on it a couple of times, to no avail. Through the window I could see that Mila was still sleeping and Sergei had also dozed off in his wheelchair. I looked at my denim jacket hung over the back of the kitchen stool, then at the sky that seemed angrily pregnant and began walking away, through the field.

On the way back, I paused by a curious barn with a wooden gargoyle of a rooster on top of it. I thought, "We are made of three kinds of tissues. A tissue that feels. A tissue that acts. And a tissue that looks inside itself." As I walked I kept asking myself a koan of a question that would last me years, "What does it mean to look inside? Who is looking? And at whom? What am I looking at when I am looking

268

inside at myself?  What does it mean to see with your eyes closed?"

These are the questions that only a self-seeing eye can answer.

The clouds have finally strained out a few harbinger rain drops. The wind died down and an electric scowl of lightening rapped across the low sky. Left behind were Mila's insatiable erotic overtures, Sergei's endless, self-referencing parentheticals and defensively timed metaphors, and something of myself, a *something* that I shed in the course of that encounter. A layer of duality, perhaps.

# Poseidon's Blues

*"I opened myself to the gentle indifference of the world."*

*"I looked up at the mass of stars in the night sky and laid myself open for the first time to the benign indifference of the world."*
— Albert Camus, L'Étranger

*"... and we would say that the child was playing with the things, were it not equally true that the things are playing with the child."*

— Eugen Herrigel, Zen in the Art of Archery

Gods are misanthropes. They tend to abandon their creations too soon. The reason is simple, creation is recreational. They owe us nothing. Gods have no more of an obligation to finish their creations than you have to finish a game of solitaire. Poseidons, among gods, however, are renown for their tenacity. They tend to hang on for a while.

"I am Poseidon," is how this incarnation began for him. To know one's name is to fall into a destiny. To name is to give form. To give form is to set limitations. Limitations are destiny.

Was he a colossus amidst a planet-sized water world or a mere space faring microbe that landed atop an oily speck of cosmic dust? He didn't know. Self unaware as befits a god, he stood waist deep in what seemed like shimmering silver, underneath the fading denim of the sky, alone. As engineered, or shall we say, as divined, his form immediately calibrating itself to the parameters of his landing site, exactly in proportion to the Significance/Insignificance Ratio (S/I-r).

There are at least two existential universals for life − metabolism and worship. Metabolism is a method of existence; to live is to surf an energy gradient of some kind. Worship is a reason for existence; life, once extant, needs no objective justification. Subjectively, all lifeforms strive for a purpose, however illusory, and that's where worship comes in; thus, all worship is a palliative defense against meaninglessness.

Poseidon was both a part and a whole. He knew that much. Or, shall we say, that little. The rest of his self knowledge was to follow.

Each lifeform is holarchically surrounded, on one hand, by lifeforms that are too infinitesimal for us to relate to, and, on the other hand, by lifeforms that are too monumental for us to relate to. The former, the infinitesimally small, are food. The latter, the monumentally big, are gods.

For metabolic and existential reasons, we cannot afford to feel bad for every damn thing that we eat. If a lifeform is infinitesimally smaller than you, it becomes progressively harder to have any empathic compunctions or moral crises about eating it.

Let's face it, to eat someone like you would feel cannibalistic. But we have to eat, right? Right. So, we eat that which is either infinitesimally smaller than us, or, as it goes with some cosmically disordered species, we eat that which we think is very different from us, even if it is of the same approximate size.

In some very cosmically disordered cases, certain species consume their own if they can convince themselves that they are *culturally* different from those "other ones." Such grotesque cases of arbitrary dichotomizing do not tend to be metabolically self-sustaining and inevitably result in a self-correcting collapse of the ecosystem and/or malignant mutations.

At the same time, if a thing is monumentally bigger than you, even if you know from the outset that a difference in quantity does not necessarily mean a difference in quality, with time it becomes progressively harder to continue to identify with it. A sense of awe gets in the way and we begin to worship it. We begin to overlook the originally self evident fact that we are all cut from the same cosmic cloth. We start to forget that we and this magnificent other are but nodes on one and the same seamless continuum of universal manifestation.

The bottom line is, just as we need food, we also need grandeur. Even gods have a need to invent gods.

Poseidon knew this. He knew that, as the S/I-r ratio holds, he, too, was inevitably somewhere in the middle. All life is. We are all nested, bottomlessly and boundlessly, inside a holarchy of form, inside a holarchy that has no outside. We are all sandwiched between indifference and awe, and we are only able to relate with empathy and love to the lettuce of body and the baloney of mind in between, that is in scale with our own.

But for now, Poseidon was alone. The nuance of his existential predicament was yet to reveal itself.

Poseidon also knew that he was a god, and that he had not always been a god.

"This story, my story, is repeated unceasingly, at every coordinate of this boundless cosmos. Eternally. Everyone, every living one gets to play god." thought Poseidon.

He knew he was nothing special. He knew that the Mother Cosmos does not shortchange its own offspring. Every living creature, if given a proper chance, and all will eventually be given such a chance, gets to evolve to become a god. Now was his turn.

There is nothing in the Universe but Matter and Pattern, mother and father. Some dichotomize this Oneness differently as Emptiness and Form. Some are pedantically correct. Emptiness isn't emptiness but Nothingness. Some clarify it further (not without some philosophical merit,) as "not Nothingness, but

No-thingness, i.e. undifferentiated, formless Matter, fatherless mother."

One way or another, that which is conceptually divided in two has to eventually circle back onto its it-less non-self. Why? Because these two are not two; these two are one and the same Oneness. We all know this but we dream different.

It was Poseidon's turn to dream dualities into existence. It was his turn to create.

Only a few life moments ago (and who the hell knows what that means in terms of a reader's time perception) the shimmering silver of the water world and the fading blue gauze of the atmosphere around it grew exponentially larger as Poseidon rushed towards his "mission post." One of trillions of panspermia, a god bomb no less, Poseidon had been traveling through the womb of space, like a ray of light in search of an eye to see it. He finally arrived. He might not have, like billions of his fellow gods in search of a planetary ovum to terraform. But he did. Was it luck? Was it destiny? The dichotomy of chance and determinism is a philosophical condition he was not yet afflicted with. To Poseidon it was simply a dream coming true.

For a moment Poseidon marveled at the calibration of his form according to the S/I-r specs. He had no more to do with this than a sponge has to do with its capacity to soak up water. This size fitting was built-in, a primordial parameter, something long instituted by Mother Matter. There was a nonnegotiable forethought of the love of a single mother that makes sure her offspring will always have something to eat and something to fill their existential vacuum with. Food and worship are the bread and butter of social engineering. Romans of every world knew it. So, too, would the Romans of this water world if Poseidon got his way, if he kept on with his cosmic arcade of playing forms, the game of kid-gods.

Poseidon's impact knocked the planetary object off its orbit, but, like a ball bouncing around the rim of the basket, the planet eventually returned back to the catchment area of its orbit. All matter does. Once differentiated into a given goose bump of form, the ethereal flesh of Mother Matter can not stand an inverted nipple of vacuity.

For a while, Poseidon hid out at the bottom of this water world, watching the waves of the original splash radiate above him on the surface until they eventually cancelled themselves out in a softening arabesque of ever shrinking parallelograms.

While he slept to reduce his metabolic demands, Poseidon dreamt of the lifeforms that he would create. He played the cosmic Lego builder of creation, until his whole inner being was fragmented into a myriad of scrambled shards of botched-up designs and abandoned ideas. Except for one form that he wished to keep, that of a horseshoe crab. He seemed to come back to it again and again, unsure of how he had arrived at the name, until he realized that the obsessive recursion of the dream meant that something was somehow awry.

Immediately, Poseidon awakened, a relative term, really, to realize that he was out of air, something his corporeal form apparently required. This was news to him, just like you, reader, at some point it was news to you that you were breathing air. Remember that curious realization when your mom and dad, or your school teacher, explained that you were inhaling and exhaling air? Are we really? What if we all have been culturally hypnotized to believe that without this air we die? What if we all have been culturally hypnotized that we die period?

The nice thing about being a god is that you are free to deprogram yourself so as to reprogram yourself.

Poseidon, gasping and frenetic, popped to the surface like a buoy. He did not like the feeling and was annoyed by having to breathe. He was going to change that, but right now he had more important things to attend to than to insist on metabolic sovereignty.

There he was, standing waist deep amidst the blue neutrality of the liquid medium that surrounded him, his legs somewhere down below, invisible; his head atop a pyramidal torso somewhere high above.

"How big am I? How small am I?" he kept asking himself. "Size is irrelevant," he kept reassuring himself. Indeed, without reference points, and he had none, his size was up to him. Poseidon turned around, seeing nothing but the shimmering silver of the medium and the fading blue of the sky, and, a bright disk of a star in the middle of the sky. There it is, realized Poseidon, an object of his own worship, something that is monumentally bigger than he.

"Bigger than I am now, that is," he corrected himself. He knew that just a few moments ago, before he was calibrated, he was immeasurable, the size of the Universe which is size-less. Had he landed in the burning medium of the sun, he would have been calibrated to the parameters of *that* landing site. Then he would be, like his panspermic cousin Ra above, terraforming the burning mass into a Sumerian brick, a dirty job as far as he was concerned.

With hands on his hips, Poseidon turned around, surveying the watery domain. There was nothing in sight. There could be nothing in sight. Like an empty mind, this water world was yet to be populated with forms. And yet, Poseidon decided to take a look-see. For what seemed like forever Poseidon traipsed chaotically in every which direction. He'd walk in endless circles in search of land. The terrestrial object which was now his playground seemed seamlessly submerged under the weight of water.

Poseidon had mixed feelings, he both wanted and didn't want this to be true. A single island, if he'd only found it, would have meant that another Poseidon had visited this dreamland before. If so, this Poseidon would feel the curious reassurance that the vision that he had been nursing in his dreams was, in fact, plausible, that his capabilities of creation would probably be on a par with his ability to dream forms into being. If so, if, in fact, another Poseidon had left a footprint of creation on this desolate water world, it wouldn't be the pristine virgin water world toy that every Poseidon god-kid asks for on his birthday.

Reassurance always comes with the cost of disillusionment, doesn't it?

In a world of watery sameness, you simply cannot tell where you are and where you have already been. You can walk in the same circles for years, overlooking a land mass on the other side without ever realizing that you are on this side. Sameness is at least perceptually side-less. One possibility is to try to orient your self to something fixed in the sky, to go by the sun. Although that celestial reference point would still have to be triangulated against some terrestrial counterpart. And no such thing yet existed. Poseidon wasn't yet ready to look up to his Ra for guidance. (Gods suck at worship, you know). So Poseidon sleepwalked on the presumption that the longer he walked, circling the water covered sphere, the less chance there would be that he had missed something. It was as good a plan as any. As with many hypotheses, it wasn't really being tested in earnest as much as it was really being confirmed.

Sleepwalking and walking are not two separate things. Sleeping and waking are not two separate things. A mind free of such distinctions simply is, knowing no time and no boredom. Such was Poseidon's state of mind on this exploratory walk-about. When he eventually stopped, he was not quite sure why. Perhaps, it occurred to him, he was finally feeling alone and starting to crave company, which involved the work of creation. Then again, he debated with himself, isn't all companionship an illusion anyway?

There are two vectors of seeing – inside and outside. But seeing isn't just seeing. Seeing is also moving. Seeing is a movement of consciousness. Thus, there are two vectors of moving – inside and outside. This dichotomy is also known as being and becoming.

Place yourself within a so-called physical space and it becomes instantly clear that you have the option to walk away from where you are. Having done so, you can return back to where you started, but, just as you return to where you had started from, you would be leaving where you had just been. It's always like that. Any physical motion, which is change, is always away from your current state of self. Among gods, this is known as socializing. To socialize is to enter into another – another being, another space, another object, another moment. Socializing, or movement away from your here and now self, is thus a form of becoming. We become the space that we enter, we become the company that we keep, and we become the stimuli that we attend to. Becoming is a change of self. A change of self is a loss of self. A loss of self is a thirst that plagues all lifeforms. Becoming is a leaving.

The other vector is that of being. Being is staying, staying put, no, not where you are, but staying yourself, staying the same. Being involves no motion, no change, and no transmutation. It begins with wherever you are, with whoever you are, with however you are. It also ends right then and there. It is a form of seeing inside. Not inside of yourself physically, but inside your phenomenological self.

There are three eyes, two belong to your body and one belongs to your mind. Two eyes look out. One looks in. The two eyes that look out see the seen. The one that looks inside sees no difference between the seer and the seen. The living awareness that pervades us, not as some kind of ethereal turkey stuffing, but through and through, without a single vacuole of emptiness, simply notices its omnipresent, un-circumscribed, un-differentiated non-Self and rests in its own am-ness.

If this is confusing, it's okay. Confusion is a prerequisite to enlightenment. A mind that knows is a door that is shut. A confused mind is an open door.

The sages of old have long understood that this is a form of socializing, not with someone in particular, but with Everything, with the Oneness itself, with that which we all share as the backdrop to our dream of separateness. This Oneness is inherently communal and self unifying. Whoever drinks from this well, even just once, never gets thirsty again. Poseidons, as a species of gods, were among the first to discover this well and, therefore, have been a kind of monastic avant garde of populating the Universe.

Sure, just like this particular Poseidon, Poseidons weren't strangers to cravings. They yearned for company in their way. Each Poseidon on a mission wanted to dissolve oneself among his own creations, only to hibernate as a latent god monad within one's own offspring, awaiting an eventual moment of

280

awakening, a moment of self recognition. As far as socialization goes, this kind had none of that trivial me too quality that is so often found among lesser gods and the less mature sapient species that are still caught up in a futile attempt to validate their un-witnessed lives. Poseidons do not wish to be worshipped. They require no halo. They are the halo that blinds the mind's eye. They are the very light that illuminates us all from within.

The craving for company, in the case of this Poseidon, was the craving for creation, a craving to manifest rather than be witnessed. And so our Poseidon began, not without trial and error. The learning curve of creation is fraught with spiraling detours of near circularity, but it does eventually wind up, like a vine, in its obsequious attempt to kiss the sun.

The first order of business was to terraform, to create land. Equipped with nothing more than divine instincts, Poseidon squatted deep down under the surface of the water and forced his powerful hands, elbow deep, into what seemed like the core of the planet. He could feel the scorching burn of lava on the tips of his fingers but winced not even once. With excavating motions, he tried to bring out the molten ore of the planet to the surface, dumping it down into the ocean to cool it off. He was building a mount, a tower, really; stacking up layers of rocks and lava like bricks and mortar. Things were going much easier than he had imagined. He had heard horrors about the unforeseen complexities of this process. Yet, strangely, things were progressing flawlessly. The layered cake of giant boulders finally pierced the surface of the water world, jutting out like a primordial ziggurat. Poseidon decided to call it a day. He climbed atop the still hot mount and jumped into the murky abyss of water. Closing his eyes, he allowed himself to sink to the bottom of the ocean, where he gathered himself up into a kind of knot, wrapping his arms around his knees and tucking his head in between his knees, and settled down into a work-sleep. There was much to dream up, much to test out in the virtual lab of imagination. Time, as always, was of no essence.

Awaking from a dream into the lucid dream of daydreaming that we call "life" can feel like a movement from point A to pointB. There is a misleading discreteness to this transition, a sense that everything that seemed so real to you a moment ago is now suddenly irrelevant fiction; and whatever is real now is really real, unmistakably real, truly real. The lucidity of our waking dream isn't that of knowing that we are dreaming but, on the contrary, that of not knowing that we are dreaming. It's the lucidity of agency. The waking life is really a dream of agency, a dream of choice and free will and self determination. Unlike the mostly egoless dreams of the night, in which an experience is lived without a particularly firm point of view, the daydream that we call "being awake" is a self absorbing fantasy of "reality out there happening to me right here." This lucidity is a dualistic illusion that I,the dreamer, can control this dream that is happening all around me. Just because we can dream that we can control the dream it doesn't mean that we are actually awake, right? Sometimes, when we experience this kind of lucid dreaming at night, we somehow write it off as "lucid dreaming," i.e. as a strange, dubiously desirable form of dreaming. But when the very same lucid dreaming occurs when the sun is up, we somehow conclude that we are not dreaming at all, that we are awake. We aren't. No one is. The Universe is asleep. And you are a dream that dreams itself at your most lucid. At your least lucid you are someone else's dream. These two are so close that even gods can't tell the difference most of the time. Neither could this Poseidon.

-

"Life," said the elder Poseidon gods, "is an exercise in playing god, a cosmic game with a learning curve that thins itself into an asymptote of near nothingness between the x-axis of ambition and the y-axis of love. This meandering moral line eventually finds it home near the abscissa of love or the ordinate of ambition. The axis that gets to keep this asymptote hostage is what sorts out good gods from bad, fools from sages, and bodhisattvas from Stalins." Our Poseidon was at the zero point of his karmic project. Or was he? Is the Universe itself free of its karmic baggage? It is improbable.

What awakened Poseidon wasn't the need to breathe but the fact that he was freely breathing. Somehow, and he didn't yet know why, he was only half submerged in the ocean. It didn't make sense. He had sunk to the deep bottom to sleep in the metallic silt of this water world earth, yet the water had somehow receded while he had been asleep. He got up to his feet, towering high enough over the surface of the planet to nearly tip its axis. The water that had been once to his waistline was now sloshing around his thighs. The horizon provided the clue as to what had happened, a column of white steam was rising up into the sky. The hole he had dug through the crust of the mantle was now evaporating the ocean into atmosphere. In no time, Poseidon knocked down the hardened ziggurat he'd built the day before and plugged the hole in the mantle to stop the process of evaporation. His hands were bleeding and peeling. He held them up to his face, as someone in the first agony of grief, the blue hemocyanin blood dripping down his forearms and into the water, diffusing into the ocean of this newfangled earth project.

The weight of the consequences forced him to sit down and close his eyes. He was looking within, peering into the light of his own being, into that curious light that is only visible with the eyes closed. Had he already failed? Had he, in his ambition, rushed? As his mind posed these questions, he knew that they mattered more than any answers he'd ever give to himself. The question of concern and caution is the seedling of love, the spawn of hovering, and maternal care.

It started to rain. The earth saved itself from its own demise. No, not Poseidon, but the planet itself! In some blind homeostatic self care, the planet refused to become another barren satellite to a god's failed ambition. The atmosphere, something in it, some fortuitous composition, was returning the water back to its watery home. Poseidon opened his eyes and began to cry, his blue tears mixing in with the sooty rainfall. The previously placid table of the ocean was now pockmarked with the rocks and chunks of baked silt that, in abeyance of gravity, were returning to earth as well. Poseidon realized that he must have slept through some powerful explosions. How careless, how thoughtless he had been! How primitive and rushed had been his calculations! Was he even thinking ahead or just acting on his first creative impulse?

"Gods are always like that," echoed someone's thought through his mind. Who said that? Who planted this land mine of a caution in his psyche; a land mine that failed to go off in time?

The crisis passed. Poseidon knew it. The ocean was now placid as before, just a bit warmer, that's all. The water had risen, not to its original level, but close enough. The ecological catastrophe had been averted. Poseidon could play again. But he didn't want to. At least, not right now, maybe, never again. He was exhausted by what happened. Like any toddler god, he was disgusted with the trivial fact that reality sometimes doesn't cooperate, even with gods.

In the days that followed, Poseidon did nothing. It was a pitiful sight, a toddler god in a sandbox full of toys, motionless, inert, heartbroken. Motionless on the outside, at least. On the inside, Poseidon was restless. In a disjointed dialogue with himself and the archetypes of his consciousness, he was maturing like a stalk of bamboo on meth. "It's just too bad," he'd think now and then, "that no one is here to witness my growth, the gold that I've made out of this shit of suffering, the lessons I have already learned and pre-learned for millennia ahead." This hunger for validation was childish and he knew it and would psychologically flagellate himself without mercy as soon as he realized he was doing it, once again turning the shit of self-pity into the platinum of acceptance.

It seemed to have been forever since Poseidon had fortified himself with any kind of food. Perhaps it had been an actual forever. Before Poseidon manifested as the amphibian colossus that he now was, he existed as a plane of purified awareness, the proto-material sap of Nature. Unlike the species of Ra gods, he knew that his was a liquid element to conquer, but he didn't live off water. He lived, as essentially all life forms do, off information. A plane of being, whether it belongs to a mature god, a god-child, or a god to be, lives off a gradient of change that is in line with its dream. A lock, to feel full, has to eat a key, so to say. The relative emptiness of our existence, the coordinate of our being, has to somehow be filled. Since this emptiness is not a true spatial vacancy but a lacuna of virgin proto-matter, it yawns with an appetite for differentiation. Differentiation, a taking of a form, is, after all, a process of individuation, a satisfaction of the narcissistic hunger that plagues the Universe.

In Poseidon's case, the hunger could only be satisfied through creation. To clarify, that would have been the shortcut. The real cessation of hunger was through hunger itself. When allowed to linger, hunger cures itself. When plumbed to its logical depths, it renders itself irrelevant, which, if you know the feeling, is true satisfaction, a satisfaction of an open ended kind. Poseidon, however, was nowhere near this level of such asceticism. He was ready to feast. He dreamt of exotic fruits and grasses and roots. He dreamt of peapods of rainbow-colored nuts, of delicious pollen wet with the dew of a storm, of chewy nougat bark and of fire hot peppers. He dreamt of pinecones dipped in psychedelic sap, of mushrooms skewered around the last ray of the sun, of a thousand and one subtle tastes, of unfathomed, unfeeling delicacies that provoked no pangs of compassion, of chicken ants that performed hara-kiri to die in the palace of his mouth, and of fleshy dragonflies wanting to melt dead on the fiery altar of his tongue.

Truth be told, none of this was original in the least. In the first three eternities of the Universe, Mother Matter was maniacally preoccupied with inventing food, which resulted in a most exhaustive Platonic menu of life forms that doubled up as food forms. The Upanishadic thinkers, on a planetary project that had once inspired our Poseidon, were right, "Verily, all is food. Eaters of food, we are food too." Or something near that. On any earth, earth is eating earth.

Designing food and designing life is one and the same. No sooner had Poseidon imagined what he would love to taste, an idea of a life form would emerge in his mind. The truth, be it sad or good, is that everything has a taste. Every part of us is of meaning to some other part of this self-devouring whole that is the Universe. Gods like Poseidon love to play the game of designing a world that joyfully and willingly devours itself in a zero regret ouroboric ecstasy. Legions of living Buddhist monks (a Platonic meme common to most worlds) climbed sequoia trees and gave themselves up willingly to buzzards and fire ants. Like a cascading nesting doll, smaller fish leaped into the mouths of bigger fish ad infinitum. Flowers with psychedelic intensity uprooted themselves and walked their own pollen to lethargic bees who, in turn, with stoic acceptance, flew into gigantic cobwebs as already satiated spiders lined up to crawl into the cavernous throats of rattle snakes. Each life form made a sacrifice of love to its predator, paying it forward on the behalf of its fellows, thus, eliminating any need for fear.

Alas, Poseidon's vision was not to be a paradise after all. As the matter of terraforming kept creeping into his mind, he'd again and again escape into the ecstatic fractals of his modeling fantasy. He knew that first there had to be land; that he'd have to revisit the nagging issue of terra firma, that life needed fiords and mountains, caves and grasses, and even deserts. Without land there simply was no point to his mission. Poseidons specialized in taming water worlds, plain and simple.

There here were also other threats to his vision, perhaps even more menacing, definitely more menacing. He knew, for example, that as soon as he'd give birth to vegetation, his green children would immediately begin to worship Ra. He knew each plant was in love with light and reified its love into sun worship. For a moment, Poseidon opened his eyes and launched himself off the bottom of the ocean, torpedo-like, into the world of light above. The dazzling fire of the nearby sun commanded instant compliance, he had to squint. Had to! He had no choice in the matter, that was the power of the fire gods. He knew nothing of the Ra that ruled the nearby sun. But he knew that the local sun had long been under divine construction. A typically passive orb in its natural state, the local sun had a nimbus of perfectly arranged fire tongues, a clear sign of "sun-gineering." Ras always preceded Poseidons – a cosmic rapid reaction force.

To say that the two god tribes worked in some kind of unison was to definitely overstate the matter. Ras and Poseidons mixed no better than oil and water. They mingled but did not mix. The tension between these two god species seemed to predate the Universe itself. The story, nowadays told less and less often, was that Mother Matter was growing cold, so she manifested a million hands and a totem pole that split the observable expanse of What Is like a diameter that cuts a circle in half. She placed her endless hands on the totem and stuck it into her own belly, right into the navel of All That Is. Naturally, if you can begin to imagine this, the pole pierced right through her, half of it on one side and half on the other side. The disembodied hands began to rub the post, but there was no agreement among these hands. To cut a long story short, the stick managed to produce exactly two effects, an expanding yin yang sphere of fire and water. Mother Matter, in frustration, broke the stick in half and birthed the two god species, the Ras and the Poseidons, to clean up the resulting cosmic mess. Naturally, all who exist on the plane of gods understand that it is nothing but a geometrically impossible myth. But we pay tribute to the past and retell the story since no other account has yet been given.

To have your offspring worship another progenitor is the ultimate wound to the ego that most mortals don't survive. For Poseidon, this was not a deal breaker. The part that gave him shivers was the responsibility that comes with the dirty business of creation. The fact is that most fire worlds and water worlds are long abandoned labs. Whenever gods glimpse the horror of the unintended, they simply run off. Most gods, you see, are deadbeat gods. Poseidon knew this but the instinct of creation was too convincing. It is something in the nature of being a Primal Cause that is obsessive and un-free. As our Poseidon returned into the far reaching blueprints of his dream world, he ran another simulation. It seemed that he was plum out of tricks. No matter what he envisioned, life, once begat, was destined to compete with each other. And that was the beginning of the end, the beginning of fear, and the end of love. The ouroboric paradigm in which the snake tail would chase the mouth of its own body to willingly satisfy its hunger would suddenly reverse and now the mouth of the snake would be chasing its own tail in insatiable hunger. That was the horror!

Poseidon wasn't ready to give up. He believed in the miracle of time. Just as time is said to heal all wounds, time is also said to solve all problems. Poseidon knew of the Rubicon of no return, and he was nowhere near it. He hadn't even created a sustainable plateau of land for his fantasies to play out. He still had time. His plan was simple, if not naïve. He would work on the matter of the land and sleep on the thorny zero sum boomerang that lurked in his dreams.

Days, which are inevitably measured with periods of rest and not necessarily through alterations of light and darkness, went mercilessly by, to no avail. The terraforming plan just wasn't coming together. Poseidon, abandoned to his mission, wracked his mind in search of a solution. But how do you square a circle? How can you create something out of nothing? He soon realized the koan nature of this challenge. This was the old problem of creation, the cosmogonic riddle of whether the Universe can have any genesis. He knew the answer, something cannot come from nothing. The Universe that he was tasked to govern, at this given coordinate, was beginningless: it had always been and will always be. To the extent that land in this water world had to be created out of nothing, the terraforming challenge was dead in the water, the problem simply could not be solved.

His original solution (to dig up some mantle rock and stack it up), as rushed as it was, proved, after all, the only solution worth considering, ecologically catastrophic consequences notwithstanding. Therein was some consolation. Poseidon, at least, stopped beating himself up. In retrospect, the overall idea was the only idea that made general sense. He spent his days running careful simulations. He did some dry runs on patching up the holes in the mantle. That worked, but only with unexpectedly small diameters. He tested evaporation rates by scooping the water and letting it patiently evaporate from the palms of his hands. He ran endless calculations, testing for such variables as multiple small scale excavation sites balanced against daytime and nighttime evaporation rates. But, he was no fan of statistics and confidence intervals. He searched for certainty. The last thing he wanted to do was to ruin this perfectly fine little water world.

Ahimsa, the ancient doctrine of non-violence and non-harm, a cosmic ethics, so to say, is after all misleading. Existence without some kind of collateral damage is a fantasy. Gods are silent about this amongst themselves. Most, by the time they reach maturity, realize that to exist, just to exist, is already violence. Existence is the taking of a form. The taking of a form is a taking of a life. The taking of a life for one's self eventually leads to taking someone else's life. Whether or not we live to see the cascading finale of our own karma, is irrelevant. The metaphysics are clear on this point, to take a form, to differentiate at point A, in this here that you call your being; something has to be homogenized, i.e. extinguished at point B.

Life is formation. Yes, of course, the Universe itself is living. And, yes, of course, no one really disappears because there is really no one to begin with, no one but the living Universe itself. And the Universe has nowhere to go, just like it has nowhere to come from. All stays, in essence, the same. Forms come and go, and the pockets of this Universe that take a form, with time, cling to it enough to totally identify with it, and for these sorry states of being a loss of form does feel like a loss of life.

While this cosmic grief is brief, it is intense. Any sentient creature, let alone a god, has, or, at least, should have. compassion for any such suffering. So, we are all guilty. If there is an original sin, it is that we chose to exist, chose to take form, and, in so doing, chose to take another life.

Yes, there is a way out of this samsaric mess, but it's not through meditation which is in such vogue on so many worlds. Meditation is a dream of release. The real release, well, that's for suicidal gods, a method that our Poseidon also has up his long, wet sleeve, a method that will, in due time, have to, by the logic of compassion, have to use.

-

Love and gravity are psycho-physical twins. They are an unstoppable duo that holds the Universe in place (not that it has anywhere to go). Any orbit is a relationship, whether macro- or microscopic. When we look out of our telescopes, we are really just looking inside ourselves, the objects we see are beings in a dynamic interplay of attachment. However, one object  that cannot be seen in this Universe, and that has to be inferred by the behavior of the objects around it, is a black hole. A misleading name since there are no holes in the seamless flesh of this boundless Oneness that is the Universe. Black holes are best understood as garbage disposals. Universally speaking, any ego, or fixity, is garbage. Any notion of "self," be it a nomadic asteroid, or a polyp in your colon; any structure, fixity, or auto-poietically self-maintaining island of stability amidst the ocean of quantum oscillation, is garbage.

We are talking about all form here. Form is the result of formation. Formation is movement away from your original self. Any formation, evolution, or growth is ultimately the narcissism of individuation. To individuate, to become an individual, a self, is to attempt to separate from the womb of All That Universally Is. The true self is undifferentiated. The true self is Oneness. Oneness (in its it-less no-self) is the only living individual, i.e. indivisible, that actually is. The rest is maya (illusion). Whatever you see, and we can only orient our vision to objects, not space, is a sorry attempt of a coordinate of this Oneness to become its own stand-alone Oneness. This, of course, is a recipe for suffering and karmic collateral damage, since any such attempt at separation involves isolation; any isolation has a perimeter; and any perimeter belongs to a shape. To take a shape is to take a life.

This is where black holes enter. Black holes de-differentiate. They strip off all form. Black holes, like your run-of-the-mill garbage disposal or meat grinder, homogenize. Black holes are gravity traps, and gravity is love, if you will recall. Egos, selves, and forms are hungry for validation of their pseudo-separateness. All forms seek witnessing and mirroring. This promise of validation and mirroring is the sticky flytrap tape that sooner or later captures the attention of the thirsting egos. After all, the best way to be noticed is to be invisible. For eons, black holes have mesmerized all forms. Over time, space faring soul collectives, atomic hives that have agglomerated into stellar dust, even sightseeing gods, anything and everything, somehow become magnetized by the insatiable hunger of gravity. If you've somehow managed to keep an enlightening distance from the black holes, they will come to you. Black holes, like traveling stains on a tablecloth, get pulled in every direction, scavenging the ego plankton of the Universe like starry bottom feeders.

Legions of thwarted Poseidons and Ras have euthanized themselves by walking the one way labyrinth of a local black hole.

-

Our Poseidon knew of this option; an option that was at his self disposal at all times. One he recognized he wasn't above in a philosophical sense. Any god is ever willing to drink the hemlock of self annihilation. Most gods eventually make this choice; each at their own timing.

Poseidon, still hungering for creation, no longer able to sustain himself on the empty calories of virtual stimulation and dreamland scenarios, was finally ready to create. In fact, he had even figured out how to solve the matter of land.

He had a plan, a plan that could actually work! But, before he could get to it, there were so many other things to pilot in his mind.

-

He couldn't wait. Gods are a notoriously impatient breed. It seems that when you have an eternity of time, you no longer feel at its mercy, instead you become entitled to it, like a child that grows up in a family with servants becomes entitled to being served. For mortals, time is more powerful than a god. There is no appeasing it and no negotiating with it through prayers. For mortals, time is a poker face carved into Mt. Rushmore. For gods, time is a servant and each now is an instantly satisfied whim.

Unless, of course, one wishes to test things out in what is sometimes called "real time." When a god, like our Poseidon, takes time to imagine how such and such scenarios would play out in "real time," he is, in fact, testing out a scenario in "imaginary time." But time, as imagined by gods, is so vastly different than the real time that is lived by mortals. Only the most astute gods are sensitive to this. In god's imagination "real time" is just time, just pure mathematical duration. Since gods know nothing about passive waiting that victimizes us mortals, they can hardly imagine the kind of time that we mortals, are sentenced to. Thus, gods take time to run their imaginary "real time" simulations and remain utterly oblivious to the fact that they are overlooking the variable of mortal impatience.

This is but one way in which things get derailed in this Universe, a way that the likes of our Poseidon couldn't be bothered with. There is only one thing that's worse than someone else's impatience and that is patiently waiting on someone else to become impatient and then waiting the others' impatience out. Any 21$^{st}$ century parent waiting on a toddler in the back of the SUV to fall asleep knows what I am talking about. Not gods! Not gods in their infinite wisdom, eh!

-

Like a kid planning a bar mitzvah, or like a teenage girl trying out a prom dress, Poseidon was giddy with planning. Most of it was akin to pick and click shopping. You see, there is nothing new in this Universe. Like a WalMart that has always been, it is chock full of Platonic ideas.

Of course, there were no shells or crates or shipping docks with truckloads of price tag revelations. All this wealth of possibilities existed at each and every coordinate of this boundless Oneness – holographically! The inventory was continuously updated. Each "new" idea, which is just a novel synthesis of the old elements, was instantly added to the holographic depository that can be accessed (by going deep within) at any coordinate of All That Is.

We find Poseidon shopping; shopping for a world that he wished to populate. He had already taken care of the basics. The wedding cake of reality was already more or less laid out. Right now he was in the process of touching up a few minor details.

He was the first reader of all the future books, because to write is to read. With delirious ease, he was downloading the cosmic favorites. "The Little Prince," "Stranger," "From Here to Eternity," "Cat in the Hat." These memes belonged to no Joyce or Camus or Dr. Seuss or Dostoevsky. Any inspired writer would tell you that inspiration is more akin to transcription than creation. The "creatives" of the world are not much more than antennae. The ones that are well-tuned, reflect the signal with great fidelity. If you were to read "The Little Prince" that is written on two different worlds by two first class antennae, you'd be essentially reading the same book. But when the antenna is not well-tuned, there is a lot of creative noise along with the signal. In which case, the little prince becomes a plus-sized princess.

-

The final touches always take longer than expected, thus, the tendency to rush through them (an easy way to tell amateur work from professionalism). Most gods are amateurs. Most gods, having played god once, never play god again. Most, in fact, abandon their castles to the sands of time. Most gods are deadbeat gods, too suicidal to pay any alimony of attention to their creations.

Was our Poseidon special? Not really. Did he think he was? Of course he did.

-

Having imagined and tested in "real time" everything that mattered to him, he was finally ready to feast on his creation (informationally speaking, that is). He was ready to bring forth what he had imagined and thought and planned. His vision, once materialized, would, he hoped, eventually be filed in the annals of godwork to serve as an inspiration to other gods about the range of worldly possibilities. The worst case scenario was that his world would be a case study for lessons to be learned – a carefully conducted experiment of collective existence, methodically supervised and carefully chaperoned by a benign supernatural hand.

What Poseidon didn't know was that manna from heaven would also turn out to be manna from hell. There is no other manna; to eat is to kill.

-

Having pre-kissed every future pair of lips and having pre-shrunk every future pair of jeans, having taken care of all possibly relevant and irrelevant future details, and, unwittingly but predictably, having ignored every uncomfortable misfire in the calculated chain of cause and effect, our kid-god, our cute little colossus, Poseidon. was now to kick off, with streamers and balloons, the birthday party of our earth.

-

Poseidon got up, bursting through the film of the surface like a rocket launch from a submarine. Water cascaded down his muscular shoulders and sculpted torso. He was a vision of a maritime god; a sea monster minus the trident. Feeling with his feet,

Poseidon located the site of his prior excavation, the rocky elevation that was the burial site of his original effort, the navel of lava.

He was returning to his original plan (which was really no plan after all); this time more methodically. Equipped with data on evaporation rates, the temperature of the lava, the flow rate capacity, daytime and nighttime atmospheric temperatures, condensation rates, etc., etc., he was finally ready to try once more. Land had to be formed. This was of paramount importance, a Poseidon imperative, no less. Without terra firma this water world was a non-starter.

-

Geology as fieldwork, is for nerds, for adventurous nerds, but still for nerds. Academic geology is for true nerds, the kind of nerds for whom a bowel movement has seismic significance. I won't bore you with descriptions of what happened. I'll fast forward through the boring part, which is also the bad part, and treat you to the end of this story. I have bad news and really bad news for you. Poseidon was wrong once again; his calculations proved to be, once again, inadequate. That's the bad news. Unlike the first time around, the planet could no longer repair itself the way it did the first time. That's the really bad news. Poseidon was shocked.

The water receded and the sky was black with soot. Poseidon, standing ankle deep amidst muddy waters, looked like a toddler who had just waded into a puddle wanting to play and suddenly realized that his socks were wet.

"This sucks," thought Poseidon and plopped down on his butt. Wrapping his arms around his knees and tucking his glorious head in between his knees, he went within, again, to escape what had now become of his world.

-

Time passed. When unattended and not waited upon, time has a way of passing fast. How much time? Who knows.;  maybe enough time for a miracle.

-

Poseidon didn't want to awaken but had to. Not because of the light that tickled his eyelids, but because of a curious warmish sensation in his posterior. Cautiously he opened his eyes. What a joy! He saw, once again, the shimmering silver of the ocean, the fading denim of the sky, and an atoll of created land mass. "How, how is this possible?" It had seemed like such a disaster, had seemed so hopeless. It actually was; Poseidon was yet to figure it out. Before he could answer the question he had just posed to himself, he had to address the now hottish sensation in his posterior. "What is going on down there?"

The answer was obvious. When Poseidon plopped down into the rakish boiling soup of the water world that was about to evaporate, he had inadvertently plugged the opening in the mantle.

The pain of heat, for Poseidon, was a curious event, an event that felt quite distant from his typical corner of consciousness. While he was acutely aware of the intensifying sensation, the sensation felt "somewhere there," but not quite where he, Poseidon, was. "Where was he, after all," he asked himself? "Where is my being, my am-ness, my sense of self?" The obvious answer was "here." But where is this "here"? Is this "here" separate from "there" where he felt the pain? How could he feel the pain "there" unless he was there too? Aren't we everywhere we feel? If we feel in our toes, doesn't that mean we are also there?

The pain had now reached an unmistakable threshold of agony. Poseidon had to have a plan. He knew that moving away was not an option. Moving away, as Poseidon knew, was always a change of state, exactly what he personally needed right now. but this change of state would also be an abandonment of his vision, of his long term plan, which by now meant a loss of self. Poseidon's only option was to go within, back to his original self, into the self diffusing vortex of am-ness that, like a built-in black hole, homogenizes the differentiated, and strips down the onion layers of ego to its nirvanic coreless core.

Again, Poseidon closed his eyes as the Ra above looked down on Poseidon's familiar predicament. Ras know infinitely more about self-immolation than any Poseidons.

-

The story of how Mother Matter rubbed the two tribes of gods – Poseidons and Ras – is, of course, apocryphal. The reality is a well hidden secret; hidden for good reasons. No 2.0 wants to remember that it once was a 1.0. Ras began as Poseidons, the way our Poseidon right now was turning into a Ra.

-

Poseidon's solution was that of a Buddhist monk, a Platonic archetype available at any point of creation and re-creation. Poseidon just sat there, in what you might call a *zazen*. His previously sculpted form has begun to melt into a radiating heap of rock. He jutted out of the water like an iceberg of plasma, a column of billowing steam rising from what Buddhist monks across the Universe call *phowa*, a hole on top of the head. Poseidon had been homogenized, liquefied into a mass of fiery water, a lava-like substance that was just a tad too cool to flow like a river. And so he sat, a liquid ziggurat of plasma, forever oblivious to his physical state.

"So, this is how I go, how I die into my future. This is how I become everything I dreamed I would be," thought Poseidon. That was exactly how it went, how he died into his future, how he became everything he had dreamed he would be, everything that you and I are currently are.

-

As always, time went by unnoticed and the once colloidal fiery mass of Poseidon had cooled off one millionth of a degree at a time, as the grateful ocean licked it with its foamy tongues. The planet went on with its own geologically mindless, terraforming business, revolving around its axis, orbiting around its sun. Tides hammered away at the cliff-like sides of the landmass that our Poseidon had once raised from the depths. The god-mad continent was now thriving. Life had gone about its business. The organic traces of Poseidon's existence had finally repurposed themselves into primordial life forms. The billions of skin cells that had been abraded off his feet whenever he had walked the rocky bottom of the water world had been sown like soul seeds all across the globe. The blue blood that had bled from his fingertips when he'd dug up the mantle rock now ran through horseshoe crabs that he had once so enthusiastically envisioned. Life was everywhere and it was through and through Poseidon himself. Not one creature, no matter the size, was free of Poseidon's presence. Many of these creatures were beginning to awaken to this ghostly presence within. Monks were busy humming, philosophers were busy picking their noses, lovers saw themselves in the stars of the night sky, flowers wove psychedelic tapestries of silent worship, and birds chirped in forgotten Sanskrit. Nothing made sense, but everything prospered.

The world wasn't free of shadows. Not at all. Everything that had haunted the dream lab of Poseidon's mind had also come true. Endless wars, among ants, among apes that called themselves humans, and between antiseptic hand lotions and hospital bacteria. Endless wars were being constantly waged. Husbands beat wives. Wives beat husbands. Parents killed kids. Kids killed parents. Eating fat was first good, then bad, then good again. Sunbathing was first good, then bad, then good again. The world seemed lost in a circle of self-imposed suffering. Books about happiness were being issued on the paper made out of 10,000 year old sequoias. Nobody read anymore and everybody wrote. Species stood in line for supremacy, first dolphins, then squids, then cockroaches. The animal kingdom waited on the curious apes that ran the planet to wipe themselves out and the doomsday clock had long been stuck on midnight.

-

Had Poseidon himself been spared the bad news that his paradise was stillborn? Not exactly. Gods have a way of lingering in disguise. Still a mountain, but now with a heavenly beach beard of white sand, Poseidon listened to the feet of the surfers, the happiest feet on Earth. But, surfers were a poor sample of what was going on, bopping up and down for hours on their boards, waiting for the big wave, they traded jokes and love stories, drank Red Bull and smoked weed. As carefree as gods, they exuded bliss, and Poseidon was proud of his creation. He liked what he saw in the mirror of his progeny. sculpted bodies and empty minds, the best of the best. An occasional beach comber, looking for shells, always gave him pause.

"How could it be," he asked himself, that people, when faced with the ineffable big picture of nature, would escape into the trivial collection of shells that only a moment ago, before they arrived on a vacation, had no interest to them. Poseidon connected the dots. Out there, out of his sight, from where tired souls made their pilgrimage to the ocean, there must be so much suffering that these life-beaten minds simply could not face the reality of their insignificance when confronted with the grandeur of space. What this meant to Poseidon is that the world, the world he made, *his* world, few exceptions aside, was more jungle than paradise, more of an arena of ambition than a cradle of love. More his agony than his ecstasy.

What it meant was that the asymptote of divine balance was clinging to the wrong axis. The gravity of love was repurposed as the magnet of ambition.

-

Poseidon did not want to believe this sneaking realization. He needed to make sure. He knew that he had been dispersed all around his world. He wished to communicate with himself, with the Diaspora of his Presence. First, the Diaspora of his Presence had to be awakened. In some ways, he was always in touch with himself, no matter how many places he was in. Just as two ocean sponges can be shredded to a cellular size and mixed in, they would still reassemble with their own kind, he, too, was quantum-entangled with all parts of himself, non-locally at any location. Backing the critical mass, each and every one of the outposts of him lacked the amplification to send a strong enough signal for the rest of him, concentrated in this far-away mountain, to hear. The signals still reached him but they were too soft, a meaningless static of worry that plagued him day-to-day. So, he devised a simple test, a test for humankind, a test for humankind's happiness, a test for the surfers whose bodies he had gilded with fine sand every day.

-

Poseidons are gods of limited magic. Strangely, they are incapable of metamorphosis on demand. While they can evolve into anything in response to the demands of the environment, they can hardly command a form on demand. What would have been simple for, say, a Ra or an Enlil or a Shiva, was impossible for a Poseidon. He needed a figure head, an actor, a proxy. He needed a human to be able to engage with another human to find out what he needed to know. He had to find one, and once had, he'd hack into his soul, into *his own* soul, with all his might, and take the person's consciousness hostage, make it his mouthpiece. It was a tricky project, but totally doable; kid's play for god-kids.

Poseidon, a maritime god, knew a couple of useful shortcuts towards this end. All he needed was a floater, a drowned man that he could revive. A drowning mind is a mind of confusion. People on fire, for example, are very focused, very intent on one thing, they run and flail and roll, completely convinced that running and flailing and rolling must be done. When on fire, the mind is not tentative, it is painfully certain of what has to happen. A mind like that is a closed door. A mind on fire is perhaps the most closed mind on Earth. Many a god tried to bang on that door but to no avail. A drowning mind is an entirely different matter. A drowning mind is confused, befuddled, and utterly uncertain, even of gravity, which is down or up. As such, a drowning mind is almost an invitation to programming, to hacking, to influence. Thus, we have the dubious utility of water boarding.

Poseidon was not going to water board anyone. He simply tickled the heels of a random surfer who was bopping up and down on small fry waves. Spooked by recent reports of shark attacks, the surfer panicked, abandoned the board and began swimming towards shore. Poseidon, whose rocky shoulders constituted the bottom of this beachhead, simply shrugged creating a powerful riptide. The surfer. in confusion. inhaled a lungful of water instead of air and began to sink. That's when Poseidon came in.

-

The acquaintance with another psyche is like vacuuming floors; easy-peasy for a god who is used to populating a space with himself. The mind in question belonged to some Dima Tokarev, a scion of a Russian billionaire, who's twenty or so years of life amounted to a whole lot of good surfing and sorting out the nuances of his sexual orientation. Poseidon shook no hands; with his presence he elbowed Dima out and high jacked Dima's body like it was some kind of RV (which it really was, was it not?).

Poseidon, clad in Dima's body, re-emerged out of the troubled waters to the triumphant shrieks of his friends who, by now, were in a full state of alarm. Half a dozen or so of his buddies witnessed Dima's disappearance and had by now given up any notion that he could still make it. Then there he was, re-emerging like some kind of Poseidon. Few surfers nowadays believe in water gods like Neptune or Poseidon, but most have a mental image of what these sea monsters would look like. For a moment Dima embodied one, the Poseidon within was in a mood to show off. He did not merely re-emerge, he burst out with a battle cry, his body a perfect cross of crucifixion, like a human torpedo, crushing his chest down into the swell of the wave and morphing into an unstoppable butterfly stroke machine that cut through the waves like a shark.

A god to himself and still a human to others, Poseidon walked out on the shore with the glorious strut of a Roman legionnaire, refused the small talk and retired to a shade of a loblolly pine that grew on the beach. He waived away his girlfriend who came out with a drink and settled in to wait.

-

Finally the Ra above called it a day and the evening began with a volley of trembling waves and a refreshing breeze. The drama of the day was forgotten. The surfer dudes changed camp and the newly embodied Poseidon was left to himself. He stood up and began to walk. A tide pool nearby, a local crab hole, was a destination of choice. When he arrived at the place, he situated himself on the sand bar and looked around. He was alone. He waited a bit and a crew of three folks arrived with a plastic crate and some nets for crabbing. He greeted them, answered questions about his Russian accent, and waded through knee deep water as the crab gang bitched about a slow night. The two guys looked for crabs and the girl waited. She had said something about feeling bad about having to boil the crabs but added, sheepishly, that she did like the meat after all. About an hour later the crate was finally full and the crew was setting up to return to their trailer. It was test time.

-

As humans, we suck when we know we are taking a test. We suck even more when we are being tested without knowing. Poseidon didn't know that about humans. Perhaps this was unfair, but gods don't read memos. They issue them.

-

Poseidon stepped up to the crew and choosing his words very carefully said, "Listen, guys. Admittedly a very strange proposal, but hear me out." He knew he had to be brief, beach conversations time themselves to the beat of the waves. "I want to give you sixty bucks for this crate of crabs."

"No fucking way," interrupted one of the guys with the smile. It was more of a "fuck you" than a "no." "Get your own crabs, pal!"

A not necessarily awkward moment of silence ensued. Poseidon wasn't surprised, he'd been counting on this, Dima's lips were simply not fast enough for him to finish his thought. Poseidon continued, taking no offense: "You've got me wrong, bud. I'm not trying to exploit you. Not buying this

310

shit for myself. What I was saying is this, would you guys be willing to dump these crabs back into water for sixty bucks?"

He was now peering into the eyes of his own children, will they pass the test? He was looking at himself. Only time would tell. When it did, it did so non-verbally. The two men looked at each other, then back at Poseidon, and shook their heads.

Poseidon raised the bar "How about a hundred?"

"Why?" asked the younger of the two.

Poseidon offered a careful but quick explanation, the last thing that he wanted to do was to come off as if he was lecturing: "I just feel bad for these creatures, you know, they way they go, wouldn't want to wish that upon anyone" His voice trailed off into the ocean breeze.

The two men smirked the way the carnivores tend to smirk at vegans. The answer was more than informative and they felt they had his number, a dumb ass intellectual, some misguided academic out of touch from the brutish realities of life, an Obama voter no doubt.

Poseidon interrupted their thought process before they weighed in on his last offer, "How about two hundred?" After rummaging through Dima's backpack he knew he had more, much more, a whole brick of cash held together with a yellow Lance Armstrong wristband. But, he wasn't going to better his latest offer a penny, since, if he had to, he'd already know the two morons in front of him had already failed.

Two hundred was a magic number. It made practical sense. Only a fool would refuse more money than that for a half hour's worth of crabbing. And Poseidon wasn't interested in testing their intelligence. It was evident from the sharp way in which the two had sized him up after all, they weren't wrong. Yes, he was an intellectual of sorts. Any god is nothing but a disembodied philosopher.

Poseidon was testing for something entirely different, he was interested in the ego thresholds of the world that he had built.

The two men once again exchanged a glance and, with a laugh, issued their final verdict: "Fuck off, pal!" This time the tone had a clearly toxic dose of hostility. But the "pal" part was supposed to blunt the blade of this hostility, motivated by self-preservation, of course. The Dima-avatar was a formidable sight to see and the guys didn't want a fight if they could help it. They turned away and started to walk up the beach, still laughing.

-

What this means to you and I is arguably not much. What this meant to Poseidon was everything. A reasonable offer of two hundred on a god forsaken beach could not turn off human ego. This was an unacceptably low ego threshold by Poseidon's estimation for his creation to be imbued with love, as he had once imagined.

The psychology of this moment was obvious. The two guys clearly felt that the offer was more than fair, after all, in half an hour they could pack up their empty crate with another batch of crabs for their evening meal. Money wasn't the issue. If it had been about money, not ego, there would not have been such a caustic "fuck you." If it had been about money, there would have been an attempt to haggle for a bit more. The decisiveness and the aggression with which the two ended the conversation meant only one thing to Poseidon; as he had feared he had found himself on a collision course with their ego. The two said "no" to him because they did not like the intuitively hierarchical dynamic of the moment. Whether they could have verbalized it or not, the two didn't want to suddenly realize that they had been unwittingly in the employ of someone else. Sure, they'd get up the next morning and be willing to work for the proverbial man, possibly even for a near minimum wage. But that would be different. That would be part of the social contract, part of what everybody does from Monday to Friday. To work for some schmuck with an accent, who had watched them work, knowing that they are working for him before they know, that was too ego threatening for them to swallow, even in the light of easy money.

-

I don't know if you are aware of this oft-overlooked fact or not. Poseidon, being the designer, certainly knew – a neuron is a neuron is a neuron. What lives inside your skull is fundamentally no different than what lives inside the carapace of a crab. Wherever you find a neuron, and you can find one even in a non-cephalized neural net of an anemone, there, as a species, you are.

It all comes down to food. To eat is to kill. On a deeper level yet, to exist is to kill. To kill is to play god. Gods make the mistake of focusing on creation, conveniently overlooking the fact that any act of creation, the taking of a form, begets a domino effect of causality that inevitably results in suffering.

Poseidon could not have been oblivious to this. This is the basic Kantian software that all gods share. But somehow even gods keep repeating the same mistake, the mistake of optimism, by falling into the trap of something-out-of-nothing, which is only an imaginary workaround the cruelty of the zero sum reality that something is always out of something.

-

Poseidon was crestfallen. Destroyed is probably a better word. He was done. Done with this game and done with humanity. A world that could not be rationally incentivized to notice the living humanity of fellow neural sojourners is an unpardonable blemish on any god's resume. If gods were samurai, they'd tickle their bellies with swords on the spot, at the exact time of realizing how badly they fail. Immortals have no option of suicide, only an option of homogenization, an option to return back home into the womb of the undifferentiated.

A voice, who knows who's, perhaps, his mother's, whispered inside his mind, "You can't save everyone." It repeated like a beacon of reassurance that was pre-installed to go off at the exact time of this devastating disenchantment.

"But I can," said Poseidon and, leaving Dima's body, he reanimated the latter, a parting gift that came wrapped in anterograde amnesia.

-

Now a living mountain again, Poseidon felt a sense of self-pity. He recalled how eons ago, on a different Earth, in his cruder incarnation as a human boy, he went riding on his bicycle after a summer rain and to his horror realized that the hybrid tires of his bike were cutting apart earth worms who got flushed out of the ground that had swollen with water. The boy that he was back then, stopped his bike. He was frozen with the realization of what he had just done, but there was no escape. Even as he stepped off the bike, his feet landed on worms, squishing them to death. He realized he had dismounted right in the middle of a busy street, and started back to the side walk, having to walk over more worms, and having to ride his bike over more worms, and having to watch cars that slowed down to pass around him, flat-ironing even more worms. The sidewalk was, of course, not free of this horror. Nor was the walk home.

At that moment he, not a Poseidon yet, must have been noticed by some cosmic chaperone and through cycles of life and death, his tender-hearted soul was prompted along this vector of compassion until one day, he cognized himself as a god.

Gods are here to test their creations, to test themselves, to attest to their misguided compassion, and to attest to their misplaced idealism.

-

Poseidon, in a final act of will, went inside, that curious loophole of built-in homogenization. He dove into this abyss of formlessness as a man that broke every promise he had ever given himself, leaving no breadcrumbs of second thoughts or doubts. Poseidon, the god of water, mind you, and not the only god that had played in the sandbox of this earth, returned his eternal proto-matter into the womb of the unborn and the undying, with a hope of never amounting to anything more than an empty shoe box. He was done playing the water polo of compassion.

-

Ra, the Ra, the one with protuberant swords of fire in the sky, the Ra that Poseidon was yet to become one cosmic day, nodded an un-witnessed farewell of a magnetic storm at our existentially comatose Poseidon, with gentle indifference, since it's the only kind of indifference that exists.

-

As for you and I, Reader-Writer, it is time we exchange a passing glance as well. Know this, however, as you go. The space of awareness that you are is many games to many players. Each and every one of us is an infinite number of things and non-things to a proportionately infinite number of beings and non-beings.

Congratulations and condolences to you on your dubious achievement of existence. I'll see you from the inside of the womb, as we flow with the hemocyanin blood of Poseidon, with the blue blood of benign indifference.

# Parenting Gods

## (as Told by a Bottom Feeder)

"*W*hen you reach the final stage of life," Stan continued, "it maybe nothing more than a lovely cottage house on the edge of the world, a white picket fence on a dead end dirt road. There might or might not be a lake that is really a pond, with a rickety boat slip, at the bottom of the hill . There you find yourself, on a veranda with a cup of coffee, startled by the sudden visit of a hummingbird. You are for a, moment, totally mesmerized by its sudden appearance. Then a door opens and out comes your sleepy kid, a four or five year old girl, barefoot in pajamas ... Startled, the hummingbird moves on, and the child, your child, wants you to come inside to play tic-tac-toe on the wet condensate of the windows. You have to put your ego aside. You have to give up your wonderful aesthetic Sunday morning and respond to her, attend to her, parent her."

Stan looked human although he wasn't. He was laying in a nursing home bed, his wife somewhere else in the same facility, the Green Valley Assisted Retirement Home. Neither seemed to miss the other, yet both seemed to decline down a carefully coordinated asymptote of functioning. They had been married for thousands of years, Stan claimed. So it was no surprise, said Stan, that they neither missed each other nor raced each other towards death. Entangled by time, they crept along like two parallel lifelines.

She had a full suite; Stan had opted for a Spartan hospital-looking room with a better view. His upper body was elevated most of the time so that he could see out of the window. The view out the window was, indeed, better but not by much. A narrow lawn, always mowed too short, breaking into an abrupt downhill, with an unremarkable suburban view in the distance. In ten or so years, long after Stan would be gone, a line of picturesque oak trees would feed the eyes of a future inhabitant of this bed space.

A couple of layers of blankets, one a hospital issue, the other a quilt made from various t-shirts his kid had worn, were tangled in his feet. He didn't seem to care. These here and now problems were his body's problems, not a problem for his mind which seemed to inhabit some other realm most of the time, a world of its own, another space time, the space time of reminiscence.

Stan reached for a cup of water, took a sip, spilling most of it on his unbuttoned gown, and withdrew back into what must have been a flashback. His eyes moistened and he looked up at me as if with reproach and continued. "All of these choices are not suffered, they are almost automatic, effortless. You just get up and leave yourself behind and you follow this innocent lead from your child. Because you must. These moments are far and few in between, the moments of your child's initiative. The little heart wants to bond with you and reaches out, and you know this moment will vanish in the onslaught of time. It's not bliss, no, bittersweet agony-ecstasy is what if feels like. The pitiful best that the Universe saves for dessert. You know that the point of all these parenting moments is not for you, really, but for your child to bond to one's own self. Not to you, because before too long, historically speaking, you won't be there to hold this little hand. You won't be there at all, for an eternity of time."

Inside his mind, Stan was back in his little cottage on the edge of the world, seeing the inky shadows of the trees on the green surface of the pond, the sudden rain of nighttime dew from the tree leaves stirred up by a breeze, and the radiating circles of the catfish as they poked out of the water to feed on bugs. He could see a pair of rusted bicycles. The details were endless. His mind was full of them, the details of that morning in his mind, that morning in the life of his child, when he chose the wrong thing to do. He chose to linger on the veranda, to finish his coffee while the child, feeling privately betrayed by her parent's lack of reciprocity, went inside to play tic-tac-toe on the condensate of the windows all by herself.

Life is like that. Here on Earth, we know this ordinary perfection. And accept it. But Stan had a higher,

320

extraterrestrial, even divine, bar to meet. Here's what I had gathered from him in the brief hours of our acquaintance.

In my therapy sessions with Stan, I had learned that he was of a race that, he said, lived hundreds of thousands of years. In fact, their lifespan was unlimited. Only a very few of their race had dared to experiment with eternity. These few oldtimers were only known of, heard of, but never seen beyond a certain point of their existence. Those daring few would vanish into the proverbial hilltops of uncharted cosmos, into an un-witnessed hermitage of immortality.

Not Stan. Stan wanted to follow in the tradition of his ancestors.

An intercom broke into our moment. "Dr. Somov, front desk, please."

"Excuse me, Stan, I'll be right back," I said. He nodded nonchalantly.

I went to the nursing station where Emily, a new head nurse, asked me to check in on Mr. Hamsun, room # 6. "I think he's getting very agitated," Emily explained without lifting her eyes from a stack of charts on her desk. I went to check on Mr. Hamsun and came back in a few minutes. "He's okay. He's shadow boxing again." Mr. Hamsun, laid out in his bed like most of the folks here, was punching the air above him, like a speed bag. "That's his approach to reminiscence, you know, reliving the good ol' days. He's all right. Let me know if there's anything out of the usual." Emily nodded, her eyes still buried in the paperwork.

As I walked back to Stan's room, I took another passing glance at Mr. Hamsun. He was definitely winning, a silly grin on his face, apparently picking up the pace in the last 30 seconds of the 3rd round. I had spent time with him before, asking him about this curious routine of his. "I just go through it in real time, Doc; fighting through it round by round, just like in the good ol' days. I remember it all, you know."

"I remember it all," was a common refrain here. It seems that when the mind decides that there is nothing new left to learn it shifts into a life review mode, a harbinger of death. Another common refrain was "I don't remember a thing," a sure sign of nirvanic rebirth.

I reentered Stan's room. "Sorry, Stan," I said. He was as I had left him, on his bed, head to the side, looking out the window. He finally shook his head as if to dismiss the apology.

"I remember every detail, Doc," Stan continued without prompting, "of that morning, you know. A pair of her flip-flops, so tiny, one with a Hawaiian floral design, the other one with sea horses. She never noticed, you know, that they were mismatched. She was hellbent on getting a pair from a store as we drove out to that cottage that summer, and they only had that pair. She never noticed. Her toes so cute in them. She was still putting them on the wrong foot all the time and I'd catch up with her and swap them around while she'd insist that 'they are right, Daddy,' it was part of the ego tug-of-war always between us."

I made a note in his chart.

He suddenly boomed, "Why do you take these notes, Doc?"

"To remember."

"It's idiotic, Doc, you *cannot not* but remember," he emphasized, "Everything that happens leaves a trace, that's the very problem, you know. The Universe is a memory foam mattress and we're asleep on it."

"I know, Stan, it's just that taking notes helps me create an access point to my memories. I'll probably never look at these notes again. It's just the mere fact of writing something down that creates a portal into the past, a gateway into a memory. Iit's like machining a key, you know."

"Well, Doc, you got a point there, you are not half as stupid as I thought you were."

I looked away. I knew Stan tended to get abrasive with me whenever he felt it was time for me to go. He wanted me to stay longer but he was bracing for my departure, driving me away. A control thing, not unlike the moments he had with his daughter over the "wrong foot" thing with the flip-flops. Cosmos is really Chaos. To Greeks, the word "cosmos" meant order, the order that they tried to see in the Actual Chaos of What Is. When we, here on Earth, learned to see the Cosmos in the Chaos, the order in the disorder, we became the control junkies that we still, as a civilization, are. Stan, albeit of a reportedly different civilization, was a control junkie like the rest of us. He admitted that freely. In fact, his very existence seemed to be a detoxification from the high of control.

"Tell me more about how you became a parent, Stan. I want to hear it again."

Stan scowled. "You are a silly fella, Doc, you know?"

"I know, Stan. Indulge me, I like listening to you. There's always something to learn."

"It's about unlearning, not learning, Doc, don't you understand? 99% of what we experience in life is left un-witnessed, and that's exactly how it's supposed to be! We are here to witness, not be witnessed. When you realize this, you no longer feel like a fish out of the water, and you settle down. The cosmos in you relaxes back into its primordial chaos of real time

324

randomness. Any lesson you learn is moment specific, it doesn't generalize to the next moment because each moment is its own reality. 'Wu-zhi," Daoist sages used to say, "is unprincipled learning. Learn how to survive this moment, but retain no lesson lest you wish to repeat mistakes of the past in the future."

Stan never needed coercing. He was a storyteller, so he went on, delving into a new level of details. I didn't interrupt. The last several weeks were a professional high for me. Ever since Stan had arrived at Green Valley, I felt like I had came back to life. Finally, I was witnessing a life-narrative whose ending I knew absolutely nothing about. Stan went over the same old basics that I had heard him describe before, but in greater detail. The more I listened, the more he seemed to trust my interest. The more he trusted me, the more he seemed to share.

His race, he claimed, lived as long as they wanted. Anyone could be immortal, for all they knew. But almost nobody chose to live forever. Hundreds of thousands of years were more than enough. Life began as it would on any planet, with a family, a family that loves you. This was a realized ideal. Each child was born into an idyllic circumstance. This kind of auspicious beginning of life was the very centerpiece of their entire civilization. This was a race of Parents. God Parents, to be exact. Although Stan would insist that "we are all nameless, these truths, these epiphanies, these aspirations were non-verbal for us, pre-verbal even."

By cosmic standards, they came of age quite fast, a child became an adult in a span of 240 years or so. Each parenting couple was to have only one child and each couple was to die together, non-traumatically when the child reached the age of sovereignty at around 250. Parenting was the crowning achievement of their almost infinite life spans. It was simply metabolically and genetically impossible for them to become parents until a very advanced age. This was entirely on purpose. The Cosmos, Stan claimed, suffered from immature parenting, from children parenting children.

Each couple had only one shot at this, one shared life, and one child, a convergence of two lifelines into a third, with a divergence soon occurring,. The two parenting lifelines would come to a final stop like geometrically abstract parallels that ran out of cosmic paper; and a new lifeline would continue onto to the next page.

Once the children reached the age of sovereignty ("Not to be confused with maturity!") they moved on with their lives. That meant they lived through an endless series of reincarnations. They were expected to change locales and languages, professions and circumstances, with each change erasing the memories of the bygone eras.

"The irony was that for us, my wife and I, parenting our child was everything. The moment we decided to have her was the moment we began to die, literally.

That's how it works with us, on a metabolic, cellular, and ontological level. A cause that begets an effect eventually ceases to exist. We've been dying every day for the last 250 years. For us, she was everything, the love of our life, a love we had been preparing ourselves for, for all these lifetimes of self-oblivion. Everyday that we lived with her, she grew in geometric importance. On our end, this growth of significance was unbearable. Everyday we felt like we'd explode with warmth and affection. She was becoming our god. We - her worshipers; but we couldn't show it. The goal was to slowly vanish, to become irrelevant to her. Love, you see, is bondage. When you love someone, they love that, they love being loved, and that is bondage. They cling to that feeling of unconditional acceptance. They become trapped in love like flies in tree sap. Even gods can be corrupted by worship. As she became the world to us, we, to her, became two ol' fogies, two nobodies, with strange stories and strange histories. That's how it should be and that's exactly how it was."

I needed time to understand this, to process this, so I asked Stan about languages, just to keep him talking.

Stan explained that "language is a tongue that kisses itself."

I didn't get it, so he clarified. "Language programs the body. It is the ultimate tool of self-serving, it is internally coherent, and therefore totally useless if you are trying to explain the Grand ol' State of What

Truly Is." Stan explained that language enables subjectivity and therefore is a source of perpetual distortion.

"How many languages have you spoken in your journey?" I once asked him.

"I cannot tell you, I know I speak English now, because that's where I chose to be a parent. But English is not a language. No language is just a language. Each language is a land, a map that has its own topography of associations and meanings. When we decide to learn a new language, we enter a realm, a conceptual realm, a worldview, a matrix, a web of inter-relations. I don't speak English, English is where I live, where my mind dwells, where my mind is right now trapped."

At another time he had mentioned that he had spoken "sound," and "touch," and "light." He said that these sensory modalities are also languages. Stan explained that, as he had traversed the cosmos, he had to learn new modes of communication, and the effect was that each and every worldview that he had previously acquired was subsequently rendered moot. "It's all absolutely relative," he'd say again and again, "absolutely relative to the time-space you are in."

"Language is a necessary evil," he'd also say, "a lullaby with which the Universe put itself to sleep."

This talk of language was a lullaby that woke me up.

--

Sometimes I couldn't help but get clinical with Stan. My justification was that I was checking the internal consistency of his narrative. For example, I'd ask, "Stan, you mentioned that you were of a myriad of different forms, that you spoke god knows how many languages. If so, how could you possibly remember where you came from or what you were or anything about your past?"

He'd chuckle, as if challenged by a toddler. "Forgetting *was* the point, Doc. Don't you understand? Of course you do, Doc. You are just teasing me, right?"

I'd stay noncommittal, awaiting elaboration. And he'd always come through.

"That was the point, to erase the past. To extinguish it. To eviscerate it. You know, consciousness comes into the world rough cut, with an agenda. It comes in dirty. You call this karma here. Being parenting gods involves a complete commitment to the present; real time action. You have to purify yourself first, and you have to detoxify yourself from your own agenda lest you pass it on. If your consciousness has a vector, if it has any vestige of past programming, you are never in real time, you are only projecting past reality onto what currently is, in a kind of invisible overlay of expectations. You taint your offspring, you end up programming them, even if unwittingly. When your mind is impure, you're in no position to parent a god. To parent a god, you have to be a god. Gods have no minds."

"Parent a god?" I repeated after Stan. This was a new one to me. He hadn't said anything of this sort before. Was he finally becoming grandiose as we all do when our senses begin to fail us, as we slip into that final feedback loop of solipsist self-referencing? Alien – I could take that. But a god? Stan was surely losing it. But, then again, aren't we all?

"Yes, Doc. You see in our life, I mean our life, not your life, the very point of existence was to eventually reach a point of such non-duality, such a real time precision of spontaneous action that you could finally embark on a parenting project, a project of parenting a god. By then you had to have completely erased any vestige of the past, you had to have completely extinguished any trace of past programming. You had to totally liberate yourself from your past. Your Greek philosopher, Lucretius, called it "clinamen," an unpredictable swerve of an atom that would account for there being "something" instead of "nothing." But your Greeks misunderstood gods. Gods are not in the business of creating "something" out of "nothing" by giving atoms a swerve. Gods leave "nothing" alone. They protect the Nothingness. Nothingness is our womb, our mother, the Undifferentiated Proto-Source of All That Is.

Gods erase swerves; they detoxify the Universe of its clinamen. Your Buddhists are closest to understanding what we do, they talk about erasing karma, expunging it like you would expunge a DUI."

"Lucretius, huh? I have heard of him, Stan."

"Well, I actually heard him, Doc." Stan shook his palm in the air in a so-so gesture.

"But all in all, Stan, you lost me again," I said realizing that my eyebrows were in the middle of my forehead as if I had just bitten down on a Trinidad scorpion pepper.

"It's simple, Doc. If you have a past, your child will have your past too. But gods, if they are to act with the freedom that comes with immortality, have to be free of the past. They have to feel unborn if they are to feel undying. There are only two things that constrain our freedom, the past and the future, determinism and teleology, wounds and desires. These are all the same. So my wife and I, we had to launder ourselves through innumerous lifetimes so we could leave the past behind. Otherwise we'd run the risk of giving our offspring a spin, a clinamen, that would create either a devil or an angel. That's not what the Universe needs. What the Universe needs is just a fair god, a balanced god capable of acting in real time, without a bias. A god without a past, or a future."

"Are you then, Stan, saying that a god is a being that has no past or future?"

"I am saying that. I am also saying that any mortal who is free from the past or the future, say, through meditation, is a god. If only for a moment…"

Stan closed his eyes and continued in a monotone.

"Parenting is the first and last mistake that the Universe made. You see, all parenting is conditioning. Conditioning is a reduction of freedom. With each and every condition you place on a child, you rob them of a degree of spontaneity. The Universe has been losing spontaneity for billions of years. Unconditional parenting is the best chance for the Universe to regain its original stem cell-like pluri-potentiality. The difference between human parents and god parents is that humans program and gods deprogram. You and I – by the way, do you have a kid, Doc?  Are you a parent?"

I nodded, "I am."

Stan continued, "You human parents, and we god-parents, are on the different sides of this project. You and I, we are in a dialectic dance  of programming and deprogramming, conditioning and de-conditioning. Your human love, even if you call it 'unconditional' is conditional. Our love is a non-love, which is what makes it unconditional."

"I am lost, Stan."

"And found, Doc."

We both settled into a long pause. There were plenty of distractions to entertain us, sounds in the hallway, the incessant intercom, and the monotone of news on the TV behind the wall. Stan kept his eyes closed. Was he napping? Do gods nap? If they do, who's minding the house in their absence? Is that when things go sour for us mortals, when gods sleep on the job?

Stan finally opened his eyes. He stuck out his jaw just a bit, like some kind of deep water fish trolling for plankton, a strange mannerism of his, perhaps, a neurological tick. He was ready to emphasize something; he did this every time when he wanted to reiterate a point. "This is what is actually meant by omnipresence. Omnipresence means 'being always present,' not being present everywhere, but being always present, present in your child's life, to witness it as it is, without a smile, without a scowl, like a mirror would. Omnipresent doesn't mean that I am in the trees, that I am in the sky, that I am in your colon or under your finger nails. Omnipresent means that whenever you are, I am there attending to you. Because time is space."

There was much too much to process here, so I limited my scope, as usual. "Why not with a smile?" I asked.

"Because functionally speaking, a smile is as bad as a scowl, either is a judgment, a form of conditioning. Any reaction you have to your child programs your child…"

Once again, I took notes.

--

Stan's religiosity, which is how I thought of all this god-parenting-a-god business, was new to me, a development that seemed too clinically significant not to explore further. Of course, this was pure rationalization on my part. The nursing home didn't really give a fuck. As long as he was progressing (meaning dying), as long as there was something to bill for and write notes on, his narrative idiosyncrasies were of no interest to anyone, but me.

"By the time you reached your midlife, that is, hundreds of thousands of years of age, you'd have absolutely no memory of your parents, whatsoever. By then you would have lived through an endless series of circumstances, like wax in a lava- lamp that had been on for hundreds of thousands of years. Time is a de-programmer. Time is the original god."

"Wait a sec, Stan," I chimed in. "You are saying that your child is destined to forget you?"

"Forgetting is a minimum. With any luck, she will

334

have completely unlearned every word of English that my wife and I had ever spoken to her. With any luck, she will be utterly unable to bring up even an echo of emotion at the mention of her parents. If we've done our job right, our daughter will one day experience herself as a pure undifferentiated state of consciousness, a veritable coordinate of oneness, liberated to be whatever she needs to be at any moment. This, Doc, is the baseline of gods, omnipresence, not omniscience. Omniscience, total knowledge, incarcerates. That, which informs us, forms us. Gods are nothing but a baseline of am-ness. What you now consider to be your breath is just god. What you consider to be your being, is really just god, the body of god, to which you add your own mind. This is true at every level of abstraction, true for an atom, true for an organism, true for a mountain, and true for a black hole."

Stan asked for a glass of water. He hardly ever ate. It was his way of controlling the process, he explained. "I don't want to waste my last moments on indigestion." He cleared his throat, "A god has to be free from the past. No name, no form, no obligation."

"But don't you want your child to remember you?"

"Ha!" he exclaimed in open dismay. "Of course not! She will have known her parents for 250 or so years out of the hundreds of thousands of years of her technically unlimited lifespan. We have long arranged our genetics to work in such a way so as to minimize the overlap between a parent's and a child's life. By the time she reaches her midlife, we, my wife and I, will have become nothing but an autobiographic fact without any episodic memories attached to it. She will only 'know' that we existed, in the way in which the last falling domino knows that there must have been a causal effect, perhaps a finger, that pushed the original domino eons ago."

--

Bewildered and overwhelmed, as usual, I focused on the comprehensible. "Genetics, Stan? Gods have genetics?"

"Yes, Doc, gods have genetics. Genetics is just the fault lines in the fabric of oneness, illusory origami scars of what once was."

In moments like this I asked Stan questions at random, in a kind of what about such and such diarrhea of inquiry. Stan never failed. Each question burned up like a moth in a flame.

--

"What about legacy, Stan?"

"Legacy? Legacy?" Stan's voice boomed with disapproval. "Legacy is a dirty word. Legacy is ego,

336

another dirty word! There is nothing, absolutely nothing that my wife and I need from our child when we are dead. Not a thought, not a memory. We won't be there to collect these imaginary dividends of legacy. Legacy obliges and undermines spontaneity. Legacy is a 'should.' Gods must only want, never feel like they 'have to'."

Questions populated my mind like mosquito larvae, each wiggling its inquisitive tail. But that morning I chose to stay true to my clinical mandate, as I picked where to go next with my inquiry.

"Do you remember anything about your parents, Stan?"

"Not a thing. I know I had them. But I neither know where I was born, nor when. This information can be accessed, nothing's really forgotten or erased. I can be prodded to remember, but I'd need an external trigger. I myself, however, have no internal rappelling rope of associations to climb down into that historical abyss of my origin. I neither can nor want to. A lifelong habit of letting go of the past turned me into an arrowhead without fletching. Whatever memories I have are of this lifetime only, they come with parenting. These memories, this past, it has no future, it will die with me. Nameless we start and nameless we end. You call me 'Stan,' but it is only a name that I myself chose for my eternal namelessness as I made my home on your Earthly plane of existence. This is where my wife and I chose to parent our god, our daughter; this is where we both reached our own divinity. We'd been waiting for this moment our entire lives, through each and every stage of our respective evolution. Our race is deadly serious about this. You live your lives to the utter max, addressing each and every conscious and unconscious whim until you feel you have reached a state of total satisfaction. Then you die in that form and rebirth yourself again and again to live again and again, until there is nothing unfulfilled about you, until you are completely realized, without any fantasies or daydreams, finally and irrevocably free to be here, now, which is what is required if you are to parent a god."

"But, Stan, correct me if I am wrong, you seem to have regrets, right? That story you told me earlier today, about your daughter wanting to play tic-tac-toe and you procrastinating because you wanted to finish your coffee, while she felt betrayed. That wasn't real time, was it? You weren't agenda free, were you? That wasn't parenting perfection, was it?"

Stan shed a tear or two. He cried often by the way. When his eyes moistened, as they did now, they seemed sparkly and piercing. They shone. Stan's explanation for crying so often was that he constantly saw beauty. Beauty, he had previously explained, was symmetry. And symmetry releases the tension of asymmetry. When reality becomes symmetrical, it becomes effortless, as we no longer have to "hold the contradiction." "Everything cancels out in a perfect symmetry," he'd say, "like mini-leaves on a fern."

338

And that's when you cry, from the relief of all that conceptual tension with which you had pre-judged the reality as unfair or ugly.

"Why are you crying, Stan?" I asked, nevertheless.

"Because you are missing the point, Doc. What happened on that veranda that day, that, too, was perfection. Imperfection, you see, is subsumed within perfection. Her sense of being betrayed was the beginning of benevolence. She had to, at least once, realize that the reality does not just include her, that there are other beings with needs. She will spend countless millennia trying to extinguish that lesson. The pluri-potentiality of gods is the negative of all the lessons that they had learned. By unlearning the lesson, we restore our ability to act in accordance with it."

"I am sorry, Stan, I am not sure I understand," I said, looking at my watch.

"You don't and you do, at the same time; you are not just the conscious part that you think you are. The part of you that feels uncertain is the least important part, Doc. The rest of you already knows everything I ever have to say, which is why you are drawn to me. You are not learning anything here; you are here to confirm what you have already intuitively known. But the conditioned, programmed part of you still resists. As it should, because here on Earth, it's been evolutionarily adaptive to think the way you consciously do," said Stan, returning to his sideways glance out the window.

--

A couple of weeks went by like this. I'd sit in his room, while he reminisced. "The crazy ol' cook," as Emily called him. He left me notes and showered me with generous details. He was clearly dying and there was no stopping that. His lab results were coming back as progressively negative and his physician would sometimes grab me by my sleeve and say, "Stan's dying, you know."

"I know," I'd say.

"Well, as long as you know."

"Yes, I know."

The most curious thing was that Stan's wife was dying at about the same pace, their vital signs both improving and declining at the same time. Neither was eating, so their weight was dropping. But both were showing improvements in blood pressure, etc. I asked Stan about that.

"Roz and I, we know what we are doing. This body, this Earthly body, is a cellular collective. It consists of many different cellular tribes. They are all fighting

this process, the adipose cells, the muscle cells...
Except for neurons. Neurons are our allies. Roz and I
are trying to starve ourselves to shut out the other
cellular tribes, to break their metabolic will to live.
Cells, as you know, can commit suicide. It's called
apoptosis. By not eating, by forcing the body to eat
itself, Roz and I are trying to kickstart a kind of
apoptotic wave, a wave of cellular suicide. And when
the body is sufficiently weakened, we can will
ourselves to die, when we are ready. But we are not
ready yet, Doc."

I listened.

"You are not gonna write this down, Doc, are you?
We don't want to be force fed or any other kind of
nonsense of that sort?"

"They are not gonna do that here, Stan. It's a pre-
hospice facility. You can die when you are ready," I
reassured him. "But do tell me more about this
method you have chosen."

"It's a Jain thing. They call it sallekhana, an open-
ended fast. We taught them that, I must say."

"So, you just stop eating and that's it, Stan? You
mean to say, you'll never eat again?"

"Correct. It's actually easier than it sounds. The thing
about not eating is that it actually prolongs your life,

up to a point."

"Yes, Stan, I've heard of calorie restriction."

"That's right, calorie restriction. Initially, you feel a kind of euphoria and then a kind of detachment. You begin to not care either way. It becomes effortless the longer you go. Gautama taught that, remember? Desire is the source of suffering. When you decide not to desire any longer, when you decide to stop wanting to eat, bliss ensues. So does lethargy eventually, so, timing is everything here."

I sized up Stan. He was still a strapping man, I could tell by his frame, his long, powerful fingers sprawling across the linens like the exposed roots of an Australian ficus tree.

With revelations like this, what was I going to do but take what Stan was saying at face value?

--

Another week went by and Stan started to repeat himself. I didn't mind. I didn't get most of it on the first go anyway. The very point of their existence was to attain a state of purity necessary to parent a god. *Check. Got that.*

They had lived their countless reincarnations with a single purpose in mind, to purify themselves of any vestiges of their own developmental past, so as to one day embark on a parenting project which doubled up as a dying project. *Check. Got that.*

By the time they reached the age of wisdom, there was nothing else they wanted to do more than to parent a god. They had fulfilled their every wild dream, lived every scenario, passed every test, loved themselves and everyone they had ever wanted to. They were fulfilled, except for one last wish – to parent a god. *Check. Got that.*

By the time they had arrived in that last phase of their life, they were finally able to be completely devoted to each and every nanosecond of their child's life. They were single minded about this, one focused, one track. *Check. Got that.*

As soon as they reached their childbearing age, which was hundreds of thousands of their years, they'd announce their intentions of parenthood, and would subsequently be tested by those very few of their own race who had chosen to live forever. *Now that was sounding new to me.* "You see, it was worth hearing it all again," I'd say to myself and open my notebook.

Those consultants of eternity would size them up and determine their fitness to parent a god. Most of the time, the first assessment was negative. The god-parents had many more lives to undertake so as to launder their unconscious presets and defaults. They didn't mind. They never minded. In fact, they took this kind of disqualification as invaluable feedback and went about reincarnating until they no longer knew themselves from Adam.

One thing, however, bothered me. What were their years based on? A year is the time it takes for the Earth to rotate around the Sun. It's a provincial unit of measurement, parochial and   coordinate specific. Elsewhere in the Universe, depending on the orbiting specifics, a year could be long enough for ten Earth based lifetimes. And since Stan, per his claim, had gone through limitless reincarnations of this sort, in different locales, how was he keeping track of all this nonsense? So, I asked him.

"There is a pacemaker within us; within you too. All life comes with a peristaltic compass, with its own time. We all, whether here on Earth or elsewhere, time ourselves through moments."

"So, then what is a year? A 1000 moments?"

"No, Doc. A year may be 1000 moments or a trillion moments. It's not about how many moments. It's about circularity – the orbit of awakening. It all begins with a kind of square one moment, a moment of waking up. Then we begin to fall asleep. Moment by moment we are losing consciousness, until there is no consciousness left. At that point, we are on total autopilot, timelessly. Then comes a moment in which we realize that we are asleep. Call it lucid dream onset. From the first moment of waking up to the first moment of realizing you are deeply asleep is a year. We orbit ourselves, you see?  Each mind is a satellite of sorts, orbiting the peristaltic sun of awareness. We wake up when we see this light of awareness and we are instantly blinded. So, we squint (sort of) trying to control this bittersweet rendezvous encounter with ourselves; and we begin to fall asleep, moment by moment. And so it goes, year after year after year."

"Hmm," I said, squinting.

--

Stan and his wife, Roz, qualified for god-parenting on the first try. At least, that's what he said. "It was rare but not uncommon," he added.

I tried to understand what this sort of statement really means – "rare but not uncommon."  What shade of gray is that?

"Definitely not unheard of, but, for sure, rare," he added, but it didn't help.

"Rare but not uncommon … definitely not unheard of but, for sure, rare …" I kept mulling this over trying to somehow quantify this vague statement of probability. But Stan wasn't waiting on me to catch up, he went on.

"The wise ones recognized themselves in us. In fact, that's how we learned of it," said Stan. "They literally told us, 'We recognize ourselves in the mirror of your consciousness,' and that was it. No silly blue ribbons or graduation diplomas."

"Is that how they typically announced this sort of thing?" I asked Stan, not sure why I had to probe such a subtle point.

"Sometimes. Sometimes they'd just nod in approval. But typically, they'd invite you to your own baby shower," Stan chuckled. Yes, he tried to be funny sometimes.

--

"Then what?" I asked.

"An immaculate conception. We were instantly pregnant. Then Pralaya was born and we began to die."

"Pralaya?"

"It's a Hindu term for Cosmic Dissolution. The only name that seemed appropriate, you know."

"Began to die?" I echoed.

"Yes, Doc, when our daughter was born we began to die. In fact, when we made the decision to have her, we began to die. The Universe is a zero sum place. The opposite of oneness is not nothingness but no-thingness. When one thing is born, another thing has to die. The balance has to remain the same."

--

One morning I went to visit with his wife, Roz. She was being followed by another psychologist, who had called in sick that morning. This finally gave me the chance to check in with Stan's better half. Unlike Stan, who had opted for a Spartan room, Roz had a full suite, although it didn't look like she made much use of it. The kitchen was clean with a little college room fridge that was empty. No paper towels, no stick of butter to cook with, no personal items at all. Roz did have a generous sliding door that opened up to a small patio. I suspected that this door was the main selling point for Roz. She was now sitting in a rocker with the sliding door ajar. Her slippers were neatly lined up to the side of the rocking chair. A still graceful, even erotic, arc of her foot caught my eye. It is amazing, I often thought, how some parts of our bodies don't seem to age. A snake of a breeze was meandering through the bottom of her oversized hospital gown. An unfinished tray of food on her bedside table was of growing interest to a couple of flies.

As I came in, I introduced myself. She oriented herself to the sound of my entrance, nodded, smiled and returned to her view out of the sliding door. I squatted down by her side to get on the same level.

"I work with your husband, Stan," I said, suddenly wondering if, perhaps, I should have obtained a release of information to allow me to share that with Roz. "A ridiculous notion," I thought to myself. They both know they are here. They nearly share a wall.

Roz showed no reaction to what I had said. A hive of questions were humming in my head. What did she think of Stan's stories? Were they stories? Did she share the same system of beliefs? Was she, too. going to tell me that she was of a different race, that she was a god-parent of a god? I was jonesing to either confirm or disconfirm Stan's assertions. But I knew better. I was here for her, not for myself. This kind of relationship boundary is always easier in the beginning. I stayed silent. Before too long the bursitis in my left shin began to act up and I had to stand and find a more comfortable place to sit. A large black ant crawled into the room and began to explore the soft cave of one of Roz's slippers. The ant crawled in and out, in and out, as if bewildered by this generous discovery. A cave! A comfy cave! A vacant cave, what possibilities!

Anthropomorphizing, by the way, is a good habit of mine. As a species, we need to anthropomorphize more. We shouldn't fear teleology. Yes, nature is purposeful; nature knows. It has goals and aspirations and ambitions and it constantly moves towards some kind of adaptive ideal. Just like this black ant that – strike that! – *who* was on his way somewhere, with some task in mind, until he stumbled upon this soft and seemingly vacant cave to explore.

Suddenly, Roz moaned out a word: "World …" "World …" she said again with a tone of painful disillusionment. She might have as well said, "Oh, the world …"

I listened. There came another "world," and then another. Worlds came and went. She was intoning seemingly oblivious to my presence. There was a mantra like rhythm to this chant, her breath elongated and calming.

"And all these un-witnessed daughters and sons …" she suddenly added, throwing me completely for a loop.

"Excuse me?" I said.

Roz turned and looked at me with utmost lucidity: "Are your parents still alive, Doctor?"

"They are not," I said, standing up for some reason.

"How well do you remember them?"

"Quite well, Roz. May I call you Roz, by the way?"

Roz nodded and smiled. She inserted her feet into the slippers, trapping the ant inside, I think, and got up. We were now both standing face to face. She was a tall, graceful woman, of indeterminable age. Unmistakable signs of beauty were in her face and in her swimmer-straight shoulders. Her almost totally gray hair had that tight Italian curl to it that cascaded all the way down to the hairs' end, a natural perm. The wave of her upper lip, strong white teeth, and a myriad of quick, short, brusque wrinkles around her eyes; her face came into my focus with sudden intensity. I had clearly underestimated her level of awareness. She was more alert than I was, for sure.

"Do you think your parents, Doctor, knew you?" she asked point blank.

"Hmm. How do you mean, ma'am?"

"Did they know you the way you knew yourself?"

I didn't have to ponder the question. I knew the answer to it right away. It is this feeling of being always misunderstood and invalidated and demonized that drove me into counseling in my earlier years, and, through the ironies of nature, paved the way for me to become a psychologist.

"They did not."

"That's what I thought, Doctor, that's what I instantly understood about you just as you came in. The world, this world, I mean, the one on Earth, and, frankly, in most places, you see, is full of unattended, un-witnessed children, just like you."

She had just answered all my questions without my having to ask any of them. Stan and Roz were on the same page of a very strange book.

"Why do you think that is, ma'am?" I probed, justifying my curiosity as having the clinical benefit of stimulating this resident's intellectual functioning (which was clearly intact).

"I am sure Stan can explain. I am not big on intellectualizing. That's his forte. But as for you, Doctor, I am afraid you have been selling yourself short. There is a subtlety to your presence, a nuance that tells me that you are not nearly as invulnerable as you tell yourself. Tell me, do you ever cry at night?"

"I do. And in the daytime, too," I complied. "I cry in the movies. I cry a lot. I don't mean 'rivers,' but often."

"Of course you do. And that's because you see beauty, right? Everywhere?"

"I do. Exactly."

Roz knocked off her slipper. "Bugger! How did you, little rascal, get in there?" she demanded, letting the ant out of her slipper onto the patio. I followed her, she was standing on the warm paving stones; one foot clad, the other bare, her skin still glowing with that Adriatic olive sheen.

"Do you think you are beautiful, Doctor?" Her eyes were looking right into me.

"Do you think your parents saw your beauty, Doctor? Did your spouse? Did Stan? Have you, you yourself, ever looked in the mirror and thought of yourself as beautiful?"

With each question, I felt as though I was being hypnotically regressed down some kind of staircase of pain in which each lower step offered a sense of increasing visibility. A tear formed in the corner of my eye. She saw it and with her right palm cradled my face, letting the tear drip through her fingers. I didn't move.

"I see your beauty, son," said Roz, and returned to her rocker as suddenly as she had gotten up from it a moment ago. It felt as though she had powered down, like some kind of bodhisattva-robot and I knew the moment was over. I had nothing left to do in her room. I walked out, having learned nothing of the mirror that so perfectly reflected my long forgotten beauty.

--

I never went back to Roz. She saw me. She saw through me. The whole thing was a total non-starter, clinically speaking. I could never be a mirror to a mirror. Stan was much, much easier. There was a familiar narcissistic self-involvement. He didn't see my beauty. He only saw his own. And, that was a cup of tea I drank a lot from.

We picked up where we had left off, with parenting gods and the death of ego. Stan, as he often did, began with an emphasis.

"Parenting is a true death, a true death of ego, when you do it right. The body dies everyday. But the ego is a cliffhanger. Parenting, if you do it right, is just about the only way to kill ego. Zen training is for patsies. Nothing compared to the vivisection of parenting."

"What do you mean, Stan, when you say the body dies every day?" I asked, hiding out in the all too familiar role of a pupil. I knew what he meant. I was just restoring the dynamic, the hierarchy between us, if you wish.

"The body is 'already and always' dead. Made of inanimate, lifeless matter, the body is never alive in the first place. As matter launders its way through a series of reincarnations, it homogenizes itself even

353

further, beyond recognition. It's the mind, Doc, the mind that has to keep dying, until it no longer is. When we reached that sought after stage of enlightenment, when we were finally ready to parent, there was nothing, or almost nothing, left of us. We were free to be in real time, to attend to a new consciousness of our child without molding it or shaping it, with that unconditional acceptance that only you humans have for the smell of a new car (no matter how obnoxious it is) until it finally wears out, without any assistance from us. Our job was to keep her safe, not to program her, not to shape her or mold her, but to just keep her safe. Gods have to be free, if they are to be gods. Free of programming, since they are the ones who program."

--

By now we had a routine where I'd spend an hour with Stan every morning and every afternoon. My sessions consisted of mostly just listening. I had long given up on any attempt to point out any inconsistencies in his narrative. Reality checks are overrated, particularly, when you are working with someone who has very little time left. At this point in his life, there was only one reality that mattered to Stan and that was his internal reality, his subjective truth.

Yes, subjective. The fact is there are no facts. I think Bob Marley said that. Or, perhaps, Krishnamurti. I agree. What we call facts are time specific, moment specific, coordinate specific points of view, i.e. opinions. What objective truth is there to assert? Truth, contrary to our beliefs, doesn't unite. Truth divides. Truth doesn't liberate. It imprisons. Truth is a pseudo certainty, an illusion of objectivity. Einstein trashed that idea, didn't he? Have we not been paying attention since 1905?

Now and then I sensed that Stan was very hard on himself. That was both objectively and subjectively true. It wasn't my place to question his basic assumptions (you know, all that stuff about immortality, being of a different race, and parenting gods). I did have to earn my paycheck now and then, so I had to intervene. The humanist in me insisted that I do so. In fact, I struggled with this high bar of parenting that Stan had set for himself. I tried to make a difference in how he thought about all of that, the clinical fool that I was.

--

"I want to make a point to you, Stan. I think you might appreciate it."

Stan swiveled his head on the pillow, away from the window, to face me. "Go ahead."

"Stan, our life here on planet Earth is so incredibly short in comparison to your lifespan. Time wise, we are moths; we die on the same day we are born. No past, no future, just one lifelong now. That's all, right? There's barely enough time for anything. One day you are playing pretend with your dolls or Tonka trucks, the next day you are thrown into a maelstrom of duties and responsibilities. It's high stakes with no margin of error. As a psychologist, I can tell you this, Stan. Here on Earth, we are all fucked up, fucked up by fucked up parents who, in turn, were fucked up by their fucked up parents. Most of us, certainly the ones in my field who end up doing therapy, were therapists to our own parents first. Unlike in your world, we, as children, end up parenting our own parents. And it feels like we are parenting gods! I say 'gods' because that's what parents are to kids. Kids see their parents as all powerful. Parents are adults; they are big, and strong, and they seem to know everything. And they keep reminding us that it was them who decided to bring us into this world; that they had this unfathomable power to materialize us out of nothingness, to manifest us out of their consciousness. One day we weren't. Then, bam! They made up their minds to shack up and here we were, a consequence of their action. How are they not god-like to us kids? Yet, before too long, we figure out that these gods are broken, fallen, beyond repair. As kids, we still love them, no matter what. We also hate them because they are so broken. It feels as though we were brought into this life only to care for them, to carry out their unfinished business, to tend to their festering ego wounds, and to fulfill their unmet fantasies. Then, Stan, we get so hard on ourselves for doing a shitty job with all this. A job we never asked for! We get so hard on ourselves that we spend many

356

of our measly years feeling guilty, seeking passing reassurances from random minds. Some of us, grown up kids, feel that we failed, that we do not deserve to be happy because we failed at parenting our own parents."

I stopped. I had to stop; I could feel the tremors of emotion in my voice. I held the pause, while Stan held my gaze, then I continued. "Then we just move on with the business of life, we become gods ourselves, parenting gods themselves, parent-gods who themselves need to be parented. We mess up our young; we cannibalize our children's souls with our own unfinished issues. We shape them and mold them and remodel them as we please. We suck them into the same beautiful mess that we ourselves have been drowning in for generations. I guess you could say that we like to drown together. Some of us even kill themselves. We create an option of suicide as though we ever had an option not to die in the first place. That's how it is here, on Earth, Stan."

I was running out of steam. Stan's eyes, however, seemed fuller with quiet acceptance. He was tearing up. Was he witnessing me? Parenting me now? Was I, a psychological orphan, still groping in the dark for an ideal parenting moment for my own good?

"And then, Stan, we die. There is no option of immortality for us, you know. We burn through our lives like bank robbers through a suitcase of cash, knowing that we are about to get caught. We live knowing that time is always about to catch up with us. Like day moths, we are on an inevitable collision with the fires of pain. Yet, through it all, we try to forgive ourselves. We are far, far better at forgiving others, however. Like closeted gods, we hold ourselves to a higher bar."

Stan finally spoke: "I know all this, Doc. My kind knows this very well. The Universe itself is an orphan, by definition; metaphysically. The Universe is beginningless, it is unborn. The Universe has no parents, it cannot if it is to be everything that ever was So, the Universe tries to parent itself, it has no option. The Universe is a god of oneness that parents oneself by breaking itself up into shards of pain. And it miserably fails along the way. As you have, as we all have… All races, all civilizations, struggle with this, Doc. This isn't just how it is here on Earth. This is a systemic issue that is cosmos wide. So, I get it. We all get it, Doc. Progress in parenting, not progress in technology is the main preoccupation of all advanced societies across this Universe. We, the race that I am from, we, too, were like that. What you described, that nightmarish trans-generational feedback loop of fucking up one's offspring, is what we have long set out to avoid. That's why I am here, on Earth. We come here because this place still needs gods. Because the reality here still sucks so much that you people still need gods."

I couldn't help but smile; we had reached an understanding. It was a namaste kind of moment; the divine humanity in me recognized the humane divinity in Stan. We were fellow sufferers.

--

"The happiest day of my life?" repeated Stan. I had asked him to think about that the other day and he has. I was still on that reminiscence therapy shtick, still trying to do my job. "Yes, I had one of those days, Doc. I had many, many of those days but this one – this one…" Stan disappeared into a long pause, his right hand strangely gripping the side of the bed and twisting.

He continued, "We were coming home from the cottage, the one I mentioned. We used to stay there a lot in the summer and fall. Fall was our favorite time. It was just the two of us, my daughter and I, coming back home on a midweek night. She had a gymnastics class next day in town and she didn't want to miss it. It was raining, hard, very hard, 'torrential downpour,' as they say. We turned off the parkway and looped around under the overpass to get on a side street and suddenly found ourselves stalled in rising water. I rolled the windows down just in time. A pond had formed at the intersection. The car hit upon something under water and wouldn't move. I unbuckled myself and unbuckled Pralaya from her child seat in the back. The water was probably three feet already and rising. She had been taking swim classes but still couldn't swim on her own, without a float and, of course, we didn't have a float with us, we had left it back at the cottage. I told her, 'I am gonna climb out of the window, then get you out and carry you to safe ground.' She was calm. She is always calm when we get tense. I got out; the water was up to my waist, too deep for her. I came around to the other side and got her out through the window. So far, so good. There wasn't much of a current, so I felt safe. I knew it was still dangerous, you know, manholes float up and you can get easily sucked into them. Then you are a goner for sure; bad way to go. The whole thing, the risk of it, still felt theoretical. I wasn't afraid for either of us at this point. Confidence is an adaptive illusion, you know. So here we are, Pralaya in my hands, I am wading through water, it's getting shallower but still too deep for her. Suddenly I stumble, I think something hit my ankle. I didn't feel any pain at that moment but I lost my footing and Pralaya slipped out of my hands. She is in the water but ok. She is standing, and the water is right up to her neck, to her clavicles, but ok. I'm thinking that I'm just gonna pick her up and in a few steps we'll be safe."

Stan paused, his right hand again gripping the mattress by his thigh and twisting it. "The thing is her foot got stuck in the drainage grill underwater. She couldn't get it out and the water was rising, slowly but still. I start trying to pull her up but her foot is stuck. I try again and again, I am hurting her as I stretch her up. I put her down. Now the water is probably to her mid-neck. I know I have no options here except... I tell her: 'I am gonna get you out but it's gonna hurt, sweetie. But you'll be okay, I promise.' She nods with that innocent calmness. It's

360

that calmness that gets to me, total trust, you know, total faith, like faith in god, you know. I got down on my knees and stuck my head under the water. I couldn't see anything, I just had to go under so that I could do what had to be done. I reached for her foot, felt it, got a mental image of how it's stuck, and I realized what I needed to do. I needed to turn it sideways, against the ankle. I needed to break her ankle."

Stan's hand once again grabbed on to the mattress and twisted it; the body memory now in sync with the memory of his mind.

"I pulled her out, her foot just hung there, limp. Just in time, the water still rising. I looked at her. She's not crying. Trying, I think, to protect my feelings. She could tell I felt awful about what I had to do. She understood the hell that I was in and ignored the hell that she was in. The little Stoic. I got her to high ground and put her down saying, 'You have an amazing, self-repairing, self-healing body, Pralaya. Your bones will grow back just as they were. Your body knows how to fix itself and it will.' She fucking smiled. She knew what I was doing. I had been telling her these things all her life, every time she bumped her knee or hit her noggin on something. Then I said, 'The rest is up to you, love, up to your mind. I know that was scary but it doesn't have to change anything about how your life will be. If you decide right now that you will be ok, then you will be ok. And it's totally ok to cry, girl, you know. Crying *is* how we get ok.' You know what she says? She says, 'I am ok, Daddy. I choose to be ok, Daddy.' Then she started crying. 'I choose to be ok,' Doc, is what she said. "

I nodded but stayed silent for a while, watching Stan.

"What makes that the best day, Stan?" I asked.

"Because I was able to teach her what 'ok' means, Doc. Understanding what 'ok' means is one of the hardest lessons in life. Only gods know that."

"Why only gods, Stan?"

"Because gods have to be ok with the suffering they cause and witness, with their inability to fix the world. I taught her that gods must sometimes hurt those they love. That, too, is ok, even necessary. In fact, that's the hardest part of the job, if you wish."

--

I thought about Stan's hand still gripping the mattress and the hold that the memory still had on him – "the best day of his life." Was he free of the past? Of course not; the past was painfully strong in him. But it was a new past, the past he acquired after his daughter was born. I was still looking for inconsistencies in his narrative. But, if he wanted to, the story could still add up. He'd just say that he and his wife had, in fact, reached a level of freedom from the past to be finally in a position to parent a god. What followed were the memories of parenting a god, the memories they were finally allowed to have, a past they were finally allowed not to expunge. Since parenting was a single shot opportunity and since parenting meant that their own existence would soon come to an end, they would no longer need to fear the programming side effect of having a past. They weren't going to screw up any more offspring with their past, that is, if they could finish out their current parenting project with that divine nonchalance that Stan had been talking about. It was becoming clear to me what this whole thing was about. Stan and his wife had purged their programming, they parented a god, and now they could enjoy their baggage without having to let it go; all of it, the pain, the angst, the guilt, the bliss, and the triumph. This hard earned experiential baggage was their end of-life reward, they finally had a "past" that they didn't need to erase. The reward of the gods was to finally get to be human. The more I thought it through, the more it added up.

All except for one thing. If Stan and his wife had, in fact, reached freedom from the past, a kind of prerequisite for parenting a god, why would they need to birth and then parent a new god? After all, they didn't have to die. If they were purified of the past, they could keep on running the whole thing themselves. If they didn't want to die, as Stan said, they didn't have to. So, it wasn't some kind of vacancy thing. This part didn't make sense. This part wasn't adding up. Indeed, why did they need more of their own kind?

It finally dawned on me. This was a case of divine perfectionism. Stan and his wife, in fact, his race, in general, couldn't leave the Universe alone to its own devices. They were trying to purify it further with better and better gods. And that's where parenting came in, it was about birthing and parenting a perfect god. They wanted to birth a god that gods themselves would worship. A real god.

The truth was staring me right in the face. They themselves weren't true gods yet. Yes, they were unborn and undying. Yes, they could be everywhere and they could be everything. Yes, they were all knowing and all powerful, whenever they chose to; all those "modalities" of being were available to them on demand. But they still weren't true gods. The very fact that they were trying to perfect themselves had to have meant, must have meant, that they still thought they were imperfect.

Just like us, they were still evolving. Evolving alongside their own creations. Alongside the orphan Universe that has no option but to parent, and perfect, itself. That's what evolution means, I realized; a ceaseless process of unfolding perfection. I was witnessing an evolution of gods. And participating in it myself through my own parenting and through the therapy I provided. I realized that the evolution of gods is a system wide project. All of us, from an ant

364

to a sequoia tree, here, on Earth, and elsewhere in the Universe, all parts of the Universe, are trying to somehow come together into that primordial divine state when the word "universe" and the word "god" meant one and the same thing-less thing. All of us are fragments of this puzzle of celestial perfection.

I thought of what Stan once said to me in passing. "All that can be is." That meant that the Universe is always at its best. The Universe is the Spinoza's god who doesn't know any better, an orphan child who doubles up as its own god-parent. I cried when this became clear to me. I cried for all of us.

--

It was an unremarkable Thursday morning when Stan and his wife died, both on the same day, at the same time, just as he had prophesized. It was no accident. It was a matter of choice. They had long entangled their life, like two particles forming a wave. And it was that Thursday morning when Emily's voice summoned me once again over the intercom. I went up to the reception area to see what Emily wanted.

"What's up, Em?" I asked. I've grown less formal with her over the last month. "His daughter, Pralaya, is here for a visit," said Emily, looking up from the chart. Then added, bitterly, "Finally."

I didn't know what to feel. I had heard so much about

her and now I was going to meet her. What was she really like, this presumed goddess? Would she be perfect, more perfect than Stan?

"Show her in, Em, I'll talk to her in the conference room," I said and walked out into the corridor.

--

Pralaya was sitting, exuding calm composure. A summer dress, one leg crossed, a flip-flop hanging off her toes, long, strong fingers clasped over her knee. She looked at me, as if to establish a connection, immense intelligence in her eyes. There was no denying she was embodied perfection, and somehow soulless. Just as we imagine our gods and goddesses to be. She seemed prepared for everything. Divinely numb. I introduced myself and sat down next to her. "Has anyone said anything to you?"

She shook her head, her eyes somehow motionless with quiet attention. It was clear she knew and was at peace. Could it be that Stan and his wife had, in fact, succeeded? If their goal was to be forgotten, to not matter, to fade into insignificance, it seems they were well on the way. There was a curious touch of nonchalance to her presence. Had she, in fact, been alive for 240 or so years, had she come of age long before I myself was born? She looked barely 24, except for that intriguing quiescence in the dead center of her pupils.

"Last night both of your parents passed on," I finally uttered looking down at the floor.

"Not 'passed on, but 'passed away'," she corrected me. "There is no after life, you know, sir. Just this life. We live as long as we choose to live. Which is why there is absolutely no need for another life, for an 'afterlife,' as you implied." She said all this with chilling confidence. At the last moment, she demurred, "At least, that's what my parents have always told me."

I nodded, respectfully deferring to her point of view. Who was I to challenge others' assumptions about life, about existence, about how this curious cosmos lived and breathed?

I redirected, "Do you think you'll miss them?"

"Me? No. I'll be ok. I know that."

She stood up. "Thank you, Doctor. As I said, I won't miss them. To miss is to lack. That's what I think. And I lack nothing. My parents made sure of that. I knew what it was about for them. I didn't ask to be born. The fact that they had me is on them. I owe them nothing, not even a memory. For now I do still remember them, perfectly, in fact. They have taught me how to pay attention, how to engage with reality so very completely that each and every moment is encoded in its entirety. It is this perfect mindfulness that completely and irreversibly erases everything that preceded it. But that's neither here nor there. I have a bad habit of lecturing. The point is I know they loved me, and they died the very moment they knew in their hearts that I was complete and no longer needed them. I know what is ahead of me, in general terms, of course. Life cannot be known in advance. It is to be lived, not to be known. It is my hope, just as it was theirs, that one day I will find a partner, as liberated from the past as they were in parenting me, so that I can have the experience that they had in having me, in parenting me. That one day I, too. will be in a position to parent a god."

She talked a lot, just like her father, and not at all like her mother. She binge-talked. Like her dad, she seemed to find solace in this verbal diarrhea of self-reassurance. Speech, as it comes out of us, is a kind of reverse virtual thumb we suck on, it fills us up as it springs from within. I found her matter-of-factness phony and disturbing. Stan was dead but I was still dueling with him, through his proxy, through his daughter. It was a shit move but I couldn't help it. I knew he'd find a way to verbally castrate me and put me in my place, but I wasn't letting go, not just yet. I guess, this was my time to grieve, to grieve this curious encounter with Stan (and now his daughter), this shared illusion I had allowed myself to become engrossed in.

"So, you didn't love them?" I wouldn't relent.

She shot a look of profound disappointment at me: "Yes, Doctor, I loved them once. Of course. When I was young, I loved them more than the world. But love is bias, it's a preference of one over another, don't you understand? Love is partiality, it's subjectivity. It is the only mistake the Universe ever made, the mistake that the Universe is still trying to undo. To stay in love, to allow yourself to love is an impasse. We have to transcend our arbitrary attachments. We have to learn to love without a bias, to love everything and everyone. And yes, you could make an argument that to love everyone is to love no one, that to love without attachment is just another name for indifference or nonchalance. I am not expecting you to understand this, Doctor." She paused for a beat, abandoned the last thought and simply added, "Gods, if they are to be fair, cannot love."

Everything she was saying sounded familiar. I had heard Stan say the same things. Except that he was gentler. His daughter, however, had the ram like ferocity of an early bamboo shoot, ever ready to plow through miles of granite. I knew it was developmental, a familiar human characteristic. What we might call "youthful maximalism." I said nothing, but she continued.

"You see, sir, as the Universe grows older, it carries more and more programming in its past, it is losing its degrees of freedom, its spontaneity. Gods, if they are to be fair and unbiased, have to be free from the past. Later today, when I am done here with you, I will

369

take a signal breath. Did my Dad explain this to you?"

I shook my head.

"It's a ritualistic breath, a rite of passage, if you wish. With this breath, I will begin my own journey. The Universe began with an out-breath, you know, not with the original sound, as they say. I mean, with the sound of the out-breath. It was the out-breath that caused the sound. I apologize, unsolicited lecturing again on my part. My point is I do not plan to stay on your planet for much longer. I am anxious to reset, that's what we call the transition."

I understood, I had heard Stan use the same terms, speak the same ideas. I realized that I wasn't just looking down at the floor, as if to hide from this philosophically precocious mind, which, if you asked me, as a clinician, must've been trapped in a curious folie a deux of her parents' delusion. No, I wasn't just looking at the floor. I realized I was staring at her tanned feet; she was wearing a pair of mismatched flip-flops, just as Stan had described them from the cottage days. One with a Hawaiian motif. The other with seahorses. They were, of course, a few sizes larger than the ones Stan had described. It was clear, the choice was demonstrative; the sentimentally adhesive past was still with her, influencing her choices. She was not yet free. She still needed to exhale the past, to exhale the echo of determinism. To reset.

"I wanna ask you something," I said, and paused as if to let her pause for a challenge. "So, you actually think of yourself as a god?" This question belonged to Stan, but I had never asked it.

"Not yet," she said. "But I will be."

I took this at face value. I didn't judge the veracity of the statement, just the implications of it. I did allow myself to wonder if she was the next god that we needed here on Earth. Was this poise, this collectedness, this precociousness, divine? I've known many a therapist with similar traits, closeted rescuers, closeted bodhisattvas still working out their own salvation through some clinical Mahayana tactics. There was a youthful abrasiveness to her, but was that not also indicative of gods, of these Promethean and Sisyphean goodie two-shoes martyrs?

She must've seen something in my poker face that wasn't there and reacted to it.

"You humans are silly. You think of gods as magicians. It's not like that, not at all. God is just freedom. Freedom is the original state of the Universe. If I am free, wherever I am, I liberate whatever and whomever is around me. It's like melting the ice of form back into the living water of potential. That's what gods do, without doing. When a human prays, the god on duty does not give but takes away, takes away whatever it is that stands in the way of the one who is praying; not some external obstacle but the internal barrier. When prayer works out it's because a block has been removed."

"Sounds just like therapy ," I said. "By the way, can you do that now? Melt the ice, I mean?"

"I am doing it right now," she said and unexpectedly pointed her index finger to the right temple of her head. She then turned towards the door. "One more thing," she said, reaching into her purse. "This is for you," she handed me a key ring with a couple of keys. "It's for the cottage house, where I grew up. I am sure Dad told you all about it. It's a rental cottage now. Stan thought that you might want to visit. Just call the office, the number is on the back, to make a reservation. Dad and Mom used to run it as a b-and-b, but we have an agent to handle reservations now."

"The one at the end of the country road, with the lake-that-is-more-of-a-pond at the bottom of the hill, and a night sky full of eyes?"

"Yes, that one, the one on the edge of the world."

She was done with me. There was nothing holding her back. Nothing left in this "now" to savor, to process, to understand. She was ready to rodeo, a cosmic wind in the making.

As she left, I watched her fade into the blurry

morning light of the hallway, her demonstratively mismatched flip-flops pacing out her journey. Perfect ankles, perfect calves, and not the slightest trace of a limp from that flooding injury.

It was clear that she would be ok, no matter what. Stan and Roz died with easy hearts; I could now see why.

I lingered the way people who are stood up on a date linger. I eventually turned around and walked past Mr. Hamsun's open door, he was shadow boxing again; it looked like round seven, he was breathing hard, dying in his own way, as we all do.

Emily, with her nose in yet another chart, paid me no attention. I walked into Stan's room, and sat down on his bed. The room was already cleaned out, and the bed remade. I looked out of the same window that had held his attention for the past several weeks and I saw a familiar corner of the Universe that was most certainly unborn and undying and, most importantly, edgeless inside and out.

On the drive home from the Green Valley facility, I kept thinking about what it meant to be a god. What would Stan have said in response to this question? "God is freedom. It's an undifferentiated state of mind, a return to pluri-potentiality, an infinite capacity to witness whatever is. It's when the Universe parents itself" Or something along these lines, I am sure. For a moment I watched the eddy of

Stan-referenced consciousness spin around inside my skull. I knew all this would eventually pass, there has never been a thought or a feeling that didn't eventually go away. The mind river takes care of its own garbage.

--

Next day, I got a call from Emily. She wanted to tell me that she had to cancel my 9:00 am because the medical team "urgently needed" to discuss my "documentation practices."

"I think he wants to write you up, Doc," said Emily. It was said with the tone of a guess, but I knew it was no guess: I knew Emily called to gloat. "Your notes are horrible, Doc. You must've known that they were going to audit you sooner or later. Dana is furious. He says he can't authorize your billing with notes like that and you know what that means, right?"

"I do, Em," I said into the phone and hang up. Em had finally snitched me out. It was just a matter of time before she'd stick her nose where it didn't belong. The psychologist in me knew from the first moment that Em was programmed for justice and fairness. She had the personality of a cop but was too risk averse to actually become one. Just another "certainty junkie;" the world is full of them. Those charts she was looking at, right under my nose, was an audit of my progress notes, on her own initiative. The problem: there were no notes. No notes yet, that is. What could've I written down after my sessions with Stan? Of course, I was going to get them done eventually. But it was going to be a pain in the ass. I had to translate Stan's philosophy into the language of geriatric delusion, into symptom checklists, diagnostic impressions, and all that clinically pathologizing jazz. It still probably would not have helped. It came down to the fact that I didn't like Em and Em didn't like me. Nor could she stand Stan, or the shadow boxing Mr. Hamsun, for that matter. If you ask me  (and who else can you ask at this point), Em had unresolved daddy issues; perhaps. I don't like being sure about things like that.

The Universe is love. Love is bias. Bias is the way of life. Em was biased, against me. So was I, against her. It is what it is.

A decision emerged as soon as I poured myself a second cup of coffee. "Fuck it," I wasn't going back. I was done; done without frustration, without bitterness, just emptied out like the first cup of morning coffee. Somehow, without Stan, the place was empty to me. I knew I'd miss the cosmic son-of-a-bitch. I also knew the Green Valley facility wasn't going to miss me. They've seen dozens pre- and post-private practice psychologists breeze through their hallways over the years. End of life facilities have a high turnover of both patients and staff.

--

All of us are cosmic sons-of-bitches. Stan, Em, me, you. The Mother Universe, an orphan herself, moves on in her ongoing metamorphosis, like a spooked bottom feeding catfish, jettisoning yet another ballast of her fish eggs like karmic ballast. Some of us hatch in the murky waters in the roots of a lotus stem; others on arid planets yet to be discovered. Once born, unattended, and un-witnessed, we parent ourselves. It's god-training, Stan would say. The Orphan way. The Cosmic way.

I walked out onto the porch, and sat down on the steps. I realized I was jealous. Stan died well, really well, his story finally witnessed. May we all die like that, surrounded by living mirrors of attention. For the rest of that morning I just sat outside and listened to the remote tenor of traffic behind the woods, thinking about humanity, as usual. I was once again a mirror, a mirror to the ineffable triviality of What (nonstop) Is.

--

There are stellar nurseries in the cosmos, places that birth stars. And then there are nurseries of gods, places where gods are born. I know that we, here on Earth, are one such place. After all, wherever you find immense suffering, you find a need for gods. We birth gods in the millions; innocent little boys and innocent little girls. They burst into this world utterly free and spontaneous; the best of what the Universe has to offer itself. Then we fuck them up. We fuck them up beautifully every damn day. Some of them become Nabokovs and Hesses, some turn into Ted Bundies and Hitlers. But they all begin motivationally innocent. They all mean well and they all do their shitty best.

Yes, we, the parents, horribly fuck them up. We should turn April 14th, Hitler's birthday, into a global day of repentance. Hitlers don't become Hitlers without parental help. We, the parents, should repent on this day, every year, as we pollute the Universe with our parenting mistakes.

And that is ok. We, the parents, just like our children, mean well and we, too, are doing our shitty best. Nonstop. The drama is built-in. Because there is no love without bias. And bias means programming. Programming for conflict, for tension, for subjectivity. It's a feedback loop that keeps the Universe cycling from big bang to big bang.

Gods get it. Do we?

--

Time passed. And I don't mean moments. I mean years. But these years passed like mere moments. I was busy parenting. My own child was growing up fast. And I was regressing just as fast.

My daughter, bronze legs, angelic hair blowing in the wind,  was now running down Observatory Hill, with her arms outstretched like the wings of a plane. Eight, going on 20, she seemed ready to take off into a life of her own, any moment now.

I was lying on the ground, my head propped up on a backpack, my aching, aging body feeling every knob under my back. I was an older parent, like Stan, but in human terms, late 40s. I was feeling my age every day, it seems. I was beginning to play the part, being an older parent even when I wasn't. The realization that I could never match the energy of my eight year old was growing every day, ominously, like a widening gap between she and I. I heard her say, "Daddy is always tired." It was a hard thing to hear, but it was true. This widening discrepancy was eating at me every day, our respective appetites for life moving in diametrically opposite directions. My child was accelerating, like a plane before take-off, and I was slowing down, soon to be grounded forever.

The day was sunny and autumnal; the best of what Earth has to offer, as far I am concerned. Nature had no patience for my melancholy. It tickled me with ants that crawled over me. Prodded me with the crackle of the sticks under my back, and caressed me with breezy fingers. The sky was a Dutch harbor of billowing white dirigibles anchored in the unmoving ocean of the blue.

While my eyes were watching this beautiful creature, my daughter, run up and down Observatory Hill, my mind was watching a shadow show on the shoji screen of consciousness. I was recalling one of the last conversations I had with Stan.

I remembered Stan's words, almost verbatim.

"You know, at some point, Doc, I said to myself, fuck it, I am not gonna die, I don't have to, I don't want to, so I am gonna stick around and we, my wife, Pralaya, and I, we'd live another eternity together like you fools here on Earth expect in the afterlife. Yes, heaven on Earth. It was and is still an option for us three, Deep in my gut, I knew that this whole limitation of aging that we place on ourselves, this notion that once we become parents we begin to die, I knew that it was programming. There is absolutely no cosmic necessity to this. We, the gods, convinced ourselves that this is how it works. Of course, it doesn't, Doc. It absolutely doesn't. We are gods after all. Gods, for fuck's sake! Enough of this divine self-hypnosis, you know?"

I remembered that Stan shed a tear when he said that.

"Cells, doc, cells in your body, they don't want to die. We all have an option to not die. You too, by the way, doc. My wife and I, we could both, right now. reverse what is happening to us. She wouldn't, though. Roz is a better god than I am, a true god. A warrior goddess. Athena."

The screen of reality eclipsed the shoji screen of

memory once again. "Let's run, Dad," my daughter was standing in front of me, totally breathless and totally indifferent about the state of her body. The evidence was right in front of me, here, right in front of me, stood a human body completely at the mercy of its mind. No matter that it was breathless, it had no option but to behave. The body is a dollar, the mind is the thriftless spender. Yet we somehow allow this relationship to flip-flop, we somehow begin to feel frail, we begin to re-prioritize, we begin to deny the mind in favor of the body.

"I am sorry, sweetie, I am tired, run and I'll watch you, my love, just be careful, ok."

"Ok, Dad," and there she went running fast enough to leave her disappointment in me behind, as a festering guilt trip, as a psychological landmine that would surely awaken me one day in the middle of the night with profound regret. And I would sob, pissed at my shitty, human, parenting best.

I was back in the room, with Stan, bewildered. The distance between Stan and Roz finally made sense to me. They could have had a family suite at Green Valley, but they opted to die apart. There was a tension between them. The gods were in conflict.

Stan kept on, chirping in the halls of my memory; he was speaking in maxims, as if dictating, or as if reviewing key pieces of programming code. "We owe our health to our children. Our health belongs to them and only them. Our health is their health. When a child is born, you become a resource to them, in every aspect. That includes your health. You have to be able to match their energy with yours. If they want to get down on the floor, you should be able to meet them there. They don't want to play at the table like you do. If they want to run down the hill with you, you have to be able to do it and not worry about your aching ankles. Your vitality is a mirror, a mirror for their energy. Being able to engage with them on a physical level is also part of mirroring and validating. Furthermore, you can't die young because that totally fucks them up. You cannot die before they are ready to be without you. They have to carry in their head this sense of immortality. Intuitively they know that they are immortal but you have to model it for them. You have to demonstrate that aging in time does not mean loss of capacity. You have to take the sting out of aging. You have to teach them that aging is irrelevant, that it doesn't subtract, it only adds capacity. You have to teach them to envy your age. If you die young, before they are ready, they forever carry that notion that there is a cap, that there is a ceiling, an insurmountable limitation, a limitation that their own all mighty parents couldn't surpass. As they come up on that age, they can't help but wonder, will I live longer than my parents did?  Will I outlive them?  And, if so, by how long?  The toxin of time creeps into their mind, the toxin of temporality and transience. Gods, if they are to be gods, have to not give a fuck about time."

Stan's words were like a drumbeat inside my skull. I

was stuck, so stuck in the past, in that moment with Stan. Every moment you think about what no longer exists you are missing out on what still exists. I was missing out, missing out on the sun, on the breeze, on this day now, on connection with my daughter.

Back inside, in my head, the virtual memory figure of Stan paused for a sip of water. It was more of a hunger for water than thirst. After he emptied out the glass, he kept tipping it over to see if he could get yet another drop. I remembered that I stood up to pour him another glass of water but he waived me to sit down.

The drumbeat resumed.

"Of course, with us, Doc, it's a very different matter than with you here on Earth. We already live way too long. If I were to model a statistical immortality to my daughter, I'd have to stick around for another billion years. I would love that, I would totally love that! I'd watch her good deeds from afar, I'd help her out when I could, with advise or resources. But then the whole thing wouldn't work. Gods have to be orphans, beginningless, without a genesis, unborn and undying, or at least approximating that. I mean, would you believe in a god whose parents are still around?"

I remained quiet. I have never liked rhetorical questions.

"I know, Doc, you don't believe in our kind of gods. You don't believe in anthropomorphized gods, right? Right. You are a strange bird, you know. I've heard you anthropomorphize ants but you refuse to anthropomorphize gods. But I get it; I know how you get there philosophically. For you gods are not gods and everything is god. You are a pantheist. Like that Spinoza, that thorn in the Christian thigh. Humor me and imagine yourself as a monotheist, a believer in a single god, just for the sake of conversation, ok? As a monotheist, would you trust a god-child whose god-parents are still around? Would you? I don't think so. If you did, you'd be right back in that polytheistic confusion of the ancient Greeks, with all that storytelling sky drama."

In my head, in the black moldy vaults of my memories, Stan was even more rhetorical than in real life. I guess that's how self-talk works. Would we pose most of the questions that we pose if we didn't believe that they are answerable in the first place?

My little girl, left to her own devices on Observatory Hill, ran up to have a sip of water from a bottle in my backpack. The reality of the moment was in strange sync with the virtual reality of my reminiscence; inside my head, Stan was also getting thirsty. He was now ready for another glass of water. I refilled it and he rolled over to his side, nearly falling out of bed. He didn't fall out; he caught himself with that well practiced twist of his wrist, screwing his hand into the mattress, the very motion that he had once used to break his daughter's ankle, when he taught her that gods must be ok when they are hurt and must be also ok with hurting others. He picked up the glass, brought it to his lips and suddenly burst into tears. He wasn't thirsty after all. He was simply on the verge of crying. As it is with many men, he was uncomfortable with that. Not befitting of the gods, I guess. But it was normal, completely normal. Everyone alive grieves. We all grieve, and we start early, too. I know it, because on the way home, from Observatory Hill, my four year old was singing a silly little song, she was making it up as she went, a song about people dying. In it there was a realization, I remember it clearly, a realization that "everyone dies." I'd tell you the lyrics but you'd first need a tall glass of water to re-hydrate, to make sure you have enough for your tears to flow.

That day on Observatory Hill eventually ended. The real intertwined with the virtual and became one in my mind. That's how we remember life, "I remember being here thinking about this." Our most poignant moments are not necessarily moments of total presence, but moments of total absence from the here and now. In my mind, Stan now lives alongside my daughter, the two of them, in that moment, anchored in the same space time.

If the memory of that moment that is buried in my consciousness, has a tombstone with an inscription, it reads something like this: "Death is a hypnosis. A post-hypnotic suggestion that we program into our children as part of our parenting. A self-hypnosis of the self-less Oneness of All That Is. Yet another round of the divine game of Lila that the Universe plays with its it-less non-self. Gods and non-gods alike have to entertain themselves, and there is no ecstasy without agony."

--

The Universe is an orphan. This is no throw-away thought. I picked it up from the silent despair of those I witnessed. We are all orphans. All of us are unattended and un-witnessed, misunderstood in our essence. And we are all Universe.

Stan's cottage, I eventually went to visit it, has a pond stocked with catfish. It's a catch-and-release paradise for them. One afternoon I watched the catfish come up to the surface, one at a time, gulping down the mosquito larvae. When I went for a swim, I could feel them poke me to see what I am about. At some point, just to measure the depth of the pond, I allowed myself to sink to the bottom. And there, once again, I saw Dimka Tokarev, his decomposing body leaking monad bubbles of consciousness into the churning champagne of existence.

I don't know if you know this or not, but these bottom feeders, these catfish, are all tongue, their skin is said to be laden with taste buds. They feed on everything because everything is food. You and I, we are also food. The Universe eats itself. It has no one else to eat. Catfish feed on the debris of life; as does the Universe. So do I, a 500lb Mekong catfish that I am.

385

As a bottom feeder, all my life I've lurked in the depths of others' suffering, not sadistically, but therapeutically or just because I happened to be there; learning my metaphysics from believers and nonbelievers, from bliss and pain, from the philosophical crumbs of existence that rain down to the human depths. I am a lucky bastard. I've been enriched by what I've witnessed. I've been unbelievably lucky. Bottom feeder that I am, I've been yanked out of the depths of my own murky mind, and released back into the mindless shallows of Now. A couple of times I've been understood; just a couple of times. Real understanding is rare. That's when I finally felt loved. The French say that to understand is to forgive. No, to understand is to love. To love is to forgive. In those moments of being understood, after being so used to the murky waters of solipsist solitude, I glimpsed the blue sky, the space that we all share.

The Universe is a fish out of water, a form out of formlessness. The Universe is the biggest bottom feeder of them all. It is the food, the eater, and the process of eating; the formless space, the object form and the process of change of former into latter and latter into former. This entire beginningless, unborn, undying, boundless, ever morphing thing-less thing is an orphan fish. It dwells inside its own self-less non-self, running from its own shadows, and falling in love with the very parts of itself it had previously disowned. Like the last and only cosmic fish that has nothing else left but to chase and hunt and love its own tail.

The entire thing, this Universe, is a god, a god divided. A Oneness fragmented into plurality. It is its own womb, its own mother, its own child, and its own parent. It births its forms out of its own formlessness. It suffers through them. It loves through them. As each fragment, as each living and nonliving self-thing dissolves back into the womb of self-less no-thingness, all experience is erased. With the exception of one aspect; that trace is love, Zeno's clinamen, the aspect that gives the whole system its spin, its swirl, its twist.

The Universe is only interested in love. Love is what it seeks, and love is what it suffers from. Since love is relational and the Universe has no Other to love it, it creates its own love, a flawed love, the love of bias that begets suffering which it then seeks to allay. This kind of love births and kills, it programs and de-programs. It is self love. And it is self hate.

It's a torturous fabrication process. The Universe first hurts itself through fractal division. It tears its monolithic oneness asunder, shredding itself into things and non-things, into material objects and the space in between them. Then it walks on its own broken glass. It hurts itself and suffers, then relates to its own parts, and finally feels love for itself, a part at a time. And then it hurts *through* love. Just as it loves its parts, it hurts them, molds them, programs them, treats them as special, puts them on a pedestal, and makes them exceptional. In so doing, it further isolates these self-parts into monadic selves, into suffering un-witnessed pseudo wholes.

387

The tragedy of oneness is that it divides itself. What makes it even more tragic is that this self-fragmentation stems from loneliness. Universe is a living hospice.

It has to be this way. It can't be any other way. Love is inescapably relational. The orphan dreams a parent to love it, and loves itself, wherever it can see itself, in its rare moments of enlightenment. The Universe creates the Other, through fragmentation into infinite parts, and, at least, experiences some partial love.

The 500lb Mekong catfish that I am, I have picked up my metaphysics in the silt of mind-streams, filtering the sediment of life for ontological truths. I am comfortable with the ones who drown after swimming upstream. Although I am a good swimmer, I rescue not. Who am I to stand in the way of your homecoming?

We return to where we start, to the cosmic bottom of undifferentiated proto-matter, to the cosmic bottom of undifferentiated proto-consciousness. To a time-space depth that is only reachable by our fleeting shadows.

That is when we get to be god, to be the loving formlessness of space that is always eager to take the form of you and me.

We misunderstand death. Death is not nothingness, death is no-thinngess. No-thingness is the womb of things. From no-thingness, we living and non-living things, come forth, forge from, and into no-thingness we return and recycle. The first and the last; the one and only bottom feeder chasing, hunting, and loving its own hungry tail.

Bottom feeder that I am, I know I have been enriched by everything I have had to digest, by pain, and by anger. The Universe and I, the Universe and you, we are recyclers. We turn the shit of divisive form into the gold of accepting formlessness. That is the alchemy of love.

The Universe is the Mekong catfish, the boundless bottom feeder with a bottomless appetite. It digests and detoxifies. The Universe is a bhakti catfish, it worships love for the sake of love because love is the only "thing" it lacks. Since love is relational, at least one part of the fragmented, divided Universe will be always without love. It will be the part that loves some other part but has no counterpart to love it. Fair to itself, the Universe churns itself over, rotating the martyrs, one pixel of oneness at a time.

The Universe doesn't care about the money you make, the music you listen to, the pictures you take, the books you read, or whether you recycle trash or not. It is only interested in love. What else would you expect from an orphan? As forms melt back to formlessness, the Universe sifts out and retains only one aspect, you guessed it − love. The space that you walk through on your morning walks isn't space, it is no-thingness and this no-thingness doesn't judge, it embraces you with utter acceptance. That is love on a physical level, on the ontological level. The space you walk through, the space I swim through, the air we fly through, all this pseudo emptiness, is a field of eagerness that takes on the forms that we are. Ether is mirror, an invisible three-dimensional mirror that lovingly validates the form that you are by embodying it.

Surely, you don't think that you are walking through some actual nothingness. The word "nothingness" exists but it has no referents in reality.

Gravity is love. It's a force of love, an attraction, a bias. In your case, what was born on Earth stays on Earth. Here, where you are and where I am, the Universe loves itself by staying loyal to its parts, like a grief stricken mother with a still living son on death row, she moves into a tent by the prison walls, knowing that her son is ontologically innocent even if he is legalistically guilty.

The Universe doesn't care about the money you make. It cares about whether this money allowed you to love. It doesn't care about the music you listen to. It cares about whether this music helped you make love to someone.

And so I sit, waist deep in the silt of the murky depths of existence, covered with whiskers and taste buds, listening to you tell me the story of how you, too, came to be god. I know that it is a collective effort. Eventually all parts come together into the mosaic of oneness and the catfish pond empties itself out of all its suffering. The Universe becomes an uninhabited womb balancing for a moment between the abysses of ecstasy and agony. Almost … I say "almost" because there is always one part left unattended; the part that has been sacrificed for the wellbeing of the whole, the part that still hungers for love, the part to be loved again. The trillion-year-old Mekong catfish, finally too full, regurgitates the undigested. Big bangs ensue.

"First, you are a god. Your kids look up to you and worship your almighty power. You gave them birth and you can kill them. They know your might. They know the power you wield. They know it long before they know anything else. It's instinctual. Those are the breaks. And then you begin to transmit this power to your kids. You praise them. You build them up. You make them golden. Each pat on the back, you transfer this immense power that you have onto them … and eventually the powerless become the powerful and the powerful become powerless again. That is the story of parenting – that is, when it is done right – it's a story of empowerment, a story of creating gods. Only gods can make gods. Powerless have no power to give. Each parenting moment is a voluntary zero-sum exchange: your power wanes, your kids' power gains. It's the thermodynamics of love, a dissipation of heart-heat into the Universe. In the end, roles have fully reversed: parent-gods are nothing but fallen angels, to be reminisced in passing through psychoanalysis, as the newborn gods edit their origin stories. And the kids, once helpless, powerless, and frail sail on into the future, with the confidence of immortals, leaving behind two broken parent-hearts, powerless to stop time. And then, again, a moment comes – the wheel of cosmos makes yet another turn – and the new power-drunk generation of gods gets bored with playing and the kids – they always remain kids to you – your kids go on to have their own kids, repeating the cycle of parenting Samsara. Whether you are there to witness it or not, doesn't really matter. You are powerless to stop this cosmic centrifuge. The undifferentiated proto-matter of sentience needs a monkey wrench to keep stirring it into becoming. Beings are born. The agony-ecstasy of love continues. The restless Universe keeps chasing its own tail. And, yes, sometimes – in fact, often, in this human realm, - things break down. When parents refuse to give up their power, they breed groupies, not gods. Groupies that worship them. That is what you folks on this planet call narcissism. And these empty ghosts, ever yearning for power, set everything on fire. With no fuel to burn, with no heart-heat to power their own lives, they see everything and everyone as kindling, not as kin … "


Stan was tired of preaching, I was tired of being preached to. We looked at each other with a perfect balance of belief and disbelief. A smell of backyard fire somewhere was sneaking into his nursing home room through the cracks in the caulking around the window frame. Stan got up to open the window. He struggled a bit with the window-lock. I had an impulse to help him. But then, wisely, I decided to not get in the way of this power demonstration. Heat-death was upon him. Who am I to get in the way of a dying god.

# Morbid Curiosity (Part 1)

Andrew was dying. Andrew Turner, I mean. The three of us – Andrew, and a Digambara Jain named Anand, and I - were sitting on the still cold granite slabs of the Jain temple at Sravanabelagola, with our backs to each other, awaiting the sunrise, with the black vanity mirror of the square Belagola "white pond" down below, in the middle of the city, all ready to reflect the Barbie-blond curls of the Indian sun. Anand was dying too. He was in the last phase of his sallekhana vow – he had vowed to fast himself to death – and it was a very slow fast, going now on its second month. Slow because people who live a slow life tend to take their time dying. Anand, of an indeterminate age, had to be between 50 and 90, probably a solid 70, with the body of a 40 year old. A life of ascetic starvation has a surprisingly rejuvenating effect on us.

Anand's physique was, of course, on display – a Digambara, he was sky-clad, permanently naked, all year long, true to our monkey nature. Andrew, by this time of his life, had traded in his Patagonia and Goretex mountaineering gear for a white robe. He was a Svetambara, a white-clad lay Jain, following his own sallekhana vow. In his previous life, Andrew was my post-doc supervisor out West but he eventually left academia and refocused on his lifelong passion which was walking, aimlessly and contemplatively, in a Thoreau kind of sense. Sometimes he sky-walked, with the help of paragliding.

As for yours truly, I too was dying but I wasn't dressed for the occasion. As I sat at the eye-level of the horizon, awaiting the sun, I was "sporting" your run-of-the-mill secular tourist garb – beaten up New Balance shoes (extra wide), a pair of loose cargo slacks (size 36, I was finally down to 36 after a couple of months in India, with the help of nearly chronic diarrhea), and an old Gap t-shirt from their (RED) campaign. No, it didn't say "Inspi(RED)" or anything noble like that. It was a knock-off which read: Ti(RED), which I thought was funny. I still do, in fact, even though I've long lost track of the t-shirt in my recent travels.

I said "I too was dying" because we all are, all the time. Are we not?! Dying and living are but two words that describe the exact same process. There is not a hair's worth of difference between these adjectives. But, boy, did we create a gulf between the concepts of "life" and "death"! Beware of nouns: nouns reify – nouns abstract us – extract us - from the indivisible concreteness of All That Is.

We were sitting with our backs to one another, because in some cultures eating, just like shitting, is a private matter. Andrew and Anand, of course, were done with eating, done for good, but not me. In my hand, I had a scatter of hard dried Goji berries, just as red as my (RED) Gap t-shirt. And I was trying to eat them one at a time, but it was no simple matter. The fingers seemed to have a mind of their own, a mind of optimization. Every two or three bites, I'd forget my "mindful eating" intention to eat one Goji berry at a time – (Jon Kabat Zinn would be compassionately disappointed in me, I am sure) – and I'd suddenly pinch off a cluster of three or five berries at once and toss them into the trash-disposal of my mouth. Mindful-living intentions have a quick way of dying, unless continuously renewed.

"The sun's about to rise," said Anand into the fading darkness of the Indian morning. The windswept cumulus clouds were strewn along the horizon like mauve saris, or, perhaps, folds of stage curtains after being brushed aside by a powerful invisible hand in the opening moments of a grand show.

"Nope," said Andrew, and I instantly knew what he was referring to: the Sun doesn't rise, you fools, it hangs up there where it's at, minding its own angry business; it's just us, little monkey-ants on top of this fuzzy tennis ball, called Earth, rotating daily away from the Sun and back towards it, in a circadian rhythm of an ancient optical illusion. Sunrise, sunset – what a joke of language. Like I said, beware of nouns: they reify the non-existent.

But do pardon my irritability. Even now, as I write this, with a handful of same kind of Goji berries on a paper towel to the side of my laptop, their sweet tartness is quick to allay my hypoglycemic "hanger."

Andrew said "Nope." That's all he said, as I remember. Anand said nothing, which is typically all he had to say. What did I say that morning, the verbose chatter-box that I am? I think I asked a question … No, that doesn't sound right. Oh, I remember now. I think I asked Andrew if I could read something out loud from a book, *The Abstract Wild*, by his namesake, Jack Turner, a passage that I wanted Anand to commend on. After all, that was the very point why I trekked along with Andrew, and a group of his friends, on what was his last, one-way mountaineering expedition.

Andrew wanted a sky-burial. And so I read to him and Anand about the Tibetan sky-burial:

*"The human body is cut up and the bones broken to the marrow and left for animals, mostly birds. Later the bones are pounded and mixed with tsampa – a roasted barley – and again offered to the animals. Finally everything is gone, gone back into the cycle. We should have the courage to do the same for ourselves, to re-enter the great cycle of being. The moose incorporates the willow, taking the life of the willow into its own life, making the wildness of the willow reincarnate. I kill the moose, its body feeds the willow and grouse wortleberries where it dies, it feeds my body, and in feeding my body, the willow and the moose feed the one billion bacteria that*

*inhabit three inches of my colon, the one million brontosaurus-like mites that live by devouring the goo on my eyelashes. This great feeding body is the world. It evolved together, mutually, all interdependent, all interrelating ceaselessly, the dust of old stars hurtling through time, and we are the form it chose to make it conscious of itself."*

"Yeah," Andrew said and, after clearing his throat, added with amplified gusto: "Fuck yeah!"

"Indeed," Anand chimed in, his voice calm and unaffected, and offered a verse from Taittiriya Upanishads:

*"Oh wonderful! Oh wonderful! Oh wonderful!*

*I am food! I am food! I am food!*

*I eat food! I eat food! I eat food!*

*I am a maker of verse! I am a maker of verses! I am a maker of verses!*

*I am the first-born of the world-order,*

*Earlier than the gods, in the navel of immortality!*

*Whoever gives me away has helped me the most!*

398

*I, who am food, eat the eater of food!*

*I have overcome the world!*

*He who knows this shines like the sun.*

*Such are the laws of mystery!"*

I remained silent for a moment, milling Goji berries with my teeth on autopilot. Then I swallowed, waited a second, and chimed in, quoting my own fricking self from *Reinventing the Meal*.

"I am Earth, eating Earth, becoming Earth. I am Earth eating itself."

"Yeah!" Andrew issued forth another raspy utterance, void of meaning, but full of vibe.

The Sun that never rises started to stand up, burning off its morning-glory eye-boogers, getting ready for its daily sky-walk. Anand too got up, deftly brushed the place in front of him with his peacock-feather whisk to make sure he wouldn't step on any insects, then he put his flat brown feet together, and started to raise his arms above his head, into a sun salutation. For a moment Andrew and I both watched Anand, fold gracefully and effortlessly, his palms flat on the ground next to his feet, revealing the original agility of an inner quadraped unburdened by cultural conditioning.  Then we too got up, lined up to Anand's side, and joined in the cycle of gratitude.

The Sun, like a Daoist sage, is neither flattered nor insulted by human attention.  Like a sky-clad Jain, the Sun that morning went about its own business of blinding all those who care to see into the darkness of enlightenment (you can read this last sentence two different ways, by the way).  And the three of us sat back down on the warmish granite slabs of the Jain temple, this time facing each other to talk a little more.

## Morbid Curiosity (Part 2)

Once again Andrew tried to clear out crud from his throat – was the peristaltic snake of his GI tract sloughing off its lining from within? – and asked: "Who did you say wrote that, Paul?"

"You mean that passage about the sky burial?"

"Yeah," said Andrew.

"Your namesake, some guy named Jack Turner, do you think you might be related to him?  He too left academia, dropped out just like you did …"

"I don't think so," said Andrew and unceremoniously took the copy of The Abstract Wild from my hands. He flipped through it, read the dedication from the front, then flipped to the back of the book and read the brief author's bio.  "Hmm," he muttered, "It's curious, this guy dedicated the book to Kathleen Thompson Turner, must be his mom, and I have a sister, Kathleen, you met her, right, she is in the movies … And, this guy went to Cornell, just like me, and then taught at the University of Colorodo, and I, as you know, at the University of Wyoming … If I didn't know any better, I'd say one and the same character but two different time-lines …"

"That's part of the reason I wanted to share this with you and … you, Anand, too. I am curious about this guy, just like I am curious about the two of you …"

"May I keep the book, Paul?" Andrew asked, referring to me by my English name, the one I used to introduce myself before I re-claimed my Slavic name.

"Of course, Andrew. And I'll get you a copy too, Anand, if you wish," I said looking at Anand.

"I do not wish, Paul, but thank you. I do not have much time left to read, maybe two, three more weeks of life, tops. I'm done eating, done reading, done with mind-food, done digesting …"

"Hmm," said Andrew, smiling and stretching, "Food is information, information is food, I like that … Eating, reading, same shit, huh?"

"Yep," said Anand tryng to sound slangish, reminding us of how the three of us met, back in Pittsburgh, where Andrew came to visit with me during his vagabond days. Back then, Andrew and I decided to check out a Jain temple in Monroeville, right outside of Pittsburgh, which is where we met Anand who was a visiting Jain scholar at that time.

Andrew was the type who climbed moutains so as to descend deeper into himself. Sometimes he would paraglide for the same reason. He was an explorer, an artist of consciousness, and he was tired of battling an annoying recurrence of a certain cancer that plagued the last decade of his life. "In fact," he said to me one day, "I see no reason why I should continue to aggress against these cells inside of me, with chemo and radiation … They are innocent, just like the rest of the cells that I collectively am … Why am I trying to kill them off? It flies in the face of everything I believe … These cancer cells probably long realized that I am depressed and suicidal and cannot be counted on as a vehicle of life, and they probably just decided to build a Noah's arc inside of me and get out when they can … Misguided, uninformed, but what am I to expect from these dumb little cells … They are not trying to kill me, they are just trying to survive me in case I try to kill myself … "

That's how Andrew reasoned in those days and that is why he then decided to accept what was happening to him and stop fighting. In fact, he decided to accelearate it by going on a spiritual fast, another Western lay Jain going pro. Ever being a champion of precedents he figured he'd do a two-fer – a sallekhana fast and a sky-burial. Fortunately, there was no one to stand in the way of this self-liberated bachelor.

But right now, in that moment on the self-heating slabs of the Jain temple in India, Andrew was still looking through the pages of Jack Turner's book. He suddenly looked up and said: "I am pretty sure I gave this to you back in Pittsburgh, don't you remember? I bought it at Caliban, in Oakland, that quaint independent bookstore that never went out of business, the one near CMU. I bought but realized that I wasn't going to read it and gave it to you, don't you remember, Paul?!"

I tried to remember. I was pretty sure he was wrong. We did exchange many books over many years, but not this one. He'd feed me books on "flow" and I'd repay him with books on Sumerian cosmologies. But we'd always sign them to each other. This one – in his hands - had no inscription. I wondered if his cancer had finally metastized to his brain, or was he getting confused from many days of fasting. Truth didn't matter. One of the biggest kindnesses we can do to each other is to let each other have our illusions. I quickly made my mind and decided to agree: "You know what?! I think you are absolutely right! You did give this book to me, I remember it now …"

Anand, strangely attuned to the small-talk insinserities of Western ways, must have picked up on my unusually upbeat and supportive tone. He looked at me, more into me than at me, but said nothing, which was in his non-violent style of life. After all, speech too can be violence, unless it's samma vacca – righteous speech.

We sat like this for a while, Jain tourists and non-Jain tourists coming and going all around us. Eventually, Anand said: "There is a scripture I want to tell you about, a secret teaching, it hasn't been translated, unknown in the West, about how Jainist philosophy began ..."

"Oh, yeah?" said Andrew, trying to look eager, but only succeeding in looking tired.

"It's unorthodox, even disputed among Jains …"

"Do tell, my friend, do tell," Andrew mustered up some curiosity, and looking up at me, added: "Are you up for this, Paul?"

"Am I up for this? This is all I am up for, buddy. Feed me some new thoughts, pal! Take it away, Anand, and I hope you don't mind if I take some notes," and not waiting for permission I pulled out a small, faux-leather-bound notebook and a pen (you don't show up in sheepskin loafers to a date with an animal-loving Jain mind!)

Anand took hold of the cotton mouth mask that had been resting on his neck and reaffixed it over his mouth. His eyes gleamed with a smile behind the mask – he knew that we knew what was going on. This little moment took all three of us back to that time in Pittsburgh when Anand, a lay Jain scholar decided to go pro. As he told us then, he was outside the temple in Monroeville, talking to a group of kids about the Jain principle of ahimsa, which means "non-violence," and while talking he swallowed a fly. An inadvertent act of violence, but an act of violence, nevertheless. Right there and then, struck with the irony of this, he decided to stop talking the walk and start walking the talk. Ever since, as befits a devout Jain monk, he'd do his best to keep his mouth shut or, at least, covered.

With this precaution in place, Anand related the following teaching.

"Jains didn't invent veganism, it was modeled to us. A light-skinned, cone-headed man, not from these parts, taught our people about a race of gods who practice ethical eating. In their world, the man said, there is vegetative life, animal life and human-like gods. And in that world, there is a voluntary hierarchy of eating. Flora, the vegetative life, begs fauna, the animal life, to eat them. And the fauna, the animal life, begs human-gods to eat them ..."

Andrew cleared his throat, indicating that he wanted to break in. Anand paused.

"But that makes no sense! What do plants eat? Who begs them? And why do plants want to be eaten by, say, deer, and why do deer want to be eating by human-gods? This makes no sense to me. All life wants to live, no one wants to die. That's ontological. An axiom. A built-in vector of wellbeing. Nature knows no masochism."

Anand nodded along: "Good questions, Andrew, and very good points. Let me address them, please. First off, you are right.  All life wants to live.  But all life also wants to live in enlightenment.  Plants know that animals know more and so they seek to know more by incorporating themselves into a higher plane of sentience – "

"Just like Jack Turner was saying, right?  In that quote that I read to you guys earlier …"

"Right, Paul," continued Anand, and, addressing Andrew with his eyes, proceeded: "Then you said that no one wants to die, right again!  No one wants to die unenlightened.  Then you asked about who begs plants – about what plants eat … That's where it gets interesting.  Plants, as you know, are considered to be auto-trophs, which is in contrast with hetero-trophs, like us, who eat others.  Plants, as we think of them here on Earth, do not eat anyone, they just photosynthesize and therefore they are peaceful, not predatorial.  But according to that man that taught about ethical eating, it's not quite like that.  There is an important point here that has been lost over the last several thousand of years of teaching.  Plants do eat others and these others are photons, light particles.  Mani, an Iranian sage from long time ago, thought of light particles as soul-particles.  But plants too, in that system, don't eat photons against their will – according to the teaching, photons too beg to be eaten, and plants concede, out of compassion and mercy, and taken them in, and this process – this invitation inside – is what we know as photosynthesis … "

"Wait, wait, wait, buddy!" Andrew jumped, his voice full of crud and impatience. "You are telling me this cone-headed dude taught you guys about photosynthesis three thousand years ago?"

"He did," said Anand, and added, "Just like he taught us about the microscopic organisms in water, which is why we filter water before we drink it, and have been for centuries …"

Andrew shook his head, then nodded: "I know, I know. I know about water and all that jazz. Never mind, continue, Anand, you have my interest."

"Good," said Anand, the cotton cloth over his mouth puffing up as he exhaled another forceful vowel. "So, back to your questions about why … The man told us that plants see animals move and they realize that to know more you have to move around, and so they offer themselves to be eaten so that they can experience movement and the knowledge that comes with it. Now, when animals witness human-gods, they can tell that human-gods, unlike animals, are very passionate, they laugh and cry and fight and cheer and mutter mantras and sing hymns … and they realize that there is something inside human-gods that moves them from inside … and they offer themselves to be eaten by human-gods so that they can experience emotions … An emotion, as you know, is when you feel moved from the inside, endogenously, from within. Thus the "e" in emotion."

Anand paused to make space for question but none came. I was wiping off sweat from my forehead, squinting in the still low but already bright mid-morning Indian sun.

"Now, you might wonder how animals know that plants want to be eaten and how human-gods know that animals want to be eaten ... It's simple, really. If you ever tasted garlic and mellons, you'd know right away. Garlic is pungent, right? What's it saying to you when you put in your mouth? It says: spit me out. What about grape? Grape is sweet, right? It says: eat me. Same with deer: they ones that run away from you on a hunt are still too afraid to know more, but the ones that suddenly stop when you are chasing them and look back at you, they are ready to die ... they are dying to know what you know ..."

Andrew once again made his presence unmistakably clear: "No, no, no ... You gotta backtrack a bit, pal. What about the photons – why do they want to be consumed and how do they make their desire to be metabolized known? And, more importantly, who is the apex predator in this little scheme of yours? Now, that's what I really wanna know, Anand."

You could see Anand smiling under his white mouth veil, the ears moved up just a notch and the cotton cloth flattened against his nose as his face broke into a broad smile beneath the white curtain.

"I am getting there pal, and, as always you have most

excellent questions, dear friend! About photons –
about why they want to be metabolized. The answer
is the same: light wants to know where it comes from
and it can only do so by bouncing back. In fact, light
wants to return to its place of origin. As you know,
when you look at a green leaf, the reason why you see
color green is because the green side of the light
spectrum is the only type of light frequency that a
typical plant cannot metabolize, so the leaf rejects the
green light and the photons that vibrate at the green
frequency of the light spectrum bounce back and head
back to whence they came from, to see who or what
emitted them. Light too, as you see, seeks
enlightenment. It too is chasing its own tail of
genesis, if you wish … The rest of the photons – the
ones of the yellow, red, and blue and purple wave-
frequencies turn into sugar and get inside the plant so
that they can later get inside the animal eyes so that
they can too look at their home stars … So, they all –
all of the photons – either get to mechanically reflect
and see where they came from or they get to reflect
on their origins through the consciousness of the
animal or of the human-god …"


"And they just know all this in advance, huh? These
little photon-fuckers, right?" asked Andrew
rhetorically.


Anand, no novice in dealing with Andrew, ignored
the rhetorical question and continued: "Now, to the
most interesting part, the one also intrigues me …
You asked: what about the apex predator in this
pyramid of self-sacrificial eating? There are two

410

ways to look at this, friend. One way is that there is no apex predator here, only apex prey. In this eating model, no one preys on anybody – all die when they are ready to know more. All get to eat but no one has to kill anyone. That's true ahimsa – unlimited, uncompromised non-violence. Our type of ahimsa is not really non-violence but harm-reduction. Even you and I – in our vow of sallekhana – as we fast ourselves to death, in this ritual of non-violence of non-eating we are killing trillions of innocent cells that constitute our bodies … Did you know that a typical human body is about 13.5 trillion cells and only 100 billion of them are the neurons with which you and I made a decision to end our lives. We – the cellular minority – the neurons that decided to go on this open-ended death-fast – didn't consult this multicellular microcosm that we are about what they want. So, despite our pretensions at non-violence, we are still very violent, but … but we are doing our shitty best, the best we know … But these other life-forms, in that non-predatorial hierarchy of self-sacrificial eating, never kill. Their eating is akin to an invitation, a compassionate incorporation into a larger sentient self. In that life, a blade of grass when it's ready, begs the cow to eat it, and the fish, when it's ready, looks for a fishing hook to swallow. But … but I want to get back to your question. So, as I said, one way to answer it is to say: no apex predator, just apex, top-most prey. But there is another way to look at it …"

Anand paused. And continued: "The other way to look at it is to say that there is an apex predator, and it is Death.  The cone-headed man told us that in that world Death spares the ignorant and takes the wise and the informed ones.  The ones that don't want to learn, the human-gods that want to live forever, which is ignorant, they stay ignorant, they learn nothing, and they outlive everyone they love, and end up being alone in the world, living long meaningless lives.  And Death ignores them because it has nothing to learn from them.  Death leaves them alone, until eventually these stubborn ones, who keep eating others, finally decide that they owe it to all the billions that they had eaten during their endless lives, a final show of enlightenment.  Think about it: in that world, not to learn is to break a promise to the flora and the fauna that became your flesh in search for knowledge.  Each and every day that you resist the invitation of Death, you are keeping the myriad of souls inside in the dark, only knowing what they already know and not an iota more.  And that is unethical.  It is an epistemological betrayal.  Finally, according to the cone-headed man, the stubborn ones, the ignorant ones too decide to wise up and Death begins to notice them and eventually Death takes them too, in part, to learn about the ignorance of ego …"

Andrew, almost spitting through his loosening teeth, fired off, half-seriously, half-rhetorically, but with unmistakable anger.

"Who eats Death?  What the fuck is death?  There is no death.  There is dying, which is the same as living.  But there is no Death!  Show me this thing you call

412

Death.  Death is just a word, a noun.  Beware of nouns: they reify.  You taught me and Paul not to do that yourself.  And here you are reifying Death, turning this concept, this construct into an Entity … Explain it to me!"

Anand demurred.

"Ok," he said with a sigh.  "I'll explain it but it is your responsibility to understand my explanation.  If you don't get it, it's not my responsibility to to re-explain it to you.  When you make a decision to swallow, it's then your responsibility to chew and digest.  Otherwise, you are like that fifty feet long python that swallowed a porcupine and died from a hundred needles sticking out of your gut."

"Shoot!" said Andrew to a man who never held a gun in his hands.

"Death is the light that hasn't yet reached your eyes.  Death is the morbid curiosity of the Cosmos that is already on its way into your mind.  Death is when the forked tongue of the uroboric cosmic snake is so far out of its leathery snout that it can almost taste its own tail.  Death is the birth of ego, which is a desire to see yourself as a separate self, as a self other than all these others that are not others but same old you … Death is when life is dying to know itself … When life just lives, it's just living, and this kind of living isn't the same as dying, as you and Paul tend to think.  When life just lives, living is just living.  But when life wants to know, which follows the birth of self, life embarks on the process of death, and living becomes indistinguishable from dying. Do you understand what I am saying?!"

Andrew shook his head, then nodded, while I first nodded and then shook my head.

Anand picked up the peacock-feather whisk and, while still sitting, swept around him as he prepared to stand up.

"I'll just say one more thing – take it or leave it - … To know is to die. And to die is to know."

He stood up and, while staying half-way bent, walked away, sweeping clean an invisible path of theoretical compassion in front of him.

# Morbid Curiosity (Part 3)

Andrew and I sat there for a long moment. I could hear him breathe.

"I love that guy, Paul," he said, "I love how he walks away when he sees no point in arguing. And he does so without feeling defeated. Ahimsa in action. Nonviolent communication, you know ... You and I, friend, we are different. We lock horns until one of us bleeds. Me more so than you ..." Andrew suddenly stopped, wiping his mouth with the fold of his white robe. His lips were parched, cracking, but the starving body inside of him was eating itself and turning itself into moist mush.

"I think he is right about motion, about our curiosity ... Curiosity is motion. We try to get outside ourselves. And Death – the Epitome of Motionlessness – sucks us in, like a black hole. Yeah, it makes sense that plants want to experience animal-type motion, and that animals want to experience human-type emotion. And then we, humans, not gods, of course, want to figure how motion is even possible. How is it that the Universe that is full of itself allows for an illusion of space? If all is one, if the Universe is one boundless, unbroken continuity of oneness, then how is it that we can move from Point A to Point B?! Nothingness, emptiness, space has to be an illusion. The space between you and I, my friend, is not a nothingness but a no-thingness, not a void but an undifferentiated, formless expanse – "

"Aether," I chimed in.

"That's right, aether, that imperceptible, luminiferous elastic medium that is the womb of everythning. The Akashic field. And to hell with Michelson and Morley and their misguided 1887 findings that aether doesn't exist – of course, they couldn't find it because it is not findable. Of course, there wasn't going to be any measurable friction for them to detect it because ether doesn't – can't – won't resist anything! Aether is the ultimate ahimsa, the ultimate pacifist, the cosmic medium of non-protest – "

Andrew's breathing was getting heavier as he spoke, he too was becoming aware of that. Not wanting to push it, he broke off his anti-physics litany and grew quiet. And he knew that there was nothing left to discover, no new insights to glimpse. He and I had spent years riffing on the metaphysics of this sort. No doubt, the candle-wick of his benign narcissism was still smouldering and, yes, of course, he didn't mind one last audience, one last silent ovation, but he was on the cusp of not needing to air his thoughts any more, particularly, to someone who had already heard them time and again. He shot a strange look in my direction. The look of someone who knew he needed to shut up – he was tired of listening to his own conclusions about reality. Words are violence, and he understood that now more than ever. And while ready to add a vow of silence to his vow of starvation, he was unsure of how to time this. Should he announce this and say: "Paul, I am done talking … for good." Or should he just not say anything else anymore and let others arrive at that conclusion. He wasn't sure and I could tell that my good old friend was confused. I held his stare as long as I could and finally offered a punctuation nod as if to say – on his behalf – "Period." My chin dropped and bounced back, while my eyes closed and re-opened, and that simple nod of understanding swept the space between us clear, like a debugging Jain brush.

Andrew got up and limped over to the edge of the hilltop temple platform – endless steps down below leading to the famous Belagola. I knew he was sizing up the drop through the eyes of a paraglider. The other day when we first climbed to the top of the hill, he was mesmerized by the view. "A great place to launch from," he had said then. I knew he had his wing shipped from US, just in case. He hadn't paraglided for years, certainly not since he had crash landed on the hood of a vintage Mercedes somewhere in the fields of upstate New York. He had almost lost his leg then, but never his desire to sky-walk. Right now he just stood there at the precipice of existence, his silhoutte cut against the azure-white backdrop of the sky, finally and forever saying nothing.

I knew in my gut that we'd never talk again, and so I just sat there, watching him and squinting at the Sun, my own mind now and then dipping in and out of the white pond of Akashic nihilism where everything is nothing and nothing is everything. And where the impersonal black anvil of death forges motionlessness out of our self-spiraling emotionality.

# Other books by Pavel Somov

*Present Perfect (self-help)*

*Lotus Effect (self-help)*

*Monkey Mind of Being Human*

*From Skinthink to Kinthink*

*Prairie Mind*

*The 6$^{th}$ Battle of Acedia*

*Totem of Taulogy (poetry)*

*Veneer of Certainty (poetry)*

*Eating the Moment (self-help)*

*Reinventing the Meal (self-help)*

*Mindful Emotional Eating (self-help)*

*Anger Management Jumpstart (self-help)*

*Anapanasati 2.0 (self-help)*

www.pavelsomov.com

www.drsomov.com